A Woman of Gallantry

Elisabeth McNeill was a long-established freelance journalist and broadcaster who wrote five non-fiction books and 26 novels. She lived with a miniature dachshund in the oldest inhabited village on the Scottish borders, where she spent most of her school days.

Also by Elisabeth McNeill

Elisabeth McNeill

A WOMAN OF GALLANTRY

CANELO

First published in Great Britain in 1989 by Century Hutchinson Ltd

This edition published in the United Kingdom in 2022 by

Canelo
Unit 9, 5th Floor
Cargo Works, 1–2 Hatfields
London, SE1 9PG
United Kingdom

A CIP catalogue record for this book is available from the British Library.

Print ISBN 978 1 80032 760 3
Ebook ISBN 978 1 80032 759 7

This book is a work of fiction. Names, characters, businesses, organizations, places and events are either the product of the author's imagination or are used fictitiously. Any resemblance to actual persons, living or dead, events or locales is entirely coincidental.

Look for more great books at www.canelo.co

Printed and bound in Great Britain by Clays Ltd, Elcograf S.p.A.

1

To Helen Darling and Pamela McNicol for telling me about Veronica Hay

1788

At the first peal of the bell from the crowned steeple of St Giles, a frisson of excitement swept like a wave through the huge crowd. They had waited in the High Street, huddling up their shoulders against the drizzling rain, since early morning. Now, in anticipation, every man and woman – old and young, rich and poor, healthy and halt – turned their eyes towards the nail-studded door of the grim Tolbooth prison.

The voice of the bell sounded again, slowly, solemnly, and the watchers became strangely silent, hardly daring to breathe, as the battered old door creaked slowly open. Out of the darkness of the void came a procession of town councillors and ministers of religion, splendid and awful in their official robes. Acutely conscious of the eyes of the crowd, they stepped, one by one, on to the worn stone treads of the short stairway that led to the street.

When the bell struck a third time, a sigh swept through the watchers like a sinister wind sweeping over the branches of trees at night. Then the man they had all come to see stood framed between the grey plinths of the ancient doorway.

He wore a cockaded hat on his carefully powdered head and he was tall enough for his hat to brush against the stone lintel on which was carved a crown, a thistle and a rose signifying the authority of the state, the authority which he had so outrageously flaunted. Beneath the symbols ran an engraved legend in squared-off lettering:

The Lord Of Armeis Is My Protector.

Blissit Are Thay That Trust In The Lord.

Deacon William Brodie, once very blessed indeed in the things of the world, had lost his Lord's protection for he was stepping out of Edinburgh's Tolbooth into the grey October day that would see him hanged.

Intent on reaching the front, Helen Cameron used her sharp little elbows to cut a way through the tightly packed crowd. Ruthlessly she jabbed and prodded at the bodies obstructing her path and when she struck a particular looped-up skirt in a very sensitive part, its wearer squealed in anger, hitting out with her wicker basket at the ragged child. 'You impident wee scart! There's no room to move. You just stay where you are like the rest of us,' she yelled.

The blow reached its target and Helen reeled as the basket sharply connected with her tousled head, but it did not stop her. In an instant she dropped to her knees and scuttled through the forest of legs like a mouse heading for its hole, but, before she went, she exacted a revenge on her attacker. Reaching up one hand she grabbed the carefully tied rumple knot of scarlet ribbons which the woman wore pinned above her bustle. Though the theft was not immediately noticed – Helen's hands were for too skilled for that – the angry woman was suspicious of the cheeky child.

Prodding her husband who was jammed tightly against her side by the press of the crowd, she demanded, 'Did you see that impident bairn jabbing me in the behind? Check your pockets, Willie, and see she's not robbed you. There's a lot of gey funny people about.'

But her Willie only nodded for he was far too absorbed in the scene at the Tolbooth door to worry about his pockets. He said to his wife, 'My word, isn't he a real dandy, the Deacon? I'd heard he was a fancy fellow but I never thought he'd be so grand!' There was wonder in his voice and the man on his left nodded in proud agreement for he was from Edinburgh and eager to display his superior local knowledge to visitors from the country.

'Oh aye, the Deacon's a fine dresser. I used to see him paradin' up and down, this very Street done up in a grand white suit like a lord. Nobody thought for a minute he was a robber!'

The people within earshot nodded their heads in agreement. 'Never guessed a thing,' they concurred in sibilant whispers. 'My, he was a grand actor was the Deacon – going out at night in his black mask. Who'd have guessed it?'

No one took their eyes off William Brodie. Still the dandy, even on this most terrible day of his life, he was wearing a spotless suit of finest black broadcloth, black silk stockings on his shapely legs and shoes with sparkling silver buckles. A sigh of admiration swept the crowd and he almost strutted as if he enjoyed being the centre of attention even at such a macabre event. He knew they had turned out in their thousands to watch *him* die, for few of them were much interested in the man condemned to hang with him, one of the gang of thieves that Brodie had led on his nefarious robbing expeditions, a low-bred fellow called George Smith with a domed idiot forehead. Smith was of little interest – he was the sort of felon who could be seen swinging from the gallows any time.

St Giles' bell was still tolling slowly, a funereal voice frightening the timid hiding away in the high tenement buildings that loomed along the length of the High Street. The bell's voice echoed up the Lawnmarket and the Grassmarket, down into the Cowgate and the Canongate as far as Holyrood. It was telling the city the sad story of pride fallen... how a highly respected town councillor and Deacon of the Guild of Wrights and Masons had been seduced by greed and the lust for danger into a life of crime that was to end on the scaffold.

The people on the street raised their heads and listened to the bell's brazen tongue, adding their own comments. 'The Deacon wasn't just a thief, he was a fornicator too,' said a whey-faced minister in a stained black coat to a man who had come from Dundee to witness the spectacle.

3

'How was that?' Like everyone around, the stranger was eager to discuss Brodie's career.

The minister lowered his voice. 'He kept two women, both here in the High Street! And he never married either of them. What's worse – he had two sets of bastard bairns. Oh, aye, he was devilish clever at it too – neither of his women knew anything about the other, at least not till they caught him in Ostend where he ran to after his last robbery.' There was a note of sanctimonious satisfaction in his voice that not even a flight abroad could remove Brodie from the consequences of his evil-doing.

The listener sighed in fake-pious disapproval. 'Oh, aye, he led a double life,' he said, but like many in the crowd he had a certain amount of admiration for Brodie. The scandal that had swept Edinburgh when one of its most respected citizens ran away after trying to rob the Excise Office for Scotland had provided endless gossip for every street corner, ale house and coffee room.

The minister was eager to instruct his captive audience. 'If you look down, there,' he said, pointing with a bony, chilblained finger, 'you'll see the entry to Chessel's Court. That's where the guard interrupted him and his men trying to break into the Excise Office. They got nothing that time, but they'd stolen plenty before – plenty, even from people who were the Deacon's friends.'

Brodie's hanging was attracting a bigger crowd than had ever before attended a public execution in Edinburgh. People had travelled for days to view a spectacle that they would remember all their lives and with which they would thrill their grandchildren. The rain and the long hours jammed in a smothering crowd were worth suffering for such a sight, and so now they waited patiently for the last act of Brodie's tragedy to begin.

The chief actor did not let them down. His demeanour was magnificently cool and his dark-skinned face untroubled as he courteously gestured to Smith to precede him up the ladder to the gallows platform. Then, with one elegantly shod foot on the first rung, he paused to wave to a friend in the press of watchers. 'Good day, Mabon,' he called in a firm and resolute voice like a man on a gentle stroll. 'How goes it with you?'

The friend, embarrassed at having the attention of the crowd switched to him, flushed red but replied in tones of genuine sorrow and respect, 'I'm well, Brodie, but I'm sorely grieved to see you in this situation.'

William Brodie raised his heavy black eyebrows and flashed an ironic smile. 'Oh, it's only *fortune de la guerre*, Mabon,' he called back, with a laugh and climbed on up the ladder after Smith. The crowd sighed again – a long, long sigh.

–

Scuttling on hands and knees through the press of people, the street sparrow Helen eventually reached the open space in front of the gibbet where she would have the best view. The official procession stood there in solemn array with their eyes fixed on the gallows rope swinging slowly in the silent air. They had all known Brodie well in better days; they had drunk with him; laughed at his sallies; enjoyed his hospitality. Now they were collected together to sanction his hanging. Their faces betrayed a still continuing disbelief that this was really happening. A black-robed minister of religion stepped out of the line and with a sorrowful shake of his head climbed the ladder after Brodie.

'That one needn't bother himself,' said an evil-smelling old woman behind Helen. 'The Deacon won't want any prayers said over *him*. He's written out a grand will bequeathing charity and good deeds to the ministers of the city – *to be put into practice amongst themselves.* He's still a joker is Deacon Brodie.' She gave an approving cackle that was quickly quelled by hushing sounds from her neighbours as the black-hooded hangman began checking the halter rope.

Some women in the crowd pursed their lips at the unsuitability of a child as young as Helen witnessing a hanging, but everyone was engrossed in the scene and she was not pushed away or told to go home.

The little figure in tattered bits of clothing stood transfixed. Though she was only seven years old, she felt the solemnity of the occasion very deeply and her feelings were in turmoil for, like all inhabitants of the High Street, she knew Deacon Brodie well by sight. He was one of her neighbours, with a flat just across the Lawnmarket from the tenement where her own family crowded into an attic on the tenth floor of Baxter's Buildings. Brodie's eldest daughter Cecil was one of her friends – at least, Helen was on chatting terms with the girl, who often gave her a twist of toffee in a bit of paper or an apple if they met on the street. The child knew that if she were to turn her head, and if the crowd were miraculously to part, she would be able to see the roofs of her home, of Brodie's home and Cecil's too. She wondered if the condemned man up there was watching smoke rising from the chimneys of houses where the various members, of his family sat waiting for the bell of St Giles to cease its awful tolling.

Though she was so young Helen knew the details of Brodie's story, for no one in her family curbed their tongue in front of her and it had been talked about constantly over the past few weeks. She knew that the Deacon was being hanged because he went abroad at night with a mask of black gauze over his face, robbing local houses and shops. She heard them say that the Deacon's fall from grace was due to his fondness for cock fighting, gambling and women. She appreciated the ironic twist to his tale, that only a few weeks ago Brodie had sat as a juryman in the very court where he would himself be condemned to death. She also realized that, though they recognized his errors, the people of the High Street still entertained a sneaking respect for their Deacon. The man whose opinion she rated most highly was her grandfather and whenever he talked about Brodie, he always added, 'Poor chiel, he got in with bad company.' She could tell from his tone that, in spite of what the Deacon had done, the old man liked him.

6

She scanned the crowd for her grandfather, who would be standing somewhere in the press, leaning on his stick and held up by his friends. His bent and aching legs were no longer capable of supporting him. A shadow passed over her face when she reflected on the change that had come over him recently. Now it was hard to believe that he had once been the fastest and most nimble of Edinburgh's street messengers, the men they called the caddies. In spite of the pains that racked him, today he had forced himself down the twenty flights of twisting stairs from their attic to watch this execution, not for the ghoulish enjoyment of seeing a man die, but to bid farewell to Deacon Brodie. Caddies were privy to more secrets than anyone ever guessed, and the breaking of Brodie's story had not been such a revelation to her grandfather as it was to other, more sheltered, citizens.

Boom – booom – boooom, went the bell, and Brodie took off his black hat and slipped a white nightcap on to his head, pulling it down to conceal his face. It would not be seemly for the crowd to witness his last grimaces in death. He stepped under the swinging noose, but in the moment before the rope was lowered over his head he addressed the executioner.

'Before you do your work, my friend, I'd like to check that this gibbet's working correctly. After all I helped to design it.'

That was true. Brodie, in his days of respectability, had redesigned the gibbet on which he now stood. With his eyes still covered, he raised one hand and pulled expertly on the, rope. To universal horror, it gave way with a sharp crack that reverberated off the tall buildings like a pistol shot.

The least confused councillor in the line-up at the gallow's foot collected his wits and called out, 'The rope's faulty! Bring down the prisoners till it's fixed.' The crowd murmured in a kind of muted horror. They were getting more than they had bargained for today.

The first man down was George Smith, sallow-faced and shaking, who staggered when his feet touched the cobbles. He was soon joined by Brodie who leaped from the ladder as nimble and insouciant as Captain MacHeath in John Gay's play.

A man near Helen gave a murmur of reluctant admiration and said, 'He's still play-acting. He thinks he's a character from *The Beggar's Opera*.'

People in the crowd remarked to each other that indeed, Brodie had modelled himself on John Gay's carefree high-wayman MacHeath. The jailers in the Tolbooth had talked in the ale houses about how Brodie passed the tedium of his last days by singing MacHeath's song:

Let us take to the road.
Hark, I hear the sound of coaches
The hour of attack advances.
To your arms, brave boys, and load...

But everyone knew that he was never to take to the road again and it seemed bitterly cruel that the start of his next adventure, what he himself called his 'leap in the dark', was being so delayed. The more sympathetic members of the crowd seemed to resent this more than the prisoner himself who, while he waited, chatted carelessly with the people around him, stirring reluctant admiration even in those who had disapproved of him most vehemently. In fact his complete composure high-lighted the hand-shaking anxiety of the executioner who now hurriedly climbed up the gallows-tree to untie the faulty rope and, conscious of the eyes of the crowd upon him, awkwardly re-knotted and re-hung it. He fumbled as he worked and tried to do the job too quickly.

The signal for starting again was given. Once more Brodie ushered Smith up the ladder before him. Once more they stood side by side beneath the swinging rope. Once more Brodie was to hang first, and when he raised his head to receive the noose, to universal horror the, rope failed again. Over all the dreadful bell kept on tolling as a shudder swept the crowd. Was this some

8

sort of omen? Was some power above telling them that Brodie should be allowed to keep his life?

The cruel turn of events took its toll on even the Deacon's iron nerve and he showed impatience for the first time, pushing the executioner roughly aside with one hand as he stepped to the edge of the platform to call down at the waiting councillors, 'This fool you've sent up here to hang me should be punished for incompetence!'

The crowd made angry noises of agreement. Their anticipation of the spectacle was beginning to lose its edge as the hanging looked about to become a pitiful farce, not the solemn and awe-inspiring event they had expected. It was obvious that their sympathies were veering more and more towards Brodie, and the officials looked for reassurance at the shabby old men of the Town Guard, lined up along the scaffold foot with their blunt Lochaber axes at the ready. If this was to continue, much longer, the mob might take it into their heads to rescue the Deacon, and Edinburgh mobs had a fearsome reputation. Each town councillor quaked inside his fine robes as he thought of the terrible outrages that had been perpetrated when the street people went on the rampage in the past. The Town Guard were alerted to raise their axes at the ready and the mob's dissent slowly died away.

Now there was a long wait, for the rope-checking had to be more thorough this time. People shuffled and leaned on one another in weariness as pedlars began pushing their way into the crowd, selling sweetmeats and souvenirs.

The woman whose rumple knot had been stolen by Helen bought a toy gibbet with a little figure swinging from its string; her husband, overcome with hunger for he had not eaten since early morning, bought a piece of gingerbread from a young man who adroitly picked his pocket at the same time as he handed over the cake. The honest pedlars and the thieves of Edinburgh all enjoyed a profitable day and silently thanked the Deacon as they pushed and shoved a passage through the press of bodies.

'I don't think I can haud on much longer,' said Willie's wife at twenty minutes to three in the afternoon. 'We've been standing here since half past ten and they said they'd hang him at twelve.' She made it sound as if the Town Council and the Deacon had deliberately conspired to discomfit her.

'They're nearly ready to start again,' her husband said. 'They're telling him to get back up. It won't be long now.'

'I wish they'd stop that bell banging away, it's giving me a terrible pain in my head,' she complained, for St Giles' bell had not ceased its doleful tolling throughout the long-drawn-out drama. The clanging was getting on everyone's nerves.

The crowd was thinning out, for even the hanging of a deacon could not put off normal business for ever, and some had to get back to their everyday concerns.

'Oh, be quiet, woman,' said Willie impatiently, 'I tell you he's climbing the ladder again. He's looking gey tired is the Deacon.'

'It doesn't matter if he's tired, he'll be resting soon,' said the man at Willie's side. They shook their heads solemnly, assuming demeanours of great solemnity. What they had come to see was about to happen at last.

'Oh, Willie, I need to pee,' whispered his anguished wife, but he didn't hear her because, at that very moment the noose was slipped over Brodie's neck, the chair quickly kicked from under his feet and he was launched into eternity.

As the body twisted and jerked like a terrible puppet on the end of the rope, the crowd gave a long wail like children in pain; the bell of St Giles gave its final, most awful peal; Willie's wife convulsed and let a sudden stream of warm water run down her legs and puddle around her feet; and Helen Cameron, pinioned by staring people in the front of the crowd, covered her enormous eyes with dirty hands and began to weep.

–

In the embrasure of a window overlooking the Nor' Loch, Veronica Hay, a tall slim girl with thickly curling dark hair that shone with a reddish hue in the strong light, was staring out at the drizzling rain. One finger traced patterns in the mist her breath made on the window glass and the other hand was on her forehead.

'I wish that bell would stop its ringing. Surely they've hanged him by now,' she said, glancing over her shoulder at her mother who sat sewing by the fireside. Lady Huntingdon, as tall and as stately as the girl but with pure white hair under her lace cap, shrugged her shoulders.

'It'll stop when it's over. But it's strange that it's taking so long. Something must have held them up.'

'It's been three hours,' exclaimed the girl, turning back from the window and throwing herself down in a chair. 'All that bell ringing has given me a headache. It's awful. Just think what his people must be feeling. Poor Miss Brodie and poor Jamie!'

'We'll go across to them when it stops,' said her mother, drawing her needle, through the fine cloth. 'We'll walk over and give them our sympathy. Poor things, they'll need friends, because plenty of people won't want to know them now.'

'People are cruel, aren't they? Why are people cruel to each other?' asked the girl. She was greatly in awe of her mother and always looked to her for an opinion or a lead before committing herself on any question. The youngest of the family, for far too long she had been treated as a baby who was incapable of making her own decisions. The mother was considering her answer when suddenly both women started. The silence could almost be felt, a tangible thing. St Giles' bell had stopped tolling. The terrible voice was silent at last and they knew Deacon Brodie was dead. The older woman's needle paused in mid air and she stared at her daughter.

With a gasp of relief Veronica stood up and stretched to her full height. 'Thank heavens it's over, Mother. I feel much better. Let me get your shawl and pattens and we'll go across to Brodie's Close.'

Lady Huntingdon was a woman of some social standing in Edinburgh. The widow of a Law Lord, she had four children who were all much afraid of her, for she had a sharp tongue and imperious ways. Her only son Thomas was a successful doctor; her two eldest girls were suitably married to men of property and she was left with sixteen-year-old Veronica, the most beautiful and the one who looked capable of making the most brilliant match if the admiration of young men was anything to go by.

The mother and daughter occupied a comfortable fourth-floor flat of four rooms and a kitchen in a tall tenement at the end of Lady Stair's Close off the Lawnmarket where Lady Huntingdon had lived all her married life and where she had brought up her family. It was not cramped now that the other children had moved away but at one time they had filled it to capacity and their one maidservant had slept on a palliasse under Veronica's bed. Though Her Leddyship, as the neighbours called her, was English born, she had grown to love the ancient wynds and passages of old Edinburgh; she loved her flat with its tall windows overlooking the Nor' Loch and the coast of Fife; she loved its panelled rooms and the painted beams of its ceilings; she loved the close-knit society in which she had lived for more than thirty years and which she had no intention of ever leaving. Some of her neighbours had recently been moving from old tenement flats like hers to the smart new houses that had begun to appear on the south side of the city or, even smarter and more expensive, to the New Town on the north bank of the loch beneath their windows, but Lady Huntingdon stayed resolutely in the Old Town.

Thomas Hay, who had social pretensions, sometimes tried to prevail on her to move, to keep up with fashionable people, but her reply was always the same: 'I like it here. I'm comfortable. Why should I go away and live in some smart house, all lonely with no neighbours? There's still some ladies of very good birth living round here.' Everyone knew her in 'her part of the High Street and she loved its busy bustle; she loved watching the passing throng crowding the pavements when she walked up to the Castle Esplanade to take the air on fine days. Most of all, she loved the convenience of her life, of being able to walk to her friends' flats for a dish of tea and a game of cards in the late afternoons; she loved hearing all the gossip of the district from Mary Cameron, the water caddy who dragged up her buckets of water from the well at the top of the West Port. Thomas said she owed it to Veronica to move into smart society, it would be easier to find a well-off husband that way, but Lady Huntingdon felt that her youngest child's beauty did not have to sell itself. A girl like her daughter would have young men flocking to her whether she lived in a flat or a palace. Meanwhile she stayed with her mother and did as she was told.

'I'm too old to change my ways. It's not worth moving now,' Lady Huntingdon said firmly when a look of longing crossed Veronica's face at the news of someone else moving out of their High Street society. Another reason for her reluctance to move, and one which she did not care to discuss with her daughter, was that she felt her income was insufficient to support a grander way of life. Lady Stair's Close was cheap. Her rent was only £15 a year. Even a modest house in the New Town would cost at least £50 in rent and that was money she was reluctant to spend because of her constant anxiety about finances. Her late husband Lord Huntingdon – advocate Willie Hay when she married him – had enjoyed his bottle even more than was usual among the hard-drinking lawyers of Edinburgh, in fact he had been famous among his contemporaries for always having a bottle of port on the bench with him and boasted that he gave his best judgements after seven bottles of claret. In the last years of his life he was never really sober and when he died, the bills presented by his wine merchants (for there were more than one) had made Thomas gasp with shock. The widow, forever given to worrying, dreaded penury and forced herself to live frugally. She took care to conceal her financial circumstances, however, for she feared that if the news came out that the family was short of money, no well-fleeced man of property would court Veronica even though she was a spectacular beauty.

Veronica was looking particularly lovely that October afternoon as she helped her mother to negotiate the sharp bends of the turnpike stairs. In the courtyard they shivered in the drizzling rain and then clattered across the grey paving stones in their high wooden pattens. A blast of wind carrying rain in its breath hit them, bringing with it a foretaste of the bitterness of winter, and they drew their plaid shawls more tightly around their shoulders. Veronica paused to straighten her mother's bongrace bonnet that the wind had sent awry.

'You shouldn't have worn this today. It's too pretty and the rain'll spoil it,' she said, smoothing the soft silk with her long fingers.

Lady Huntingdon tutted in reproof, 'Of course I should wear it. We're going on a very important call, and besides, no woman of any class is seen in the street with her head uncovered. Why, when I came here first, ladies of quality used to wear masks when they went out. You pull your shawl over your head, Veronica, in case anyone sees you.'

They hurried, daughter in front and mother behind, up the dark passageway to the main street, clutching their wide skirts over their arms so that they could pass safely through the narrow space without tearing their silks. When Veronica reached the Lawnmarket she paused only for a second and, without looking to right or left, was about to dash across its wide breadth when a cry from some men on the pavement stopped her.

'Wait, miss, wait, don't cross!' they cried and she drew back just in time to avoid being hit by a dashing cart drawn by two foam-flecked horses whose hooves sent sparks up from the cobbles.

The women stood holding each other in terror and Lady Huntingdon found her voice first. 'Who's that driving so fast? They shouldn't drive like that through the town. They could have killed my daughter!'

Veronica was shaking and ashen faced but not because she had so nearly suffered an accident. 'Didn't you see what was in the cart, Mother?' she asked in a trembling voice. 'Oh, didn't you see? It was Deacon Brodie's body. They're driving around with the Deacon's body!'

Miss Jean Brodie, in her early fifties and seven years older than her brother, had always lived with him in their parents' home in Brodie's Close, approached through an arched gateway between two wooden-fronted tenements, facing on to the Lawnmarket opposite Lady Stair's House. The Brodies' father had been a rich and highly respected cabinetmaker whose furniture graced the best houses of the town, and their home was large, and comfortable, a first-floor flat up a turnpike stair with its windows overlooking a busy wynd leading to the West Port.

Next door, on ground-floor level, was the cabinetmaking workshop, still a thriving concern, that had been inherited by William. Like his father, he had been a skilled craftsman and left evidence of his artistry in the ornately carved front door of the flat at which Veronica paused.

She turned to her mother and asked, 'Are you sure we should be troubling them? Don't you think it would be better to leave them alone?'

But Lady Huntingdon had not put on her pattens and bongrace bonnet for nothing. She gave a peremptory gesture and snapped, 'Rattle the risp, Veronica. They need friends to show they care for them – especially now.'

The girl lifted the metal bar of the risp and it made its familiar grating sound. Like her mother's flat, the Brodies' still had its old iron risp, not so fashionable as a bell but less liable to be snatched off by drunken revellers on their way home when the taverns closed at ten o'clock. After a few moments the carved door opened and a scared-looking serving girl stared out at them.

'Where's the ladies? Are they here?' asked Lady Huntingdon.

The girl nodded, indicating a closed door behind her with a shrug of one shoulder. 'They're in there,' she said, opening the door wider. It took a brave person to withstand Lady Huntingdon.

The room was dark, lit by only one candle and the glowing embers in the hearth. Veronica blinked and, as her eyes adjusted to the dimness, she could make out a tall stone mantelpiece with a smoke-darkened painting of the Magi above it. Miss Jean and her younger, gayer, married sister Jemima Sherriff – Jamie as everyone called her – sat side by side at a table with the candle. The family Bible was open in front of them and they had been crying. If they were surprised or annoyed to see their callers, they did not show it. Jean sprang to her feet and immediately assumed her best social manner as if this were an ordinary visit on an ordinary day.

'Lady Huntingdon! How kind of you to come. Sit down. I'll tell the girl to bring tea,' she said, bustling towards them and wiping her reddened eyes with the back of her hand.

Veronica wanted to put out her arms and hug the poor woman, to tell her to stop, to sit down and weep if she wanted to, for everyone knew she had been devoted to her brother.

The tension was broken by Jamie, who stood up abruptly and ordered, 'Sit down, Jean, they know fine that Willie's been hanged. Don't pretend.'

Lady Huntingdon and her daughter stood awkwardly in the middle of the floor and for once the older woman was put out of countenance. 'We just came to say we're sorry, to give you our sympathy,' she offered to the bereaved sisters.

Jean was now standing gaunt and terrible beside the huge fireplace. 'Sorry?' she repeated. 'Oh, we're all sorry. What I want to know is why did he do it? He couldn't have needed the money. Our father left fifteen properties in the Canongate and ten thousand pounds! Did you know that?'

Veronica gasped. It was a fortune. The Deacon indeed had no pressing need to go out stealing at night with all that behind him. She was acutely conscious of the mounting tension and desperately wanted to break it, to fill the terrible silence with words. Common sense told her to keep quiet but she was in a highly charged emotional state and said the first thing that came into her head.

'Oh, Miss Brodie, when we were crossing the Lawnmarket, I was nearly ran down by a cart. It had your brother's body in the back.'

The sisters and her mother stared at her in horror for what seemed like an age.

'Yes, we know,' Jamie said at last. 'William wrote to the Lord Provost for a favour, asking that his body be released at once and not kept in the prison like other – like the others who are hanged.'

'The men were driving very fast, like madmen.' Veronica could not stop talking.

'They're trying to revive him,' said Jean bleakly, leaning down to light a taper from the grate. 'Yes, they're trying to wake him up, you see. He's arranged for a surgeon to wait down there in my father's workshop to operate on him, to bring him back to life when they cut him down, but they're trying to see if he can be jolted back first…'

'Who's trying?' asked Lady Huntingdon, who found it difficult to believe what she was hearing.

'His friends. Our brother had plenty of friends, you can be sure of that. And his, two sons – the one by the Grant woman and the other by Agnes Watt.'

'But they're only little boys,' blurted Veronica, who was not meant to know about the children Brodie had fathered on Agnes Watt and Anne Grant but had heard it all from Mary Cameron.

'Boys or not, they're out there trying to revive their *father*,' said Jean Brodie in a bitter voice, stressing the last word. 'They'd be better to let him stay dead. The shame he's brought on us! I swear that after this day is finished. I'll never say his name again and I'll thank you all not to speak it to me.'

In the lower part of the High Street the taverns and pie shops were doing a roaring trade, packed to the doors with the people who had come to see the hanging. Men and women stood in clusters on the pavements discussing the spectacle they had just watched. Solemn-faced, they went over and over the story of Deacon Brodie. If the object of a public hanging was to persuade the populace of the advisability of keeping within the law, this one had been a resounding success. The catharsis of watching human tragedy enacted before their eyes made many people ravenously hungry, and pedlars were busier than ever hawking cakes, toffee, bread and apples. All sorts of hucksters had come to town for the event, and outside the Tron Church a grizzled old showman was standing in front of a big metal cage in which sat a friendly-looking young lion.

'Fresh from the lands of the Dey of Algiers, this *man-eating* lion, this *killer*!' he was roaring, flicking at the beast with the end of his whip. But the lion sat impassive, ignoring the incitement to roar and draw a crowd. Passers-by hardly gave it a glance. They had been surfeited with sensation for one day, and a lion, even a man-eating one, was an anti-climax after what they had witnessed.

With a dirty tear-stained face, Helen Cameron slowly walked the short distance downhill from the place where the gallows stood west of St Giles. She held her nose at the opening to evil-smelling Fleshmarket Close where people were already spilling out of the door of James Clark's tavern. It had been a favourite haunt of Deacon Brodie and all the visitors wanted to see what it was like inside. She would normally have lingered longingly outside the lion's cage but today she passed it without a turn of the head. She passed the Tron with the cluster of enticing stalls of flower sellers and herb women who were happily disposing of their goods at a tremendous rate.

She greeted no one and looked neither to the right nor the left till she reached Cant's Close where she knew Cecil Grant lived. In her hand she clutched the stolen rample knot ribbons for she had made up her mind to give them to Cecil. On such a terrible day surely it would be a comfort to receive a present from a friend.

A shadowy archway led into Cant's Close, a long narrow wynd leading downhill to the Pleasance, and she saw a small crowd of women and children clustered at the entrance of the building where the Grant family lived. Of course, they were talking about Deacon Brodie.

'He was singing that highwayman's song of his on the scaffold,' said one tousle-haired woman.

'No, he didn't. He knelt down and begged the minister for forgiveness,' contradicted another. 'He'd learned the evil of his ways!'

The other listeners looked incredulous. 'Knelt down? Deacon Brodie? Who'd have guessed it?'

Helen heard all this as she pushed her way to the front of the crowd, trying to make a way to the stair door. She turned on the gossipers, her face angry. 'He never knelt down at all. He never even said he was' sorry once. He was very brave. He didn't seem to care that they were going to hang him.'

The women stopped gossiping and looked at her. They all knew who she was because she lived most of her life in the street and her family were well known.

'Did you see the hanging?' asked the red-faced woman disapprovingly.

'I did that, I saw everything that happened,' replied the child.

'What a scandal to let a bairn see a hanging. My bairn were kept in the house while it was on, but you might've guessed as much of the Cameron gang,' said one young wife…

Skinny little Helen made easy work of the climb to the eighth floor. She skipped up like a mountain goat, never once pausing for breath, for all her life she had lived in a tenement attic as high up as an eagle's nest, and steep stairs were no problem to her. The dark corners where the stairways turned round and where there were often secret alcoves or window ledges never frightened her. A child could hide there and watch people go by without them realizing they were being spied on. In her own stairway there was an alcove above the fourth floor where her grandfather said there had once been a holy statue, and she spent many hours there spying on the other families in the building. But now in Cant's Close there was no time to waste with lingering in alcoves. She had come to give Cecil her present.

Bonny, blonde Anne Grant was the mother of eleven-year-old Cecil and two younger boys, ten-year-old Peter and six-year-old David, fathered by Deacon Brodie. She loved her man, had accepted everything he told her without question and never pressed him for marriage. She respected his mania for secrecy and never talked outside about her lover, warning her children as soon as they were able to understand that they too should keep all details of their private lives to themselves. Privacy was difficult to maintain in the crowded tenements but she and Brodie were moderately successful.

Only Anne's immediate neighbours knew that the Deacon visited her at night and that he was the father of her little family. Unsanctioned unions like theirs were quite common in the High Street and she felt sure that he loved her although he often disappeared from her life for days or weeks at an end. Anne had been a seamstress when Brodie met her and because of her skill with a needle, her children were always neat and well turned out. 'Well brought up bairns,' approved the neighbours when the details of the children's parentage were revealed in the hullaballoo of gossip that followed the Deacon's arrest. Illegitimacy was no slur. If Anne had kept her children dirty or ragged, that would have been a greater shame on her.

Cecil, a solemn-faced, studious girl, was dark-haired like her father, with much of the Deacon's commanding presence in her face. He made no secret that she was his favourite child and while he languished in the Tolbooth prison awaiting execution, he had requested that she be allowed to visit him. He did not ask to see any of his other children or either of his 'wives'.

She had gone to the Tolbooth and calmly sat with him in his cell, letting him hold her hand. The only time her father had betrayed any emotion was that morning when they parted for the last time, when he held her close to him, sobbing into her hair.

The child seemed stunned when she returned home to her mother and a strange blankness settled over her from that moment. She moved around like a puppet, her face expressionless, and she alone shed no tears on the afternoon of the hanging.

It was easy for Helen to know which was the Grants' flat because of the sound of weeping coming from inside, where a frenzied-looking Anne sat sobbing in a wooden chair, with stiff-faced Cecil holding her hand. The youngest child David was lying face down on the box bed beside the fireplace, his shoulders heaving with grief. None of them paid any attention to the child who pushed open their unlocked door and stepped forward to thrust the bundle of crumpled scarlet-ribbons at Cecil. The older girl stared down at the offering, then slowly let go of her mother's hand and took them without speaking.

The rumple knot looked incongruously cheerful in that sorrowing household but Helen found her voice to say, 'They're for you, Cecil. I thought they were bonny so I got them for you.'

Cecil stared blankly at the ribbons. The significance of the gift was not lost on her. In the High Street she had often seen and pitied Helen Cameron, who looked so thin and poor that sometimes Cecil gave her a piece of candy or a bit of sugar bun. Till now she had not realized how much the ragged child appreciated these attentions.

There was an awkward atmosphere in the room with David and Anne continuing to sob, and Helen did not know whether to stay or go away. Cecil made no move to detain her or even to thank her, so she was turning back to the open door when there came the sound of running feet up the stairs. A blond boy came bursting into the room. His face was white and his hair rumpled. Because he wore no coat she could see marks of blood on the sleeves of his white shirt. It was Peter, Cecil's brother, as blond as she was dark and already taller than his sister. At the sight of him Anne gave a loud wail, jumped from her chair and ran to take him in her arms. If Cecil was the Deacon's favourite child, Peter was obviously hers.

'Oh Peter, what happened? Did Degraver save him? Where is he?' The urgent questions poured out of her, hope shining in her eyes.

The boy shook, his head and gave a gasping sob. 'Be calm. Mam. He was dead when they cut him down. They drove him through the streets, round and round the Castle, but he didn't wake up so they took him to the workshop. The surgeon lanced him in all the special places – but he was dead, his neck was broken. They're burying him in the Buccleuch ground tomorrow.'

Anne raised her hands above her head and gave an awful eldritch scream that set the hairs bristling on Helen's neck.

'Oh my God, it didn't work! It cost him a hundred pounds and it didn't work! I never thought it would work... I didn't trust that Frenchman. Didn't I say it wouldn't work? Oh my God, what's going to happen to me and my bairns now?'

Her screams went echoing down the stairwell, transfixing the interested crowd in the wynd. The Grants' flat was no place for a stranger and Helen, embarrassed, slipped out of the door and started to run back down the stairs. She wished with all her heart that she had not gone to see Cecil after all. Her visit had only been an intrusion, the gift of ribbons like a mockery. There were tears in her eyes when she reached the bottom of the stairs and she was shouldering her way through the press of people there when she heard a voice calling after her.

'Wait a minute, wait a minute.' Peter Grant appeared out of the door behind her and took her arm to lead her up the alley where they could speak privately.

'You're Colin Cameron's granddaughter, aren't you?' he asked and she nodded in agreement.

'Could I come to speak to him tomorrow?' asked the boy.

'He's always in. He can't get out much now. Do you know where we live?' replied the little girl.

'It's in Lady Stair's Close, isn't it?'

'Yes, it's up that close, on the top floor of Baxter's Buildings. I'll tell him you're coming.'

—

Sheets of rain drifted like ghosts down Edinburgh's High Street on the morning of Deacon Brodie's funeral. The water dropped steadily from the leaden skies like tears, making the grey slate roofs and the bleak fronts of the tall houses glisten as if they had been iced. There were only a few people about as the black-clad men carrying the coffin on their shoulders slipped and slithered down the precipitous wynd from Brodie's workshop to the West Bow. Once there, as if they were anxious to get the whole thing over as quickly as possible, they struck up a jogging pace with the plain deal box bobbing on their shoulders till they reached the wrought-iron gateway of the Buccleuch kirkyard.

Only a handful of people came to see the Deacon laid to rest. His two oldest sons, Peter Grant and Andrew Watt, stood behind a cluster of dark-suited men, one of them the chief councillor who had officiated at the previous day's hanging. The boys were ten years old, the same age almost to the month, but they were determined to act like grown men. They fought back their childish tears and kept their faces rigid as the black earth was thrown on top of their father's coffin. It was hard for them because they had good memories of Brodie, who had been generous and caring to all his children though insistent on keeping his relationship with them secret. Both boys had been brought up in an atmosphere of secrecy, with their mothers warning them never to talk outside about the man they knew as father.

But there had been a link between them for as long as they could remember. As soon as they were old enough to play in the street, they had gravitated naturally towards each other. All their young lives they had been best friends, and in the gangs of children who roamed up and down the alleys of Edinburgh they always ran together. They sat side by side in the dame school down at the bottom of the Canongate; they were always at each other's side during the forbidden games of throwing cabbage stalks down the chimneypots of the houses clustered on the terrace beneath the high walls of the Castle; they played tag up and down the steep closes; they rang the bells of people who were upstart enough to have such modern things installed and then ran away laughing and clutching each other when the angry householder came rushing out. Their mothers had known of their friendship but, not realizing the Deacon had a double life, neither woman had any reason to forbid the boys to see each other. When the revelation of Brodie's double life burst on them all, however, the boys were bombarded by outbursts from their angry mothers.

'Never speak to that Watt laddie again,' Anne Grant ordered her son.

'You keep away from the Grants,' Agnes Watt told Andrew.

The boys were confused and troubled because, since they were the oldest sons, their mothers used them as confidants and railed to them against the rival family.

Anne Grant called Agnes Watt a whore and told Peter, 'She was the one that gave your father an alibi. She said he slept the night of the robbery in her bed. She's just a street walker shaming me in front of all the people! But it didn't save him, did it? Who's to believe her when she says those bairns are his? They could be anybody's.'

Her son bent his head, wishing she would be quiet. When he thought about his friend, he realized that everyone should have recognized long ago that Andrew was the Deacon's son. He had the same black hair and eyebrows, the same shining dark brown

24

eyes, the same strutting way of walking that distinguished his father. Oh yes, Andrew was his father all over, far more so than Peter who was fair like his mother.

Agnes Watt, who had indeed been a street walker before settling down under Brodie's protection in three rooms in Libberton's Wynd, had a coarser line in invective than Anne Grant, and entertained her neighbours with accusations against the Deacon's other family.

'She thinks she's a lady does that Annie Grant but I ken her for what she is – she's nothing better than a slag. My man was tired of her or he wouldn't have come into my bed, would he? And there's another thing. I'd like to know who it was that told the councillors he'd gone to Ostend? Who showed them the letter he wrote to her? If they hadn't seen it, they wouldn't have known where to go to catch him, would they? Oh, aye, Madame Grant must be at the back of it. I wonder how much they paid her for the information.'

Loyalty to their mothers, who were both in a state of shock, confused the boys. They also suffered themselves from mixed feelings towards their father of love and betrayal, and over the weeks that passed between the Deacon's arrest and his hanging they had carefully avoided each other. But when his body was cut down from the gibbet they found themselves side by side as they helped his friends to load him onto the cart. They felt no rancour towards each other, in fact they found it comforting to be together at such a time though it was impossible for either of them to talk about his feelings.

Now they stood together at his graveside, drawn to the same spot and once again strangely comforted by the knowledge of their shared shock and sorrow.

Andrew slid a look at his brother's face, normally pert and cheeky, now unnaturally solemn. He longed to talk over his thoughts with Peter and was not to know that the other boy felt exactly the same way.

Remembering their weeping mothers, however, they kept their eyes fixed on the dwindling mound of wet earth being rapidly shovelled back into the ground. Both of them knew that the responsibility for their mothers and the other children in their families would fall on them now that there was no money and no provider. Their days of going to school and playing in the street had been abruptly terminated.

When the gravediggers finally threw down their shovels and mopped their brows, the men of the funeral party exchanged a few words among themselves and then turned back to the gate. The Deacon's sons trailed on behind. They were shoulder to shoulder when they reached the gateway and there they paused to look directly at each other. Andrew's lip quivered as if he were about to weep.

Peter thrust out his hand to say, 'Goodbye, Andrew. We won't be able to be together any more but I'm still your friend.'

His brother grasped and held it firmly. 'Goodbye, Peter,' he replied, 'I'm glad we're still friends. I hope we'll be able to talk about this one day when we're grown men.'

Then they parted, deliberately walking off in different directions. Anyone watching them would have seen how difficult they were finding it to fight back their tears. After all, they were still very young.

–

The ancient city of Edinburgh always reminded Helen of a dragon in a fairy tale because it stretched along its ridge of volcanic rock like a mysterious animal from one of her grandfather's stories. The dragon's head was the Castle, high on its steep perch, stout walls studded with sally ports like watching eyes. The dragon's tail was the snaking High Street leading down to the Canongate and the deserted but still impressive Palace of Holyrood with its fountains and courtyards where Mary Queen of Scots had held court and where her lover Rizzio was stabbed to death before her eyes.

Along the dragon's spine, church spires stuck up like fins marking the Royal Mile which had seen so many kings and queens riding up and down it in solemn procession from Castle to Palace. The Royal Mile was never quiet, never empty. Feet clattered along the cobbles from early morning till late at night because Edinburgh was the most populous city in Great Britain – nowhere else had so many people crammed into so constricted a space.

Helen loved the evenings best because that was when the women leaned their elbows on the window ledges high above the street and chattered like starlings to their neighbours. While they talked they hauled in their multicoloured rags of washing that had been hung out to dry on wooden frames sticking out from almost every window.

The child, her head full of magic, wandered around listening to the music of the street: women screeched and shouted; beggars played bagpipes or banged drums; shopkeepers stood in the doorways of their open booths drumming up trade, stallholders hawked food and flowers, cheap toys or lengths of cloth; pigs, hens and scavenging dogs chirped, squealed and snorted as they rooted about among people's feet; carriage drivers, carters, sedan-chair carriers and water caddies hustled about their business.

When the smoke from the tall chimneys began rising into the air as people prepared their evening meals, Helen would sit on a stone step at the top of the Grassmarket and soak in the drama of the street. She was waiting for her tired mother to come trudging up the hill. When the familiar figure appeared, the child rushed up to take her hand and they walked home together.

One of the best-known characters in the Old Town was Mary Cameron who worked as a water caddy, carrying buckets of water from the five town wells to the flats of her customers up and down the High Street, for there was no piped water. She was a sharp-tongued, big, raw-boned woman with straggling dark hair and a hooked nose. Her back was permanently bent with hard work and her body ruined by constant childbearing.

Little Helen, the last in her family, was her thirteenth child in fifteen years. The rigours of her life and the constant anxiety of living with a husband who drank all the money he made when he *did* go out to work as a sedan-chair carrier, had coarsened Mary so much that it was difficult even for members of her own family to remember what a fine, upstanding girl she had once been. Though she looked rough, and sounded even rougher when she stood in the queue of water carriers waiting for their turn at the well, Mary Cameron had a soft heart and Helen was her favourite child.

It was important to her to have a daughter for she was one of a close Edinburgh matriarchy who, like squawking rooks, inhabited the attics of various tenements up and down the High Street and the Canongate. They had been living there since time began, it seemed, and there was a camaraderie among the women of the tribe that overcame all other considerations and loyalties.

They banded together against their men and their enemies from other families; they shared each other's sorrows and avenged each other's slights. Should any outsider hurt one of them, the whole gang of screaming viragos would turn out on the cobbles, yelling, rioting and throwing around excrement of which there was always a bountiful supply in the alleyways of Edinburgh.

Her sisters, aunts and cousins had sympathized with Mary when she kept on giving birth to sons, most of whom died in infancy. Only three boys survived before she eventually had Helen, a skinny changeling of a baby who looked to be not long for this world. It was a constant anxiety to Mary that her daughter would succumb to one of the many diseases that carried off the bairns of both rich and poor in the cramped tenements where the poor lived on the top storeys and the rich beneath them. They were neighbours and equals and social divisions impressed no one very greatly. They knew far too much about each other for that.

Every day Mary told her cronies at the well head, 'I'm bothered about my wee lassie, she's all skin and bones, and so fine that it looks as if the sun shines right through her.'

The other women eyed the tiny baby and shook their heads. 'She'll not make old bones,' they agreed gloomily, for optimism was not their style.

When Helen reached the age of four and was able to trail along behind her mother they were still shaking their heads about her. 'You're lucky to have got her up to this age,' they told Mary.

Now aged seven, Helen was as, bright as a button, could read and write and knew every street and alleyway in the city, but she was still a skinny wee thing without a picking of meat on her, and the wiseacres marvelled at her resilience. 'It's a miracle,' they told her proud mother. 'She should be dead by now.'

Mary had grown more relaxed about Helen's chances of life over the years though she had to agree that she was not the healthiest-looking child in the district. Small for her age, with excessively thin arms and legs and a translucent skin, she was yet noticeable because of her pretty heart-shaped face and her enormous pale blue eyes, eyes which had a rim of darker blue around the iris to make their impact even stronger. Her eyes showed the spirit and intelligence that glowed and burned inside the child. Sometimes when she lifted them to people, they faltered in what they were saying though they did not know exactly why.

'Once you've looked into my wee Helen's eyes, you'll never forget her. She casts a spell with them. She's got magic eyes,' said her proud mother.

The chief friend of the child with the magic eyes was her grandfather, Colin Cameron, who looked after her when her mother was working and who fed her imagination with his stories of long ago. Though now an invalid, the old man still had a grave and proud air and Helen loved his voice, which was soft and sibilant. To strangers it sometimes sounded as if he were talking Gaelic all the time though in fact he only sprinkled his conversation with Gaelic words, mainly endearments addressed to his granddaughter.

He, called her things like *thasghaid* or *mo ghaoil* – my darling – but the name she liked best was *a luaidh* – my dearest little one.

Colin Cameron was a Highlander who had arrived in the city in the army of Charles Edward Stewart on its way back from Derby and, sensing the hopelessness of the Jacobite cause, had settled down in Edinburgh where he worked as a street caddy, carrying messages and undertaking all manner of commissions for the better-off inhabitants. His intelligence and astuteness were legendary even among the other caddies, a body of men renowned for their quickness of wit.

When the strange disease struck him, ageing him rapidly and withering his limbs, his fellow caddies, because of their respect for him, elected him their Constable and arbiter of their disputes. Every week they came to the flat to carry him down the stairs to a tavern where they held their meetings, so he had not lost touch with the life of the city he loved so much. Nothing surprised him, nothing escaped his notice or the notice of his friends. Ask Colin Campbell about any citizen or any place and he would instantly have the information at his fingertips, though he might not always be prepared to share it with you.

The child and the old man had a strong bond. Today, because the weather was bad, she sat with him beside their smoking hearth and listened entranced as he talked about his own child-hood away up in the Highlands where tall mountains swept down into the sea and the glens were full of fairy people. He had the Gaelic love of romance and an ability to weave spells with words.

Helen pressed herself against his withered legs and asked for her favourite story. 'Tell me about Charlie, tell me about how you came to Edinburgh,' she pleaded.

Lighting up his clay pipe, Colin began telling about the day in 1745 in when as a young man fresh from the wildness of Lochiel he marched into Edinburgh behind Prince Charles Edward Stewart, the Young Pretender.

'When they saw us coming, all the men of Edinburgh ran away, just took to their heels and ran. We didn't have to fight as much as a dog. We must have looked a wild lot – Highlanders out of the glens, some of us without any shoes. But we each had a broadsword, oh aye, each man had a blade and he wasna feart to use it.'

The child closed her eyes. In her imagination she could see her tall grandfather among the marching column of kilted men striding up towards the Castle.

'And Charlie, tell me about him,' she pleaded.

Colin looked sad as he always did when he talked about Charles Edward Stewart. 'Oh, he was a grand enough young fellow was Charlie, a real Stewart, a charmer and free with his men, no fancy airs and graces. We loved him and we were glad to die for him. Too many did – but he was a Scotsman, not like those German johnnies they've put over us now.'

'What did Charlie *look* like?'

'Bonny brown eyes and a fine face he had on him. Tall as a pine tree and straight as a pikestaff. He wore the kilt like we all did and a grand plaid in the finest material with a black jacket and decorations on the breast – here – sparkling in the sunshine. His hair was powdered and tied at the back in a black ribbon. He didn't wear a wig.' Helen gave a shiver. The mention of powdered hair brought back the memory of Deacon Brodie waiting for the noose to go over his head. She pressed herself against her grandfather's leg and grasped his hand.

He was sensitive to her moods and asked, 'What's the matter, *mo ghaoil*?'

'Nothing,' she whispered.

'Tell me, *thasghaid*,' he insisted and she gave a little sob.

'It's just that every now and again I remember seeing the Deacon... you know.'

'You've to forget that,' he ordered firmly. 'Put it out of your mind. You shouldn't have gone to that hanging. But forget it now, I'm always here to watch over you.'

–

The rain had stopped and a watery sun was silvering the blue-grey slate roofs far below him when Peter Grant finally reached the tenth floor of Baxter's Buildings. Through the tiny window of the Camerons' attic room he could look out across the Nor' Loch to the glittering river Forth and the shores of Fife.

'You've the best view in Edinburgh,' he said to the old man who was sitting hunched up on a stool at the fireside. On the floor beside him sat his granddaughter, the thin child who had been at Peter's house the previous day.

'Och, aye, the view's fine as, long as you look outwards and not inwards,' agreed Colin.

Peter stared around. Though his own family were not rich and his home was nothing like as grand as some of the other flats in the High Street, this room spoke only too clearly of poverty. There was no furniture except a couple of stools and a battered table. There were no beds and the family obviously slept on the floor wrapped in rags, for there were bundles of tattered coverlets neatly piled up beneath the window.

The child and the old man saw him looking and he flushed red at the thought that his pity might have showed.

'I came to ask your advice – and your help,' he told the old man.

Colin Cameron nodded gravely. 'Ask away,' he said.

'I wondered how you went about becoming a caddy. You're their Constable and I thought you'd be able to tell me.'

'You'll have to keep your mother and the other bairn now, won't you?' Cameron's voice was understanding, and the boy nodded.

'We need money now, we can't wait till I serve an apprenticeship for something,' he said flatly.

'You're a smart lad, I can see that, and you're strong enough looking. How old are you?'

Peter was going to lie and add on a few years but the directness of the old man's stare prevented him. 'I'm ten, nearly eleven, but I'm strong, I really am.'

'That's old enough to start, there's no shame in being a caddy, you know. Lord Haymount, who sat on the bench when I was a young man, sent his two sons to work as caddies so that they could learn about life. He said it was the perfect training – better than the Grand Tour – and so it is.'

Peter nodded in agreement and smiled for the first time that day.

Colin Cameron was watching the boy's face closely and he added, 'But we're a close crew. We like to keep it amongst ourselves. We're nearly all Highlanders, you know. Can you speak the Gaelic? That's what many of us talk amongst ourselves.'

Peter shook his, head. 'No, but I can learn. My mother's family's from the. North. Her father was from Appin and spoke the Gaelic so she knows some words.'

'Oh yes, of course, I mind your grandfather. He was in Charlie's army with me,' said Cameron. It was obvious that this was the clinching matter as far as Peter's acceptance as a trainee caddy was concerned. 'I'll speak to the others and get someone to take you on with them.'

'When will I know?' Peter was anxious to start right away.

'Soon, soon,' sighed the old man. 'I'll send my little *thasghaid* here to tell you when.'

Peter looked at the child sitting silently beside her grand-father. 'What's a *thasghaid*?'

'It means my treasure,' said the old man. 'That's your first lesson in Gaelic. If you want to learn more, come to me and I'll teach you.'

Many beautiful women had lived in the High Street throughout history and the people in the buildings and alleyways that housed them took pride in their beauty, celebrating them even after they were old and wrinkled or dead and gone. They were debated over and discussed by all the lingerers and users of the streets, even by the solemn-faced lawyers who clustered round the door of the court house, or the judges, resplendent in official robes and with wigs well settled on their heads, who marched along the pavement from their homes to the courts, surrounded by a few old men in the shabby uniform of a Town Guard.

There was always one girl who was esteemed above the others. At night the young bloods toasted her in the drinking clubs, and by day passers-by smiled at her, taking pleasure in her loveliness. In the year 1790 Miss Veronica Hay brought the honour of housing the town's greatest beauty to Lady Stair's Close.

It was not only that she had a beautiful face with a Grecian profile and pale cream skin, but she also had her mass of curling hair, her tall and lissom figure and an admirable sweetness of expression and address. Even her rivals in loveliness found it hard to feel resentment about Veronica for she was without guile or suspicion.

If she had a fault indeed it was that she was too trusting, too malleable, too much under the influence of her dominating mother who looked on her now, in the bloom of her beauty, as a saleable commodity at the peak of its marketable possibilities.

Daily she was warned against throwing herself away on some low-born fellow; daily she was rehearsed in the bloodlines and family connections of the town's most eligible bachelors and even the mother's customary reluctance to spend money was thrown aside. She called in dressmakers and seamstresses who knelt on the carpet around her statuesque daughter and robed her in the finest silks and satins. When she went to the society balls held by a redoubtable pair of maiden ladies of good birth, young men vied and bribed for the honour of drawing her fan out of the hat. The ladies would not allow the young people to pick their own partners but if they had done, Veronica Hay would have been overwhelmed.

Lady Huntingdon frequently consulted her priggish son Dr Thomas about a possible marriage for the girl. Dispassionately they weighed up her chances of a brilliant match – high on the plus side were her loveliness, her sweetness and malleability. But on the minus side was her lack of learning. Not for her the clever conversation of ladies in high society. Her mother had thought it unnecessary to have her tutored too intensively because the girl showed little interest in learning.

As they sat debating her future over the tea tray, Veronica slipped out of the flat on an illicit rendezvous. When she reached the bottom of the stairs, the water caddy's child was sitting on the step. Her enormous eyes were fixed on Veronica and it was obvious that she was waiting to run errands or carry a lantern for her.

Every time she went in or out the child was waiting, but Veronica was not annoyed at this evidence of devotion. Her good nature made her pause and talk to the little thing. She had seen the child around for years, but did not know what she was called, so she said with a smile, 'Good evening. What's your name?'

'It's Helen.' The reply was accompanied by a grin that brought the pinched wee face to life and Veronica was surprised to see that the ragged child really had the most amazing eyes –

so big and so very blue… and there was something else, they looked like the eyes of someone who had been alive for a long time and had seen and understood all sorts of things. The effect of them was quite uncanny.

'It's getting dark. Can I light your way?' asked. Helen, jumping up and preparing to lift a tar-soaked torch from a pile in the corner. They were standing in a pool of brilliance cast by a guttering oil lamp on the wall but all around the gathering darkness was painting deep velvet shadows in the corners of the square.

'Oh, that's not necessary. I'm only going down to Advocate's Close to meet a friend,' Veronica replied.

But Helen would take no refusal, for she worshipped Miss Hay. From her dark alcove on the stairs she spied on the older girl continually, admiring her lovely clothes, her graceful style and the devotion shown towards her by the streams of young men who climbed the stairs to pay their respects.

If Helen could have chosen to be born in another body, she would definitely be Veronica Hay. But when she said this to her grandfather, he snorted and told her, 'You're fine as you are. Beauty like hers doesn't always bring happiness, you'll find that out in time.'

'Let me light you to Advocate's Close, *please*. If you like, I'll wait and light you back as well. There's some gey rough folk on the street at night and the lamp at the head of the close's gone out.'

Helen ran to light her torch from a brazier burning at the half open door of the blacksmith's shop on the corner of their square and Veronica almost laughed aloud at the unlikeliness of her protector. The child looked more in need of protection than anyone else about that evening.

'Do you think you can keep me safe?' she inquired with a smile.

Offended, Helen turned, wearing her bravest face. 'Of course I can. I'm a braw fighter and I can yell louder than anybody in the High Street. Please let me light your way, Miss Veronica.'

Veronica gave in. The poor little, thing probably wanted the tip usual for such a job. 'All right,' she said. 'Go on, show me the road with your torch, but you needn't wait. I'll get the nightwatchman to bring me home.'

At nightfall the drama of the streets was more muted although the alleyways were never empty, never quiet. Feet clattered along their cobbles from early morning till late at night. Down the dark street Helen, who had not grown very much over the past two years, guided the tall young woman in her silken gown like a small tug manoeuvring a stately ship of sail. As they went, she called out instructions:

'Mind this pile of muck here, mind you don't get your shoes dirty, keep to the middle of the road.' Full of self-importance, she waved her torch over the rough cobbled surface, past an unending line of high-fronted buildings, their façades dotted with windows. There was not a vacant inch of ground that had not been built on. Magnificent old mansions of the Scottish aristocracy were jostled by ramshackle tenements that looked as if they were about to fall down – and in fact from time to time some of them did just that because from the early Middle Ages they had been thrown up without proper foundations and only managed to stay upright by leaning on their neighbours.

At street level the buildings were pierced by frequent barrel-vaulted tunnels, leading into mysterious alleyways, some of them dark and sinister – the haunts, it seemed, of thieves and robbers. Others gave access into what looked like a different world to the noisy bustle of the main street because, peering along them, passers-by could catch sight of the tops of trees reaching for the sky behind high stone walls.

These alleys – vennels, as they were called – gave Edinburgh a herringbone pattern because they branched off the main thoroughfare like the ribs off a fish's backbone. On the north side they led precipitously down to the rubbish dumps on the steeply sloping bank of the Nor' Loch, partly drained now but still with a pool of shining – but too often stinking – water in the middle. On the south side the alleys and dark passageways led just as steeply downhill to the open space of the Grassmarket, the dark Cowgate and the green Pleasance, where once upon a time the gentry had their orchards and pleasure gardens.

After a short walk which the proud Helen did not want to finish so quickly, they reached Advocate's Close, a long and low-roofed gully that appeared pitch black as they looked down it. Not waiting to be told to go home, the bearer of the light dashed ahead like a rabbit disappearing down a burrow. 'Come on. I'll show the way,' her voice came echoing back and at the doorway of the house where Veronica's lover Henry Stewart was waiting, the child stopped proudly with the brand guttering in her hands and lighting up her pleased little face.

'How did you know I was coming here?' asked Veronica with misgiving. If the child knew about Stewart, how long would it take the news to reach her mother?

'I've seen you coming down here before.'

The young woman said nothing but reached into her silk purse and brought out a farthing. 'Don't tell anyone about this, will you?' she requested, holding out the money, but the child gestured it away as if offended.

'I don't want paying. I just wanted to help you. Of course I'll not tell anybody anything. It's your own business.'

–

St Giles' bell was ringing eight o'clock, closing time for the crowded courts, offices, shops and booths of the Old Town when Helen re-emerged from the mouth of Advocate's Close. She stood for a moment pressed against the wall watching people hurrying out of their places of business and into the taverns for their nightly refreshment. Most of them would stay there, chatting with their friends, for a little while before setting off for home and supper. Others would continue drinking until the ten o'clock bell rang and then they'd reel out into the street, making a lot of noise and causing quieter folk to open their windows and yell out in anger.

But now, as she watched and listened to the eight o'clock bell, the pavements became very crowded with white-faced clerks rushing along, pushed aside by women burdened with bundles who shoved their way through the crowd. Tired journeymen, still wearing the clothes that showed their calling, straightened their shoulders when they saw the door of their favourite hostelry opening before them.

The 'Wha' Wants Me?' man, standing outside the Luckenbooth stalls that faced across the road towards St Giles, was giving his usual loud call: 'Wha Wants Me? Wha Wants Me?' But there were no customers tonight for the chamber pots he carried under his cloak for the relief of anyone caught short on the street.

Happily watching the passing throng, Helen saw Andrew Watt, the Deacon's dark-haired son, coming out of a silversmith's booth built against the wall of St Giles. She had heard he was working there as an apprentice to the smith, and tonight he was wearing a short leather apron tucked up into his belt and had small hammers tucked in at his waistband. He looked tired and anxious as he heaved up the shop shutters and pulled the heavy iron securing bar into position. Wearily he stepped back from finishing the job just as his half-brother Peter came running up the road and collided with him, knocking him to his knees. From the ground Andrew stared up at the other boy and they stayed frozen in their individual positions for a few moments until Peter leaned down to help his brother up off the cobbles.

'I'm sorry, I didn't see you in the dark. I hope you're not hurt,' he apologized.

Andrew picked up a fallen hammer, brushed at his legs with his hands and smiled. 'It's all right, Peter. I'm not hurt.'

They stood awkwardly together, words unspoken on their lips, and they were still smiling when they walked away from each other. The watcher in the shadows could see how badly they wanted to stand for a while and talk but their fear of being seen made their old ease and friendliness no longer possible.

Collecting herself, she ran down the road after Peter Grant and caught him by the tail of his coat. 'Where are you going, Peter? Can I come with you?' she asked, for she had come to know him well through his visits to her grandfather.

Startled out of his thoughts, the boy said, '*Dhia!*' – a Gaelic exclamation of surprise which he had learned from Colin. 'Oh, it's you, you imp. I was on my way to deliver a note to a woman in Blair's Close but she's not in. I'm going back to the Mercat Cross to see what's doing.'

Peter was kept busy with caddying jobs now and he had grown even taller over the past two years, so people regarded him as a man and trusted him with their commissions.

Helen hung on to his coat and pleaded, 'Come up and see Grandfather. He's not well today and he's not been out for a long time, the cold weather's bad for him.'

She knew that Peter was good company for the old man, far kinder and more considerate than her own three brothers or her father. The boys worked as porters in the Fleshmarket and thought of their grandfather as a nuisance because he made no contribution to the household. Her father rarely came home at all and was never sober when he did because he spent most of his time and all of the little money he earned in Lucky Middlemiss's tavern in the Grassmarket and only came home for food or a fight with her mother.

'In that case, I'll come with you. What are you doing out so late yourself? You should be in your bed.'

She grimaced. 'Don't be silly. I've been lighting Miss Hay down the street.'

'The bonny Miss Hay? The one who lives in your building?' Like all young men he had seen Veronica and admired her desperately. 'Where was she going?'

Helen shook her head. 'I promised not to tell but she's gone to see a friend.'

Peter laughed. 'I know which friend that is, it's the lad who lodges with a woman in Advocate's Close. He works in a Writer's office in Parliament Square.'

She was impressed by his knowledge but reluctant to give away Veronica's secret so she kept quiet.

Peter went on, 'He's tall, with ginger-coloured hair. His name's Stewart and he's from Inverness. He's a bit of a lad for the ladies.'

Helen shook her head in admiration. 'My, you're going to make a grand caddy, Peter, you know all the news already and you're only starting.'

'I've had a good teacher in your grandfather,' said the boy and she walked proudly along beside him trying very hard to act like a grown-up and make interesting conversation. It would be polite to ask after his family, so she said, 'How's your mother and Cecil?'

But the question seemed to depress him and his face darkened. 'My mother's sickly. She's been that way since – for two years now. Cecil's helping her with the sewing and they're kept busy. Your Miss Hay comes to them for bits and pieces.'

'I haven't seen Cecil for a long time, she used to be kind to me,' Helen told him. It was true that Cecil no longer walked along the High Street as she used to do, and thinking about the past made the child remember the terrible day she took Cecil the rumple knot. The shadows of the street suddenly seemed more threatening and she gave a shudder, pressing herself closer to Peter.

'Cecil's changed. She doesn't go out much now,' said Peter shortly. It was obvious that he did not like his sister very much.

–

'Helen, Helen!' Her mother's angry voice came down the stairs and the child in the alcove clutched her arms more tightly round her legs and tried to make herself invisible. She had not gone into their attic with Peter but had stayed behind, secreting herself in her favourite place on the stair, waiting for Miss Veronica to come home. Just a glimpse of her idol was all she wanted, just the reassurance that Miss Hay was safe back from Advocate's Close.

But her mother always knew where she could be found and now she came plunging down the stairs, swearing to herself, and pulled her daughter out. 'It's nearly gardy loo time, you ought to be asleep,' she scolded. Mary Cameron was wan-faced with the efforts of her working day, and longed for sleep. It baffled her why the child liked spending hour after hour in that alcove watching people go in and out.

Dragged upstairs, Helen could not sleep until she knew Miss Veronica was safe home. After ten o'clock it was not safe for anyone, especially not for a woman, to walk the streets. Curled up on her nest of rags, she kept her sharp ears open. The door was slightly ajar and she could hear all the noises of people preparing for the night in the flats below. It made her feel safe, as if she were an ant in a huge ant hill, surrounded by others living their lives, being sad or happy.

Boom, boom, boom – went St Giles' bell, telling all the people under its care to go to sleep in peace. Tonight its voice was friendly and reassuring, not solemn and portentous as it had been on the day they hanged Deacon Brodie. The bell told her that it was ten o'clock, and all down the street the inhabitants of the tall tenements would be opening their windows and emptying their chamber pots on to the pavement with cries of 'Gardy loo!' The cry was meant to alert anyone passing below to the danger of being deluged with an unspeakable downpour. People in the street were meant to call out 'Haud yer hand' but too often the tenement dwellers poured before they called, and unfortunate passers-by were drenched.

At the sound of the bell Mary Cameron rose with a sigh, grabbed her father-in-law's brimming chamber pot, took it to the window and poured it out. The deluge narrowly missed a couple lurking in the shadows at the door and a sharp cry of anger rang out: 'Take care, take care!' It was Veronica's voice and, hearing it, Helen turned on her side and dropped off to sleep at once.

–

In the ensuing weeks Helen did not fail to notice the bloom of beauty that shone from Miss Hay. She sparkled and shone in the grey city like a radiant star; she gave off a feeling of charged emotion that infected even the oldest and most cynical greybeards on the Street and made them smile indulgently upon her.

'That lassie's in love,' said Mary Cameron with a shake of the head when she saw Veronica pattering over the courtyard in her pattens one summer morning, and she was right.

Oblivious to what people were saying about her, Veronica moved in a dream of romance, so wrapped up in it that she even failed to notice the child dogging her every step. Each time the lovers had one of their clandestine meetings, Helen would be lurking round a corner or hanging about in a darkened doorway. But they were so far gone in their ecstasy of desire that they had almost abandoned caution and did not look for spies.

Veronica thought of nothing except Henry Stewart and his delightful urgency when he pressed her to him and asked her to yield, coaxing her, petting her, pleading with her. The power she had over him intoxicated her, made her capricious at one moment and appealing the next. She wanted him with a fervency that matched his own and the passion that arose in her when he touched her skin, when he let his lips linger on her white neck, brought a weakness that almost overwhelmed her so that she trembled uncontrollably and wondered if she might faint.

She was sure that she was the first and only woman in the world to have felt the force of such desire, and laughed to herself when she speculated about her mother and her straight-laced sisters, married to their merchant husbands away in the West of

Scotland. They did not know what it was like; they could not know or they would not be so sober-sided, so disapproving of passion, so tolerant of their dull husbands. She thought of her father reeling home at night and remembered the Edinburgh saying: 'Every drunkard's a gentleman and every gentleman a drunkard.' Not for her. Her lover was not a drunkard. He was the perfect man because he loved her so much. No other woman could know what love was like.

When they were apart she lay in bed and longed for him, longing so much that she could almost feel him beside her, feel his hands on her. At that dangerous thought, she tossed beneath her quilt and cried out in anguished longing. She was a woman made for love and having to deny it made her frantic.

She knew that he was as badly smitten and that it was affecting his work. He told her with a downcast face how, almost every day, his employer, a grey-faced Writer to the Signet, had reason to chastise and threaten him for his mistakes. The man said, 'You needn't think because you're my cousin that I'm going to keep you on here if you continue in this way. I'll send you back to Inverness, my lad, unless you stay out of the ale shops and come in here brighter every morning.'

Neither of them was cautious; neither gave a thought to the consequences of their actions. Only fear of her mother's wrath prevented Veronica from giving herself to him.

'My brother came today and told Mother that the son of some landowner near Perth is interested in making an offer for me,' she told her lover one evening when they lingered in the shadows at the back of the Tron Church. The effect was everything she desired and he groaned in genuine pain.

'I'll kill myself if any other man gets you, we love each other, we must be together,' he told her and the thought of being apart made them both nearly weep.

'I love you too,' she told him, safe and secure in his arms.

He held her tighter before saying in a resolute voice, 'I've made up my mind. We'll marry. You're old enough and so am

I. They can't stop us. If we go out and marry, they'll have to accept it.'

The first doubts gripped her. She was used to a comfortable life and knew how poor he was; she had been told only too often how marketable her beauty was and now she was on the verge of throwing that all away on a man who lived in a lodging house. She knew he had no family behind him and she could imagine the wrath with which her brother would receive the news of her marriage to a pauper. He would not give her as much as a groat for her dowry, and life without a cosy flat and fine clothes would be a hard penalty to pay for love. But Henry was more urgent than she and knew how to coax her, so within a short time she was prepared to cast almost all her doubts away.

'But who would marry us?' she whispered. 'Any minister in Edinburgh would instantly tell my mother. They all know me.'

He had thought it out. 'My sister and her husband are living in rooms in Princes Street and they know a man who'll do it – for a consideration. Don't worry, I'll find the money somehow. You order yourself a new dress and we'll be married next week.'

–

A few days later Miss Hay came out of her door and called up to Helen in the alcove, 'Go down to Mistress Grant's and collect an underskirt she's making for me.'

It was the first time that Helen had been in Cant's Close since the day of the Deacon's hanging and there was a feeling of dread in her heart as she climbed the staircase. She found Anne Grant looking pale and lined, with wings of grey in her blonde hair, but Cecil had grown into a tall young woman, swarthy-skinned though like her father, and unable, it seemed, to look you in the eye. Her hair was no longer glossy and attractive but looked strangely flat and repellent, as if she washed it rarely.

The two women stared at Helen as if she were an unwelcome intruder, and Cecil challenged, 'What's it you want?'

'Miss Hay sent me for her underskirt.'

'Oh, we're just finishing it off,' said Anne in a kinder tone. 'Sit down there till we put on the rest of the rosebuds.'

Between them on the table was spread a large white cloth covered with dozens of little pink satin rosebuds which were so attractive and realistic that Helen longed to pick one up and sniff at it. She put out a hand towards them and sighed, 'They're lovely. It looks like a bride's dress, doesn't it?'

Cecil snatched the corner of the cloth away as if terrified. 'Get your dirty hands off that,' she snapped, 'the likes of you shouldn't even be carrying a fine skirt like this.'

Cut to the quick, the younger girl sat down abruptly. There was a terrible silence in the room and she noticed the urgency with which Cecil was sewing, stitching on the pretty rosebuds as if her very life depended on it. Peter was right, she was no longer the kind of girl she had been before her father died. The bitterness of her soul poisoned the very air around her.

–

'Something terrible must have happened to Miss Veronica.' Helen's face was worried as she confided to Peter Grant after one of his visits to her grandfather. As she spoke she glanced up to the window of Lady Huntingdon's flat but there was no sign of life inside. For the past few weeks the child had rarely seen Miss Hay going up and down the stairs. Her mother reported that there had been a terrible row downstairs late one night, with Lady Huntingdon shrieking at her daughter and even Dr Thomas being called in to add his wrath to hers.

'What's the matter with her? Is she sick?' Peter had the true caddy's interest in other-people's lives.

Helen nodded. 'She could be. The last time I saw her she had a face as white as a ghost. She looked as if she'd been bled.'

Next day Peter stopped Helen on the street with some news. 'I asked around about your Miss Hay and it seems that she must be lovesick. Thon fellow who was courting her has been sent away to India. They say he took money from the Writer's office where he worked. The Writer's a relation of his, though, so he didn't prosecute – just sent him away.'

'Oh, poor Miss Hay, no wonder she's so miserable. I wonder if she ever got a chance to wear her bonny underskirt with all the roses on it?' sighed Helen.

It was sad to see the change in the pretty girl downstairs. She looked dispirited and cowed whenever she did go out – and always under the strict chaperonage of her grim-faced mother who was obviously not prepared to trust her on the streets alone. The winter passed without any gaiety returning to Miss Hay, and the young men in the drinking clubs began toasting other nubile beauties.

On one of the first fine days of spring Helen was hanging around the building entry, warming herself in the fitful sunshine that slanted down from a gap between the high canyon walls of buildings around her, when she saw Dr Thomas, immaculate in a black suit with shining silver buttons, coming down the passageway in company with a stumbling, red-faced man in buff breeches, brown gaiters and a blue top coat. Even to the child he looked like a country bumpkin come to town but Dr Thomas was treating him with great condescension and politely ushered him upstairs to Lady Huntingdon's flat. Neither gave a glance at the urchin on the step but her sharp eyes missed nothing, and something told her that the visit of this stranger was important. They stayed upstairs for a long time, and when they re-emerged the red-faced man was beaming delightedly. Even Dr Thomas looked pleased and clapped his friend on the shoulder when they parted at the mouth of the close.

When the stranger came again on his own, Helen's suspicions were even more fully aroused and so it was not much of a surprise to her a month later when her mother came rushing up the stairs to announce that Miss Veronica was going to be married.

'She's not marrying that big red-faced man with the wee eyes who came with Dr Thomas, is she?' Helen asked. Surely her lovely Miss Veronica would not be thrown away on such an unattractive suitor? Things, didn't happen like that in the stories of romance told by her grandfather.

'I don't know anything about that,' replied Mary. 'All her mother said is that the groom's a farmer in a big way in Berwickshire. He's got a house in Berwick and a great spread of land just outside the town. There's plenty money there.'

'That's him, that's the one, they must have forced her into it,' groaned Helen, and her disappointment was very real.

The bridegroom-to-be was John Ker of Broadmeadows, Berwickshire. Peter saw the announcement in the newspaper and brought the broadsheet for Colin and Helen to read. On the same day the child saw Miss Veronica, in a new silk dress, out walking on the Castle Esplanade holding on to the arm of the big man with the little eyes.

–

The more Helen saw of Miss Hay's future husband, the less impressed she was, for John Ker was past thirty years old, thick-set, coarse and awkward. Though he was tall he seemed incapable of controlling his own body and was ponderous on his feet as if he needed to think all the time about where he was going to lay down each foot. His eyes were indeed small and cunning, like mean little currants set close together in a raw-meat-looking face. When he came courting to Edinburgh he walked along with a stunned expression as if astonished at his own luck in finding so handsome a young wife from such a good family.

It was obvious that he was dazzled with her, though she did not bother to turn on him the arts of coquetry that she had polished at the society balls and soirées of the city. She did not flirt, tap him with her fan or lower her eyelashes, but treated him as if he were indeed lucky to have captured her. Those months of their courtship – if it could be called that – set the tone of their marriage for the future. No one thought to warn

Veronica that Ker had the sort of nature that reacted with blind, unintelligent fury when pushed too for.

Her brother Thomas tried to take him into male society but soon gave up the effort because Ker, almost totally silent, occasionally and painfully produced a banal remark, let it settle into the company and then sat back in silence to see how it was being received. Though he was sharp about money he was devoid of wit and any kind of sensibility, and Helen was not the only person to wonder aloud at why Veronica was marrying him.

–

On the morning of her wedding Veronica lay and gazed at the piles of pretty clothes heaped around her bed. She was going off with a dazzling wardrobe, her mother had seen to that – silks and gauzes, striped taffetas and smoothest broadcloth, shawls and fichus, caps of the finest lawn and exquisite straw bonnets trimmed with flowers and feathers. Only a few months ago the display would have thrilled her to ecstasy, but on her wedding morning she contemplated her fine clothes dully because in order to possess them she had to give herself to John Ker. Her soul shrank at the thought of the night that lay before her and she turned on her bed in anguish, burying her face in the pillow. As she lay sobbing, the door opened and her mother came in.

'Aren't you up yet? It's nearly ten o'clock and the ceremony's at twelve. His family will be here before you're ready, get up at once.'

Veronica raised a tear-stained face and asked desperately, 'Do I have to? Must I marry him?'

Her mother was silent for a moment and then she gathered her forces. 'Of course you must. You know you're lucky to get him in the circumstances. What if it got out? Who'd have you then? He's a rich man, Veronica. His, father's one of the most prosperous farmers in Berwickshire and he's the only son. You know that I'd have preferred you to marry into a family of a superior class but Thomas thinks that this is a very advantageous union. Your husband's his friend.'

'Thomas doesn't have to live with him. Thomas doesn't have to marry him...'

Lady Huntingdon made a disapproving face and advanced on the bed, picking up bits of clothing as she came.

'That of course has been your trouble from the beginning. You're far too *sensual*. You'll soon discover that Ker's as good a man as any other. All the nonsense about love is moonshine, take it from me.'

–

It was a strain even for the determined Lady Huntingdon to be cordial to the Ker family when they arrived for the wedding – a quiet affair, privately celebrated at home. They sat stiffly on the heavily carved chairs which had been among Veronica's mother's wedding presents over thirty years before, and stared around at the looped silk curtains, the pictures on the wall and the shining silver on the white-clothed table. Mary Cameron had been called in to help the Hay maidservant serve the meal after the wedding, and she was in the kitchen, peering through the door, curiously sizing up the bride's new relations. The Ker party was small – only the groom's parents and his garishly dressed sister Susan. The bride's snobbish sisters with their prosperous-looking husbands could not prevent criticism of the clothes of the other women being very obvious in their eyes. If Veronica was not marrying style and class, she was apparently marrying money, they said in a consoling sort of way among themselves, and no one seemed more satisfied with the situation than her brother, who had introduced Ker to the family and who acted like his close crony. If any of the Hays thought this surprising on the part of class-conscious Thomas, they did not say so.

In spite of the sophistication of the Hays, however, the most impressive member of the wedding party was old David Ker, the groom's father, a gimlet-eyed, satirical-looking greybeard who was impressed by nothing and nobody. He had worked his way up from poor ploughboy to owner of more than a thousand acres of high-quality land, all achieved by shrewdness, determination and unscrupulous drive. His name was a by-word in the cattle markets of the Borders and Northumberland for never letting an opportunity of enrichment, no matter how minor, pass him by. Unlike some other farmers around him, he was in the vanguard of those who were prepared to try out new methods and ideas. He had never been too proud to walk behind a plough himself till late at night, draining and irrigating land that other farmers said would yield nothing. His industry made the ground fertile and as time passed he was able to snap up every parcel of land, and every animal, that came up for sale in the district. During the agricultural depression of the 1780s, when other farmers were selling up in despair Ker was buying at knock-down prices. By the time his son was ready to offer for the hand of Lady Huntingdon's daughter, the parents – who had started their married lives in a one-roomed cottage with a hole in the thatch to let out the smoke from the fire – were installed in the mansion house of Broadmeadows.

At fifteen minutes to twelve when the black-robed minister arrived, a shiver of anticipation went round the gathering. The groom, who had been sitting quietly in a corner, trying to steady his shaking hands, stood up and revealed himself dressed in a magnificent scarlet jacket with gold lace, white buckskin breeches and tasselled top boots. This semi-military outfit was explained by his mother:

'John's an army muster master. That's why he doesn't live with us at Broadmeadows but has his own house in Berwick near the barracks,' she told Lady Huntingdon.

A muster master was an army official who toured the various barracks and camps of his district, checking that the sums the officers claimed to have paid out as wages to the soldiers tallied with the number of men in their force. It was a political appointment, obtained through jobbery by Ker's shrewd old father who had friends in high places and knew how to bribe.

The groom, in his finery, stood awkwardly in front of the minister and everyone waited for the bride to appear through the folded-back double doors that divided the reception room. Lady Huntingdon felt her throat go dry in dread as the seconds ticked by, but Veronica's training was too strong for her to break it now.

There was a rustle of silk at the door and heads turned to see the bride coming in with her oldest sister bringing up the rear.

Veronica wore a beautiful hooped dress of pale blue with the skirt caught up by pink ribbons, but she looked like a wraith and seemed almost to be sleepwalking as she advanced towards the clergyman, whose face at the sight of her also took on an expression of extreme unhappiness and disquiet.

It was a very subdued wedding. Dr Thomas moved in at Veronica's side and held her elbow in a firm grasp, prompting her in a whisper if she showed signs of faltering when taking her vows. Ker stood four square with his eyes fixed on the minister's face like a schoolboy repeating a lesson and pronounced his vows in a rough voice, never once looking tenderly at the bride.

During the ceremony Helen sat huddled in her secret alcove, watching all the comings and goings. She saw a succession of trunks being carried to the Kers' old-fashioned coach by two sturdy menservants and every time the door to the Hays' flat was opened she heard the sound of voices and clinking cutlery. Her mother, she knew, would be full of stories afterwards but meantime she kept her vigil, waiting to catch a last glimpse of Veronica.

She did not have too long to wait. The party broke up early, for old Ker was reluctant to spend much time away from his farm, even for the wedding of his son. By two o'clock people were trooping down the stairs and through the close into the Lawnmarket where the heavy coach, drawn by four sturdy horses, was waiting to take them to Berwickshire.

'We'll be at our own door by midnight,' said old Mr Ker to Dr Thomas. 'We've posted relays of horses along the road and we'll make good time. No expense has been spared, you see. This trip has cost me a good two hundred pounds with one thing and another. I hope it's a good investment.'

The doctor knew what was meant. His sister was to start producing sons as soon as possible.

'I'm sure it'll be a very good investment,' he replied suavely. 'The bride comes from a healthy family. Both of her sisters have fine children…'

'So I'm told, so I'm told,' said the old farmer, climbing into his coach. 'Let's hope she does as well, eh?'

Last out of the house were the bride and groom. He was flushed and she looked more animated than earlier as she threw her arms around her mother and kissed her.

'Oh, Mama, I'm going to miss you,' she sobbed.

Lady Huntingdon reassured her, 'You're not going to the ends of the earth, my dear, you'll come back and see me soon. God bless you. I love you.'

And she was telling the truth. She did love her beautiful youngest daughter very much.

About twenty poor children from the buildings round about were gathered to see the bridal couple leave because it was an Edinburgh custom for a bridegroom to empty his pockets of small change and throw the coins to the children of the street when setting off with a new wife. Little boys and girls without shoes on their feet or proper clothes on their backs clustered chanting at the carriage door as a smiling Veronica and her embarrassed-looking husband climbed in, but the hopeful crowd were to be disappointed. John Ker only looked at them blankly and turned his face away as he settled himself down in the corner of the coach. It drove off without the children seeing as much as a farthing. They jumped up and down and yelled in disappointment, then ran down the street at the back of the coach, shouting ribald insults after the stingy bridegroom. It was a bad start to Veronica's marriage.

1792 — 1794

In the stuffy attic at the top of Baxter's Buildings old Colin Campbell was dying. He lay on a bed of rags, his faded plaid that had gone to Derby with Charlie wrapped around his legs. The breath came rasping painfully from his chest but the sun glinting through the window gilded his wrinkled face like an icon. The skin looked dead already, as yellow and dry as ancient parchment.

His granddaughter Helen, who had never left him throughout his last illness, knelt beside him.

'Can I get you something. Grandpa?' she whispered, but the old man shook his head slowly and painfully.

'Nothing, nothing, *a luaidh*,' he said, holding up a hand. 'Just sit by me. Tell me what you saw in the street today.'

She leaned against the wall behind his head and racked her brains for something interesting to say. She knew he loved hearing about the day-to-day events of the life of the High Street, so she began, 'That big Maggy Watson had a fight with the washerwoman on the corner of the West Port. She got hit with a wooden stool and she bled like a stuck pig. Serves her right, she's aye looking for trouble.'

'She got it then,' whispered old Colin with a stifled laugh.

Encouraged, Helen continued, 'Oh and there was a grand fire in one of the tenements down the Canongate, one of those where the gentry live. All the folk from the Lawnmarket were running down to see the fine furniture carried out. It was put out, though.'

Her grandfather nodded silently, his eyes pleading for more. She felt insufficient, she didn't know enough of what was going on in Edinburgh to divert his mind from the terrors of dying unshriven, for in his last days he was returning to his original Catholic faith and she knew he longed to see a priest.

'Miss Veronica's back. Grandpa. She's out to here with a bairn. She's come back from Berwick to have it in Edinburgh beside her mother. Dr Thomas is to look after her.'

'That's fine. You'll be glad to see her.' Colin Campbell had always known about his granddaughter's fascination in the beautiful Miss Hay.

The girl nodded. 'I was that. She's as bonny as ever, and she seems happy. Not like the day she was married.'

'Folk settle down usually,' said the old man, but then he gave a sharp cry as another spasm of pain gripped him.

Helen was anguished. She would do anything to divert him from the agonies that were torturing his racked body.

'Would you like to see Peter Grant, Grandpa?' she asked. 'I saw him this morning and he was asking about you. I know he wants to come up to have a wee talk with you.'

The old man nodded. 'Yes, bring Peter. He's a grand laddie. So's his brother Andrew. The Deacon had a fine pair of lads there, though he was never to know it.'

Helen ran down to look for Peter, who was usually to be found with the other caddies waiting for business at the foot of the Mercat Cross near St Giles. She saw him at once for he had grown so much that his fair head overtopped the other men already. With all the exercise he took, running here and there all day and most of the night, his body was lean and well muscled, so that he looked older than his fourteen years.

She grabbed his arm. 'Please come and speak to my grandfather. He's awful bad and the pain's terrible. Come up and talk to him.'

He came at once, solemn-faced. Back in the attic, she left him cheerfully telling the old man all the gossip and scandal of the streets, and when Colin eventually fell into an uneasy sleep, Peter came down the stairs and sat on a step beside her.

'He's going,' he said sadly. 'You're going to lose him soon.'

'I know that, but I just wish I could help him go easy,' she agreed dry-eyed, for in their society there was no room for sentimentality or avoidance of the truth. She nodded upstairs with her head and suddenly said to Peter, 'He's afraid to die. I wish I could help him.'

The boy stared at her, his eyes wide with surprise. 'Oh, no, you're wrong, Colin Campbell's not afraid of anything,' he protested.

She nodded vehemently. 'He's afraid to die unshriven. He's a Roman Catholic, you know, and he wants a priest before he dies, but I don't know where to find one.'

Peter stared at her and then leaned his head on his hand, thinking. In staunchly Presbyterian Edinburgh where the ghost of John Knox still walked the High Street and preachers in the pulpits railed against Catholicism even more than they did against the Devil, a priest was not easily found.

'You want me to find him a priest?' he asked after a bit, and the girl nodded.

'When?'

'Tonight, I think. He'll be gone by the morning.'

Peter rose to his feet and looked down on her with respect. 'All right. I'll try, but don't say anything to him. I know a family down near Holyrood that might tell me where there's a priest. I'll bring him if I can.'

Later that night he returned with a dark-cloaked stranger. No one noticed them because of all the fuss going on in Lady Huntingdon's place. Veronica was in labour and her brother, with his assistant young Dorsey, was rushing around, making a greater din than the labouring mother.

When Colin Campbell died in peace holding the priest's hand, little Edward Ker, Veronica's firstborn, came bawling into the world.

While a radiant Veronica Ker was giving the breast to her lusty son for the first time, Helen Cameron was weeping as she followed her father and another man carrying her grandfather's stiff body down the stairs before laying it on a stretcher for its last journey to the paupers' burying ground. She followed them into a sunlight that warmed her body but failed to make her heart joyous. The brilliance of the light and the blueness of the sky only heightened her pain. She wept even more as she thought how her grandfather would have enjoyed the sunshine if he could have seen it. Tears flowed unchecked as she walked along, the only other family mourner, for her mother had to do her day's work as usual. People eager for their daily water would not wait.

In the burying ground Peter Grant came to stand beside her and watch Colin Campbell's body being slung into its shallow grave. When it was all over they walked back together along the sunny High Street.

'How's your family, Peter? How's Cecil? I never see her now,' Helen said.

'She's gone strange. David, my wee brother, died this winter and that's made her worse. She won't go out, she says people are pointing at her and talking about her.'

Helen laced and unlaced her fingers as she listened. 'Oh, poor Cecil. What happened to your father was very bad for her.'

He nodded. 'But not just for her. I try to tell her that she's not the only one involved – there's all of us and there's the Watts as well.'

'What's happened to the Watts?'

'Andrew's having trouble, they tell me. The silversmith he was working for lost some things and blamed him. He said because he was the Deacon's son, he must have tarry fingers. Andrew was very angry and he hit the man, so he hasn't any work now. One of the other caddies told me that he's going off to Leith to join the navy. It's a hard life but he wants to get away from Edinburgh. He wants to forget he's the Deacon's son.'

It struck Helen that the Deacon's legacy to all his children had been one of sorrow.

She left Peter and ran back home, keeping to the dark closes and avoiding the brilliantly revealing sunlight. Her route took her down into the West Port and then back up through Libberton's Wynd where she paused for breath because of the steepness of the ascent and saw Andrew Watt with his mother Agnes at the door of their building. The boy had a cloth-wrapped bundle over one shoulder and he and his mother looked awkward, as if they wanted to embrace but were afraid to show their feelings.

The mother held out one hand and touched her boy's cheek. 'God bless you, laddie,' Helen heard her say.

The boy grasped his mother's hand for a few moments and then, with a convulsive movement, he turned and ran for the opening of the close, bumping into Helen as he did so. Knocked breathless by his bundle, she fell back against the wall and he paused to apologize.

'We always seem to meet when one of us is getting knocked down,' he said, putting out a hand to steady the girl. 'I'm sorry, I didn't see you there in the shadows. It seems gloomier in here when it's sunny outside.'

She nodded in agreement. 'Yes, it does.'

He looked closer and saw that she'd been weeping. 'Is something wrong?'

She nodded. 'My grandfather died last night.'

Andrew looked sympathetic. 'That's bad. He used to sit out in the close over there, didn't he?'

'Yes. That was him.'

'I remember he told me not to be ashamed of my father after – after he died.'

'He liked your father, he told me so. And your brother Peter's just told me that you're off to join the navy.' They were walking slowly and when they reached the head of the close, the sunlight shone down on them revealing that, like Peter, his brother had grown into a man. Though his hair and skin were still very dark, he seemed to have none of the swarthiness of his father or Cecil. His skin was a lighter, golden colour.

The remarkable eyebrows that were such a characteristic of the Deacon's face were just as strong on his son's but instead of being straight and bushy, they arched elegantly across his brow like the wings of a raven. She thought him very handsome and wished him well.

'I hope you keep safe in the navy, Andrew Watt,' she said solemnly as they parted.

–

All that afternoon visitors trooped in to see the returned young wife and her new baby. After the people had gone Veronica and her mother were left together admiring little Edward and talking about the things that had happened since the day of the wedding.

It was not the older woman's way to remind her daughter of past sorrows and she did not directly ask if the marriage was a success, for Veronica seemed happy enough and bubbled over with stories.

'Life in Berwick's very gay and busy because of all the soldiers being billeted there,' she told her mother. 'There's always balls or soirées being held by the officers and I know such a lot of people. Mother! It's almost as social as Edinburgh.'

Lady Huntingdon studied the young woman's face, as lovely and unblemished as ever. Perhaps John Ker was not so sullen and dull as he had seemed, for Veronica had no direct complaints against him. In fact she hardly mentioned him at all and her conversation was full of references to young Kellock, Captain and Mrs Southern or Major Browne and his lady.

'What about your husband's family? Do you see much of them?' asked her mother.

Veronica pulled a face. 'They're so unfashionable! His mother never leaves the farm and that old-maid sister of his stays with her. They're not used to life in society and it frightens them, I think. Broadmeadows House is three miles from Berwick and though my husband goes there about once a week, I don't go every time – and since I fell with a baby, I don't travel. It's a wonderful excuse.'

'Will you stay here long?' was the mother's next question.

Veronica's face changed slightly. 'Well, it would be nice to spend a little time, at least till the baby's strong enough to travel and I feel better.'

Her mother was reassuring. 'That's good. You'll stay with me until you're fully recovered. Thomas and his assistant will look after you. Dorsey's a good young fellow and very clever, Thomas tells me. Your brother's doing well, you know. He and his family are moving to a house in St Andrew's Square next month. It's a fine house and very fashionable.'

Veronica clasped her hands in delight. 'Oh, I long to see it. As soon as I'm able we'll hire two sedan chairs and go over. I know you love this old flat, but a house is much smarter. When old Ker dies we'll live at Broadmeadows and that's a lovely house… so big. There's room for dozens of children there.'

–

All the gossips of the courtyard had their eyes on Veronica. They leaned their arms on their window sills and called out to each other over the lines of washing. Some of their windows were so close together that they could hear each other even when the news was given out in whispers.

'That bairn's three months old and she's not gone home yet.'

'If you ask me she's not keen on married life. And I can't say I blame her, thon's a gey tumshie-headed-looking fellow she's married to.'

John Ker paid one visit to Edinburgh to see his son and was so delighted that he was putty in Veronica's hands.

'He's going to be busy all summer with his muster master business, so there's no need for me to go back to Berwick till September. I'll stay in Edinburgh with you,' she told her mother.

She had recovered her looks and maturity suited her; the fullness that maternity brought to her figure gave her an added appeal. Money flowed through her hands like water, she bought cloth of the most expensive kind, fans, parasols and fine silken shawls. The rage of that year was to have one's miniature painted so Mrs Ker made an appointment with Caldwell, the portrait painter, and went to his studio in Princess Street once a week for a sitting. He so enjoyed painting her that he did an extra portrait for nothing.

Heads were shaken and lips pursed by the neighbours who watched her goings-on with disapproval. Veronica had always made a good subject for gossip and speculation even before she was married. Now that she was Mrs Ker she was not letting them down.

Helen was recruited to watch baby Edward who grew fat, pink and contented, so contented that it was easy to leave him and go off for a few hours between each feed. His mother bloomed more delightfully with happiness every day, and whenever she appeared it seemed to Helen that a halo of radiance shone around her. The last time Miss Vee – as Helen had come to think of her – looked like that was before the lad from Inverness was sent away to India for stealing. The memory, of that year came back vividly when she watched Edward's young mother rushing off to another tea party, another portrait sitting, another concert, another outing with her friends.

Veronica loved to flirt and there was no barrier against her going about in polite society without her husband. Hearts were broken once again by her, she teased and dimpled, and the admiration that she received gave her confidence. Her mother had insisted for so long that her only marketable quality was the way she looked, that Veronica had come to believe it herself. It was so pleasing to hint, to smile and drop her dark fringes of eyelashes over her sparkling hazel eyes, to lay a gentle hand on a man's arm and feel him shiver at her touch.

It made her relish her power and feel that, in spite of everything, she was still the beautiful Miss Hay.

Beneath her insouciant exterior she hid her innermost feelings, speaking of them to no one, and when the thought of going back to Berwick came into her mind she resolutely thrust it away. Her husband had never courted or complimented her. From the beginning he acted as if he had bought her, with the same beady-eyed bargaining power that he and his father used when they went to market and looked over the sheep and cows huddled in the pens. After their first row he had not hesitated to point out to her that she was his chattel, he owned her: her brother Thomas had offered him her hand in marriage in return for writing off a debt that the Hay family owed old Ker, who supplemented his income by the odd bit of money lending and who had been used by Thomas in the matter of purchasing his fine new house.

'How much?' she asked, dry-mouthed.

He grinned. 'How much do you think you're worth, my lady?'

'I don't know, tell me.'

'One thousand pounds, you didn't come cheap,' he said and made a grab for her.

From their first night together he had bedded her without tenderness, grunting away on top of her in urgency and rolling off when he was satisfied.

Though she said nothing to him, she knew that lovemaking did not have to be like that; she knew that it could be urgent but also ecstatic, gentle and delightful. She knew that making love in the right way with the right person could cast a spell over a woman so that she walked proudly through life like a princess. But her husband's idea of lovemaking left her bruised, sore and yearningly unsatisfied. In the morning the only thing she wanted to do was put it out of her mind. Now, safe in

Edinburgh and far away from him, the memory of his touch made her shudder and she threw herself into flirting, demanding admiration like an addict demanding opium.

She was playing with fire. Soon the gossips began bringing tales back to her brother, for she had begun seeing his assistant, young Dorsey, on the afternoons she was supposed to be sitting for Caldwell.

'I saw your sister yesterday outside Register House making eyes at that young assistant of yours. If her husband hears about it he'll take her home quick enough,' one of Thomas' fellow club members told him.

He charged her with it and she denied it, but the rumours grew stronger. Soon it was plain to see that Dorsey was smitten with her; in company he never took his eyes off her, he followed her in the street and sent her loving letters. Her mother scolded in rage, her brother stormed but she still made a joke of it and denied any impropriety. Dorsey was sent away to Glasgow to work with another doctor and Thomas, in a fit of spite and urged on by his jealous wife who had always been resentful of her sister-in-law's beauty, wrote a note to Ker advising him to come and take his wife home before she brought scandal on the family.

Ker came storming into the flat one afternoon and headed towards her, scarlet-faced with the rage that had been building up inside him for all the hours of his long journey. Only the presence of her mother prevented him hitting her as she sat calmly sipping tea. Thomas Hay had unwittingly unleashed a raging demon when he wrote to Ker.

'I hear you've been carrying on with some young fellow,' Ker said angrily.

Veronica carefully laid her teaspoon in the deep saucer before saying to Lady Huntingdon, who was looking shocked, 'What does he mean, carrying on? I'm not carrying on with anyone.' But she was frightened. That was plain to see.

Lady Huntingdon was wearing a white lace cap with long lappets hanging down the back and they visibly quivered as she stood up and said, 'Let us all keep calm about this. Sit down, John. And you, Veronica, you've always been frivolous, you mean no harm I'm sure but people talk so about the way you behave. You're married now and it's up to you to make the best of it and not bring any scandal on your family. Thomas said he was going to write to your husband to come and take you home as soon as possible, so you'd better make your preparations.'

Wide-eyed, Veronica turned on Ker. 'What did Thomas tell you? If it's about Dorsey, it's nothing, he's just a boy. He means nothing to me...' She was frantic.

John Ker looked from mother to daughter, not knowing what to say except to bluster, 'Make yourself ready, fetch the baby's things. I'm taking you home where you belong – and it'll be a long time before I let you come back, either.'

'Don't let him hurt me,' Veronica appealed to her mother. 'Oh, don't let him hurt me, you don't know what he's like.'

Lady Huntingdon stared at the furious Ker and a chilling inkling of what could happen to her daughter struck her. 'Don't you dare lay a finger on her,' she warned him. 'If I hear that you do, I'll be down to bring her home. She's not a bad woman, she's really done nothing wrong, I'm sure. If you treat her tenderly, she'll be a good wife to you...'

It was a subdued procession that set off along Lady Stair's Close in the wake of the burly, sullen-faced farmer. He did not even bother to hand his wife into the carriage but let her clamber in on her own at the back. The sleeping baby was handed up by his grandmother, and Helen waited at the back of the line with his wicker basket and soft cobwebby shawl. She felt very sad to see Veronica and Edward go – over the summer weeks she had become even more caught up in wonder and admiration at the beauty and high spirits of the lovely Mrs Ker, and her devotion to the baby had grown with every day. Life in Baxter's Buildings would revert to being dull and uneventful now.

Lady Huntingdon seemed anxious and worried for several days after her daughter left. She looked for letters from Berwick but none came and as the days grew into weeks, her anxiety deepened. Coming back from an evening stroll one night, she saw Mary Cameron's ragged daughter and it struck her that the child was looking very forlorn too.

'You miss the baby, don't you?' she asked and Helen nodded her tangled head dumbly, for like most of the people in the building she was a little afraid of the formidable lady.

'What do you do with yourself now?' was the next question.

'I help my mother carry the water buckets.'

Lady Huntingdon nodded and looked reflective, then all of a sudden she seemed to make a decision. 'Ask your mother to come to see me tonight when she comes back from work,' she said and disappeared into her doorway.

'Can that daughter of yours write?' was the first question Veronica's mother asked the weary Mary Cameron.

'Aye, a wee bit. Before he died her grandfather taught her to read and write, she likes copying things out of books if she can get them. And my word, but she's a wizard at the counting!' Mary, who was illiterate herself, was proud of her girl and could not keep herself from boasting.

Lady Huntingdon nodded approvingly. 'Yes, I thought she was a clever little thing. What I want her to, do is simple enough. If you'll agree I'd like to send her down to Berwick to work in my daughter's household. She was good with the baby when they were here and you must be wondering what to do with her now she's growing up. How old is she?'

Mary looked confused. She had not considered sending her bairn so far away, but to go to work for Mrs Ker was a good chance. It would be better and easier for Helen than hauling water buckets up endless flights of stairs.

'She's twelve years old past.'

'That's old enough. Would you let her go?'

'I'd have to ask her first,' said Mary slowly.

When she went upstairs to find Helen she did not beat about the bush. 'Would you like to go to work for Miss Veronica in Berwick?' she blurted out.

Helen's eyes grew enormous with surprise. She had not expected such an exciting thing to happen to her ever. Of course she'd go. Her delight was so obvious that she did not even have to say yes.

When the mother and daughter went back downstairs to accept the offer Lady Huntingdon seemed pleased, but she had another request to make. There was a special reason for sending Helen to Berwick. She wanted a spy in the Ker household.

'She's to send me messages about my daughter. She's to let me know what happens down there. She's to go to the Berwick coachman and give him any message she has for me and I'll tell a caddy to meet the coaches and carry them up here whenever they come.'

Helen nodded, she'd be able to do that quite easily, she said. Eventually the two older women sent her up the stairs, but Mary turned back to ask Lady Huntingdon to explain her requirements more fully.

'What sort of thing is she to tell you?' The idea of a spy being planted in Veronica's house seemed a doubtful undertaking to her.

The two women could speak frankly for they had known each other a long time.

'I want to know if my daughter is behaving herself; she tends to philander a little, I'm afraid. I want to know if my son-in-law and my daughter are living happily together. I want to know if he ill treats her – most of all I want to know about that. Helen's to watch him, for Ker worries me. You needn't say all this to the girl. Just tell her to send me a message if there's anything she thinks I should know… She's bright and she's fond of Veronica, she'll know what to tell me.'

Lady Huntingdon had chosen her spy wisely. She knew quite well that the granddaughter of Colin Cameron, whose sharp eyes missed nothing, would be ideal for her purpose.

-

Helen was to be tidied up for her new position in life and Lady Huntingdon had strict instructions for her daughter's new maid. First of all, she insisted that Helen comb her hair and get some decent clothes. The hair combing was the worst bit because impatient Mary pulled roughly at intractable tangles that had not been tackled for years, and broke several combs in the process. When she came to a particularly difficult knot, she just cut it out.

In the end the job was done, but not without tears on Helen's part. Lady Huntingdon gave them money to buy cloth for a skirt and blouse, and Mary took the material to Anne Grant to make up for Helen.

Summer was over and a chill northerly wind was blowing cold down the High Street, making people huddle together under the overhanging fronts of the buildings for protection, as Helen in her grandfather's old plaid ran to Cant's Close to collect her new clothes. She was excited and pleased with herself for it was good to feel clean and to know that soft hair was blowing attractively around your face. Even her mother had said with a certain amount of surprised satisfaction when looking at her, 'My word, you're getting quite bonny!'

Cecil put a blight on her happy feelings, however. The girl's face was ghostly white, she was skinny as a skeleton and openly hostile, handing the bundle of clothes in a surly way through the crack of the door and taking the money without as much as a word of thanks.

'I'm going down to Berwick to work for Miss Vee,' Helen offered as the door was closing, but Cecil was not prepared to chat.

'So your mother told us,' she said and slammed it hard.

The hostility cast a blight on Helen and her trip back up to the Lawnmarket was less cheerful. She walked along thinking how she was leaving behind the people she had known all her life and going off to live in a distant place among strangers who might all be as odd as Cecil. And what about the strange new town? Every alleyway of old Edinburgh was familiar to her and she loved it, even the old wynds and houses which were reputed to be haunted. As usual, acting out of habit, she crossed the road to avoid walking past the black mouth of Mary King's Close where her brothers had told her there was a ghost that insisted on shaking hands with people, and a pair of chopped off feet that danced a wild jig on their own. They did not really frighten her any more but she was not taking any chances.

She liked feeling so easy in a place, knowing where everyone lived and, like her grandfather, storing in her retentive mind more details about their private lives than they realized. She knew where she could pause for a friendly chat and where it was best to hurry on by with only a smile. She was as familiar with the ancient streets as one of the scrawny cats that prowled the courtyards – but what would it be like in Berwick? Would she be lonely? Would she miss her family? Her mother was taciturn and undemonstrative but the bond between them was strong and they would indeed miss each other. Her father, drunk most of the time and sleeping when he was not, would be hard to miss, and her brothers were only transient visitors in the house. Since her grandfather died she had enjoyed no close companionship with anyone.

–

At twelve years old and never having been very far from the house in which she was born, Helen was at first thrilled by the long journey in the mail coach. The road snaked down the coast and she gaped with astonishment at the pounding, white-frilled waves and longed to alight and explore the deep rocky inlets cut into the coast where seabirds whirled and mewed, turning circles in the turbulent air. After six hours, however, the cold and the boneshaking motion began to tell on her and she wished for the ordeal to end. Her only companion among the baggage on the roof of the coach was a sleepy old man who smelt of whisky and by the time the postboy turned towards her, called out 'Berwick' and gestured to a distant town with a tall spire rising from its centre, she had almost reconciled herself to travelling on for ever.

Used as she was to hearing only the Edinburgh dialect or the soft Gaelic of her grandfather, it was difficult to understand what people were saying when she asked directions for Silver Street, but she found the house eventually. It was built of bright red bricks with a pretty white-painted portico arching over the door and curved railings leading up each side of the whitened steps.

Clutching her small bundle she mounted the steps and lifted a heavy brass knocker which made a thunderous sound that echoed and re-echoed through the house.

Somehow she had expected Miss Vee to open the door to her. That was what would have happened in the High Street but it was a stranger who asked, 'And what do you want?' The voice of the woman was intimidating and the effect was backed up by her appearance: a grim face under grey hair tightly scraped back under a frilled white cap. An enormous apron shrouded her tubby body.

Helen had to swallow hard before she could bring out the words: 'I've come for Miss Veronica. I'm her new maid.'

'You mean Mistress Ker. There's none of your Edinburgh ways here. She's out – as usual. Get round the back like the rest of the maids.'

And with that she slammed shut the door and Helen could hear the sound of her determined feet receding.

It was growing dark and she could see no gate or entry leading to the back, for the house was joined on to its neighbours in a long line, so she set off up the street looking for a back lane. For the first time since her adventure began, she felt frightened, for she had seen many groups of soldiers wandering around Berwick, nearly all of them drank. The town was packed full with a roistering garrison, a fortified post against the Scots in case they should try to rise again as they had done in 1745.

At last she found a muddy entry leading to the back of the houses and she turned into it only to be met halfway along by a trio of reeling soldiers, not much older than herself, who whooped in delight when they saw her. She knew it was useless to ran so she flattened her back against the wall and stared fiercely at them out of her enormous eyes. The biggest of the three, whose scarlet coat was swinging open revealing a half naked chest, came towards her with his arms extended and she hissed like a fierce cat, 'You touch me and I'll kick you in the balls.'

He drew back, nonplussed for a second, but the bravado of beer took over and he came on again. 'So you'll kick me in the balls, will you? Oh, I like a dirty spoken lass… come on, let's have a hold of you.'

His friends, giggling, backed him up as he advanced towards Helen, whose heart was thudding in her throat. When his hands were almost touching her, she doubled up like an eel, dropped her bundle, and at the same time grabbed with talon-like hands at where she knew it would hurt him most. Her street childhood in Edinburgh had taught her useful things like that. With a scream he bent forward, red hands clutching at his crotch.

'Oh, the little bitch,' he gasped. 'Catch hold of her, get her.'

But she had scored through the element of surprise and she was too fast for three drank men. Picking up the bundle again, she ran at full tilt down the alley till she came to an open gate. Darting through, she banged it shut and leaned against it. By a miracle she'd come to the right place – through the basement window she could see the face of the grey-haired woman looking out at her.

'You took your time getting here. What do you think you've been doing?' was all that was said to her when she staggered into the kitchen.

It did not take her long to discover that the kitchen was a buzzing beehive of gossip and speculation and the subject was always the same, their employer's wife. The grey-haired housekeeper was called Mrs Eliot and she was backed up by two housemaids, Christine Branxton and Mary Weatherstone. All three came from Hutton, the village nearest old Ker's farm at Broadmeadows, and they had been recruited for his household by Mrs Ker, who was related in a distant way to Mrs Eliot. They immediately put Helen in the pro-mistress enemy camp because she had been sent by Veronica's mother. The only other servant who was on Veronica's side was the young coachman William Smith, and the women scoffed at him when he attempted to plead her case...

'You only like her because she's bonny,' said Christine in a voice that made it only too clear that Veronica's beauty was one of the reasons the maids were against her. As she listened to them, Helen remembered her grandfather's words when he said that beauty was not always a blessing.

Working in that house gave Helen her first introduction to the servant-master division of society. Though her family earned their bread by doing menial jobs, they never considered themselves to be the inferiors of the people for whom they worked, and nor were they looked down upon. Work was done in a spirit of equality and people would talk together without any forelock touching or bending of the knee. You could not live in the same building and not know the details of each other's lives or share the same problems. Good birth was acknowledged as a sort of gift from the gods, but the gentry were still accessible. The only division was that one section of society had more money than the other, but money could be earned and it was quite common in Edinburgh for enterprising people to rise from poverty to the heights of affluence.

But in John Ker's house the servants felt like servants and resented their lot. They were actually conscious that their destinies were in the hands of the man who paid their wages, and they jealously watched every move made by the people upstairs.

Their comments were riddled with a malice they took care to conceal from the people they talked about. Veronica came in for their concentrated dislike because of her city ways, her pretty clothes, her fancy voice, her airs and graces, and most of all because her husband boasted to everyone that her father had been a lord. It would have made no difference to them if they had appreciated the significance of law lord's title – she was a lord's daughter and therefore one of the enemy.

Yet, because Veronica spoke to Helen with the same ease and friendliness she had always done, the other servants were driven to frenzies of jealousy. They ostracized the girl, branding her the mistress's spy, hushing their conversations whenever she approached and openly making fun of her ignorance and mistakes, for housework had never featured in her upbringing. The nuances of fancy cooking, starching and ironing linen flounces or black-leading fire grates till they shone like jet were unknown to her.

'You're nothing but a street Arab. I ask myself what *Lady* Huntingdon thought she was doing sending you down here. You're worse than useless,' was one of the cutting comments frequently flung at Helen by Mrs Eliot on the few occasions she did speak to the girl directly. Angered, Helen flushed scarlet but kept a curb on her own sharp tongue. She was very conscious of the house being split into two camps and her loyalties were firmly given to Veronica, who needed her support. But the barb struck home. They made her feel rough and uncultured when she was derided for not knowing how to scour the copper pans hanging from the rafters in the kitchen till they shone like mirrors; for not being able to make pies with paper-thin crusts or turn out roasts of beef that made the mouths of passers-by water with longing. In Edinburgh, on the rare occasions when anyone she knew had a roast of beef, it was taken down to the baker for roasting and brought home on a tray covered with a cloth by the triumphant owner.

She did try. She quickly learned how to dress herself neatly, to keep clean and tidy and to fix her avid eyes on the ground as good maids should. She learned to comb her hair every day and tuck it under a starched white cap.

She learned how to put up Veronica's abundant hair and powder it white, coughing and choking as the chalk flew down her throat. She learned how to lace up her mistress in tight corsets and fluff out her skirts at the back over the padded bustles that were still being worn in Berwick though, from her reading of London newspapers, Veronica said that bustles were disappearing and women of fashion were wearing slim, figure-fitting dresses. But that fashion had not yet reached the provinces and in Berwick it would have caused a sensation if she turned out dressed like a French revolutionary.

So she stuck to her satin gowns with the pretty frilled under-skirts showing through the open fronts of the skirts; she stuck to the wooden-fronted stomacher that concealed her pregnancy almost till the day of parturition; she stuck to her lace caps, though sometimes, very daringly, she wore a turban of tightly wrapped striped silk with a jewelled, gently waving pong-pong pin stuck in the front.

She was pregnant again; but it was not a happy marriage, for Ker's jealousy, always latent, had become acute since the Dorsey incident. If his wife went out, he wanted to know where she'd been and who she saw. Secretly he ordered Smith the coachman to spy on her and report back her every movement – where she called, how long she stayed, who she saw.

The household was in a ferment of suspicion all the time but in fact, William Smith, a tall, raw-boned young man with sticking-up fair hair and a kind, ingenuous face, was a reluctant spy for, secretly, he sympathized with Ker's wife. He had grown up on the Kers' farm, had known his employer all his life and had few illusions about the man's character. He felt guilty having to watch Veronica and tried to keep his reports as uninteresting as possible without deviating too far from the truth.

During her pregnancy that was not difficult. When she did go abroad it was to visit other young wives in the various officers' or merchants' houses throughout the town. This was a difficult pregnancy and she spent a lot of the time lying in her curtained bed staring out of the window at the top of the trees clustering round the parish church.

'I don't really like the country, I miss the bustle of Edinburgh, all the noise and the shouting,' she told Helen in a wistful voice one morning.

The maid nodded her head in agreement. 'Aye, there was always somebody going about even in the night-time. All that you hear in this place is the clatter of soldiers.'

Veronica smiled. 'We should be grateful, I suppose. At least it's busier than Broadmeadows. There's nothing there but sheep and cattle – and the rest of the Kers.' She dreaded being exiled to the farm but it looked as if that might soon happen, for old Ker was sick, near death in fact, and his wife too was ailing. When they died, John and his family would have to live in Broadmeadows House.

Helen agreed wholeheartedly as she sat behind Veronica, brushing out her hair. Young Dr Kellock was to call soon with a cordial to make her morning sickness better, and she always brightened when he visited.

Kellock reminded Helen of young Dorsey and her heart sank at the thought. He had the same clean scrubbed look, the same pink and white face, and the same devotion shone in his eyes when he looked at Veronica, who became coquettish as soon as he sat down beside her. It was as if she could not help herself, for even in the last days of pregnancy she could still make her bloated body look enticing if she had a mind to do so.

It was a comfort to Veronica to have Helen Cameron beside her for she knew quite well that the child was her only friend in a household of disapproving servants. Sometimes, when she was alone, she allowed herself to think and sank her head into her hands in sheer misery as she realized how unhappy she was, how much she missed Edinburgh and, worst of all, how much she hated her husband. John Ker had not improved with acquaintance. He was brutish and any small tenderness he had shown to her in their early days of marriage had long since disappeared. As the months with him grew into years, she found that his mannerisms, his way of speaking, the things he said, his very opinions and frame of mind were intensely irritating to her. Watching him, sitting at table with him, speaking to him, going into society with him at her side was like torturing oneself deliberately in a bed of thorns. In her subconscious mind she cursed her brother for selling her to this man, and her unspoken resentment simmered unexpressed. If she could have taken up a pen and written a letter of bitter accusation to her family it might have made her feel better, but she had been too long tutored by her mother for that. She had no confidence in her own opinions, no true sense of her own value. Instead she lay awake in the long nights, listening to him snoring at her side, and fought with the anger that was tearing her inside like a ravening animal. The impossibility of her situation was so cruel that she could not afford to allow her mind to dwell on it. Instead she soothed herself to sleep with fantasies of a lover who would step out of a crowd one evening, sweep her up in his arms and carry her off, away from Ker, away from his family, away from everything that made her life so unhappy.

One of her retaliations against her husband was to spend his money with a recklessness that even frightened herself while she was doing it. As soon as he went off on his muster master business, buttoned up tight in the scarlet coat that matched his face, she would be out in the town, going from one shop to another, spending happy hours fingering lengths of material, speculating about what they could be made up into, dreaming her dreams of romance while ordering another gorgeous gown. It was acknowledged that, even when pregnant, she was the best-dressed and best-looking woman in Berwick, and when the bills arrived John Ker was torn between pride at her appearance and wrath at what it cost him to keep her.

—

It was the darkest' time of winter when baby Louisa was born, quickly and effortlessly, with only a midwife in attendance, so it was not necessary to summon Dr Kellock. John Ker was grateful for that, not only because it saved him money, but because he was becoming jealous of the friendship that had grown up between Veronica and the young man.

After the birth the mother lay radiant in bed with her baby in her arms and her happiness warmed the room as much as the huge fire in the grate. She and Helen looked down at the dark-haired child and cooed with delight…

'She has such a bonny face, look at her wee hands, so perfect,' sighed the maidservant, who was moved with longing at the sight of the baby.

Edward, less than two years old himself, peered over the edge of the bed with his small face solemn and tried to show the same enthusiasm for this interloper as his mother and his nursemaid, for Helen had taken over his care as well as her other duties. Being scarcely more than a child herself, she understood the things that pleased him and did not scold in the same way as other grown-ups, especially his Aunt Susan whose tongue was very sharp. Now he watched Helen's face for signs that she was going to prefer this baby to him.

Sensing his disquiet, she put an arm round his shoulders and whispered, 'You're just as bonny as the baby. Don't worry, we all love you as much as we love her.'

That however was not strictly true where Veronica was concerned. From the beginning she doted on the new child, even giving up her busy social round in order to be with her as much as possible. Her devotion became more complete when it grew obvious that the baby was sickly, and she knelt by the wooden cradle as if willing her own strength to flow into her daughter. By the time she was three months old Louisa was prettier than ever but alarmingly quiet and docile. She lay like a waxen image among her white woollen shawls, her enormous blue eyes fixed on her mother with a puzzled expression.

'She smiled at me today,' Veronica cried out to Helen one spring afternoon. 'She really smiled at me.'

Helen joined the mistress by the baby's bed but, try though she might, it was impossible to discern any expression other than bewilderment on Louisa's face.

While she was trying to agree with Veronica that the baby was smiling, in the kitchen Mrs Eliot was rolling out pastry and gossiping with the maids. 'The mistress had better prepare herself for losing that bairn. I've seen them like that before and they don't live long...'

If such a thought crossed Veronica's mind she thrust it away to join the other unwanted ideas at the back of her consciousness. She told herself that Louisa was only a little slow, but her beauty and the way her eyes fixed with such trust on her mother's face showed that she understood what was going on – she did, she did. Of course her lovely child would live, anything else was unthinkable. She lifted the tiny body out of its warm nest and held it tightly to her breast, putting her lips against the soft neck and gently kissing the sweet-smelling skin. Louisa did not turn her head or show any sign that she felt her mother's caresses. She was as accepting as a doll, a beautiful, warm doll.

In the early summer the child stopped sucking and Veronica was frantic, rising at all hours of the night to offer Louisa the breast. The baby would obligingly suck for a few seconds before turning her head away.

With deep disquiet Helen realized that the baby's head was growing while her body stayed almost the same size as at birth.

Eventually Veronica accepted that all was not well and, by dint of much coaxing and pleading, overcame John Ker's initial refusal to call in Dr Kellock. There was no better medical man between Berwick and Edinburgh, and local people talked of amazing cures he had effected on old people and children alike.

–

'Give her to me, let me look at her.' James Kellock spoke gently to the mother who stood clutching the little bundle in her arms. His heart beat quicker at Veronica's beauty and she awakened a deep feeling of chivalrous concern in him, for she looked as tragic and stricken as a heroine in an ancient legend.

Without speaking she held out the child and he laid it on the bed slowly unwrapping the layers of swaddling clothes until he revealed Louisa's wasted limbs and greying skin. He put both hands gently on the misshapen skull and kept on pretending to examine Louisa although he knew only too well what was wrong. The baby was a classic case of water on the brain, she would be dead within a few weeks or even days.

But when he saw the hope on Veronica's face, he could not tell her. It was not possible to be so cruel. With pretended optimism he said, 'I'll give you a draught for the baby, and come back tomorrow.'

Veronica clasped her hands at her beautiful breast and her whole face came to dazzling life. 'I knew you'd know what to do. I knew you'd help me.'

He came the next day and the day after, he came every day for a week. He wanted to make a cut into the child's skull to drain off the water, but when he tried to suggest it Veronica seemed unable to comprehend his words.

He spoke privately to John Ker. 'Your daughter is not going to survive, I'm afraid – not at least unless a miracle happens. But your wife doesn't seem to understand when I tell her how sick the child is...'

'I've been trying to tell her the child's a weakling ever since it was born. When it dies, she'll just have to accept it. Women are like that – they go on hoping till the last minute.'

'But I feel that we should prepare her.'

'She's not stupid, she knows that babies die all the time – like animals, the weak ones die and the strong ones live. It's the law of Nature,' Ker replied. Veronica's devotion to the sickly child intensely annoyed him. His sister Susan, who was in charge of the household during Veronica's distraction with her baby, had only that morning suggested to him that his wife's behaviour was not normal.

Kellock said, 'I'm worried about how she's going to react. She loves the child very much, she'll be deeply affected if it dies. I could try an operation to drain the water off the brain but there's little chance of success, really, and I feel you should ask her if she wants me to do that.'

Ker stamped his booted foot in open anger now. 'What a waste of money. Why operate on a child when it's dying? No wonder you medical men do yourselves so well, persuading silly folk to part with their money. If the child's as sickly as you say, it'll be better for it and for my wife if it dies sooner rather than later. Let things alone. Dr Kellock, let Nature take its course.'

Veronica came to rely on the young doctor's visits. He sat with her in the evenings and listened with despair as she voiced useless hopes that Louisa would live. It was only with difficulty that he kept himself from breaking the terrible truth and with even more difficulty that he stopped himself from voicing his growing love for her. On the day that Louisa died he did not come because he could not have borne to see Veronica's grief.

Her sobs and cries echoed through the house and silenced everyone, even Mrs Eliot and the insensitive Susan. Helen and Edward huddled together in the nursery and their blood was chilled by the wailing.

At nightfall John Ker came in, heard the weeping and bounded up the stairs to her room two steps at a time. He slammed the door open and glared at her lying face down on the bed beside the cradle containing the corpse of the child, for she would suffer no one to take it away.

'So it's over then. Be quiet, woman,' he roared, and everyone in the house heard him. 'The child was an idiot. It's a good thing it's dead. You can have another. Women lose children all the time. Get up and dress yourself or I'll have to make you.'

For the next two days she rose and dressed at the usual time but moved around like a sleepwalker, never smiling and speaking very rarely. Nothing seemed to excite any reaction in her – not Susan's malice or little Edward's anxious need for love. What was most disturbing to Helen was that every few minutes Veronica would leave whatever she was doing and run to the bedroom, searching for the dead Louisa, and when she found no cradle there she covered her face with her hands and wept most bitterly.

When Helen returned from taking Edward out next day she heard a terrible shouting going on upstairs between her mistress and Ker. The servants were all crowded together in the hall listening avidly, and the figure of Susan could be seen on the first-floor landing with her attention fixed on the bedroom door.

Helen's first reaction on hearing the din was relief that Veronica was able to shout again, was able to rouse herself sufficiently to fight, and when Ker left the house she ran upstairs to her mistress. To her disappointment Veronica was weeping as copiously as ever, slumped in the same attitude of bowed sorrow as she had taken up since Louisa's death. Helen ran across the room to put her hands on the bent and heaving back. 'What's wrong? Is there anything I can do to help?'

Veronica said in a shaking voice, 'Oh Helen, Helen, he won't put a headstone on her.'

'What do you mean?'

'My husband, Ker – the brute – he won't put a headstone on Louisa's grave. He says it's going to cost too much, she doesn't need a headstone for no one will know she's been alive, for less remember her.'

The next day Louisa was buried without a headstone or any marking on her grave in the churchyard at Hutton near Broadmeadows. Her mother was not at the burial for she had fallen into a state of nervous shock that rendered her partially paralysed and she lay on her bed in Berwick, staring at the ceiling with tears slowly trickling down her white cheeks.

–

Christine burst into the kitchen and said dramatically, 'He's up there with her again. He told me to go away. He said he'd give her the medicine himself. I know what sort of medicine that is!'

Mrs Eliot turned from the huge fireplace to say, 'He knows the master's away or he wouldn't dare – nor would she. It's a scandal what's going on in this house.'

'I think we should tell her that we're all going to leave unless it stops. There's plenty of work in Berwick just now. We'd soon find other places.'

Christine looked at her friend Mary who put on a pious face and agreed, 'It's not right for us to be working here, taking the master's wages and not telling him what's going on between his wife and the doctor. All of Berwick knows except him.'

The cook and the two maids looked at Helen who was cleaning Veronica's shoes in a corner. 'She'd not leave,' said Mrs Eliot with a shrug of the shoulder in Helen's direction.

'*Would* you?' Christine directed the question directly at the other girl.

'No,' said Helen shortly.

'No, she'd not leave. Her sort don't mind things like that. That's the way they go on in Edinburgh,' sneered Mrs Eliot.

Helen kept her head lowered and curbed her tongue but she was worried. Though Veronica had recovered from the crippling hysteria that had prostrated her after Louisa's death, she was changed, and not for the better. She was harder and more desperate, careless of her reputation. When she spoke to her husband in public she was openly scornful and cutting, but Helen knew that he still had the power to frighten her. No one in the house doubted what sort of storm would erupt if he thought she was betraying him with the doctor.

When the trio of self-righteous maids confronted Veronica her first instinct was to cuff their ears and send them about their business, but a small voice told her to be careful – life was teaching her circumspection. Though it was humiliating, she found soothing words to reassure the old harridan of a cook.

'You're mistaken. It's all very innocent. The doctor only comes here to treat me. There's nothing wrong between us.'

When she saw that her avowals were not believed, she swallowed her pride even more and went on, 'I'll tell him not to come back to the house. I'll not have him here again...'

But she had every intention of going on meeting him at the homes of sympathetic friends. Why should I give him up? she asked herself. I'm starved of romance and he loves me so, he's obsessed with me and he's so kind. He helped me after Louisa died. If it wasn't for him, I'd have perished from grief. Ker had no idea how I was feeling – and he didn't care a jot.

Kellock's admiration was healing her. Her beauty was like a plant that had shrivelled during a bitter winter but was once again showing shoots of green. Their long conversations helped her to acknowledge her deep feelings of anger against her brother – and, even more deeply, against her mother – about the circumstances of her marriage. When she told him about her husband's brutalities, he cursed with rage against the man that made her feel truly protected for the first time since she left her mother's house.

I need him, I need him to watch over me, she told herself fiercely, for Lady Huntingdon's daughter had never been encouraged to stand alone.

It was inevitable that they became lovers, but Veronica felt little guilt. At first he was more reluctant than she, but her gentle coaxing overcame his misgivings and in her marital bed their mutual ardour had swept away the last of his scruples.

The memory of making love with him acted like a drug on her, easing her mind and boosting her confidence. Intrigue energized her, she enjoyed the secrecy and tension almost as much as she enjoyed the loving coupling of their bodies, and she guarded the memory of that like a precious jewel, calling it up to delight herself when Ker was hectoring and bullying her or when she had to sit for hours in the window waiting for the time to meet Kellock again.

She knew that Helen was watching her with anxiety but she pretended not to notice, and all caution was gradually thrown away. She felt justified in what she was doing – she needed Kellock's love more than she needed food. She needed his tenderness, she needed the reassurance that life had more to offer her than the brutalities of Ker. To think about the future was pointless.

I will not worry about being found out, she told herself. For once I'm going to live in the present and let the future look after itself.

–

Ahead of her on the street Helen saw the figure of William the coachman, who was wandering despondently along with his hands sunk deep in his breeches pockets. She ran to catch up with him and said, 'You're looking very sad, what's the matter with you?'

'You'd be sad too if you were taking orders from two sides,' he told her.

'I don't understand.'

'The mistress sends me off to Quay Walls with notes for that doctor fellow and the master tells me I've to report everything she does and everywhere she goes. What's a fellow to do, I ask you? Mrs Eliot and the girls would say I ought to tell him – but I can't...'

'Have you been carrying notes for Ver – for Mistress Ker to Dr Kellock?'

Smith nodded.

'I should have guessed as much,' she said angrily. 'I should have known from the way she's been behaving...'

The coachman looked at her obliquely. 'I'm not saying I don't blame her. I've known Johnny Ker since he was a laddie and he's not a good one.'

'But she said she'd sent the doctor away.'

'She only sent him as far as the house of those folk. Captain and Mrs Watkins. That's where they meet. And I carry the notes between them.'

Helen turned and ran back to the house in Silver Street. She was on fire with a mixture of emotions but the chief one was fear at the danger her mistress was putting herself in. Her confusion was so deep that the deference which came naturally to her in speaking to Veronica was cast aside when she burst into the parlour. 'I met Smith on the street. You shouldn't do that,' she burst out at her mistress.

'What do you mean?' Veronica looked coolly up as if she had no idea what she was talking about, and Helen realized that her mistress thought she was disapproving of her, taking a moral attitude like the other maids.

'I don't mean that what you're doing is wrong – it's not that. It's just you're running a terrible risk. Smith told me about your notes to Kellock, it just came out of him. If it reaches your husband there'll be trouble.'

'Why should he tell Ker? I pay him well.' Veronica was as prickly as a thistle.

Helen's face was white as she continued, 'It's dangerous, don't you see? He hates the secrecy. You don't understand the position he's in. He and his family have worked for the Kers for years. His father's old Ker's steward at Broadmeadows. His mother works in their kitchen. He has a lot to lose if the master finds out he's been carrying your notes. You shouldn't ask him to do it – it could come to the point where he has to choose, and he'd probably choose the Kers. I'll carry your notes if you must send them.'

Ker would have to tear her tongue out before she told tales on Veronica.

Veronica sighed and shrugged. 'All right, I won't do it again – I won't send Smith with the messages.'

–

As it turned out Helen could have saved her breath. When William was out he became drunk and, staggering back into the kitchen late at night, blurted out his worries about the notes. Mrs Eliot, very righteous, told Miss Susan, (but without implicating Smith who was a favourite with all the kitchen women). Susan, even more sanctimonious and self-satisfied, told John Ker. What happened after that was so terrible that everyone forgot how it all began.

The screaming woke the house. Helen sat up in bed and clutched the covers to her chest. Edward awoke, sprang from his cot and ran to climb in beside Helen, burying his head in her lap. Mrs Eliot's first thought was that she was dreaming but when she realized the screams were real – and where they were coming from – her immediate reaction was remorse. Christine and Mary huddled together in the bed they shared in the attic, shaking in terror. Susan Ker smiled with satisfaction and lay awake, waiting for the final outcome. William did not hear the screaming at first because he slept in the hayloft above the stables, but eventually even he was awakened by the din and sat up with his head in his hands, trying to close his ears with his clenched fists.

Helen and Mrs Eliot collided on the stairs. The cook shoved the girl aside to pound on the locked door and shout, 'Let me in. Don't kill her, let me in.'

As they thumped their fists together on the door they could hear the sounds of someone being beaten and still the terrible shrieking, howls of agony as a heavy stick thrashed down time after time.

Mrs Eliot's face was white as she turned to Helen. 'Go and get Smith to put a ladder against the window. We must stop him or he'll kill her.'

The ladder was too short so Smith came pounding up the stairs and put his shoulder to the door. Thud, thud, thud – again and again he ran at it like a human battering ram until in the end it gave way and the panel splintered down the middle. By this time the screaming had stopped and Veronica was lying in the middle of the floor covered with blood, her tattered nightdress hardly covering her body. Her husband stood over her with a cudgel in both hands, raining blows down on her even though she was unconscious. His face was red and contorted with fury and Smith had to fight with him to force the weapon out of his hands.

Helen and Mrs Eliot lifted Veronica and at first the girl was afraid that her dear Miss Vee was dead, for her face was ashen and her body completely limp. One arm was twisted under her in a strange way and there was a huge contusion on the side of her head.

'He's killed her, oh my God, he's killed her,' whispered the cook as they carried her between them to the bed and laid her on the tumbled covers. But as Helen wiped the blood from the battered face with shaking hands, she saw that Veronica was still breathing.

Ker was standing sobbing like a child in the middle of the floor with his head hanging down and Smith was beside him with the bloodstained cudgel. No one spoke or knew what to do until Helen cried out, 'She's not dead yet. Fetch some brandy, we have to bring her back to life.'

Her right arm was broken, one shoulder dislocated and her whole body battered and cut. It was a miracle that he had not fractured her skull for she was especially badly beaten around the head, both eyes were closed with terrible bruising and her nose was bloodied.

She was only semi-conscious for two days but little by little she began to fight back and they breathed with relief when they realized that she was not going to die. On the day that she opened her eyes and recognized Helen, the girl took a piece of paper and wrote a note to Lady Huntingdon: 'He beat her almost to death. You must come and warn him not to do it again.'

–

It took Helen a few moments to recognize the old woman who climbed down from the Edinburgh coach. Lady Huntingdon had shrunk and shrivelled with age; her mass of white hair had grown thin and lank; her fine-featured face was drawn; her body was skeletal and badly bent. There was not long left for her and she was well aware of that, but with the time she had she was as determined as ever to put everyone on the right road.

First of all she lectured her daughter who lay propped up with pillows on the great bed. 'From what I hear, it seems you gave your husband great provocation. All this nonsense must stop. He's agreed to take you back and forget what happened but you must promise me that there'll be no continuance of this ridiculous affair. You're very lucky that Ker is doing nothing about it… he could divorce you for it, you know.'

Veronica wearily turned her aching head on the pillow and said, 'He won't divorce me for Kellock, Mother, he's told me as much. He says the puppy has no money and couldn't be sued. He'll wait for a man of substance… He says if he divorces me he's going to make money out of it.'

Lady Huntingdon was shocked. 'Oh Veronica, how you've changed! Of course that's all just talk on Ker's part. He's bitterly jealous or he wouldn't have beaten you like he did.'

Her daughter stared coldly up at her from blackened, blood-shot eyes. 'Is a beating a sign of love? Is that what you think, Mother? Ker beats me because he enjoys hurting me... not because he loves me. It's not the first time he's hurt me – oh my God, Mother, you don't know what it's like sharing a bed with a man like him – but it's the first time he's really allowed himself to enjoy it to the full. The next time he could kill me.'

The mother-in-law went downstairs to confront her son-in-law who sat shaking in his drawing room. Her tongue was sharp with anger and she left him in no doubt how she felt about a man who raised his fists to a woman.

'If this happens again we'll take Veronica away from you and sue *you* for divorce. You're lucky that you're not in gaol right now for murder. Promise me it won't happen again or I'll blacken your name up and down the length and breadth of Scotland, John Ker.'

She must have guessed that the promises both of them gave her were worthless, but she was old and tired and only wanted to go home to Edinburgh, where she died less than two months later.

1794 — 1799

Two days after the departure of Lady Huntingdon there was a great bustle in the house on Silver Street. Susan Ker, looking unusually animated, was in charge of the operation and all the servants except Helen ran around under her orders, loading china and silver, window hangings and pictures into huge wicker hampers.

'What's happening? Why are you clearing the house?' Helen asked Christine Branxton in amazement as she watched each room being systematically emptied.

'We're going to Broadmeadows. The master's going home. Didn't you know?'

Veronica was in bed when Helen burst into her room, for the bruises were still too terrible for her to be seen in public. Even the noise from below had failed to rouse her to animation.

'We're moving to Broadmeadows, did he tell you?' asked Helen.

Veronica wearily shook her head. 'We haven't spoken to each other since my mother left. He'd know that I'd not want to go so he wouldn't tell me anything about that. I'm not surprised, though. He's trying to make me a prisoner.'

She made no protest when a flushed and triumphant Susan came in and told her to dress. Meekly she put on her clothes and, assisted by Helen, went slowly down the stairs.

At the door stood a huge cart harnessed to russet-coloured oxen. It was loaded to the top with her household furnishings.

Edward, in a fever of excitement, was capering around for he was delighted that they were going to live on the farm. The child loved Broadmeadows and on his visits there he followed his father and grandfather around the outbuildings and the fields, soaking in everything they said and everything he saw. The farming blood of the Kers was strong in him and he instinctively felt a deep link with the broad lands of Berwickshire.

Helen travelled the three miles from Berwick to the farm in the gig with Veronica and Edward. A very subdued William was driving and he seemed afraid to catch Veronica's eye, but she was too deep in her own misery to notice his embarrassment. With tears sparkling on her cheeks in the summer sunshine, she looked out at the ancient town as they drove up the main street.

Helen placed a hand over hers on the gig seat and said, 'It won't be so bad. It's a lovely place, they tell me.'

Veronica gave a strangled sob. 'I don't know what's happening to me. Is my whole life going to be spent in this misery? Will I die as unhappy as I am now?'

'Of course not. Things will change – anything could happen.' Helen's childhood in poverty had taught her optimism. If you did not believe things would be better there was no point going on.

But to Veronica, with all her memories of happier days behind her, life with John Ker looked like an unending bleakness stretching to the grave. She had sent a note to Kellock, imploring him to communicate with her, but that was yesterday and nothing had happened so her last hope of rescue was fading fast.

It was a short journey and the nearer they came to the farm, the more excited Edward grew. 'We're nearly there, we're nearly there!' he exclaimed at every corner, bouncing up and down.

Even town-loving Helen had to admit that the countryside looked lovely that morning for the road was shaded by tall beech trees and lined with tangled hedges spangled all over with cream and pink wild roses.

William noticed her interest in the flowers that lined the roadside and he summoned enough courage to say, 'It's bonny right now. All the flowers are out.'

The maid turned her elfin face towards him and asked, 'Do you know what they're all called? I think they're awful pretty.'

He shared her enthusiasm and he did know their names, he'd learned them as a child wandering those hedgerows with his father and brothers. The last part of their journey was made brighter by him pointing out clumps of yellow and purple vetch, tumbling clover with strawberry-coloured heads, pale mauve storksbills, tall spikes of foxgloves and yellow mullein standing like sentinels in shady patches, spiky thistles, ox-eye daisies and the tall umbrels of hedge parsley and sweet cicely that scented the air deliciously.

At one place where the grass was thick with flowers of different colours he drew on the reins and said, 'I'll bring you a bouquet.'

While they sat watching, he carefully gathered a selection of flowers – one little bunch for Helen and the other for Veronica. Back at the gig, he stuck a sprig of heavenly scented honeysuckle in Edward's straw hat and solemnly presented each of the women with his offering. Helen happily stuck her nose in hers and sniffed up the different scents but Veronica was surprised to see that her bouquet consisted of only one kind of flower, spikes of bright blue bells hanging from a thick stem and enclosed by leaves of greyish green, all covered with fine hairs.

Thinking she was disappointed at such a plain bouquet, William said, 'I brought you borage, mistress, I picked it specially for you because it's a magic flower. People say it gives you courage.'

–

After many false alarms, Old Ker was dying at last. Even that formidable man, who with all his iron will and craftiness had carved success out of the most unpromising beginnings, could not deflect death. Round his bed stood his son John, even more russet-faced and bulkier than when he married; his dyspeptic daughter Susan who would never catch a husband now and knew she was destined to a life of bitter spinsterhood; and his little wife Mary Ann, crinkled and brown as a nut but still reminding the old man of a squirrel, with her sharp little eyes and folded paws, idle for the moment but not usually for long.

His grandson Edward was brought in, a fine-looking little lad, a good heir for Broadmeadows even though he was the child of that city-bred woman who was lying in her bed upstairs. Through the long window of the downstairs room where his bed stood he could see the acres of grazing land that had given the place its name stretching before him. The park was dotted all over with browsing black and white cattle and clusters of ancient oak and beech trees stood here and there to provide them with shelter.

Turning his head with an effort he looked up at John. He knew this son of his would never be capable of doing what he himself had done, but it was important that he husband their hard-won resources until Edward was old enough to take over. His last words were, 'Look after the place, lad, look after Broadmeadows.'

Mary Ann Ker had been born in a hovel in the village of Hutton, the roofs of which could be seen from the first-floor windows of Broadmeadows House. Hutton was still full of her friends and relations and she had not grown too grand to visit them, to sit in their kitchens, sip a draught of ale and admire the flowers and herbs in their gardens. For she had green fingers, an almost witch-like capacity for making things grow. Cuttings she nipped from friends' flowerbeds would blossom and thrive in her own, outdoing the parent plants in size and magnificence. She had an eye for picking out sickly plants that could be revived, and her husband had always relied on her to rear the runts of litters. Feeble little lambs, stunted pigs, poor-looking puppies and miserable kittens always thrived if she took them under her care. There was something about her daughter-in-law's maid that woke a healer's response in her. Wee Helen Cameron, with her pointed white face, her bairn's body and her enormous eyes, was a good subject for Mary Ann's alchemy.

'Come with me to the garden. I can't bend down so well now and I need someone to do it for me,' she asked the girl one morning.

Helen flushed with surprise. She was slightly frightened of the wizened old woman with the black gypsyish eyes and, moreover, she distrusted any approach made to her by a Ker.

'Miss Vee – I mean Mistress Ker might want me...' she mumbled, thinking of Veronica still abed upstairs. Last night, in an effort to induce sleep, she had drunk too much brandy. In fact over the past weeks, since they came to live in the country, Veronica had taken solace in the brandy bottle for Dr Kellock had made no move to contact her.

'Was she at the brandy last night? Oh, don't worry, I don't expect you to tell me. Let her be for the meantime,' said old Mrs Ker. 'Come with me. I need your help.'

Together they walked into the flower garden which was Mary Ann's creation, and she stood, leaning gently on the girl's arm, casting her eye over the beds, missing nothing.

Helen was surprised at how small the old woman was, a good three inches shorter than Helen herself, and she felt a sudden surge of sympathy with Mary Ann but suppressed it, feeling she was betraying Veronica by softening towards the enemy.

'Do you know anything about gardens?' asked the cracked old voice as they wandered along the box-trimmed paths.

Helen shook her head. 'There wasn't any gardens where I lived. There wasn't even any trees or any grass. All this is a surprise to me.'

'Do you like it?'

'Yes, I think I do but I don't know anything about it. It's pretty and the flowers smell nice.'

Mary Ann gave a surprisingly sweet smile. 'They do, don't they? They're good for other things too. You can cure people's sickness with some of them – and you can cure your own by working with them. I've always been happy in my garden. Come down here. I'll show you the roses...' and she pulled Helen's arm so that they turned off the main path into a narrow twisting one that ran under bowers of spice-scented roses and bushes of white flowers. In a cleared bed by the side of a huge rose bush covered with star-like white flowers, she paused and pointed to clusters of spears of pure white lilies raising their trumpets from the black soil. 'My lilies,' she said simply. 'Look at my lovely lilies, come up and smell them. There can't be a better smell than that in heaven.'

The girl bent over the flowers. The scent that came off them made her feel intoxicated and her head swam in a strange ecstasy. She forgot all her troubles in the sheer delight of it. 'Oh, how wonderful,' she sighed, gently touching the waxen whiteness of the curving petals, and her obvious delight pleased her old companion.

'You come with me every day and I'll teach you about gardens,' she said, 'I think you have the gift of learning.'

–

'I hate them, I hate them all, I hate this place...' Veronica could only give open vent to her feelings when she was alone. From the windows of the old rambling house she looked out over a vast spread of open countryside. Away in the distance, dreaming in a heat haze, rose the ramparts of the Cheviot hills. It was a magnificent vista but she was blind to its beauties because of the misery in her soul. To her the lands around Broadmeadows looked empty and lonely, a prison.

Downstairs she could hear the shrill voice of Susan instructing the maids in their daily tasks. Even her house was under her sister-in-law's control, there was nothing for her to do and nowhere to go. Tears filled her eyes as she stared sightlessly out of the window. A string of the usual questions ran through her mind: Will I never leave here? Is my entire life going to be spent in this misery? Will I die as unhappy as I am now? In her despair it seemed that the answer to them all was yes.

Shoulders bowed, she walked back to the sofa and slumped down on it. In memory she remembered the happy days before she married, days and nights of going to balls, flirting with handsome young men, taking tea and making calls from house to house. Misery overwhelmed her when she thought of her mother, her only protector, now dead. Ker had not allowed her to go to Edinburgh for the burial for fear that she would not come back – and he was right, she thought with vehemence, if she once escaped, it would be difficult to make her return.

Idleness hung on her, for the friends she had were left behind in Berwick and in this lonely place she had no calls to make and no callers to solace her. The wives of surrounding landowners looked down on her because of the Kers' low position. In such an enclosed society it would never be forgotten that they had worked themselves up from the labouring class. The wives of farmers like her husband were afraid or jealous of her because of the way she looked, the way she talked or the boasting of Ker about her upper-class background. Worst of all, everyone down to the farm servants viewed her with suspicion, for the Kellock story had reached the countryside from Berwick before she did.

Because of her disgrace Susan treated her like a leper, scarcely able to speak a civil word to her. Mrs Ker was polite enough but she did not seem to care what happened as long as she was left to potter about in her garden and her stillroom. Helen, the water caddy's child, was being taken over by the old lady and in the garden below her window she had seen the pair of them walking down the path between the flowerbeds, deep in conversation. Even Helen, her only friend, was abandoning her.

Her throat tightened in pain as she remembered the hopes she had once entertained, hopes of being happily married to a loving man, with a pretty house and lots of cheerful society around her. Instead, she was shut up here, watched by beady-eyed jailers and with her only prospect that of being thrown into bed and roughly used by a hateful husband.

There was one solace that eased things for her. Trying to make no noise, she went downstairs to the dining room – where she took a decanter of brandy from a corner cupboard and poured out a full glass. She downed it quickly and then poured herself another. When she had drunk three glasses the pain in her heart was slightly muffled and the fourth glass made her so sleepy that she spent the rest of the afternoon in dreamless slumber.

Drinking to forget rapidly became a habit, and when she was slightly intoxicated her demeanour changed completely, making her excessively affectionate to her little son but more than usually cutting towards Ker and his family. Her efforts at wit flashed forth at them as she came sweeping in to meals, stepping haughtily like a duchess attending a levee. She liked dressing up in her finest clothes then, powdering her hair and putting beauty patches on her face. Sitting at the dining table among the plain-clad Kers she looked like an actress in a masquerade.

'Brandy gives her airs and graces,' said Susan to Mrs Eliot, but they did not seriously try to stop her because Susan's sharp eyes detected a deterioration in Veronica's looks after she had been drinking heavily for a month, and that gave her enemies special satisfaction. Ker did not stop her either because when she had drunk herself to the semi-comatose stage, she was quiet and incapable of fighting him off or saying cutting things about his performance in bed.

Helen was the only person who tried to push the decanter out of her way, the only person who mourned the change that had come over her. When Veronica slurred and stumbled over her words, when she staggered up the stairs with scarlet blotches on her face and neck, her maid looked anxious. If they were alone together, she tried to warn her mistress about what was happening. Eventually, when Veronica started reaching for the brandy bottle in the morning, Helen stopped being tactful.

'You're killing yourself. Have you looked in the mirror recently? If you don't stop drinking you'll be a hideous, smelly old soak like the tramps in the Grassmarket. Take it from me, you're nearly there now...'

Veronica stood with her hands on her cheeks and stared at herself in the mirror above the fireplace. It was true, she did look terrible. The insistence of her mother that her looks were the only thing of worth about her came back to her mind. She must not throw that away, for without her beauty she had no bargaining power, no chance of escaping from Ker. In her secret heart she still hung on to the hope that, some day, someone would come into her life and transform it. That someone would have to be a man – and without her looks no gallant rescuer could come along for her. For a moment she almost allowed herself to be sorry for Susan, her pikestaff-plain sister-in-law, for Susan would live and die at Broadmeadows, no man would whisk her away to another life.

'I must hang on. I have to fight,' she whispered to herself. It was a struggle not to take solace in brandy every time her spirits flagged but she fought and she fought, watched with admiration by Helen who alone realized what Veronica was going through – and in the end she won.

The battle exhausted her and almost sapped her of hope. Now that she was sober all the time, she could see her situation more clearly. She could see that it was essential to make a sort of peace with her husband because only by doing so would she be allowed a modicum of freedom. He was not an imaginative or introspective man and when she turned her coquetry on him, he was startled at first but gradually accepted that his wife had seen some sense at last. She smilingly climbed into bed at night with him and did not resist his clumsy advances; she did not shudder openly in disgust at his lovemaking; she curbed her tongue and let him think that they were reconciled. She was laying her plans.

When autumn painted the trees of the Broadmeadows park with russet and gold, she said to Helen, 'I want you to do something for me. The old lady often sends you into Berwick on errands, doesn't she? Next time I want you to take a note to Dr Kellock for me.'

The maid shook her head, 'No. I can't. It's not a good idea.'

In the kitchen Helen, had heard the servants talking about how Ker had threatened Kellock with ruin unless he stayed away from Veronica. She knew too that if the young doctor had wanted to contact Veronica he would have done so by now.

'You must do this for me,' pleaded Veronica. 'You're my only friend, Helen. I just want to write to him to tell him that I'm well. I just want to send him a note.'

But Helen continued shaking her head.

Veronica wept, 'Please, please, don't let me down. You can't imagine what my life is like here. I just want to know that I still have a friend...'

Against her will the maid finally agreed to carry the note.

Veronica saw her off with delight and with another order: 'Make sure you bring me back a reply from the doctor. If he's not in, wait until he comes back. I must have a reply.'

Berwick was shimmering in the autumn sun, with flashes of blue and silver glinting off the satin-smooth waters of the Tweed estuary. The streets were packed – the garrison in the barracks was bigger than ever. There were crowds of ships at anchor in the harbour, and streams of packhorses laden with bundles were crossing the humpbacked bridge as Helen and William headed for the centre of town. Her spirits rose as she surveyed the throng – she liked towns, she liked crowds, she liked bustle and business. Living in the country was all very well and she loved spending time with old Mrs Ker in the garden but she was a town-dweller to her backbone, her blood was the blood of generations of Edinburgh folk who would have felt lonely and threatened by emptiness in the middle of a garden.

If William knew she was up to something, he gave no sign even when she told him she did not know exactly when she would return to their meeting place – it might be quickly but it might not. There was someone she had to see. He was very remorseful for having been the instrument of Veronica's downfall but she was not going to risk the chance of him talking out of turn again.

–

Dr Kellock had moved to a fine new house in Hide Hill with a wrought-iron lamp holder over the steps and a shining brass knocker on the door. The maid who answered her knock recognized Helen and seemed apprehensive at the sight of her.

'Is the doctor in?'

The other girl shook her head.

'I've a note for him. Would you give it to him, please? When will he be back?'

'In about an hour. He's gone to see Mr Blackwell, he goes every day.'

'I'll come back in an hour, then. The person who sent the note wants a reply, you see.'

She hurried off on her errands for old Mrs Ker, collecting muslin, flower bulbs and a tin of snuff from the heavenly-scented little shop on the corner of Silver Street.

The hour passed quickly and when she returned to Hide Hill the maid opened the door only a crack and said, 'The doctor told me that there's no reply.'

Helen's face was hard as she stood her ground. 'There has to be a reply. Tell him I'll stand here on his doorstep until he gives me one.'

She stood for half an hour, obstructing the way for other callers, until Kellock gave in. He came to the door himself, tall and slim, his face flushed with anger as he said to her, 'Come in. I'll give you your reply, but not out here.'

She stepped inside the door which he closed before turning furiously on her. 'She's wasting her time. I'm not writing anything down. There's been enough trouble about all this already. Tell her to leave me alone, tell her not to write me any more letters. I don't want to hear another word about it, she was the one who chased after me, you know, and it nearly ruined my practice. Tell her, for God's sake, to leave me be. It's finished, she must accept that.'

–

'What did he say? What were his exact words?'

It was difficult telling Veronica about Kellock's refusal to have anything more to do with her. She did not seem to fully understand what Helen meant when she recounted the results of her trip to Berwick.

'He said that he can't write to you, he can't see you again – it's his reputation in the town, you see.'

'I understand. Ker's frightened him. He's told all his friends about us and if they stop going to poor Kellock, he'll be ruined.'

Helen nodded, grateful at this apparent acceptance. 'That's it. He's only starting in practice, he has to be careful.'

'But we would be careful. We were careful before. Oh, Helen, he loved me so much. You should have heard the things he said to me. He was my slave!'

'It's too dangerous,' mumbled the maid in embarrassment. 'He said it was too dangerous.'

'Then I'll write to him again. I'll work out some way of us meeting so that no one knows. I long to see him, I want to tell him that. Did he say he longed for me too?'

'He said he was sorry,' lied Helen. 'He sent his love and he said he was sorry.'

Veronica's face brightened. 'He sent his love – of course. I miss him so much. He listened to me, he really understood what I was talking about, not like that oaf Ker. We were so happy together.'

The maid stood awkwardly in the middle of the parlour floor, reflecting silently on the vagaries and inconstancy of love. How quickly it seemed to pass for some people! They were saying they would die for you one day and the next they only wanted never to see you again.

'You'll take him another note. I have to tell him how much I miss him. We must meet.' Veronica rushed to her writing desk and pulled out a piece of paper from one of the pigeonholes but Helen stepped forward and prevented her lifting the pen from its tray.

'Don't write. I didn't tell you the truth. He really wants to end it. He doesn't want to carry it on.'

'That's just how he appeared to you. Inside he must miss me as much as I miss him – a woman knows these things.' Veronica still refused to accept cold facts.

'You don't know about this. He told me you were to leave him alone. I'm sorry to be so blunt but you can't go on pestering him.'

'Pestering him? Pestering a man who swore he'd love me till he died, who swore there'd never been another woman in his life to equal me? What do you mean – pestering?'

'Please stop,' said the maid, looking directly into her mistress's eyes, and Veronica recognized the hopeless finality in her tone of voice.

'Is he another one to betray me? Is he another to use me? Does he really want rid of me? Did it mean nothing to him? Oh God, Helen, how long is this misery going on?'

–

It was a long, cold winter. The snow came in November and filled the fields and blocked the roads till February. Helen thought she had never seen anything so beautiful as Broadmeadows park under snow but it was so cold that her breath hung in front of her like a silver veil when she went to the dairy or the stillroom on errands for Mrs Ker, who was far too frail to brave the bitter weather herself.

The old woman used Helen more and more, sitting with her for hours teaching her how to keep the household account books, for her hands were crippled with rheumatics now and she could no longer hold a pen. She showed Helen how to make long columns detailing the things bought for Broadmeadows and she showed her how to work out what they sold – eggs, milk, butter and cheese had always been in her domain and she had carefully kept her accounts for forty years. The old woman was not prepared to entrust her daughter with carrying on the work for she was slow-witted as far as learning went. Neither she nor her brother could count very well and their handwriting was poor, but Helen was an able pupil, writing a good open hand and with a quick facility for numbers.

Through the winter Veronica was undemanding for she was once again pregnant, a walking testimony in her advancing size to the reconciliation with Ker. If she suffered deeply as a result of Kellock's rejection, she did not show it openly and concentrated on making an effort to calm her husband's suspicions. Becoming pregnant was a masterly stroke. He relaxed when she was with child because he felt that she was undesirable to other men, and their only quarrels through the months of winter were about her extravagance.

She had managed to wheedle him round to allowing her to send to Berwick for laces and ribbons, silks and satins. In a way, spending his money prodigally was a kind of revenge against him. Only the best would do for her, only French taffeta at ten guineas a yard for her Christmas dress was good enough for Mrs Ker. She boasted to Susan about the cost of the gown, knowing full well that the scandalous expenditure would be immediately reported back to her husband. The row between them was most satisfying to her even though she wept copiously and threatened to have a miscarriage as a result of her upset.

But she did not miscarry. Baby Elizabeth was born in the spring, a chubby, blonde child with Ker's features and Susan's high-pitched voice, a voice that jarred on her mother when she gave her first infant cries.

A week after the baby came into the world, old Mrs Ker quietly died in her sleep. 'One goes out when another comes in,' said Mrs Eliot to the servants in the kitchen.

–

After Mrs Ker's death Veronica at last succeeded in seeing off Susan, who was sent to live in a cottage on the edge of the farm near the village. She came back frequently of course but she no longer had her hands on the reins of Broadmeadows House and she resented her loss of status greatly. Her hatred of her sister-in-law grew until she found it difficult to contain, but John Ker would not listen to the poison she dropped in his ear. He wanted a quiet life.

It was enough for him that his wife seemed to have settled down and in the four years succeeding the birth of Elizabeth, she was pregnant four times.

Twice she miscarried, once the baby was born dead and on the fourth occasion it lived only a few days. However, these vicissitudes did not oppress her too much, and as she reached her late twenties she glowed and sparkled with a beauty that masked the boredom and disillusion that filled her innermost soul. She had a few friends in the houses and farms round about now, and her slim figure was the envy of all the other women. She was also admired for dressing always in the height of fashion and in the most expensive materials.

It was a miserable marriage. They had no mutual joy, no love between them, but they tolerated each other; and when he looked at his wife, John Ker was only proud of her as a possession.

He was still sexually demanding and jealous, but if she approached him tactfully, he usually granted her demands, though when the bills came in from mantua makers, hat trimmers and cloth merchants there was always a period of strife in the house. Sometimes he would beat her, though never so severely as after the Kellock affair, but from time to time the servants had to break up their quarrels for fear of the mistress being badly hurt again.

Veronica had learned to hide her thoughts, going on from day to day, dreaming her dreams, planning her trivial plans and playing with her children. Edward was still the favourite though little Elizabeth was changing and no longer resembled Susan quite so strongly. If Veronica thought of Louisa, she never said so and she never went into the graveyard at Hutton church where a mossy green mound marked the child's grave beside the flat carved stone above the resting places of old Ker and his wife.

Now that Ker no longer feared she would betray him with Kellock – for news came back that the young doctor had married and was the father of a son – she enjoyed a measure of freedom and often used to order the groom to saddle her a horse so that she could ride out to enjoy the air.

She was an excellent horsewoman and being mounted suited her for it made her look like Diana the huntress with her curling hair tumbling down under her dashing tricorne hat and a trimly tailored habit accentuating the elegant lines of her long-backed figure. She was never away from home for long and her favourite place of sojourn was Ladykirk churchyard where she would sit on the old gravestones and stare out across the Tweed Valley at the distant Cheviots while her horse grazed among the daisy-strewn grass. Sometimes she wandered into the cool old church and beneath its dog-toothed Norman arches knelt down in a carved pew, with her head resting on the shelf in front. She would stay there for a long time, not thinking anything very much but soothing herself in the silence, the peace and the tranquillity. She never prayed.

1799

Broadmeadows House and Mordington Hall were only four miles apart, separated by the pretty Whiteadder river that cut through deep wooded banks, gurgled through trout-filled pools and twisted gaily round in a tortuous course between them. Compared to its stately, slow-moving cousin the Tweed, it was only a mocking little river and its mockery and cheeky chuckling were justified because it knew how insufficient a barrier it would prove to be once the woman of Broadmeadows and the man of Mordington became aware of each other's existence.

—

The thing that Sir Alexander Renton, squire of Mordington and Lamberton, feared most in life was boredom. His enormous energy and drive, evident in his broad-shouldered, powerful figure and his bushy dark hair, made him a stimulating but tiring companion and to stay the course with him, his friends had to be as physically strong as he was himself. They also needed deep pockets, for Renton's drive was powered by a considerable fortune. In his entire life he had never failed to attain anything he set his sights on – if he could not dominate his way to it, he was able to buy it.

The only son of a very rich member of the squirearchy and a gentle, indulgent mother from a noble family, he had grown up secure in the knowledge that he was one of the blessed people. Never had a wish of his been refused, rarely had anyone contradicted anything he said. As a boy he was educated by a series of sycophantic tutors and at eighteen was sent to the Continent in the care of an easily dominated 'bear leader' to be introduced to foreign travel and gentlemanly vices. He came back dressed in the height of fashion, aware of women and the power of his money – a sensualist, a sportsman, a gamester, a connoisseur of beauty and the arts, a patriot, a snob – he was a typical man of fashion, graduate of the Grand Tour and the best society of Edinburgh and London.

He divided his time between Edinburgh, where he had a large circle of cronies and belonged to the most exclusive drinking clubs; London where he stayed with his mother's well-born relations and rode out in riotous parties to the races, the theatres and the pleasure gardens; and, less often, Mordington, his power base from which he managed his vast estates in Berwickshire. It was Mordington and its farms that filled his pocket and he was for too astute to leave the running of the estate to stewards, no matter how devoted they seemed to be.

In the summer of 1799 he came north to spend three months overlooking his estates and catching up with business matters. He was thirty-six years old, vigorous, lusty, proud and sure of himself. As soon as he set foot in Mordington Hall the servants bustled about frantically carrying out a spate of rapid-fire orders. In what seemed like no time the old house was echoing with noise, his lurcher dogs were scampering over its fine carpets, and carriages were rolling up to the front door filled with friends from all over the country. They descended on the house, filled the bedrooms and sprawled around the dining table which was soon covered with an army of empty port and claret bottles brought up from his late father's cellar. Each day, with Renton at their head, they went into the woods to watch cock fights or set their brindle bull terriers on each other; they raced their horses over Alex's wide meadows and played dice or cards for high stakes till the early hours. Troops of giggling, pretty young women were brought in from Edinburgh or Newcastle and frolicked with them throughout the night. Presiding over all this, Sir Alexander watched with a satirical eye, laughed and joked, urged his friends on to greater heights, greater excesses but managed to remain more sober and guarded than any other member of the gathering, for he was a man who liked to see other people lower their defences and show their weaknesses. But he was not prepared to do the same himself and though few of them realized it, each morning he was up hours before his cronies and had disposed of a mass of business before they were awake.

While Lady Huntingdon was alive Helen and her mother were able to keep in touch through letters to and from Veronica, but afterwards it was more difficult because Mary was illiterate and Helen, though she sent occasional notes, was tied to Broadmeadows, more of a prisoner there in fact than her mistress because maidservants had little time off and what she did have was never enough to travel to Edinburgh and back again, even if she could have afforded the coach fare. No one considered that she might sometimes be homesick, for they were so sure of the advantages of living in the country that they congratulated her on her luck at having made her escape from the sordid city. If she had told them that she often longed for the din and smell of Edinburgh they would have been truly astonished.

Mary Cameron consoled herself with the thought that Helen was well cared for and comfortable – Lady Huntingdon had assured her of that often enough. At night she lay on her pile of rags with her arms over her tired eyes and tried to visualize her bairn… so little and thin when they last saw each other. Had she grown tall? Was she bonny? Did she sometimes think of her mother who missed her so much? But her own life was too hard and unremitting for prolonged reverie. Soon she was asleep, and before she knew it the morning had come and, with it, work.

All the grand folk were slowly leaving the Old Town and their flats were filled up with poorer families, many people to a room, who could not afford to employ water caddies but hauled buckets of water up the stairs themselves. Mary however was well respected and still had a full day's work assured to her – every day, seven days a week. Sometimes she wished for a respite because her bones ached and a terrible tiredness turned her feet to lead by early afternoon when she was toiling along with her unending burden. Age was claiming her, for not so long ago she could work all day and not feel tired till nightfall.

She was feeling particularly weary one Sunday while queueing at the Lawnmarket well head when she saw Cecil Grant coming hustling down the street with her cloak flying out behind her. What a change there was in that lassie! She was not much older than Helen but she had the air of an old woman, her face was white and strained and her hands plucked anxiously at her clothes as she half walked, half ran along.

When Mary greeted her she paused, frowned as if she had difficulty remembering who the woman was, and then spoke in a frantic sort of way... 'Have you seen Jamie Sherriff anywhere? I'm looking for Jamie Sherriff.'

'Mistress Sherriff'll be at Brodie's Close. She goes there every Sunday to be with her sister, Miss Jean. You know that fine, Cecil.'

'Brodie's Close,' scoffed the girl, her eyes wide and strange, 'I'm a Brodie, you know, I'm his daughter. They're only his sisters and they pretend they don't know me.'

It was difficult to know how to reply to that because it was true what the girl said. The Deacon's sisters had completely ignored the existence of his two families. Not only that, but Miss Jean in particular seemed to have obliterated the memory of her brother. She never mentioned his name and pretended she did not know who he was if anyone spoke of him. It was truly as if he had never existed.

To avoid answering Cecil, Mary bent down to balance a water bucket on each end of the carrying bar that she wore across her shoulders. She paused with one hand in the small of her back. Oh, what a terrible gnawing pain she had just there. It was burning away all the time now, even a night's sleep did not cure it. Cecil did not notice her discomfort however because she was launched on her favourite tirade, one that the people of the streets had become used to hearing over the months since poor Anne Grant had died.

'They ignore me. They ignored my mother even when she was dying. They pretend we don't exist but I'm his daughter. My brother is his son. I want *justice*.'

Mary looked over her shoulder to see if Peter Grant was among the caddies at the foot of the Mercat Cross but there was no sign of him. That was a pity for he alone seemed able to soothe his sister, but he must have gone off on an errand. Cecil was worse today than she had ever been. This fixation about her father had grown steadily on her and with it a terrible resentment against his sisters.

It was difficult to take sides. Mary sympathized with poor dejected Anne Grant who had literally shrivelled away and died after the Deacon was hung. Neither she nor her bairns had received any help from the Brodies, but then neither had the Watts who had just as good a claim on their father's family. On the other hand Mary was sorry for the Deacon's sisters too. Poor Miss Jean's world had been ruined by her brother's disgrace. She had always been so respectable, so conscious of their social status, so prim and proper. The terrible spectacle of the hanging of William Brodie and the scandal that ensued when his true character was revealed had almost killed her. She went out rarely now and when she did, you could tell from the way she walked and the way she held her head that she was terrified of what people were saying. It was difficult for her to believe that even the death of the Deacon was soon forgotten by the happy gossips in the teeming streets, that they would grow tired of the subject and move on to another. For her the scandal would never die away.

Jamie Sherriff was a more resilient sort but then she had her husband, the merchant in Leith, and her bonny daughter to take up her mind. She was kind to Miss Jean though, coming up Leith Walk in a sedan chair every Sunday morning to spend the day with her sister, to accompany her to church and guide her back over the streets to her haven in the dark flat. It would be a terrible thing to have their quiet routine disrupted this Sunday by a demonstration from Cecil.

'I think you'd best go home,' Mary told the girl. 'Your brother might be looking for you there.'

Cecil almost screamed. 'Go home, I won't go home! I've come to see the Brodies. I've come to tell them that they can't pretend any longer that he never existed… a woman told me yesterday that his sister Jean's even cut his name out of the family Bible. She can't do that. I've come to demand his rights. He should be in that Bible – and so should we.'

Mary was angry now. 'What rights? The Deacon hasn't any rights now, lassie, he's dead. Go home and stop making trouble for yourself and everybody else.'

Sensible advice was lost on Cecil, however, and gathering her cloak around her she ran across the Lawnmarket to disappear into the dark gaping mouth of Brodie's Close.

'I've a feeling the Town Guard'll have to take her home. There's going to be some trouble today,' said another water carrier to Mary as they stood with their fists on their hips watching the girl disappear. She was right. Within a few minutes they heard the sound of shrieking coming from the dark close and Miss Jean, on the arm of her younger sister, emerged running into the daylight. The women were respectably dressed in their Sunday best with deep black-lined bonnets shading their faces but they were clutching up their cumbersome skirts and staring back over their shoulders up the close from which emerged Cecil, flapping her arms under the cloak like a huge black bat.

'You've cut his name out of the family Bible. You've cut him out of life. He was my father – you can't deny that. He asked to see *me* in the Tolbooth – only *me*! I have to fight for him. You can't cut him out, you can't pretend he never existed.'

The sisters clung to each other on the pavement. Miss Jamie trying to console her weeping older sister, but Cecil was closing in on them with more accusations. 'You go to church and pretend you're so good but you've denied your brother, just like Peter denied Jesus when the cock crowed.'

The water caddies were watching this scene with interest, and more passers-by came running to swell their number. The watchers were all muttering among themselves – 'That lassie's daft – where's her brother? – get the Guard…'

Cecil was alongside the two women now, poking at them with her finger, exultant at their humiliation. 'My mother never had a kind word from you. My brother and I are denied our birthright. What have you done with all his money? What have you done with the money you were given for telling the councillors that he'd gone to Ostend? They must have paid you well for that.'

This last taunt roused Jamie to retaliation. She let go of the huddled body of her sister and turned on Cecil with her parasol upraised. 'You leave us be, you shut your evil mouth. We, did *not* tell on William. If you say we did, that's a wicked lie!'

And she gave a wild swing with her weapon at the girl but Cecil ducked and it missed her. A full-fledged fight was averted by Peter Grant running down from the Mercat Cross followed by a group of his fellow caddies. He rushed up to Cecil and pinioned her flailing arms with his.

In a soothing voice he said, 'Come on now, let's go home, you've just become a wee bit excited. Let me take you home.'

She quietened like a lamb, and said in a very different voice, 'Oh, it's you, Peter. I was looking for you. I wanted to tell you they've cut his name out of the family Bible. They can't do that, can they?'

He led her away, nodding sympathetically as he listened to her frenzied chattering. When he had her heading in the right direction he called back over his shoulder to the watching Brodie sisters, 'I'm sorry about this. She's a bit upset sometimes.'

The sisters stood close together for a few moments with shocked expressions, and then Jamie quietly led Miss Jean back up the close to the flat. There would be no churchgoing for them that day.

–

His hat tilted forward over his eyes, Alex Renton stood in the early morning sunlight, whip in hand, surveying the ground for his new racecourse. With his steward and head stableman he had ridden out before his drinking partners of the previous evening were awake, to walk over his lands at Lamberton Toll, select the site for the finishing post in the middle of the open moor and decide where his army of carpenters should build the wooden viewing stand.

'We'll make it a mile and a half, that's a good test of a horse,' he told Hennessy, the stableman, who nodded in agreement.

'You're right, Sir Alex, it's rough ground and the end's uphill too so it'll take a strong horse to finish here.'

They spoke like equals, united in their appreciation of horses and racing and respectful of each other's knowledge. Hennessy demanded Renton's high regard because he had been specially brought up from Newmarket to Mordington and had a reputation as one of the best men with horses in the country. In return he genuinely respected his employer because Renton was famous among racing men for his eye for a horse. He bought only the best bloodstock, and horses bearing his colours had won many valuable races. Now he was planning to lay out and run his own course and the stableman was proud to be involved in the project.

The trio stood amicably together on the top of a little hillock – the horseman grizzled and bow-legged with a broken-veined face and gnarled hands; the sturdy, solemn steward with his stocky peasant's body, trustworthy open face and thick blond hair that shone like a gilded helmet in the sun; and the patrician Renton, tall, dark, elegant, slim-waisted and broad-shouldered, with a sardonic face and slanting eyes of pale blue, eyes that always seemed to have a wicked glint as if he were relishing some joke the others had not understood.

'I'm planning the first meeting for the middle of next month. It will be ready by then?' It was more of an order than a question really and the steward nodded. He had all the arrangements well in hand; the labourers, carpenters and painters were ready to start work as soon as the course lay-out had been decided.

'They'll start tomorrow,' he told the squire.

'Good man, then we'll put the newspaper notices in next week. We should have a big crowd from the Berwick garrison – there's a lot of racing men among the officers there – and my friends in England are sending horses up. We should have a good race – but Hennessy, you've to see that my fellow, the Pasha, is in top fettle. I'd like to win my own cup.'

The stableman nodded in eager agreement. 'He's on his toes, he's bursting to go. It'll take a wondrous horse to beat him.'

They walked down from their vantage point to where they had tied up their mounts against a gate, and Renton said to his steward, 'We'll ride home the long way. I'd like to see how the fields are looking on the Paxton side. Hennessy, you go straight back and start working on the Pasha.'

He and his steward made a detour across country to reach Mordington House and, two hours later while they were approaching a humpbacked pack bridge that crossed the river Whiteadder, they saw a black-clad rider on a grey horse coming towards it from the other direction.

The bridge was narrow and two horses could not cross at a time without clashing stirrups but it did not occur to Sir Alexander to hold back so that the rider on the far bank should go first. It was his bridge, it was his land, it was his right to precede everyone else. He drove his horse forward and blocked the way although the other horse was already on the narrow bridge. When he looked arrogantly across at the advancing rider he saw to his surprise that it was a woman. Even that did not make him yield and, raising his eyebrows as if surprised that she was in his path, he drew rein and waited for her to make her horse step backwards. But she was as proud as he and stood her ground, refusing to move. They stared over their horses' heads, each, taking the other's measure, and she felt her face slowly flush as his eyes openly scrutinized her. Her embarrassment grew even stronger when she detected a glimmer of a smile on his mouth with its short, curving upper lip and the measuring look in his confident eyes. She had no idea who he could be, but both his manner and his clothes made it clear that he was a man of property and assurance.

'Surely you're going to let a lady cross the bridge?' she demanded, making an effort to stop her voice from quavering. The effort was successful because the voice he heard was high and clear and – something he noticed because it was important to him – refined. This was a lady. She could not be the wife of some jumped-up johnny or low-born farmer out on a visit. His eyes scrutinized her: slim, well-dressed, refined, beautiful – damn it, very beautiful – and angry.

'I own this bridge, madam,' he drawled and had the satisfaction of seeing confusion cross her face. Without another word she prepared to reverse the grey mare off the bridge but, always one to spring a surprise, Renton beat her to it, dropped his hands, drew on his horse's bit and made it execute a smart back step that showed his skilled equestrianship in the smoothness of the action.

Then, with a scoffingly doffed hat, he sat easily at the bridge head as she came clattering over, her face scarlet.

'Good morning, madam,' he said in a cordial voice because, as she rode past without looking at him, he could not but notice what a deuced fine woman she was in her well-cut black habit, not the sort of woman one normally saw around those parts.

When she was out of earshot he asked the steward, 'Who was that?'

The other man laughed and said, 'Oh, she's the wife of Ker at Broadmeadows. An Edinburgh woman, a lord's daughter, they say, and a bit of a madam from the sound of it.'

Renton turned in his saddle and stared after her disappearing slim back. Even from a distance, its shapeliness impressed him greatly.

'Her husband's not that old rogue who bought Broad-meadows from the Mathers? Not that sharp-eyed old villain who drove such a hard bargain?'

'No, not him, he's dead. She's married to his son, the big heavy chap that works with the army sometimes. He's a muster master and tours the northern camps.'

Renton laughed. 'I'd never have believed that ill-bred dunderhead could find a wife like her. She's a good-looking woman, but I'll wager she costs him a-pretty penny.'

Beneath the bridge the river laughed and giggled its way over the rounded stones of its bed.

-

John Ker was working in his stackyard with the men when a messenger arrived from the. grand Sir Alexander Renton, who had never even looked the road he walked on before. He felt immensely flattered that the emissary had come with an invitation – it was more of an order really – to attend the first race meeting to be held at Lamberton the following week.

'Will you be able to come?' asked the messenger.

'Without a doubt,' said John Ker, who would not let anything stand in his way of mixing with the gentry in their place of pleasure.

The excitement at Broadmeadows was tense on race-day morning. Ker was out early supervising the men polishing the chaise and seeing that the two carriage horses were groomed to perfection. With a silk handkerchief he personally buffed up their silken coats before they were backed between the shafts of the carriage and he would have buffed up Veronica too, so eager was he that she do him credit among the fine ladies and gentlemen who would be at Renton's races.

She would not let him down, though, he saw that as soon as she stepped out of the house in all her finery. Not only was her appearance most pleasing to him but she was cordial and beaming, as excited as he at the prospect of this outing into high society.

Two huge ostrich feathers waved from her hat, a silken shawl with soft-coloured stripes and a deep fringe covered her shoulders, and her gown was of fine silken gauze that shimmered like sunlight when she moved. Her husband did not let himself wonder how much it had cost. That anxiety would come later. In spite of her delight at going to such a gilded gathering, however, Veronica found herself growing irritated as she climbed into the carriage.

Though she fought to hide her anger two things particularly annoyed her – firstly because John had insisted on including his sister Susan in their party in the hope that she might meet a husband there, and secondly because he was so childishly flattered to be invited to such a high-society event.

'Watch you don't crush your skirt, you have to look your best,' he admonished her as he – and Susan, looking awful in violet satin that clashed hideously with her purple cheeks – followed her into the gleaming carriage.

'I don't know why you're making such a fuss, you're acting as if the Lord himself had asked you out for the day,' she snapped.

Susan gave a pinched smile. 'Oh, sister-in-law, he almost has. Sir Alexander Renton is the most important landowner round here – a very rich man indeed. His mother was one of the Montgomeries… his older sister's married to a man of title… he owns thousands of acres.' Susan had the genealogy of everyone in the district, especially the gentry, at her fingertips.

In spite of herself Veronica was impressed. 'Oh, so that's who the local squire is! Is it him who's asked us to the races? When I was a girl I knew his sister. She used to be at the same balls as

I was in Edinburgh. She was married by then but she was still a great beauty – so many men were in love with her! They say the novelist Smollet adored her but she wouldn't go away with him.'

John Ker's usual jealous displeasure when hearing Veronica talk of her past triumphs was overcome today by delight that his wife had enjoyed some social contact with the squire's family, who were almost as grand as Royalty to his way of thinking.

'I'd heard his sister was a beauty. She's a lot older than him though – his parents thought they'd never have a son by the time he came along,' he said, plumping down in the seat opposite his wife, 'but he's turned out a handsome fellow – fine-looking and elegant and he talks very grand, a real gentleman.'

Saying nothing, Veronica looked at him, turning over his words in her mind. By now her husband was far from being either fine or elegant for he was big, too big, with his belly already lying comfortably on his knees and the knotted calves of his legs bulging in the silk stockings bought specially for the outing. As for being a gentleman – no silk stockings, no coat with silver buttons, no silk cravat knotted under his chin would ever make her husband one of those.

–

From his position on the top of the white-painted wooden stand Renton saw their chaise arrive but did not climb down to receive them. That would have been too much to ask. Instead he noted with satisfaction that Ker had risen to the bait and brought his wife along, and, yes, the steward had been right, it was the same woman and, yes, she was even better-looking than he remembered. She climbed easily out of the carriage, tall and slim in a straw bonnet trimmed with feathers and a flowing dress cut delightfully low at the neck exposing delectable breasts. His hunter's eye marked her out as suitable prey, a good diversion to banish boredom during the months of summer.

Before Pasha's race he sought them out as if by chance and addressed Ker with smooth charm. 'You're Broadmeadows, aren't you? I've been meaning to call on you. We landowners should stick together. I'm glad you could come along to my race meeting and it was good you brought your ladies. Their beauty makes them very welcome!' He kissed Susan's hand first and then Veronica's and she felt his fingers gently caressing hers as he held her glove for just a second longer than was absolutely necessary.

A palpable excitement swept the crowd as the horses came out for the big race and Veronica's heart was beating so fast that she was afraid for a moment she would faint away. Renton's horse was ridden by a jockey with a grey wrinkled face, looking like Punchinello in silks of scarlet and black, and he held the reins of the curveting black horse with confidence as the runners ranged up behind the starting line opposite the Ker carriage. The crowd gave a loud cry of glee as the flag fell and the rope was dropped, then the horses leaped off in a stream of dazzling brilliance. She blinked and put a hand to her forehead. What was the matter with her? Why did she feel so strange? At her side Susan was screaming hysterically and Ker was booming away – 'Come on, come on...' but their voices seemed far away as if they were calling from some distant cavern. They were urging on the squire's horse and their shouts grew louder as the pounding cavalcade came round the last corner and headed for the finishing post. 'He's winning, he's winning,' cried Susan, hanging on to Veronica's arm in her excitement, and as the Pasha passed the post first all eyes were on him – all that is except Veronica's. She was watching Alexander Renton, standing up in the front of the stand with both arms raised above his head and his face alight with passion as he urged his stallion home.

They were all excited and pleasantly tired when they drove home that evening. Leaning back in the corner seat, Veronica felt her head swim as she listened to Ker talking on and on about Renton's horse. Posing as a connoisseur of racehorses, he expatiated on its bone, its breeding, its stamina and its performance while Susan nodded in eager agreement. Her plain face was alight with unusual animation and her mind was busy memorizing the details of who was there – and who was not – to carry with her from house to house around the district as she boasted about talking to the squire, about being complimented by him, about watching him in the crowd with his fashionable friends clustered around him. They did not notice that Veronica sat quietly, her eyes abstracted. She was thinking over what had happened. As soon as Renton came into their company she had recognized him as the rider on the bridge, and a strange little flutter gripped her heart. Though he looked at her without betraying any open sign of recognition, she could tell by his mocking glance that he remembered where and when they had met before. I'm going to know this man very well. This man is going to mean a lot to me, said a sudden little voice inside her head.

Most of all however she was distracted by remembering the last thing that had happened when the meeting was drawing to a close. Ker was off with a crowd of other farmers and Susan was gossiping somewhere, leaving her alone in their carriage. She was enjoying the noise and enthusiasm of the crowd around her when Renton suddenly appeared at the brass carriage rail by her side.

'Have you enjoyed yourself?' he asked in a low voice, and when she nodded, he went on, 'We'll meet again, you and I, Mrs Ker.' Then he gave her a flashing, beguiling smile and disappeared before she could summon up the wits to say anything.

–

That night, in the two houses only a few miles apart, the talk was of the day's enjoyments. John Ker looked with pride at his wife on the other side of their dining table, and though compliments were in his mind he could not find the words. If he could have found his tongue he would have said that she'd been the finest woman there that afternoon, that she'd outshone the others like a glorious beacon, and he could not believe that she was his. If only he could see into her mind, he thought, if only he could find out what was hidden behind those shining hazel eyes that became so expressionless when she stared at him. He took another swig of port and resolved: 'By God, I'll bed her well tonight. Other men might admire her all they want, but I'm the one who sleeps with her.'

In Mordington Hall the fashionably dressed ladies and gentlemen around the polished mahogany table lounged in their chairs and exchanged quips and banter.

'Good racing today,' drawled one young man, 'and good viewing too. Saw some damned fine women on the course as well as fine horses.'

The host looked down from the end of the table and asked casually, 'Did you? Who was the finest, do you think?'

This was a popular kind of topic and they all had their different opinions which they discussed for a while, wrangling pleasantly until Renton, pushing away the woman at his side who was gently caressing his thigh, asked again.

'Did anyone see a tall woman with a feathered hat and a pale green dress? A woman with a red-faced oaf of a husband.'

One or two had seen Veronica and appreciated her style and beauty. 'Who was she?' asked one middle-aged roué who had made special note of her.

'The wife of a mud-caked farmer down in the valley. A damned fine woman, though,' said Renton, turning the stem of his wine glass slowly in his hands. Then he suddenly became more animated and added, 'I'll make you all a wager. I wager I can make that woman my mistress before the month is up.'

There was nothing that enlivened his dinner parties more than a wager. The guests all spoke at once – 'But you don't know her. She doesn't know you, does she? She's probably a model of wifely virtue...' they protested.

'That won't stop me. Will you wager me a hundred guineas?' asked Renton, his face tense in the candle light. Three men shouted, 'Done, I'll take your wager.'

The woman at his side gave a grimace of distaste, raised her head high and said cuttingly, 'I'll take your wager too. A month, you say? That doesn't give you much time. What if she takes longer than that to win?'

'She won't. It's long enough. She's ready for the taking. I can always tell,' was the confident reply.

–

Dalliance was a sport to both of them. Like skilled fencers they knew the next move, the next feint, taking, up their proper positions almost without thinking. Her heart was light and she had a thrilling feeling of anticipation as, two days after the race meeting, she mounted her mare in the Broadmeadows stable and headed towards Foulden ridge. Once there she drew rein and looked around – over on her right she could see the trees bowering the white façade of Renton's mansion. It was large and imposing, with fluted pillars, built only ten years ago after he came back from his tour of the Continent. A stream of thoughts ran unbidden through her mind… Was he in the house now? What was he doing? What would it be like to rule a house like that, to be a squire's lady? That was what she should have been really, not the wife of a lout like John Ker. Why had her destiny been mapped out for her when she was so young? Could she not manage a second chance?

Beside her was the little parish church with its ancient ivy-covered tithe barn nicked away in the corner of the churchyard. She looked at the tilting gravestones on the mossy grass and rapidly turned her eyes away, for she did not want to think of the transience of life, of how quickly the days succeeded each other until you were old and dying. To avoid the sight of them she slowly turned her horse round and looked out across the broad valley to the south. On the horizon rose the misty outlines of the Cheviot hills, a few patches of snow still visible on them although it was June. Nearer, on the southern ridge above the Whiteadder river, she could see Broadmeadows sitting securely amongst its sheltering trees. Big, blustering Ker would be in the farmyard; the maids would be in the kitchen and Helen would be playing in the garden with Edward and Elizabeth. Her mind dwelt on her children – handsome, affectionate babies both of them. She loved them dearly, there was no doubt of that. What she was doing today was only a game, a little diversion, and besides, she told herself, he might not come. He might not play the game the same way she did.

With the sun dazzling her eyes she turned for home. She had timed it well, for when she reached the pack bridge it would be almost the same hour as on the day they first met. Her mare slithered and slipped down the steep slope towards the river, bracing herself with her front legs, but Veronica was not tense or afraid that she would fall. She sat easily in her high saddle, letting the careful mare make her own way without interference.

For some time she thought she had misunderstood his approach, for the shadows beneath the beech tree at the end of the bridge were so deep that she did not see him at first. It was only the soft whinnying of his mount when it saw her mare approach that gave him away. Pretending to be surprised, she drew on her reins and sat upright.

'Are you crossing first?' she asked in a challenging tone and he laughed as he stepped out into the full light.

'No, you go on. I'll give you precedence today, Mrs Ker,' he replied.

She tossed her head and pushed the mare forward with an imperious jab of the heel, but he put up a hand to grab her bridle.

'I hope you enjoyed the races,' he said.

She still looked haughtily down at him before replying, 'Very much. My husband and I were most gratified to be invited.'

'Your husband enjoyed himself? Is he a betting man?' His voice had a mocking tone as if he knew only too well what game she was playing.

She liked that and when she shook her head, she permitted a little smile to cross her lips, knowing how fetching it would make her face appear under the smart little hat. 'Not he. I'm the gambler in our family.'

'Oh, I like a lady who's prepared to take a chance,' said Renton, letting go of the bridle. 'Perhaps we'll meet here again tomorrow, I usually pass this way about this time.'

She trotted off across the little bridge with her shoulders held straight and her head high. Her heart was singing a loud, loud song. She felt young again, she felt like throwing her hat in the air and turning round to blow him a kiss, but she did nothing of the sort. The game between them had begun.

They met every day for the next week. They sparred, they advanced and retreated, smiled and sulked. On the eighth day she deliberately did not keep their tryst and was pleased to see his look of relief when she turned up the next afternoon, acting casually as if nothing had happened and never giving him any explanation for her non-appearance. He paid her back though by talking about a woman he admired, describing her beauty in detail while all the time keeping a watchful eye on her face, which betrayed her chagrin in spite of her efforts to hide it.

When she went home to Broadmeadows, she always sat for a while in the parlour going over their talk in her mind. Nothing of any consequence was ever really said, for they confined themselves to gossip; to reminiscences about Edinburgh and people they both knew there; to speculations about the progress of the war (and in order not to appear too stupid she began to read the newspaper). He paid her compliments and she accepted them with grace; she flattered him and he accepted that as his due. But all the time they were riding along, talking together, they were growing more and more conscious of each other's physical presence. The sun shone down on them and as the temperature rose into the sweltering eighties, so did their mutual attraction climb to passionate heights. During the long, hot nights she lay awake beside her snoring husband and stared out of the open bedroom window. Over the ridge, over to the north, he would be lying awake too. If only they could fly out of their windows and he beside the river…

They had been meeting for nearly three weeks when an invitation arrived for Mr and Mrs Ker, along with Miss Susan Ker, to attend a summer party at Spital House, about a mile across the fields south of Broadmeadows. John, and Susan were transported with delight: in all the years their family had farmed there, none of them had ever been invited out by the local gentry. Spital House was the property of a wealthy gentleman called Alston, a man of good birth and leisurely pursuits who left his farming interests to his servants.

'I wonder why he's asked us?' Veronica speculated as she handled the note that had been brought over by a liveried servant.

'I had a word with him at the races,' suggested her husband. 'We exchanged "good days" then. Perhaps when he saw us there, he realized that we were the sort of people he could ask to his house.'

'His lady died last year. He's in want of a wife,' said Susan, who obviously thought that her chance to escape lifelong spinsterhood might have come at last.

In theory the idea of an alliance between Spital House and Broadmeadows was quite a good one, though Veronica privately wondered how Mr Alston would react to the suggestion of taking on Susan in order to acquire her dowry – a few fields. She had her own ideas about why they were invited to Spital House but, of course, was not prepared to voice them.

On the evening of the party the sky was coloured a deep purple like overripe plums, and away in the distance could be heard rumbles of thunder, rolling up the valley like the chariots of the gods. The air seemed charged with a strange tension, and when Helen dressed Veronica's hair it clung to the teeth of the comb and sparked with fire in the strange brazen light from the window. Her mistress was tense and agitated, as if the weather affected her nerves, and she seemed incapable of making up her mind which dress to wear…

'Perhaps the pale green satin.? No, I'll wear my pink chiffon with the pearl beads round the skirt. Do you think it becomes me better than the green, Helen? Or perhaps I should wear the blue silk – though it's very daringly cut. Ker doesn't like me to wear it out in company…'

In the end they decided on the pink chiffon and at last she was dressed, stepping down the stairs like a princess with the warm colour of the dress reflecting a glow on to her neck and face. In her hair Helen had put jewelled golden combs and artfully teased little ringlets to cascade down in front of her ears. 'Thank heavens no one powders now,' she said to Helen, 'I could not have suffered breathing in all that chalk on a stuffy night like this. It's so nice to wear one's hair *au naturel*…'

When Susan saw her sister-in-law she gave a grimace and knew even more clearly than usual why she so disliked Veronica. What chance had she of netting a husband if everywhere she went she had to stand beside this full-blown goddess of a woman?

'Is it quite proper for your wife to show so much bosom?' she hissed at her brother as he was showing his wife into the carriage.

Veronica heard and turned on the step to say, 'Everyone wears their dresses low now – if they have the figure for it, of course. They say Josephine soaks her dresses in water before she puts them on so that they cling to her figure – but then she's very slim and lovely.' Her glance swept over Susan's lumpy, solid body and the subject was well and truly closed.

The gathering at Spital House was small – only sixteen people and, to Veronica's disappointment, Renton was not among, them. During dinner they sat stiffly at the long table and made polite conversation. The war was a subject of never-ending fascination and the name of Bonaparte was on all lips, for he had recently come to prominence, displaying his military genius at the head of the French army in Italy. As the men in the party discussed his military tactics the women gossiped about his marriage to the widowed Josephine de Beauharnais, a woman with a very chequered past, they said. The speculations about Josephine were continued when the ladies retired with Mr Alston's middle-aged sister to the upstairs drawing room after dinner. However, this was not a house where the men sat for hours over their port, and within a short time they were all together again, trooping back downstairs to a long salon with glass doors opening on to the gardens, for someone had suggested dancing.

Miss Alston seated herself at the piano, servants were called in to roll back the carpet and in spite of the oppressive heat, the evening commenced with hearty enthusiasm.

Veronica was treading a stately measure with a lanky young man whose face looked like a mournful goat's when she saw Renton entering, in tight white buckskin breeches and a long-tailed, dark green coat. He was staring straight at her and she felt herself flushing, not with embarrassment but with desire so strong that it made her lose her breath. They could not go straight to each other – the rules of the game did not permit that – so they danced with other people until at last she saw him standing before her, proffering his hand. She was sitting with her husband and lowered her head so that Ker could not see her eyes while Renton asked permission to lead her on to the floor. She knew that John Ker would be so gratified that the squire of Mordington should show such condescension towards his wife that he would give permission gladly – so long as his suspicions were not aroused.

The watchers in the room could see that they fitted together like glove and hand. They were both tall, both slim, both elegant, both so aristocratic-looking that everyone else seemed like peasants beside them. When they stood side by side, their impact was remarkable. They were a pair of proud and beautiful people, a matching of the gods. Even innocent Miss Alston wrinkled her brows a little when she saw how they danced together, so effortlessly, so fluidly though they had never before stepped out on a floor together. She had wondered why Alex Renton had specially requested her brother to invite the Kers to his party and now she thought she knew, though she hoped she was wrong. In their dancing there was an undertone of sensuality that would have given them away completely in a less innocent gathering.

Veronica tried not to look directly at him during the dance, fixing her view over his shoulder or down at her feet, but when the music came to an end she curtsied deeply and, as he put out a hand to help her to her feet, she rose up very slowly, her gaze coming up from the floor until it finally rested on his face. His eyes were dark-shadowed and dangerous like the eyes of a man possessed by some demon.

'I'll wait for you in the garden – in half an hour. Beside the rose arbour. Come when they serve the ices,' he whispered urgently.

-

The servants came parading one after the other into the room with silver trays bearing dishes of coloured ices – pink and green and palest yellow melting in delicate blue and white china bowls. With cries of delight the guests surged towards them, fanning, themselves or mopping their brows with their handkerchiefs and exclaiming at the terrible heat.

'It's bound to thunder soon,' said cherry-cheeked Mr Alston. 'It can't go on like this much longer or the earth will crack right open.'

John Ker's face was purple as he handed a dish to his wife but she gave it back to him. 'You eat mine, John, I'm not hungry and it will cool you. Sit down there and eat it. I'm going to take a breath of air in the garden.'

She, rushed out before he could suggest accompanying her, and the dark night swallowed her up. In the velvety blackness she stood still for a moment, blinking her eyes to accustom them to the gloom. She had no idea where the rose arbour was to be found but he must have seen her come out, for away in the distance she heard a soft hooting – like a night owl, but it was saying 'Here, here, here'. She ran across the grass to a shadowy place beneath trees, but before she reached it she was engulfed in his arms and his lips were on hers – urgently pressing, biting, demanding lips that she gave in to completely.

They stood without speaking, only kissing frantically until he drew her back to the shadows. 'In here, it's safer, we can't be seen in here,' he muttered in a strangely strangled voice and led her to a stone bench beneath a tangle of sweet-smelling white roses that arched above them like a heavenly ceiling. The scent of the roses, the stillness of the night, the oppressive heat and the feeling of febrile excitement in the air acted on her like a drug. She put her lips on his and her body went limp in his arms. She made no resistance when he slipped her dress off her shoulders and she sighed in sheer bliss when he laid her down on the bench. Only when he entered her did she cry out for he was possessed with such fury and urgency that she was afraid for a moment… But he hushed her and stroked her neck and shoulders with his hands so that she quietened, only moaning softly at each move of his strong, tightly muscled body. They were far from the house and no one but the night animals and the hunting owls heard the sounds of her ecstasy.

He was an experienced lover, skilled and considerate. He brought her to heights she had never experienced before, he made her body sing under him and when he was finished they lay together on the broad bench staring up at the sky without speaking, like people in a dream.

Then, as if to remind them of the heights of their passion, the darkness was cut by a blinding lightning flash, followed almost immediately by a terrible peal of thunder that threatened to split their eardrums. The rain began pouring in sheets, and as they started to pull on their clothes, from the house she could hear Ker's voice calling her name. She tried smoothing her hair but it had fallen out of the combs and she had no time to search for them because Ker's voice was coming nearer and nearer.

Renton was watching her with the whites of his eyes gleaming like an animal's in the dark.

'Go to him,' he said.

'I've lost my combs.'

'I'll find them for you. Go now or he'll find us.'

'Will we meet tomorrow?' she asked.

'Yes.'

'In the usual place?'

'Yes.'

And she ran across the soaking grass with her dress clinging to her. When, she reached the salon door she was dripping and her hair was plastered around her face in wet tendrils so that she looked as if she'd been dipped in a river, and no one noticed that her bodice was torn or her combs had disappeared.

–

On the day after the party she did not ride out, however, because the drenching had given rise to a fever which rendered her slightly delirious and unable to leave her bed. As Helen tried to soothe her she clung to the girl's hand, murmuring some garbled message. 'I have to let him know. I must tell him...' But even in her illness she still retained caution, and when Helen asked, 'Tell who?' she only turned her head on the pillow and did not reply.

She did not come to the bridge for three days, and on the third night the month of Alex Renton's wager was up. As he prepared for dinner he was jubilant and ready to surprise his friends with his boastful revelation that the farmer's wife had fallen to him. He was looking forward to watching their reactions, to teasing them with the details of where and when the seduction happened. Old Alston was among his dinner guests and he would be specially interested that Renton had won the bet in his rose arbour.

Seven of them sat round his table as before; the candles in their silver sconces glittered, on the plate and glasses and lit up the avid faces as the old roué challenged him, 'What of our wager, then? Did you seduce the beauty?'

He enjoyed the knowledge that they were all looking at him as he leaned back in his chair, balancing it on its two back legs. He stuck his hands in the pockets of his striped waistcoat and slowly ran his eyes over the faces of his friends. Showing nakedly were curiosity, lascivious interest, envy – and in the case of the wagering woman, an actress with a touring company at Berwick, jealousy. Then, without premeditation, his mind switched back to Veronica Ker. He remembered her face, he remembered how yielding and loving she had been to him; he remembered her sweetness, her gentleness and her terrible need for love. He pitied her life with Ker, for rumours of his ill-treatment of her were rife in the district. All of a sudden, he knew that he could not betray her.

He laughed aloud and said, 'You win. I lost.' Then he leaned forward and pulled some coins from his pockets, throwing them down on the white cloth for the eager hands to lift. 'I lost the bet, she wouldn't yield to me!'

As soon as he had done it, he repented of his rashness. She'd cost him 400 guineas. I must have gone insane, he said to himself.

–

Next morning he was angry at his weakness, rejecting all the soft thoughts he had entertained about Veronica. Of course she was a woman used to love, she was too easy to persuade, she had little virtue – why pretend that she did?

Deliberately he rode off in the direction opposite to the pack bridge and did not come home till late at night. He could not guess that she waited beneath their tree for over an hour before riding home in despair.

As it happened, they met again by chance. He was riding to Berwick through Paxton village, a cluster of little stone-built houses with pretty gardens clustering up to their front doors, and she was riding back to Broadmeadows from a visit to another farmer's wife when they saw each other approaching.

Her face flushed and her heart began beating so fast that she could feel it fluttering like a trapped butterfly in her throat; his face hardened at the sight of her and he drew up his horse at the side of the road, making a mocking gesture with his whip to let her pass. But regardless of the curious eyes in the cottage windows, she stopped in the middle of the rutted path and said in a rush, 'I was sick. That's why I didn't come. I had a fever.'

His face changed as he looked at her. She did look pale and drawn but she was still beautiful, perhaps the most beautiful woman he had ever seen.

'I missed you,' he said, 'come tomorrow.'

Without more words, they rode away in opposite directions.

–

Both Veronica and Renton relished intrigue: the secrecy of their clandestine meetings added spice to the affair. What had begun as sheer madness in the rose arbour became a raging passion over the following weeks.

When Veronica rode out the day after their meeting in Paxton to the packhorse bridge where, of course, he was waiting, sitting negligently on a huge black stallion, one gloved hand on his thigh, a wicked thrill grasped her stomach and twisted it in a delicious grip. The skills of flirting, of teasing and coaxing which she had practised so well in her girlhood all came back to her.

She had not thought deeply about the possible progress of their affair, in fact she had not intended to yield so easily to him. The actual act of adultery frightened her, especially when she remembered the beating that her affair with Kellock had brought her. With Renton however she found that their mutual need was so urgent and his will so much stronger than hers that scruples were cast aside.

Still smarting from his unexpected act of altruism by throwing away the bet, he was determined not to allow his prize to escape, and he laid his traps as cunningly as a hunter.

As she tried to hold out against him his ardour grew and he courted her with an assiduity that, he had never before been called upon to use. He sent her love letters through a man who worked in his stable yard and whose mother, old Alice, was a scullery maid at Broadmeadows. Veronica's whole body glowed with love: the letters so affected her that she feared everyone around would see the difference in her.

Summer waned into autumn and the leaves of the trees that bowered the deep banks of the Whiteadder turned to gold, red, brown and orange; silver trout turned very slowly in the shallow pools, and swallows, preparing to fly off for the winter, lined the roof tree of the old stone watermill near their trysting place.

The melancholy that overcomes the human race as the year ends affected them both when they met one brilliant October day. They were shaken by the feeling that this autumn would never again be repeated, and the dying of the year brought with it a nostalgia for youth and life itself that swept them along with it. They needed each other desperately and were as emotionally strung up as bowstrings when they led their horses down into the deep glade. Once there, beneath the guardian trees, they turned to each other and kissed with passion; lips still together, they slid down into a bed of fallen leaves where once more he made love to his goddess.

—

'Give old Alice a nightgown,' Veronica ordered Helen. The maid looked at the filthy old woman standing in the kitchen hallway behind her mistress and asked, 'An old one?'

Veronica shrugged, and looked slightly shifty. 'No, give her one of the new ones.'

With bad grace Helen went upstairs to the tall, brass-handled cupboard in Veronica's bedroom and pulled out a lawn nightgown with lace decorating its neck. Her fingers lovingly touched the lines of pin-tucking on its front and she held up the long, lace flounces of the skirt so that they did not sweep on the floor. The cloth was fine and soft, far too good for dirty old Alice, the stillroom maid. The girl's only comfort was that she guessed the old crone would never wear it. As soon as she got her hands on the nightgown it would be sold to some other farmer's wife. Helen could imagine the bargaining that would go on over the price.

When Alice had shuffled off clutching the precious bundle, Helen turned on Veronica. 'Why did you give one of your lovely nightgowns to that awful old woman?' Helen was the only one among the Broadmeadows servants who could talk to the mistress with such directness, but she usually took care never to do it in the hearing of the others for they did not understand Edinburgh democracy and if they overheard Veronica and Helen talking like equals, their mistress's authority would be lowered in their eyes. But now Helen forgot that Mrs Eliot was standing, eagerly listening, in a corner of the kitchen half hidden behind an open cupboard door.

Veronica remembered, though, and she pushed Helen in front of her down the passageway to the front of the house, saying soothingly as she went, 'Oh, poor old thing, she was saying to me that she'd never had a nightgown.'

'Tch, we all sleep in our shifts except you. She'll not have a nightgown now, either. It's going to be sold for hard cash very quickly. She was just working on you. She's a sly old fox.'

The explanation did not seem likely to Helen for, in spite of Veronica's abstracted behaviour recently, she was not easily duped by her servants, and Alice was the worst of the lot – a gossiping, untrustworthy old dame who was employed to scour pots. Her husband and sons worked on various farms around the place and she had an army of relations spread throughout the surrounding villages. Alice was the fountainhead of local gossip, the Broadmeadows equivalent of an Edinburgh caddy.

Back in the kitchen Alice was queening it. She took no orders from anyone, not even from Mrs Eliot, who was jealous of her position of authority and long tenure. These days, if Alice was told off or ordered to do something she disliked, she would threaten Mrs Eliot: 'I'll tell the mistress on you.' The threat infuriated the red-faced cook and built up the kitchen resentment against Veronica.

Not that the mistress was ever very much at home, Helen noted. The servants were left to ran things to their own satisfaction except on the days when the Master's sister, Miss Susan, came visiting and swept through the back premises like a dyspeptic tornado. People were gossiping at how much Mrs Ker had taken to riding out every day, all dressed up in the black habit, and staying away for hours. They had no idea where she went but when she came back she was so affable that it was impossible to arouse her to react against anything but the most outrageous misdemeanour. Even in her private life the old domestic quarrels were over – she was tolerant of her husband, indulgent to her children and – best of all, Helen felt – she avoided brandy. While grateful for the new contentedness of her mistress, a worry nagged at Helen… She had seen it before and knew what it might signify.

–

When Veronica and Alex parted on the last afternoon of October she rode home deeply pensive and depressed about the winter that stretched before her. How could she go on without him? He had promised to continue sending her notes by Alice and sworn that they would meet, but she could not see how this might be done, and her heart was heavy.

Edward and Elizabeth were playing with Helen in front of the house when she returned and the sight of her golden-haired babies, so innocent and so loving, nearly stopped her heart. What am I doing? she asked herself, remorse and guilt seizing her as she looked at them. She jumped from the saddle to gather them in a close embrace, kneeling on the grass in her flowing black skirt, tears replacing the satisfaction of recent lovemaking.

The children struggled in her arms, surprised and embarrassed at this outflow of emotion, so she let them go and, still weeping her tears of remorse, watched them scampering off after their father who was coming from one of the cattle sheds.

Ker heard them calling his name and without turning he stretched both arms out sideways, palms open, and the children ran squealing behind him, each one grabbing on to a hand. He did not look at Veronica nor did he greet her though she knew he had seen her arrive.

He cares far more for them than he cares for me – and they love him better than they love me. It would matter very little to them if I were to go away, she realized with a sharp pang.

It was the first time she had seriously contemplated the possibility of her marriage breaking up. It was the first time too that she allowed herself to imagine going away with Renton. After all, why not? Other lovers do things like that – the newspapers are always full of scandals in high society. If a man and a woman love each other enough, she told herself, they defy society's rules in order to be together.

Old Alice was waiting in the dark passage leading from the drawing room to the kitchen. 'Have you any message for Mordington, mam?' she asked. 'I'm going over there this afternoon and I'll take it with me.'

Avoiding the old woman's satirical eye, Veronica replied, 'Yes, we're going to ask Sir Alexander to dine. You can take him the note – and wait for his reply.' Alice was not deceived but she gave a toothless smile and said the commission would be undertaken as swiftly as possible. 'And I won't give the note to anyone but the squire,' she whispered.

The grubby note was carried into the Mordington library that evening and presented to Renton who was toasting his feet in front of an enormous fire while reading a book on horse breeding.

The writing on the cover was known to him and he smiled as he turned it around in his hands a few times before ripping off the seal and opening the single sheet. Its message was short, misspelt and unpunctuated:

> *My love, My thots are all of you we must meet again tho my tirant of a husband would kill me if he found out try to find a place I will always remember this afternoon. V.*

The manservant waiting at the door coughed and said, 'The old woman who brought it is waiting for a reply.'

Renton tucked the note into his pocket and said, 'I can't reply now. Tell her to come back tomorrow.' Then he spent the rest of the evening with pen and paper, scrawling out words and then crumpling sheet after sheet of paper before he was satisfied. His memory of their afternoon's lovemaking was also intensely pleasant. She was a beautiful, sweet-natured and gentle woman; she delighted him as much as any woman he had ever known – and he had enjoyed many mistresses in the past, at Mordington, in Edinburgh and London. But Veronica was special, a lady, a challenge – and she was married, which meant, if they were careful, that there would be no nonsense about having to wed her. To cuckold a clod like Ker would be no disloyalty for either of them. With circumspection, their affair could carry on in secrecy until either he or she tired of it, but in the meantime he was going to enjoy this feeling to the full – he had not felt so lovesick since he was a lad.

Next afternoon Alice slipped into the parlour where the mistress was sitting alone, worrying that there had been no reply to her note. She could not go out because she didn't want to miss receiving his communication the moment it arrived. She was terrified in case it fell into the wrong hands. Surely he would answer quickly, surely he would come up with some suggestion for their future meetings?

The old woman handed her the sealed letter with its crested wax seal and flashed a knowing smile before disappearing without speaking. Veronica's heart was thudding in her throat when she opened it. The words spun in front of her eyes and she gasped in delight when she saw that he had written her a poem...

To the Charming V.

Thinking of you who every wish employs,
And languishing in hope of future joys,
So have I sighed o'er happy memories past,
Rememb'ring passion when I saw you last,
Scarce had I left you when my fancy drew
Your form enchanting which full well I knew,
I clasped your lovely waist within my arms
And when the Summit of my bliss was o'er,
I saw, embraced, and fancy could no more...

That was all. He did not say when they would meet again, but by sending her a love poem he won her completely. Her romantic soul, starved for so long, responded to him like an opening flower. From the moment that she read his poem, she was lost, all misgivings about her children or her adultery cast aside. Her only concern was how and where to meet him.

1800

It was New Year's day, the start of a new century, and the air was electric with excitement. Though the sun was shining and the sea a brilliant blue, the temperature hovered only a little above freezing point as an animated gathering of fashionable people from the town and its surrounding district sat in lines of carriages drawn up alongside the parade ground below the green ramparts of Berwick. They had turned out to watch the Gentlemen Volunteers perform their military exercises. Patriotism and warmongering were rife, talk of Bonaparte was on every tongue and some of the onlookers felt nervous at the thought that the French armies under their terrible leader might, at that very moment, be preparing to launch an attack on Britain's shores. The glorious sight of the Volunteers as they paraded in their colourful uniforms in front of lines of gleaming cannons was soothing apprehensions a little, but not entirely. The war was going the French way – Bonaparte was sweeping all before him.

The Volunteers were making a brave show. A long line of men, mounted on their best horses and proudly wearing their dark green jackets with scarlet facings and liberally hung around with loops of golden cord, came clattering up the road from the barracks.

Their legs were encased in white buckskins and black tasselled boots; on their heels shone silver spurs; their faces were stiff with pride and resolution as they moved on to the grassy sward to begin their parade. At their head were their colonel and lieutenant colonel, more glorious than any of the others. The colonel was Lord Dacre from south of the Border; his lieutenant was Sir Alexander Renton.

Her face glowing in the cold air, Veronica Ker sat in her husband's carriage with her children cuddling up beside her to take advantage of the thick fur that lined her rose velvet cape. She had one arm over each of their little shoulders, protecting them from the cold, and she hugged them tight to her in an agony of love. They were delightful, kind children, she adored them, and this adoration was sharpened by the knowledge that her illicit love for Renton burned as fiercely as ever. She was torn between longing for him and love for her children. If she was ever able to go away with him, would they have to be left behind? Could she bear that separation? As she tightened her grip on Edward and Elizabeth, she felt that to suffer the loss of them would be impossible – even for love.

John Ker, in his muster master's scarlet jacket with white pipe-clayed facings and gilded buttons, was sitting in front of her, puffed out with pride at the demonstration Berwick was making of its warlike determination. His face was flushed and she could see a tracery of broken veins over his nose and across his full cheeks. A vein throbbed visibly in his left temple and she watched it with fascination – almost willing it to burst and flood his brain with blood. Often at night she lay awake beside him, listening to him snoring, and asked herself why he kept on living. Why could he not die? He was forty, the age when many of his contemporaries died, leaving sorrowing widows behind to enjoy new lives if they so chose. But Ker, in spite of his faults, was an active man who walked his lands every day and drank only in moderation though he liked his food and ate prodigiously. His general health was good in spite of his bloated appearance – he did not look likely to leave her a widow yet.

All heads turned when the clattering hooves of the advancing cavalcade were heard on the frost-gripped road. She saw her lover instantly, erect and proud on his prancing black horse. Her adoration shone out of her unhidden as she stared at him, thinking he looked like one of the heroes from the Trojan War. Her mother used to tell her stories about that when she was a small child but had not succeeded in passing on any idea of history, and Veronica did not realize that Trojan heroes would look out of place in the Berwickshire Light Dragoons.

He saw her too, her face brilliant beneath the flower-trimmed bonnet and her slim body wrapped in the rose cape. A flash of recognition shone from his eyes as he rode past the Kers' carriage but he looked neither to the right nor the left, staring straight in front, his features set in a determined frown. If Bonaparte was to face up to Alex Renton, Veronica believed, the war would be over instantly with Great Britain as the victor.

They had not met for nearly two months, and the strain of separation had nearly made her mad. Notes went to and fro between them and sometimes she abandoned discretion, sending off old Alice twice a day with a communication for him. Those notes were only scraps of paper on which she wrote simple sentences like *I love you, I miss you*. His replies were more infrequent and when his apparent neglect annoyed her she consoled herself with reading and re-reading his love poem… *So have I sighed o'er happy memories past* was the line she loved best, for it summed up what she herself was feeling.

The Gentlemen Volunteers trotted and cantered in a huge circle, wheeled into a long line, drew their sabres and advanced at a gallop towards the sea as if repulsing the French invaders. Then, as one, they turned their horses and came cantering back to the delighted cheers of the onlookers.

The line of cannons fired, sending bursts of flame after their missiles, which hurtled in high, trajectories to the sea where they splashed down in distant spumes of white spray. The excited watchers cheered even more loudly, and Edward and Elizabeth, eyes shining, gasped in delight and clutched their parents for safety. It was a marvellous display, perfect for raising morale on New Year's day.

During the journey back to Broadmeadows Veronica remained in a high state of exaltation, longing to discuss

Renton's magnificent appearance at the head of the Volunteers, to hear someone else compliment him. The horse pulling their gig struck sparks from the hard road as it dashed along, eager to reach the warmth of its stable, and Veronica questioned her children – 'Did you see anyone you knew? Who did you think looked the finest?'

Edward thought a portly old man on a white horse looked best of all; Elizabeth was taken with the drummer boy in the regimental band. It was her husband who gave her most gratification when he said, 'Sir Alexander looked very fine. That's a grand horse he has. It was the same one as won the race that day – Pasha it was called, wasn't it?'

She nodded and said, 'I think it was.' How could she tell him that she knew Pasha as well as she knew the keen little mare that was pulling them home so bravely, that she had leaned against his satin coat and been kissed by an ardent Sir Alexander?

–

The nursery fire crackled up the chimney and the children slept peacefully in their beds while outside the window, the flowerbeds and the broad grass park were covered with crisp snow that sparkled in the moonlight like icing on a cake.

Helen sat in the pool of light cast by a tall candle and painstakingly wrote in a large leather-bound ledger. Since the death of old Mrs Ker and the departure of Susan, Veronica had passed over the keeping of all the household accounts to her maid. She trusted Helen so completely that she never asked to see the household books. Instead of being flattered, this omission pained Helen because she was proud of the way her handwriting had improved and of the neatness of her account pages. The pleasure that it gave her to add up a column of figures and make them match exactly with the column on the other side could be shared with no one but the children.

The weeks of snow had been a slow time in the house and on the farm, though Veronica seemed agitated and still conducted strange, whispered consultations with old Alice in dark corners and empty passages. Helen resented not knowing what secret they shared; she felt excluded and angry as she watched old Alice queening it among the other servants.

She acted like a woman with special knowledge, and her hints and sly looks frightened Helen, for she guessed that the old woman was not trustworthy. If Veronica had shared some important secret with her it would eventually be let loose.

You're just jealous, she told herself as she sat alone with her account book. You're jealous because Miss Vee's not spending so much time with you… But it' was not just jealousy: something was wrong, she knew it in her bones.

There was a light step on the creaking board outside the nursery door and it opened slowly to reveal Miss Vee herself, peeping her head round to see if the children were asleep.

With a finger on her lips she tiptoed towards their beds and stared down at them. When she turned to Helen her face was alight with happiness. 'They're so lovely. I love them so much,' she whispered, with a strange emphasis as if she had been doubted.

Helen nodded. 'They're good bairns,' she agreed.

Veronica came over and sat in the fireside chair. 'You seem sad, what's wrong?' As she looked at her maid it struck her for the first time that Helen was no longer a child for, almost overnight it seemed, she had grown into a woman, tiny and slim with a pretty pointed face, softly curling brown hair and those enormous eyes. The wee brown duckling had turned into a swan. Now the eyes were fixed on Veronica's face and they seemed capable of reading everything in her mind.

'How old are you now?' she asked.

Helen frowned as she replied, 'I'll be twenty this year. I'm not sure exactly when my birthday is but it's in the summer. My mother said it was very hot when she was having me.'

'Twenty! You've grown up without me noticing. I'm twenty-nine this year…' Veronica's voice lost its cheerfulness when she talked of her own age but she was not silent for long. Soon she was questioning Helen again.

'You're always busy, little Helen, but do you have a beau? I've seen you with Smith, he's a solid young fellow. You could do worse than him. I think he likes you too.'

The maid shook her head very definitely. 'He's my friend – he could never be my beau.'

What she could not say to Veronica was that William Smith's face showed, whenever the mistress appeared, that there was not a woman in the world to equal her as far as he was concerned. His adoration of Ker's wife had grown over the years, and to divulge his secret to the object of his devotion would be a terrible disloyalty.

'Is that why you're sad? Because you haven't a beau?' persisted Veronica.

'No, I don't think so. I've been thinking that I'm lonely here, though. I'd like to go back to Edinburgh if you could spare me.'

'For how long?'

'For always. I'm not a country person really, Miss Vee. I miss the city – you know what it's like.'

Veronica's own longing for Edinburgh had disappeared since she met Renton. Nothing now would wrest her from proximity to him. She looked harder at Helen and saw that the girl's eyes were troubled – and also guarded. All of a sudden she felt how impossible it would be to lose her.

'Oh, Helen, don't go. Don't leave me. You're my only true friend here – and what would the babies do without you? That awful Susan would try to take them over, I know she would,' she pleaded.

Why should their mother not undertake their care? But Helen said nothing. Edward, who was eight years old, wouldn't need her much longer. He was a sweet child, kinder than the Kers and with much of his mother's physical beauty, but he was very much a farmer's son, a sturdy boy who was happiest when following his father around the farm, avidly learning all he could about Broadmeadows and the country life. He shared his father's pride in the place, and already he knew that it would be his one day.

Elizabeth was more in need of loving because Veronica had never managed to feel the affection for her that she had for her Louisa. Because Elizabeth sensed that she was very much a second best in her mother's eyes, she turned to Helen and it was on to the maid's lap that she climbed for cuddles and affection. Veronica was right, it would be hard to leave her.

'But I heard last week that my mother's not well. One of the carters told me she'd had to stop working. She's sick,' said Helen. It was true, Mary Cameron was ill but Helen had faith, that her strong mother would recover once the better weather came. The carter had also said that Edinburgh was deep in snow and it was bitterly cold there. In the spring Mary would recover.

Veronica sprang to her feet. 'I know what We'll do. I'll write to my brother to go and see her. He'll cure her. In spite of what he's like as a brother, Thomas is a good doctor. Don't worry about your mother. When he's seen her, he'll write and tell us how she does. Besides you couldn't' travel in this weather.'

–

So Helen stayed but her disquiet increased as spring approached and Veronica's agitation grew worse.

When John Ker went off on his first muster master's trip of the year, the mistress was seized with energy and ranged through the house ordering the maids to sweep and clean, to polish and scour as Broadmeadows had never been cleaned or scoured before. Before two days were out the reason for this orgy of cleaning became obvious. Sir Alexander Renton came riding up to the front door and before one of the maids could open it to him, Veronica was running there herself and welcoming him in.

There was scandal in the kitchen at this behaviour. 'The mistress answering the door herself like a maidservant!' said

Mrs Eliot with disapproval. 'You go through to the parlour, Christine, and see what's going on.'

Christine came back very quickly, her face excited. 'Oh, Mrs Eliot, they've locked the door but I went outside to see if I could peep through the window and she's closed the shutters.'

Mrs Eliot's face was a study. 'It's like she was with Kellock. It's just the same. My word, she's not starting with the squire now, is she?'

Old Alice was up to her elbows in greasy water in a stone sink in the back kitchen and listening to everything. She gave a cackle of laughter. 'So now you've guessed it. That's been going on for a long time. You women, here are as blind as mowdies if you haven't known about it. It's the talk of Mordington.'

–

Renton had not intended to fall in love with Ker's wife. Love was something alien to his nature. A man of considerable experience as far as women were concerned, he fully intended to marry eventually and provide an heir for his vast estates, but was not in any hurry to do so. His taking of a wife would be a calculated decision, like the buying of a brood mare. The woman who would please him as a wife would have to be young and fertile, and, most of all, to come well provided with money or land. The idea of falling in love as a pre-requisite for marriage, had never occurred to him.

But Veronica Ker was so sweet, so lovely and so trusting that she wakened in him feelings which he never knew he possessed. When she told him of her ill treatment at the hands of John Ker, his blood surged in his ears with anger. How dare that low-born fool treat a woman with such cruelty? One day she showed him her bruises, livid marks on her white arms and legs, and he wanted to commit murder on her behalf. 'I love you, I love you,' he told her with terrible vehemence and she believed him completely. He believed it too.

During the winter their affair had faltered and nearly ended as far as he was concerned. He took himself off to London and lived his usual carefree life there. When he was at home, he stalled her requests to let them meet at Mordington House, explaining the need for caution.

Servants talked, he had no confidence that a meeting at his home would not be known in the entire countryside within a matter of hours. But when he saw her at the Volunteers' review, his heart was strangely moved. He longed to hold her in his arms again, to hear her gentle moaning as he made love to her, and he resolved that he was not ready to give her up.

It was Veronica who found the perfect trysting place for them – a deserted cottage in a tiny field tucked away on the Broadmeadows side of the river. It had two rooms, a fireplace and, best of all, a bed recess that they filled with straw for their lovemaking. While Ker was away they met there at night and loved each other with growing passion while the moon shone down and the night owls hooted in the trees. They would clasp each other in a frantic fever of desire, throwing off their clothes as they sank into the sweet-smelling bedding. When he rose to go, she would always reach out for him and whisper, 'Don't go, wait a while, don't go yet.' Then he would sink down again and lose himself in her once more.

They were as compatible in desire as it was possible for a couple to be and even he, the hard-headed dynast, permitted himself to speculate about the possibility of being with her always – if only, if only, if only his lovely Veronica was not already married to that brute Ker; if only she did not have two children to make demands on her affection; if only she was not poor and without an inheritance to sustain her.

She walked around in a dream of love, transported and changed by the knowledge that she was so adored. Every moment that she was away from him was a moment wasted; every second they shared was a second to be saved in her memory and dreamed about till they met again. Her love for him obliterated all her other duties and responsibilities. This new attachment was the culmination of her life, she had been waiting for Renton since she became a woman, and she was blissfully grateful that they had met at last. If they had not been so entranced with love they would have realized that they were bound to be discovered.

–

The gossipers were gathering around like a cloud of wasps. Renton came to the house several times – Ker was still away – and the women of the house missed nothing. They noted the disorder of her clothes and hair; they noted the exaltation on her face; and they spied on her, pressing their eyes to cracks at the parlour shutters and rushing in to see if the sofa cushions were disordered when her lover left.

The first person outwith the servants to hear the rumours was Susan. She drank in every word Mrs Eliot told her, questioned and re-questioned her on specific points and then went from cottage to cottage in Broadmeadows, Hutton and up near Mordington gathering her own information. When her dossier was quite complete she confronted her brother with the damning evidence.

His first reaction was to beat his wife. That night he took a stick to bed with him and when the door closed upon them, thrashed her so soundly that the frightened servants broke down the door to rescue her.

Sobbing and bloodstained, she assured him that his suspicions were wrong, that he had been misled by his jealous sister – and he appeared to believe her.

But John Ker was learning caution and he too was laying his plans. First of all he wrote a stiff little note to Sir Alexander Renton and sent it over by William Smith who gave it into the squire's hand in Mordington's vast stableyard.

He opened it and read: *Sir, I have by this to acquaint you that your visits to this house can be very well dispensed until. Signed John Ker.*

Smith watched as the squire laughed, tore the sheet of paper in half and threw it away on to the dung heap. He was not going to be warned off by a lout like Ker. The knowledge that her husband was jealous and suspicious only made him more eager to make love to his wife. The affair had become a game again. Ker deserved all he got, he told himself.

The meetings in the little house at the foot of the meadow became more frequent and Veronica found that they alone made her life endurable. At Broadmeadows she and Ker no longer shared a bed – or even a room – and for that she was grateful because it spared her both his attempts at taking her by force or his sudden outbursts of brutality in the middle of the night after he had been lying awake, brooding on his wrongs.

The atmosphere in the house was continually strained. Susan closed up her cottage and, took over the household management, displacing Helen who gave up her account books without a murmur and concentrated her attention on the children. Edward and Elizabeth sensed that something was terribly wrong, though no one spoke to them about the rift between their parents, and they ran anxiously from one to another as if seeking reassurance. Their mother was very loving one day and apparently distracted and indifferent the next; their father was morose and did not seem to notice them. The only anchor in their lives was the maidservant who never changed.

Veronica was surprised at the way her husband was behaving. After sending off his letter to Renton, he lapsed into a kind of calm – ominous calm, she guessed. He rode off into Berwick several times during the weeks before harvest and came hack looking solemn but satisfied. She could not guess what he was about, though as the corn ripened under the brilliant sun and the workers began making preparations for bringing it in, she relaxed in the knowledge that Ker would be too busy to concentrate entirely on her for a while. Afterwards she realized that she should have guessed he was having her followed. She should have known that he would browbeat every confidant she had – except Helen, whose affections were unshakeable. She should have realized that every time she went out of the house, if only to walk in the garden with the children, eyes followed her and reports were made. Ker was setting his trap. Sometimes she caught sight of an anguished look on his face and thought that he was near breaking point, but she was wrong – he had reached his breaking point and gone beyond it.

Proud in her beauty and the knowledge of the love Renton had for her, Veronica was confident of the future now, sure that even if she and Ker were to break their marriage, her lover would stand by her. It seemed possible that she would be Lady Renton, mistress of Mordington, leader of fashion, adored wife of a dashing, handsome husband – and rich, rich beyond the dreams of anyone else in the district. She listened with delight when Renton swore eternal love for her, she stroked his face with her hands and coaxed him for more. The lovemaking they shared during the warm nights of late summer was more sensual even than their first snatched encounters. It seemed that there were ever higher heights of passion for them to reach together.

Letters of assignation and notes of love passed between her and her lover almost every day, still carried by old Alice who was bribed by both the mistress and the squire. They were sure that her avarice would overcome her fear of Ker.

After one September night in the meadow house, making love in the straw and watching fireflies dancing outside the half-open door, he rode home, his mind full of her, and sat down to write her another poem. It was carried to her by Alice and she read it with a palpitating heart:

Roses refreshed with nightly dew display
New beauties blushing to the dawn of day.
So by the kisses of a RAPT'ROUS NIGHT.

149

Thy vermel lips at morn blush doubly bright.
And from thy face that exquisitely fair
That vermel brightness seems more brightly appear.
Deep purpled violets thus a deeper glow
Held in some Virgin's snowy hand will show.
And early ripening Cherries thus assume,
In the last Blossom a superior bloom.
Oh let that CRIMSON on thy lips remain.
Till back I'm brought to thy dear arms again.

Though his ardour had overtaken his rhyming power she thought it the most beautiful poem ever written and thrilled at every word... 'Till back I'm brought to thy dear arms again,' she whispered to herself as she folded up the paper and hid it between the leaves of her journal. It never struck her that Ker – and soon his lawyer – would read every word in that book.

When they met again, Renton came slipping down the steep path from the road to the cottage, not knowing that two men were lying in the ditch watching him. They stayed for two hours, straining their eyes at every sound and raising up at every crackle made by badgers and hedgehogs in the undergrowth. Eventually the door opened and the man they were trading re-appeared, pulling on his coat. But he did not leave because from the inside of the cottage came a woman's voice and chuckling, confident laughter: 'Stay awhile, don't go yet, stay awhile.' So he went back in and closed the door. It was two o'clock in the morning when they finally saw him leave.

Next morning Veronica was awakened by Helen whose face was white as she whispered, 'Miss Vee, Miss Vee. The Master's in the parlour with another man and he wants you to go down to them directly.'

It was a painful interview. Ker had risen early. After meeting his two spies in the stackyard, he saddled his horse and rode to Berwick where he was waiting outside the office of his lawyer when the clerk came along to open the door. The lawyer and he rode back to Broadmeadows before breakfast and summoned Veronica.

As she walked into the room Ker stood in the window with his back towards her while the lawyer stepped forward and showed her to a chair.

'Mrs Ker,' he said in a solemn voice, 'your husband has proof that you have been conducting an adulterous affair. He feels that your behaviour for the past two years has rendered your marriage null and void. He says you are a woman of gallantry.'

She stared up at the lawyer's face. She knew him well but there was no sign of recognition or friendliness on his chubby, usually smiling features. 'A woman of what?'

The lawyer looked uncomfortably at his feet, wishing he had not been entrusted with this delicate task: 'A woman of gallantry, Mrs Ker. Your husband has reason to believe that you have been adulterously involved with several men and that you are a woman of – gallantry.'

'Gallantry? Do you mean splendour – fashion?'

'I'm afraid that gallantry has another meaning in law. A woman of gallantry is a woman given to amorous intrigue…'

'A woman of gallantry.' She seemed stunned for a second but as she tried the words on her tongue, she was enjoying them in a way, he thought. Then she collected herself and said, 'He can't prove it.'

'I'm afraid he can. The servants have all sworn to it and your husband has been having you followed these past two months. The letters you sent to your lover have been intercepted and read. You were watched last night – he knows all about your affair…' The lawyer was finding all this very embarrassing and gave a little cough as he spoke.

She traced the pattern on the carpet with the toe of her pump as she tried to muster her thoughts. 'Who am I meant to have been committing adultery with?' she asked, but in a way she was exultant that it had come to this at last. She could see her freedom opening up before her.

'With various men,' said the lawyer, gathering up his papers and thinking it a pity that a lovely woman like Mrs Ker should have stooped to such acts of folly.

She did not deny it. Instead she looked up at the lawyer's face and asked, 'So what's to happen?'

'Your husband is divorcing you.'

In spite of her apparent calm during the interview, Veronica found her hands were shaking uncontrollably when she returned to her bedroom and sat down at the little writing desk to send a note to Renton. Now she realized that she was among enemies and there was no one in the house – except Helen – in whom she could place any trust.

She turned in her chair and saw the girl standing in the open doorway. The news of her interview with Ker and his lawyer had of course reached the servants almost as soon as the word 'divorce' was out of the lawyer's mouth.

'Have you heard? Have you heard I'm being divorced by my husband?' Veronica asked.

The girl nodded. 'I've heard. Where are you going?'

Veronica shook her head slowly and then stood up to walk across to the gilt-framed looking glass above the fireplace. She tiptoed slightly and leaned towards it, scrutinizing her face in the dimpled, flawed glass with care. Twenty-nine years old but still lovely, the skin unblemished. She turned her head slightly and admired her slender neck – he loved her neck, he stroked it with gentle hands and called her a swan. She put a hand up to her hair and tucked it up at the back where it had become unloosed, but soft little tendrils still tumbled over her shoulders, giving her a sensual thrill as she remembered the times he had unpinned it before making love to her. She stood back satisfied that she was still beautiful. She had nothing to fear. The prospect of a break with Ker, of a new life starting at last, did not frighten her now that she had reassured herself. Instead she welcomed it because it would force the relationship with Renton on to a new stage. She was completely confident of his love for her. The last time they met his ardour had been as strong as on the first day they made love, her power over him was undiminished.

Gathering herself, smiling and confident now, she went back to write her note. 'I want you to take this to Mordington for me,' she told Helen.

'Me? Why me?'

'You're the only one I can trust.'

–

William Smith took her the four miles to Mordington on the crupper of his saddle, and the farm was in such chaos that no one noticed them leaving. She swore him to secrecy and knew that, just as Veronica could trust her, she could trust him. The note was handed in at Renton's kitchen door and they were told not to wait. The squire would reply when he was ready.

He read Veronica's note with deep disquiet. It seemed as if the words snapped him out of enchantment and back into harsh reality. Although the news was devastating, her tone was strangely jaunty, a jauntiness that he could not share:

> *Alas my love ruin is certain we have both been seen and our staying so late has been the cause – my servants was on the watch. How often did I beg you to let me go yet still your LOVE got the better of your prudence, to meet tonight is impossible but tomorrow perhaps we may meet at half past eleven o'clock and I will explain the torture I at present undergo. See you I must from my heart I love you. V*

–

When there was no answer to her note all day, Veronica assured herself that her lover was away from home, and in a way she was right because, like Ker, he had ridden off to Berwick before noon and was not back till dark. When evening came, she went to bed and lay sleepless but still calm and unworried, staring at the stars glittering in the velvet sky outside the window. Owls hooted and skimmed low over the trees just as they had around the meadow house when she and Renton made love on so many warm summer nights. Comforted by her memories, she eventually slept.

Next day Ker was not at home when she rose and no one knew where he had gone, but at ten o'clock the lawyer was back again with a message for her: 'Your husband requests that you leave this house before he returns in two days' time. You can take with you all your clothes and jewellery... he is prepared to be generous.'

'But where can I go? And what about my children? I cannot leave my children...' All of a sudden the realization of what could happen burst on her. Edward and Elizabeth were very dear, very important to her, she could not face the idea of leaving them behind. He would not force her to do that, surely?

The lawyer gave no sign of yielding, however, though he looked harried. 'You must leave this house, Mrs Ker. The petition for divorce comes up in Edinburgh next month and it is up to you to make any future arrangements for yourself. You'll have to decide if you are going to contest the petition or not, but my client says he is no longer responsible for you.'

When he had gone, Susan, looking gleeful, bustled into the sitting room where Veronica was weeping with her hands over her face. Her sister-in-law had no mercy for her.

'I've told your maid to pack your clothes. My brother said you've to be out of here by tomorrow morning.' She did not address Veronica by name and she did not bother to hide her satisfaction.

There was still no letter from Renton and she did not know what to do. Frantic, she ran upstairs to the nursery where Helen was sitting with the frightened-looking children. 'I'm being put out of my own home. What can I do, what can I do?' she asked her maid with the tears pouring down her cheeks.

'Has he answered your note?'

'Not yet, he hasn't had much time. He must be away from home. The only thing I can do is go there...'

Helen looked doubtful. 'If you do, you'll be admitting to an affair with him. Your husband will know. It will tell against you in the divorce case, surely?'

'I don't care, there's no point in not admitting it. He's been having me followed, the servants have been spying on me.'

'So you're not going to fight the case. You'll let him divorce you?'

'I'll be glad for him to divorce me. I hate him. The only thing I care about now is my children – what about them? I don't know if he'll allow me to keep them... he must, he must, even he couldn't be so cruel.'

Helen looked at the children sitting on the floor, their faces shaken as they watched their distraught mother. Edward ran across to Veronica, putting his arms round her legs and burying his face in her skirt.

She knelt down and held him close, weeping over him. 'Oh, my baby, he won't take you away from me. He can't, they won't let him... I'm your mother.'

She kissed her children, told Helen to pack her clothes and then, in terrible haste, ran to the stables and ordered a groom to saddle up her mare. Without even stopping to change her clothes, she was in the saddle and off galloping down the road. The mare was foam-flecked when she drew rein at Mordington House and as soon as the door was opened to her knock, she pushed the manservant aside and ran across the hall with its gleaming alabaster statues set in curved niches at each side of the inner door. His magnificently furnished drawing room was empty but she had no time to admire the statues he had brought back from his tour in Italy, the heavy-framed pictures or the fine silken curtains. She stared around frantically then raised one hand to her mouth and loudly called his name – 'Alex, oh, Alex! Where are you, Alex…?'

On her right a heavy door with a gilded handle opened slowly and he stood there, his face impassive. He was wearing his blue coat and white buckskins but his neckcloth was undone and he fended her off with one hand as she threw herself at him, weeping hysterically.

Looking over her shoulder at the interested face of his manservant in the hall, he said sternly, as if he was embarrassed by her lack of breeding, 'Do be calm, collect yourself. The servants are all listening. Come in here, my lawyer is with me…'

Another lawyer, as grim and disapproving as Ker's man, sat at a table in the window. He looked up at her as if she were a carrier of the plague when Renton led her to a deep chair and said, 'We've been discussing this business. It's very tricky, Vee. Does your husband name me in his petition?'

She shook her head. 'No, he says "various men" – such a lie. There's been no one but you.'

The men exchanged glances and the lawyer asked in a precise Edinburgh voice, 'Did you deny that there were other men? Did you name Sir Alexander as your lover?'

'Of course not.'

They both looked relieved and Renton told her, 'Now, it's very important that you keep calm, and unfortunately you must stay away from me for the time being. We don't want to make it easy for him, do we?'

'Why not?' She was surprised at his reaction. Surely he was as delighted as she at the thought that she would at last be free?

'Well, I've been advised that if we were to admit to adultery, he might sue me. He could ask for damages.'

A terrible deadness swept over her. Her mouth went dry and an uncontrollable shaking seized her limbs. 'Damages? Of course he might. That's just what he would do. He's so *greedy*. In Berwick, long ago, he said that he wouldn't do anything about Kellock because the puppy had no money. Perhaps he's been waiting—'

'He's been waiting for a man of substance to enter your life,' said the lawyer coldly.

-

Helen, dressed for travelling, waited in the hall at Broad-meadows. Susan had told her, 'You won't be needed here any longer. I'm looking after the bairns now. Pack your box and get up the road with that woman.' The pair of them were being turned out into a cold and hostile world.

As Helen gazed through the open door of Broadmeadows House for the last time, she was seeing with sharpened eyes and truly appreciating the beauty at last. For so long she had yearned to return to the city that this summary dismissal should have been welcomed, but now she knew she would miss the view stretching away in front of the house; she would miss the ever-changing spread of sky; she would miss the green bowers of the trees; the soft-muzzled cows that nibbled her fingers for tit-bits; above all, she would miss old Mrs Ker's garden, brilliant today with its tightly furled scented roses, starry pinks, tall white hollyhocks and huge yellow sunflowers. Will anyone remember to gather the sunflower seeds for the hens when they ripen? she thought wistfully. She'd miss the garden very much, she'd miss her peaceful hours grubbing up the weeds, lovingly transplanting the seedlings, gathering the bounty when the flowering time came round.

But her most wrenching sorrow was parting with the chil-dren who now clung to her skirt, not crying, but with their little faces terror-stricken at losing her. Dear Edward, sturdy and kind-hearted, with his mother's cheerful, trusting nature and his father's frame. Elizabeth was more nervous, more anxious to please and easily influenced. Helen dreaded to think of the lies about her mother which would be told to her by Susan. Poor Elizabeth would believe them if there were no counterbalancing stories to contradict her aunt's biased account.

'Promise me that you'll be good children and take care to be a credit to me,' she whispered to them, gathering their warm bodies to her in a close embrace. 'You won't forget your friend Helen, will you?' Her heart ached at the thought that she might never see them again for she was fiercely devoted to them, far more fond than she had ever been of her brothers or cousins back in Edinburgh.

Veronica's babies were like her own children. She had bathed them, dressed them and comforted them ever since birth, and because she was little more than a child herself when she took over their care, she could understand them. They felt secure in her love and responded to her like opening flowers towards a kindly sun.

Edward wiped his eyes with the back of his chubby hand, the baby dimples still clear on his knuckles, and gave a hiccuping sob. He was trying to be a man, she could see that.

'But you'll come back when Mama comes back, won't you?' he asked. He was not able to face the idea that both mother and nurse were stepping out of his life for ever.

'I have to go with your mama now to look after her, but I'll come back,' Helen promised. They accepted that because, young though they were, they knew their mama was someone who needed care; her vulnerability impressed even her children.

When Helen heard Veronica's step on the gravel she rapidly kissed each child and turned to go, for she did not want to witness Veronica's goodbye to her babies. The pain of that would be too much to bear.

–

When Veronica came back from her dash to Mordington a pile of bags and boxes was heaped up on the front doorstep. Susan was standing beside them with her arms crossed over her meagre breast and her pinched face flushed pink on the cheekbones with excitement. 'I know where you've been,' she accused. 'You needn't think you're getting back into this house now.

The carriage will take you to Berwick. From there you can do what you like.'

Without speaking or looking at the despicable woman, Veronica swept into the hall.

The full horror of what was happening did not seem to have fully occurred to her yet. She was confused, partly energized by emotional trauma and partly anaesthetized by shock. She stood in the hallway, still beautiful although her face was swollen and blotched with weeping. At the sight of the children she gave a moan and knelt on the floor, holding out her arms towards them. They rushed to her, tears flowing unchecked now.

'Don't go. Mama, don't go away. Aunt Susan says you're going away, but don't go,' sobbed Elizabeth.

Veronica laid her face against the soft curls and her tears wetted the child's head. 'I have to go, your father is sending me away. But I'll come back as soon as I can. I'll come back to take you to live with me. Don't worry, I'll come back for you.'

She did not know that at her back Susan was pulling a sceptical face at this speech. As far as she was concerned, Veronica Ker would never see the children again. Susan was going to fight hard for that, her final revenge, against her beautiful, once carefree, so much admired sister-in-law. All Susan's jealousy, all her hate and frustration, all her own feelings of insufficiency and ugliness were now channelled into keeping the mother and her children apart.

Veronica and Helen left Broadmeadows before Ker came back, for he had deliberately stayed away until the coast was clear. Perhaps he feared that Veronica would be able to persuade him to forgive her and did not want to put his resolution to the test. It was easier to come back to a house under the comforting rule of his sister, to give himself up to her coddling and incessant encouragement...

'I don't know why you put up with her for so long. She's a really wicked woman, the talk of the district with her carrying on, we're well rid of her. She was just a drain on your pocket.

159

The babies are quite happy, they'll settle down quickly,' Susan told him over and over again.

He sat at his dining table with a bottle of claret in front of him and let her reassurances soak in. There was no good saying to Susan that Veronica's beauty had been so seductive that it had driven him almost mad with jealousy. From the very beginning of their marriage he had been conscious that she was coerced into marrying him. Without her brother's connivance, without his father's financial acumen in lending money in the right places, he would never have come close enough even to hold her hand. That knowledge, from the beginning, had made him burn inside with bitter frustration.

He filled his glass again and drank down the claret like water. His thoughts ran confused and jumbled – she'd laughed at him, she'd betrayed him with that fop of a squire, that arrogant bastard Renton who regarded men like Ker as peasants, beneath his notice. He thumped a fist on the table in impotent rage. Oh, if she were in the house now, he'd beat her senseless. At least he'd have that satisfaction. He'd not be made a laughing stock without giving her something to show for it. John Ker would have the last word. He'd make the bitch pay for his humiliation and he'd make her lover, that disdainful man of fashion, pay too. A divorce was not enough. He'd ruin the pair of them. The rest of John Ker's life was to be given up to seeking his revenge. Nothing else would ever be as important to him.

1800 – 1801

The door of Dr Thomas Hay's fine big house in St Andrew's Square was opened by a manservant in smart blue livery and brass buttons whose eye ran up and down Veronica as if appraising her financial potential. The doctor and his lady were at home and would receive her, he said when told the identity of the caller, and from his demeanour, his barely hidden curiosity, it was obvious that her arrival was not unexpected. Though the door was open to Veronica however it was obviously closed to Helen. The bags she was carrying were firmly taken from her and she was told in no uncertain terms to remove herself from the whitened doorstep.

Veronica was abashed at the treatment of her maid and gave her a warm hug, saying, 'Go back to Baxter's Buildings – your family's still there, isn't it? I'll send for you as soon as I can...'

It was more than seven years since Helen had walked along the streets of Edinburgh and in spite of her tiredness after the long journey from Berwick and her depression about leaving the children at Broadmeadows, her spirits rose as she watched the bustle all around her. She sniffed the air with pleasure and breathed in the smell of yeast and hops coming from the breweries down at Holyrood. The faces of many people hurrying past seemed familiar; she recognized the old blue-bonneted beggar who was stumping along on his wooden crutch in St Andrew's Square, which was far more refined and restrained than his old haunts in the High Street. In the square some of the elegant town houses had railed-off front gardens with clipped bushes at their entrance steps and stone urns perched high up on

fronts. Her eyes went round with astonishment, for the buildings were designed to give an impression of grandeur with their
dressed stone façades and carvings. The creamy-coloured stone
gleamed and sparkled and the windows with their huge panes of
glass glittered in the evening light. In her rough skirt and shawl
she walked slowly along the broad pavement, feeling rustic and
out of touch, stepping deferentially aside to let fashionable ladies
and gentlemen pass, and they swept unseeingly by her. The
swish of silken skirts, the tap of walking sticks or parasols, the
murmur of conversation and laughter marked their passage and
she was full of admiration at the sight of them. Edinburgh was
casting its old spell on her again.

Not in any hurry to go home, she walked up and down the
lines of new streets, astonished that everywhere people seemed
to be building houses of competing grandeur. Horses pulled
huge carts of stone or wood over the neatly laid out roads
and all along one side of Princes Street, as far as she could
see, stretched a line of new houses, each one more imposing
than its neighbour. Behind them even more were appearing in
straight lines going downhill as if they were heading straight for
the river Forth that glittered on the distant horizon. Another
town, a new Edinburgh, was being laid out before her eyes. But
when she lifted her head at last to look over Princes Street to
the south towards the Castle it was a relief to see the familiar
spires of the Tron and St Giles rising out of the comforting
huddle of ancient tenements with their peaks and precipices
of rooflines, all clustering along the ridged backbone of rock.
That was her home really, that mass of humanity huddling up
to the Castle for protection. Her heart danced with delight to
know that Old Edinburgh was still there, clinging fiercely to its
foothold, teeming with people, thriving and jostling, making
deals and sealing bargains. That was the Edinburgh she knew
and loved.

She was tired so she took her time walking over the North
Bridge, pausing at various stalls on the way, looking for familiar

faces. She exchanged greetings with some of them but even people she knew well did not recognize her at first and all exclaimed at how she'd changed. 'You were just a bairn the last time I saw you,' they said. It seemed a very long time that she had been away. Some people did not recall her at all, even when she told them who she was, and their blank eyes made her realize for the first time how great was the change in her.

A sadness and a lost feeling crept over her as she turned into the High Street and stood looking up towards the Castle from the Tron Church steps. Was it her fancy or were there fewer smart people on the streets? Where were the old dandies who used to stand gossiping outside Willie Creech's bookshop? Willie was dead of course, but his old cronies could not have been carried off all at once as well. Where were the ladies in their pretty gowns, pattering along in pattens to take tea with their friends? Where were the respectable servants bustling to and fro among the food stalls round the Tron? All the people she saw looked poor – bedraggled women hauling dirty children in their wake and many, many drunken men. It seemed as if the attic dwellers had come down from their eyries and taken over the High Street. But where had the quality gone? Then it struck her. Of course they'd gone down there to the New Town on the other side of the Nor' Loch. Even the last and most conservative of them had deserted their old flats and moved into the fine new houses that she had been admiring only a short time ago. Only the poor or the pitifully unfashionable were left behind.

Her legs were aching and her head swimming with fatigue when she finally reached the attic at the top of Baxter's Buildings, and she had to pause for breath before pushing open the door. As she put her hand on the splintered wood, she was daunted by the thought of what she would find inside. Her dear grandfather would not be sitting alongside the fireplace, his grey head bent over a bit of wood carving or an old book. Her noisy brothers would not be there – though they would not be missed particularly. She hoped her mother was at home

– her poor hard-worked mother. Perhaps she would be trying to make a meal out of bits of vegetables scrounged from the market women. A noise made her brighten and her heart rose at the sign that there was someone at home. She even heard a voice as she pushed open the creaking door. It had always creaked, she remembered, that at least had not changed.

A fair-haired young woman, not a great deal older than Helen herself, was standing by the window staring over to Fife and crooning to a tiny baby in her arms. She turned round when Helen came in and stared at her in surprise.

'Who are you? What are you doing up here?' she asked.

'I'm Helen Cameron. Is this my father's place still? His name's Ewan Cameron… My mother's Mary Cameron, the water caddy.'

'This is Ewan Cameron's place. I'm his wife,' said the girl. 'We weren't expecting anyone. If you're his lassie he said you'd found a place in the country.'

Helen reeled. 'Where's my mother?'

The girl reddened. 'Don't you ken your mother's dead? She's been dead for a twelvemonth. I'm your father's wife now.'

'Can I sit down for a bit?' asked Helen weakly, coming into the room, 'I've come a long way today – from Berwick.'

The girl pushed a stool forward with her foot and a reluctant sympathy came to her face. 'Oh aye, sit yourself down. You're gey white looking. I'll fetch you some ale if you'll haud the baby. Your father's back from his work soon. He's on the sedan chairs. He'll be surprised to see you.'

Surprised and none too pleased, according to the tone of her voice. Helen sat down and looked around. Her mind was full of jumbled thoughts – Mary was dead and she'd never even known. Her father had remarried. He was actually working, carrying a sedan chair. He'd never been keen on hard work when she was a child. All the working in the family was left to her mother. She took a quick inventory of the room. They had a bed with a coloured coverlet; her mother had never slept on a bed. They had a chest of drawers in one corner with a few bits of china ranged along its top; there had been nothing like that in the house before. There were no piles of dirty clothes or empty bottles in the corners, no water buckets stood waiting to be filled. The girl did not look as if she worked, for she was wearing a flimsy dress and was as plump as a puppy that spent a lot of time sleeping. Helen's heart was sore at the memory of her mother's lean body, whipcord muscles and careworn face...

'What did my mother die of?' she whispered.

'Oh, old age, I think,' said the girl carelessly. 'It was in the winter time that she took sick and she never really mended. Then she just died, you know what it's like.' Helen nodded, her heart aching. She knew what it was like for poor people like Mary Cameron when they took sick.

–

Thomas Hay and his wife sat at a mahogany table in the window of their first-floor drawing room overlooking the St Andrew's square garden with its pretty trees, and exchanged anxious glances. The heavy panelled door opened and the manservant showed in Veronica, who rushed towards them with tears starting in her eyes.

'Oh, Thomas,' she cried. 'Oh, it's terrible. John Ker's divorcing me. What am I to do?'

Thomas, stood up, his polished professional manner standing him in good stead, and held out a chair for her as if she were a distraught patient. 'Sit down, Veronica,' he ordered, 'just sit down and pull yourself together. We've been talking about you, because your husband wrote to me. His letter came yesterday. I'm afraid you've behaved in a very ill-advised manner.'

She sank into the chair and stared at him with fear rising in her heart. Her brother and she had never been close but he was her only male relative, the only one from whom she could expect any help now. 'Thomas, I don't know what to do,' she whispered tearfully.

Thomas turned on his heel and stared out of the window for what seemed a very long time. His voice when it came was remote. 'Am I to understand that you've been conducting a liaison with Sir Alexander Renton, the squire of Mordington and Lamberton? He's a man of property. What does he advise you to do?'

She shook her head without speaking, remembering with terrible clarity the interview with her lover and his lawyer, remembering the constraint of their conversation then. But Thomas was waiting, implacable, and she finally said, 'He and his' lawyer think it best if we do not see each other while the divorce is going on. My husband could sue him, you see, if he was seen to be taking me away from him.'

Thomas seemed pleased at this idea. 'Quite.'

He turned back from the window and walked towards her. 'I must tell you, sister, that I am fully on the side of your husband in this business. You've disgraced our family name. As far as I'm aware your husband has every intention of suing Renton for seducing you, and I'll back him to the hilt.'

The first hint of the full horror of what awaited her began to reveal itself to Veronica.

'But what about me, Thomas? I haven't any money. I haven't anywhere to go.' A hysterical note sounded in her voice. She was on the verge of screaming at him. 'This is all your fault. If you hadn't sold me to Ker in the first place, this would never have happened. My life could have been different but for you…'

Her brother was indifferent to her distress. 'You should have thought about all that before you embarked on this business. You should have shown some sense. You've always been flighty – as we both know – but this is criminal folly. How can you expect me to help you? John Ker is my friend. I feel that you have treated him abominably.'

'You mean that you're on that brute's side against your own sister? You don't even care that he beat me till I was senseless? He nearly murdered me, for God's sake. You'd let him do that and look away, but you won't help me now?'

166

Thomas looked at his grim-faced wife for support. 'I'm afraid that's exactly what I do mean. But you *are* my sister and I've a duty towards you. I'll have to help you – though remember, if you don't do exactly as I tell you, that assistance will be immediately withdrawn.'

–

At first Ewan Cameron did not recognize Helen when he came breezily into the flat and saw a stranger sitting on the fireside stool sipping ale. When he realized that this was his daughter, grown into a woman, his heart sank. He fervently hoped that she had not returned home to stay, bringing with her bad memories of the days of his drinking, of fights with Mary, of the grinding poverty of bringing up an army of children with no money.

She saw his expression before he had time to rearrange it, and noted the message. Her father had started a new life and did not want her there.

'I didn't know my mother was dead. I heard she was ill but that was all – I thought she'd recovered. I'm on my way to stay with a friend but if Miss Veronica comes looking for me, please tell her where I am...'

Her voice trailed off because she had no idea where her next stop would be. Perhaps one of her many aunts would give her a space on their floor. She'd have to go and ask.

'I'll come back tomorrow and let you know where I'm staying,' she finished lamely.

He did not argue, neither did his wife who did not want any reminders of Mary living with them. But they were both smiling and friendly when Helen went back down the stair with her bundle. She smiled too and wished them well, but in her heart she was daunted. For the first time in her life she felt alone and lost in Edinburgh.

The aunts had grown old, drunken and cantankerous. All they wanted to do was talk to her about Mary, how hard her life had been with that Cameron, how quickly he'd found himself a young lassie and started a new family. They told Helen that she'd have no home in Baxter's Buildings now with that girl in the flat, her father wouldn't want her there. Mary was dead, and as far as he was concerned all interest in her children had died with her. The brothers had disappeared, God knew where, long ago. The aunts were prepared to house Helen in their fetid dwellings but she took one look round and was reluctant to accept the offers.

Once again she found herself on the street. It was dark now and only a few black-cloaked figures were flitting about in the shadows. Old Edinburgh had never been a hospitable place after Gardy Loo time for anyone, without money to pay for a lodging, and Helen was, contemplating going back to knock on her father's door to plead for a space to sleep – for at least his wife kept the place clean and tidy – when she realized that she was at the mouth of Cant's Close. Was Cecil Grant still living there? It would do no harm to climb the stairs and ask.

The Deacon's daughter would not open the door at first but stood behind it hissing questions: 'Who are you? What do you want?'

Helen put her face against the door crack and said, 'It's me, Helen Cameron, the water caddy's lassie. The one who gave you the rumple knot... Don't you remember me, Cecil?'

There was a long pause before Cecil spoke again. 'Helen Cameron? Wee Helen, with the face like a fairy? What do you want?'

'I've no place to go. I'm frightened, Cecil. Can you take me, in?'

There was obviously a struggle going on within Cecil, but eventually Helen heard the sound of a bolt being withdrawn and the door opened – though only a little way. 'Put your face up here to the door. Let me see you. Come closer and let, me see if it's really Helen Cameron.'

Helen did as she was told, half closing her eyes as Cecil's candle dazzled her after the darkness of the stair. It seemed an age before the other girl was satisfied but eventually she said, 'Come in, you look tired. Have you come far?'

'I am tired. I'm dead weary. Let me stay with you for one night, Cecil, I'll help you with anything that needs doing.'

Cecil had a shawl half drawn across her face, as if she was afraid of being seen. 'Come on in quickly then,' she said. 'I remember the ribbons. You can come in.'

The flat was shockingly filthy, worse than any of Helen's aunts' attics. It was hung with cobwebs, all obviously of long duration, drifting from the ceiling and over the window panes. Every piece of furniture was shrouded in a thick layer of dust and the table was covered with dirty dishes, guttered candles and mouldy food. It was difficult to see clearly in the darkness because Cecil had only one taper lit and she carried it with her as she moved about, leaving the rest of the room in blackness. It was clear that the state of the place was a matter of indifference to her and she made no apologies for it, only indicated that Helen should sit in a spar-backed chair beside the ash-filled fireplace.

'When you knocked I thought it might have been someone about my father. I'm waiting for one of his friends to come. He might come tonight,' she said in a matter-of-fact voice.

'A friend of the Deacon's?' Helen could not keep the astonishment out of her voice. He had been dead for thirteen years.

Cecil was drawing off her shawl and folding it, surprisingly carefully considering the state of her home, as she spoke. 'Oh, he had many friends. He was a Freemason, you know. That's why he was not found out for so long – it was a conspiracy...' The last word was hissed out, long and slow, with sinister meaning. 'His friends knew what he was doing but they wouldn't give him up… he was one of them, one of their secret society. The Provost knew, he was a Mason too. That's why he let them take the body off the gibbet. The French surgeon was a Mason as well – but he was a fool and he ruined their plans. My father was *sacrificed*.'

There was the terrible hissing again and Helen shivered. Cecil was obviously obsessed. Watching her, the younger girl was taken back in memory to the afternoon when she watched Deacon Brodie's body swinging from the gallows rope. She had not thought about that for years but, here in this filthy flat, it seemed as if it had happened only yesterday and she trembled uncontrollably, feeling all at once very cold. Why had she come here? She would have been better off with one of the aunts, far better than with Cecil. She looked around for signs that someone else shared Cecil's home, but there was nothing.

'Where's Peter? Where's your brother?' she asked in a hoarse, tired voice.

Cecil furrowed her brow as if trying to remember her brother. 'Peter? Oh, Peter! Yes, Peter went to England to make his fortune – perhaps he's breaking into banks now as well. They'll probably have to hang Peter too – and he's not a Free-mason so he won't get away with anything. I haven't seen Peter for a long time.'

'And your mother?'

'My mother died a long time ago. Her heart was broken, she wasn't able to live without him. But Agnes Watt, she's still alive, the witch that she is! And my wee brother David, he died first. Poor wee David, what a cough he had. So now there's only me to fight for my father, I have to make them admit he wasn't bad. I have to find the others that were in it with him. I must clear his name… his own sisters pretend he never existed, would you believe that? Not me nor Peter nor David. I have to find out what really happened. Who told them he was in Ostend? It couldn't have been as easy as that.'

'As easy as what?' Helen was mystified by the torrent of words that burst out of Cecil like water from a full well head.

'Don't you go asking questions. You're just like Peter and the others. What do you think? You're wrong. I was the one he asked to see in the Tolbooth. I was the only one he loved. I'm his daughter. I've a *right*. Those sisters of his can't deny me that.'

Day or night were all the same to Cecil, who never seemed to sleep but roamed the flat, rattling the door, peering through the filthy window as if waiting for some clandestine caller, and ranting at Helen who sat fully dressed dozing in the fireside chair, wrapped in her travelling plaid.

When morning came and light fought its way through the dirt-caked window, Helen saw that the food on the table was uneatable and that Cecil was painfully thin, like a walking skeleton. 'I'll go out and buy some bread,' she offered and ran into the thin morning sunlight, grateful to be able to breathe clean, fresh air at last. For the sake of comfort she would have liked to find another place to stay but her pity for Cecil had been awakened. The girl so obviously needed someone to look after her, someone to make sure she ate and to try to persuade her to lie down at night and sleep instead of walking up and down, reciting the same old litany about her father, over and over again.

The only time that Cecil went out was in the evening when she ran up the hill to St Giles to pray in one of the churches that occupied the old cathedral building. She avoided the daylight for she hated to be seen, and like an alley cat preferred to slip along the closes when the shadows were failing. As she watched Cecil and accompanied her on the nightly outing, Helen's face was sad for she could still remember the bright and cheerful girl Cecil had been before the Deacon's hanging. She remembered being given a new-baked bun by kind Cecil just because she looked hungry – and hungry she had been indeed. Poor Cecil, it was as if all her lifelong happiness had been poisoned on the day her father was hanged.

'Wouldn't you like to go for a walk? Wouldn't you like to come with me over the North Bridge and see the fine new houses in Princes Street and George Street?' she asked Cecil on the second day of her stay in Cant's Close, but the answer was a shake of the head.

'I can't go out, you don't understand, I have to wait in case someone comes with news. They're making inquiries for me now. They could come any time.'

'But what sort of news? And what good would it do anyway? You can't bring the Deacon back. You can't change anything.'

'I'm waiting to hear how they knew where he was. I'm waiting to hear how they knew he was in Ostend.'

'But even if you do hear, he's dead, Cecil. He's been dead for years.'

The Deacon's daughter rounded on her friend in a fury. 'You're like all the others. I thought you'd more sense. You don't realize what it means. You don't realize how important it is.'

'All right then, would you like me to go and ask for you?' Helen offered because it struck her that Cecil was waiting for her mysterious news but making no effort to go out and find it. If she were really serious, all she had to do was walk up to the City office and ask. Certainly someone there would be able to tell her. There must be papers about the Deacon's trial and there were still people alive who'd attended it.

But at Helen's suggestion Cecil flew into a terrible rage, grabbing at her with angry hands and shouting, 'What do you mean? Do you think I'm not trying? Do you know more than I do? You can clear out of here and take your suspicions with you…'

But when Helen prepared to leave, Cecil's mood changed and she clung to her arm desperately. 'Don't go, Helen, don't leave me. I didn't mean it!'

On the fourth day of her stay with Cecil, Helen was wakened in the morning by a sharp tapping on the flat door.

Cecil had been asleep, amazingly quiet for hours, in the box bed and she sat up, looking terrified and pushing her hair from her face. 'Don't answer it, don't answer it,' she told Helen.

But the rapping came again and then a woman's voice. 'Are you in there, Helen? Are you there?'

Helen jumped up from her chair. 'It's Miss Vee. I'll have to let her in.'

Veronica, in travelling clothes, stood on the landing. She put out both hands in a pleading gesture and said, 'Oh, I'm glad I found you. Your father said you were here. I'm being sent to Durham to my mother's sister while the divorce goes on. My brother won't have me in Edinburgh because of the scandal. Please come with me. I need you, I need a friend so much.'

Cecil was sitting up in bed, her face white and contorted as she stared at Veronica. 'You can't take her away,' she challenged. 'Don't go, Helen. Stay here. Don't go.'

But there was no doubt in Helen's mind what she had to do. 'I'm sorry, Cecil,' she said simply as she walked over to where her bundle was lying, picked it up, drew her plaid around her and left the flat.

–

Leaving Edinburgh behind was sad but Helen sat stolidly in her seat, never turning her head to look behind as the coach clattered down the coast road, skirting the slate-grey sea. Behind her the city reared up on its crest of rock, but nothing would be achieved by staring back at it. Like everything else in her life, Edinburgh was changing. She had felt like a stranger there.

Veronica's face was strained and deathly white as she stared out of the coach window. Careless of the other ears inside the coach, she kept bending over to Helen and giving her whispered scraps of information.

'Ker's case comes up next month. My brother says it'll go straight through. I've not to contest it. Then I'll be free of him, so I don't care. I'll be able to see Renton again.'

She had heard nothing from her lover though she had written him a number of frantic notes. His silence, she explained to herself, was only sensible and when the divorce was over they would be together again. What she had to do now was keep him informed of her whereabouts so that he could come to her as soon as possible. The only comfort she had was her certainty of him. She thought over and over again of the many times he had sworn deathless love for her. He worshipped her. He could not have made love to her as he had done without adoring her. In her skirt pocket she carried the little bundle of his letters and poems, each one well creased with frequent unfolding and re-reading. When this nightmare was finished, she would be able to be with a true and tender man. He would look after her. All she had to do was survive till then.

'It's Edward and Elizabeth who worry me most,' she next said to Helen in a slightly louder voice. 'My brother says I won't be allowed to see them after the divorce. They'll keep us apart because I'll be a woman of proven wickedness. But they can't do that. I'm sure they can't. I'm not wicked. Anyone who had to live with Ker would know what a hell my life has been. They couldn't blame me for finding someone else.'

An old man and woman in the corner of the carriage stared at her in horror. They had been chatting quite pleasantly to the good-looking woman and her maid till then, but now their faces hardened and they seemed to build a wall of ice around themselves, staring fixedly out of the window and avoiding Veronica's eyes. A smartly dressed younger matron with a teenage daughter reacted as if she might faint when she heard Veronica's words. She turned frantically to her daughter and began engaging her in conversation about their dressmaker, obviously anxious to prevent the girl hearing anything that would be said next. She failed, however, because the girl's eyes were alive with interest and if ears could be seen to be pricked, hers were almost sticking up on end.

They alighted at Berwick where Veronica had many friends, but though she saw more than one of them in the street their greetings lacked spontaneity and it was obvious that they were anxious to escape. No one invited her to their home, no one lingered more than a few moments in her company and more than one cut her dead, pretending not to see her as they passed by.

When the maidservant at the door of one of her closest friends refused to let her in and said that the mistress was out of town, although she had been glimpsed through the parlour window from the doorstep, a realization of what it would mean to be a divorced woman began to dawn on Veronica. Disconsolately she went to an inn and reserved a room for the night – the coach that was to take them through Bishop Auckland to Durham did not leave, until the following afternoon. The innkeeper, a rough-voiced man in a leather apron, recognized her too, addressing her in exaggeratedly deferential tones as 'Mistress – er – Ker?'

The story of her downfall was obviously at its peak of interest in Berwick, and everyone, it seemed, had gone on to John Ker's side.

'Isn't it strange how a woman is always in the wrong in things like this?' Veronica asked Helen as they laid down their bags in the inn bedroom. 'Isn't it strange how people who didn't even care for Ker before are all behind him now?'

Next morning it was raining, and Veronica stood staring out of the window in an agitated state. She did not want to expose herself in the town again, but inactivity nearly drove her mad.

'I'm going to hire a pony cart. I'm going to Broadmeadows to see my children. I'm not divorced yet. They can't keep me away from them,' she announced.

It was a quick drive behind a smart, high-stepping pony and when they turned into the farmyard, the men almost dropped their implements in astonishment. One boy ran ahead to alert the household that the mistress was back. At a half-open stable door Helen caught a glimpse of the astonished face of William but she did not salute him – it could be hard for him later if she indicated any special friendship towards him. Purposefully Veronica jumped from the driver's seat and strode towards the kitchen door, but Mrs Eliot stepped out to bar her way.

The cook's face was scarlet and beads of sweat could be seen on her upper lip but she was determined. 'You can't come in. We've been told to keep you out. You must go away now.'

'Where's my husband?'

'He's not at home, but Miss Susan's here.'

'Where are my children?'

The cook looked shifty. 'They're with Miss Susan in the nursery.'

From above her head Veronica could hear the sound of a child crying, 'Mama, Mama, Mama!' As she realized what the child was saying, she pushed agitatedly at the cook's broad bosom. 'Out of my way. I must see them. Move out of my way or by God I'll knock you down.' Mrs Eliot reeled under the onslaught but bravely stood her ground and she was saved from further injury by a tall, heavy man from the farmyard who came up behind Veronica and gently but definitely took her arm.

'You'd best go away, mistress. You'll only cause trouble for us all if you stay here.'

He looked at Helen, who had also alighted from the cart, and said, in a sympathetic voice, 'Take her away, Helen, make her see sense.'

But Veronica would not listen and her face was ravaged with grief as she stood, head raised, listening to the crying child.

'Edward, Elizabeth, come down to Mama,' she called up at the nursery window, raising her arms as if to embrace them.

Some of the women clustered in the kitchen door turned their eyes away in pity. Behind the glass above her head she could see, but only for an instant, the figure of a child looking down and then, in a trice, it was snatched away and the crying stopped.

She turned to the embarrassed audience. 'Oh, let me see my children, just for a moment, let me see my children,' she called, looking from one face to another. 'I never did any harm to any of you. For God's sake let me see my children.'

But one by one they turned away, their faces betraying their mixed emotions, and Helen had to lead the shaking, weeping woman back to the pony trap. Then she took up the reins and drove it slowly out of the yard with Veronica slumped on the seat beside her.

–

They stood close together in the innyard watching swearing ostlers pushing and shoving fretful horses between the shafts of the coach. One horse was particularly difficult and when it was being harnessed, it lashed out wickedly with its back heels and splintered a stay pole. That meant a delay of two hours in setting off from Berwick, and even on the road the same horse continued making trouble, dropping its head and leaning outwards against the shaft, causing the other three to go out of step and endanger the stability of the coach. So they made poor time and the journey seemed both uncomfortable and interminable to the two women.

Helen was acutely conscious of Veronica's distress. Though she was silent, her face was drawn and white and tears glittered on her cheeks like diamonds in the flickering light of the little oil lamp. Her maid guessed that she was reliving her visit to Broadmeadows. Veronica's absorption in her anguish was so complete that she was totally unconscious of the other people in the carriage – a prosperous-looking old couple, who originally had shown a wish to chat but, receiving no response, composed themselves in opposite corners and went noisily off to sleep, snoring gently like a pair of happy pigs.

Helen could not sleep. She was too unhappy, grieving for Veronica but also thinking of her mother, and she mourned alone for Mary Cameron.

Darkness fell by the time they were ten miles down the road and nothing could be seen through the tiny window. This was the longest journey Helen had ever undertaken but it failed to excite her, for there were too many other things to occupy her mind. After a while she sensed Veronica slipping into sleep and she was the only one left awake, listening to the thudding of the horses' hooves, the rattling of the wheels on the rough road and the curses of the coachman and postilion. Sleep was just beginning to creep over her when the coach lurched heavily to one side. There was a wild shout from outside; all four passengers were thrown on top of each other and the horses clattered to a halt…

'What the deuce…?' demanded the startled old man as he picked himself up from the floor. Veronica was lying in a bundle of clothes, as still as a dead woman, but she was only stunned and made no complaint when they all helped her back into her seat.

'Drivers today, they can't manage horses like they used to,' moaned the old lady, adjusting her straw bonnet and spreading out her voluminous skirts with shaking hands. Helen said nothing because, she alone realized the reason for their spill and she was shocked into silence. Through the tilted window in the half-upturned coach she could see in the silver moonlight a masked man, sitting on a tall horse under a tree at the side of the road. He was pointing a pistol at the coachman's head.

The sky was clear with a sickle moon hanging away to the left, and the diffused light made the highwayman's figure look enormous and threatening in the shadows, but he had a clear and confident voice that sounded almost jolly as he called, 'Step down. Hand over your money and your jewellery. I'm sorry, but my need is greater than yours.'

The old man, grumbling loudly and threatening retribution, reluctantly plunged his hands into his top-coat pockets, bringing out some paper packets and a little doeskin bag of clinking coins.

The dark figure drew his horse nearer, reached out a gloved hand and took what was offered. Weighing them lightly in an upraised palm, he said cheerfully, 'Oh, I think you have more than this, Mister Jacobs, haven't you? You're carrying jewellery to Durham. Don't bother arguing, just look again. Try inside your hat, or I'll try there for you – with or without your head in it.'

The old man's wife was noisily weeping and she scolded her husband through her sobs. 'Don't be a fool, John. Give him everything you have or he'll kill us.'

Her husband took off his old-fashioned beaver hat with a silver buckle in the band, and scrabbled inside its lining for some time, finally producing one by one, and with little grace, more paper-wrapped packets which he handed up to the waiting figure.

But still the robber was not satisfied. 'And the fine buckle too, it has a grand sparkle. I'll need the buckle as well, I think.'

The lesson was not lost on the old man's wife who did not argue as she almost eagerly handed over her reticule and stripped the rings off her plump fingers. When it came to Veronica's turn she sighed and gave up a necklace and two rings. 'That's all I have,' she said with depression haunting her voice.

The robber's eyes gleamed behind the slits of his mask as he looked from her to the baubles she held out to him. 'You've nothing else. This is it all?' he asked and she shook her head.

'That's all.'

The highwayman stuck her possessions in his deep pocket and said, 'What a pity. A lady as fine as you should have. pretty jewellery. You haven't been looked after very well, have you?'

'No, I haven't,' she replied with feeling.

Helen had remained on the bottom step of the coach watching what was going on. Now that it was her turn to face the highwayman's scrutiny, her heart was thudding in her chest and nerves like trapped birds were fluttering in her throat so that she knew it would be difficult for her to speak.

He turned his masked face towards her and asked, 'And what do you have, little one? Come out and let me look at you.'

She stepped down gingerly, hoping that her skirt would not drag to one side because of the weight of Veronica's purse which she had grasped and tied in her underskirt. It was essential to keep up her courage so she spoke boldly as she went closer to him. 'I've nothing, and if I did, what satisfaction would it be to take away a lady's only possessions?'

Her triangular face was lifted to his, defying him, and she heard a sharp intake of breath from the old lady behind. He gave a laugh as if he relished being challenged by such a little thing, but his extended hand was implacable. 'Give me what you're carrying. You ladies have a fancy for putting things inside your skirts. Have a look there for me now, will you?'

She was acutely conscious of Veronica's purse banging against her ankle but she was not prepared to give it up and was protesting again, when her mistress stepped forward and said to the highwayman, 'She's my maid and she has my purse. It's everything I possess in the world, surely you won't take it?'

The man looked at her more attentively now. What he saw was a beautiful woman of fashion in well-cut, expensive clothes, not a pauper from her appearance by any means. 'Sorry, madam, but I hear those stories all the time,' he told her. 'I'll leave you enough for a night's lodging in Durham but I must have the purse.' Then he turned to Helen and ordered more sharply, 'Don't waste my time. Give it to me!'

Her face furious, she bent down, lifted the hem of her dress a little and untied the purse from its hiding place. Then she deliberately walked up close to his boot leg – so close that she could smell the leather of his saddle – and held the purse out to him. If possible she was going to have a look at him so that she could tell the authorities later. When he bent down to take the purse he stared into her face and his gloved hand seemed to falter. For a moment she thought he was going to draw back and she heard him give a sharp exclamation under his breath… '*A dhia!*' was what he said. She had not heard that curse since old Colin Cameron died.

'Well may you call on God,' she snapped as she pushed the purse into his hand. He recovered himself he took it and then, all of a sudden, he laughed – really laughed. Was she dreaming or did she recognize his voice?

The passengers stood fearfully huddled together and watched as the coachman and his assistant piled mail bags into the road.

The highwayman took what he wanted from them and then, remounting and wheeling his horse, he saluted them all and set his mount at the hedgerow. It soared over and disappeared with only a faint cry coming back to them as he galloped off across the fields.

Everyone became suddenly very brave and the excitement of having been robbed kept them awake and talking until they reached the ancient city of Durham as dawn was breaking. The triple towers of the cathedral rose with heart-stopping stateliness into a pearly grey sky and a wreath of mist drifted along the river at the foot of the castle rock as their coach clattered over the bridge leading into the huddled narrow streets of the city.

Some people were already up and about their business when the coach rattled into the main square. With his face blazing in excitement, the postilion jumped down from the box calling, 'We've been robbed, we've been robbed!' Because they had escaped with their lives, what had been a frightening experience was now an adventure, something to boast about. Though Helen was furious at having lost Veronica's money, when the officials questioned her about the highwayman she found to her surprise that she was not prepared to tell them how he swore in Gaelic. She kept that piece of information to herself but she did not know exactly why.

–

Veronica's aunt was a gossip without the sharp intelligence of her sister Lady Huntingdon. She was married to a clergyman, one of the prebends of Durham, and they lived in great comfort in an old house with a lovely garden tucked up against the massive cathedral walls. They were childless and set in their ways, interested only in the day-to-day events of the see and leading lives in which nothing disruptive ever happened. When their nephew Thomas' letter about his wayward sister and her scandalous goings-on arrived, the old lady had to have recourse to the smelling salts at the thought that such a scarlet woman was able to claim relationship with her. She had not seen Veronica since she was a small child and her only knowledge of the life of her late sister's youngest had come in intermittent letters from Edinburgh, none of which had given any hint that a divorce was even a possibility.

'Thomas must have taken leave of his senses! We can't have that woman here. What would people say if they knew about her divorce?' she demanded of her paunchy, easy-going husband who shook his head in agreement and soothed her with promises that when Veronica arrived they would find some way of passing her on like an unwanted parcel.

It was breakfast time when she finally turned up, dishevelled and tired-looking, with some story about being held up by a highwayman on the road from Berwick. The old couple looked at each other significantly at that – she was probably begging for money as well, said their flashed look.

Very conscious of their disapproval, Veronica sat at their laden table and sipped tea from a fragile china cup while they faced each other, one on each side of the fireplace like a pair of old firedogs. It was obvious that they were worried about how quickly they could be rid of her.

'I'm afraid we're not used to visitors, there's not a great deal of room in this house,' said her aunt, with a vague wave of the hand at the comfortable room. The house was silent and empty except for the servants but Veronica could appreciate how the old pair enjoyed their peaceful little routine and did not want it changed.

'Please don't worry,' she told them, 'I've just come to ask if you could tell me where my maid and I might find rooms. We'll go there.'

'Rooms?' asked her uncle, looking at his wife with his brow furrowed.

'Rooms?' she replied in a voice of pure terror which showed that she had hoped Veronica would only be passing through Durham and not staying.

'Some respectable lodging,' explained the exhausted-looking young woman. 'I'm very tired and so's my maid. I need a place to stay until things are sorted out – Thomas expects me to wait in Durham until he communicates with me. He'll write to you, I expect, and my maid could collect letters from you…'

Her voice trailed off. Depression and weariness were about to claim her and she doubted whether she could summon enough strength to go in search of lodgings.

Her uncle recovered his composure first. 'Ah, yes, rooms…' He looked at his wife, trying to convey the thought: At least she knows she can't stay here. The old lady rallied and nodded her head so he continued, 'Ah, yes, I'm sure our maid will know of someone who rents rooms.' He sprang, surprisingly lightly considering his bulk, to his feet and pulled the bell at the side of the fireplace to summon their maidservant, who came quickly because she had been listening outside the parlour door.

'The corn merchant's wife in Saddler Street takes in roomers and she keeps a clean house,' the maid said when Veronica's request was repeated to her.

'Then we'll try there, send the kitchen girl down to ask,' said Veronica's aunt with undisguised relief in her voice. Her familial duty was almost done.

–

'How long will you be staying?' asked the corn merchant's wife, Margaret Winters. Her sympathy was immediately awakened by Veronica's beautiful but harried face and by the way the poor thing's hands shook with tiredness as she stood nervously in the doorway of the shop in Saddler Street.

'I don't know, but several weeks I'm sure,' was the reply. How could you tell your prospective landlady that you had no idea how long it would take to be divorced by your husband, how long it would be before your lover could come and rescue you?

There's a mystery here, thought Margaret Winters. This young woman is in trouble, she badly needs help.

'You can have the big front room for a guinea a month,' she told Veronica.

'A guinea?' Veronica was trying to calculate how long her money would last and then, with a shiver of disappointment, she remembered that she'd been robbed… 'It's not that I think that's too much, it's just that we were stopped by a highwayman on the road and he took most of my money. I'll have to wait till more comes from my brother in Edinburgh. I'll write to him today.'

Extending credit to lodgers was unheard of, but this case was different. 'Don't you worry, love. You can have the room till you're able to pay.' Mrs Winters took the bag from Veronica's hand and showed her and Helen up the narrow wooden stairs at the back of the shop. She did not really know why she was moved to such generosity – it must have been the pitiful way the lovely woman looked at her, the way her eyes seemed to say, 'Help me, please help me, I don't know what to do.'

–

Mrs Winters' maid was polishing the door brasses two days later when a ragged little boy from the inn at the market, place came running up and inquired whether her mistress had recently taken in a lady and her maid.

'Yes, poor things, they were in that coach that was robbed,' she told him.

'That's right, they're the ones I'm seeking. Give the maid this package. A man at the inn sent me to find her.'

The maid called up at the window for Helen, who came down and looked surprised as the package was put into her hands.

'But who gave you this?' she asked, shaking it curiously and hearing a faint tinkle.

'A fellow at the inn, a well-set-up kind of man who came down from the north last night. He said to find the maidservant to the lady who lost her money to the highwayman. He wanted to help you. He said those rogues should be hanged and not allowed to rove the roads the way they do,' chattered the boy importantly.

'Didn't he give a name?' she asked suspiciously but the boy shook his head.

'No, and I've not seen him before. He rode off early. But perhaps he put his name inside,' he suggested, hoping that Helen would open the parcel so that he could see what the stranger had sent, but she did not satisfy his curiosity.

'If you see him again, thank him from me,' she replied.

Veronica was still in her nightdress when the maid brought in the mysterious parcel. Together they stood at the window, untying the cord and removing three layers of paper before they found a little paper box that rattled when it was shaken. They gasped in delight when the lid was removed and revealed a pile of golden coins.

'Oh, thank God, thank God,' gasped Veronica, pouring the money out on to the table top. She and Helen started to count it and to their delight finally worked out that they now had eighteen guineas, more than twice what had been lost.

'*Who* did you say brought this?' Veronica asked in wonderment.

'A boy from the inn, he said a man from the north brought it down and asked him to give it to me.'

'To you? Did he say what the man looked like?' Veronica's voice was trembling with hope.

'A well-set-up man, he said.'

'Then it must have been Renton.' The light came flooding back into Veronica's face. 'It *must* have been him. I wrote to tell him I was being sent to Durham. He'll have heard what happened and ridden down to help me. Of course he couldn't see me because of the divorce, but he wanted to help me. Oh, Helen, he hasn't forgotten me! For a while I was so afraid...'

The maid was scarcely listening, slowly turning the box around in her hands for some clue. Scribbled on the lid were two very faint words and she held the box to the light to make out what was written there. 'Mr Deacon' it read.

'What are you looking at?' asked Veronica, who had delightedly started recounting the money. She was so taken up with her own relief that she did not notice Helen's confusion as she quickly slipped the box into her pocket.

'Oh nothing, I was just thinking how kind it was for some man to send me so much money,' she replied hastily.

'For Sir Alexander to send us all this money, you mean,' corrected Veronica. 'He couldn't send it to me direct in case I was being watched so he sent it to you – but I knew my Renton wouldn't let me down.'

–

2nd December, 1800.

Sister, though it pains me to address you as such, I enclose the official notice of your divorce from my friend John Ker of Broadmeadows. By your actions you have rendered yourself a disgrace to your sex and in all probability you will now be miserable during the rest of your life.

Thomas' covering note to the divorce document was short and she could hear his sanctimonious voice as she read his words. 'My friend John Ker' was his message that his sympathies were entirely with her husband and the words also carried a threat for the future – what were they planning together now?

The divorce action had been raised in the High Court of Edinburgh in October and the decree was dated the day previous to Thomas' letter. It was also short and painfully plain spoken: John Ker, the pursuer, had married Miss Veronica Hay, youngest daughter of the deceased William Hay of Huntingdon, one of the Senators of the College of Justice in Edinburgh, on 2nd May, 1791. There were several children, some of whom were presently existing. John Ker raised his action for divorce against his wife on the grounds of her adultery with different men for at least three years.

It was a cut and dried case. The divorce was granted by Lord Dunsinane, an old friend of her father's, on the grounds of her adultery.

She sat with the crumpled papers in her lap and stared bleakly at the wall. Her whole life – her marriage, her existence up till that moment – was encapsulated in those letters. How unfair it was that no one, not the Judge, not the lawyers, not even her own brother had taken any thought of her feelings. They had not considered that she might have some protest to make against their dismissal of her as an immoral, wayward woman. Would it have made any difference if they knew how Ker had treated her? Would it have influenced their judgement if it was stated how reluctantly she had married him and what pressures were brought to bear on her? No, she realized, it probably would not. They were men; they made the laws; they thought that when a woman married she became her husband's chattel. If he beat her, she had no grounds for complaint; if she found that his very presence, every word he spoke, grated on her nerves, that was her misfortune and one that had to be borne without complaint.

And what about her children? They were not even mentioned by Thomas or named in the divorce papers. They were Ker's; he would keep them. They were lost to her like everything else that belonged to her miserable marriage. At this thought her womb contracted as if she were in labour and she clutched her hands to her belly, moaning in agony. Such pain, such misery, would it ever be assuaged? She rose and staggered over to the cupboard where she had hidden a bottle of brandy. There was only one sure way she knew that could dull her agony.

'I thought you had more sense! You know what it was like last time you did this!' Helen was furious and because all mistress-and-maid restraint between them had long ago been swept away, it never struck her that it was not her place to rail at Veronica with such vehemence.

She grabbed the almost empty brandy bottle and flung it angrily into the fireplace where it splintered into dagger-shaped shards, what was left of the volatile liquor splattering over the hearth.

Veronica, swaying slightly, stood watching the brandy vaporize before her eyes. 'What a waste,' she sighed gently, but she did not argue for she was drunk; her sensibilities were muffled against the misery of her life and it was too much of an effort to think very clearly about anything.

In her transformed mood she almost laughed at the sight of her maid rampaging up and down the room, throwing open cupboard doors, searching under cushions.

'Have you any more? If you do, tell me where it is!'

Veronica weakly shrugged her shoulders under the lace fichu and Helen saw with pain and concern how thin she had grown over the past weeks. She had been ill for some time with an intermittent fever that refused to respond to any of the apothecary's cures, and it had taken a heavy toll of her.

'Don't worry. There's no more. I only had enough money for one bottle.' Her voice was slurred.

'Did you send that silly maidservant downstairs for it? I'll tell her not to bring you brandy again. For God's sake, don't start drinking. You need all your wits about you now.'

Face red with anger, Helen bent down and picked the scattered divorce papers off the floor. She could see very well what they were and what they meant for Veronica as she put them neatly together on the table. The older woman sank down on the chair and covered her eyes with her hands.

'Oh Helen, it's all right for you. You don't know what I'm going through. He hasn't written, he hasn't sent me one word though I've written to him every day. What am I to do? Our money is running out and Thomas will send no more… What's to become of us?'

'Write again to Renton, and not one of your love letters. Write him a demand note. Tell him to send you money. He's as guilty as you are and it's not fair that he should wash his hands of the whole thing.'

So, when Veronica was sobered a little she was set to work with her pen. The words flowed eagerly from her as if she were talking to him.

> *Dear love, Your silence makes me very unhappy for God sake write and relief my mind I had a very harsh letter from my brother calling me wicked and immoral From my present trouble in body I must apply to you as a friend to assist me in my resent distress. When I take the pen in my hand it trembles sadly – I have had a shocking fever which is very expensive, if you can spare a little money I shall be very much obliged to you. I realty stand in need and know I have no friends except yourself be mercy on me at this time and remember the felicity we had together. I wish I could see you if you could come to Durham I could meet you here without it being known – I shall wait with impatience for an answer. Don't be cruel you once fondly loved the unfortunate writer – I am afraid you can't read scrale – believe to be sincere. Yours signed V.K.*

Two letters were delivered to Alexander Renton by his manservant on a bright winter morning after he returned from making the rounds of his policies with his farm servants. He was in a cheerful mood because the game in his coverts was plentiful – shooting and hunting would be good for his Christmas guests. About a dozen of his friends were arriving soon from various parts of the country and he was looking forward to the festivities.

He recognized the handwriting on the first envelope and opened it with a look of distaste: *I must apply to you as a friend to assist me in my resent distress... Don't be cruel you once fondly loved the unfortunate writer.* The woman knew nothing about punctuation. You would never think her father was one of Edinburgh's shrewdest advocates in his time!

He furrowed his brow and read the letter again: I have had a shocking fewer... trembles sadly...

There was no point in her attempting to win his sympathy. He had too many worries already on her behalf to be influenced by pleas of sickness. What did she want? Ah, here was the crux!

If you can spare a little money I shall be very much obliged to you. I really stand in need and know I have no friends except yourself have mercy on me at this time and remember the felicity we had together... His irritation grew at her references to their felicity, their lust, their passion. He wanted to forget his sweating need to make love to her on a bed of straw in a half-ruined cottage. Now that it was over he had put it out of his mind, but she never would. She was still harking back to the past.

> *If you could come to Durham I could meet you here without it being known... Don't be cruel you once fondly loved the unfortunate writer... I am afraid you can't read scrale...* She couldn't spell either... *Believe to be sincere. Yours signed V.K.*

She was so unsure of herself, so dispossessed, that she was still signing herself as Veronica Ker though her husband had repudiated her. He threw her letter down on his desk and lifted the second one. It was written in a more scholarly hand and had been sent from Edinburgh. When he read it all happy thoughts of Christmas cheer disappeared for it was a summons, issued by John Ker Esquire against Sir Alexander Renton, accusing him of acts of adultery, debauching, criminal conversation and otherwise alienating the affections of Ker's wife from her lawful husband.

Two years, ago, it accused, Renton had caused Ker's wife to alienate her affections totally and at many times and many places he had carnal knowledge of her and debauched her.

For this Ker was demanding the sum of £20,000 in damages as a compensation for the great injury done to him and his family by Renton. Not content with that fortune, he also wanted the sum of £500 for expenses.

–

William MacKenzie had been Renton's lawyer for many years. They were the same age and he much admired and envied the tall, dashing squire whose attitudes and elegance were everything that the lawyer would have liked to have been himself but never achieved. His life was circumspect and fanatically proper; he and his wife attended church three times on Sundays and maintained sober demeanours on every other day as well. His fantasy life as a rakehell squire was lived through Renton.

Now he pursed his pale lips and re-read Ker's summons.

'He knows you're a man of property. He's out to make a profit out of losing his wife to you. Are you sure they weren't in it together? Are you sure it wasn't a plot?'

Renton tilted the office chair back and frowned. 'I don't think so. She hated him – couldn't say a good word about him, called him a brute and a tyrant, things like that. Besides she's not the sort who could be calculating.' He did not add that Veronica's ardent lovemaking, her need for him, could not possibly have been faked.

MacKenzie frowned again and tut-tutted hopelessly. 'Let me think. He's asking for a fortune. A man could set himself up in style for life with twenty thousand pounds. It would buy an estate and a gentleman's income. He puts a high value on her – why?'

'Her connections, I suppose. He's only the son of a peasant himself. And she's very beautiful, the most beautiful woman in the district, there's no doubt of that.'

Of course, thought the lawyer approvingly. It was only right that she should be beautiful.

'You could afford to pay twenty thousand pounds for the lady if we made some financial adjustments,' he suggested next but Renton leaned forward abruptly so that the chair legs thudded on the floor.

'I will not! I won't pay the greedy swine his money. Why should I compromise my estate for him? Why should I sell as much as an acre for an oaf like Ker to benefit from it? I'll fight him.'

'In that case we must be careful… we need to plan our defence very carefully. Are you in touch with the lady?'

Renton nodded. 'I know where she is. She writes to me.'

He passed Veronica's last begging letter over the desk and MacKenzie read it carefully.

'Do as she asks. Send her some money. Not a lot, just enough to last her a few weeks, and tell her that when she replies she must address all her letters to Berwick post office and have someone else write the cover. Ker could have spies on you by now and he would recognize her hand. Don't arouse her suspicions, you need her on your side, so you must humour the lady. In the meantime we'll check up with witnesses who know her and her husband. We'll have to prove that she and her husband lived unhappily together and, if possible, that she was unfaithful to him before you ever made her acquaintance. How can he sue for damages of such magnitude if he is losing damaged goods?'

Every day letters either arrived or were sent from Veronica's lodgings in Saddler Street. The stimulus they provided kept her sober, and Helen was able to relax her guard a little. When winter grew less harsh she started to explore the town and found that it pleased her. The twisting streets, the three stone bridges across the river Wear, the nooks and crannies of the ancient buildings reminded her a little of Edinburgh.

They had been in Durham for nearly five months and though it was more to her taste than the country, it was quiet and unexciting. The people were so well behaved and docile, no shouting voices disrupted the peace of the streets at night, no quarrelling gossips stood outside shop doors, there was no one to talk to except Veronica – who was distracted with worry about Renton's predicament, for he had written to tell her of Ker's demand. Because of the new case he could not see her, though he sent her £20, and her letters to him had to be addressed by Helen for fear of Ker's spies detecting that the lovers were still in touch and using that as evidence against Renton.

Yet the knowledge that something was happening brought a stimulus to Veronica's life and when she and Helen were together she talked confidently about her lover. 'He loves me. When Ker's case has been thrown out, we'll be together. Oh, when I think of all the things he said to me, I know he loves me…' she assured herself through Helen.

Sometimes she would bring out his love poems and sit with them in her lap, reading each word over and over again, her eyes misty. Even when spring came she hardly ever left the lodging, afraid to go away in case she would miss the next letter. Her aunt and uncle, to their profound relief, saw nothing of her.

Helen was off wandering in the town and Veronica was alone when Thomas' next, letter arrived. Her brother was now openly interceding on her husband's behalf because Ker had promised him a share of the £20,000 if the suit should be successful. If his sister had ever entertained any doubts about Dr Thomas' true nature, these were now swept away. Greedy, cruel, manipulative and self-seeking, he cared nothing for her reputation and unhappy predicament. He enclosed a sheaf of papers, copies of Renton's defence against the action for damages... *When you read this*, he wrote, *yow will realize what your lover is attempting to prove against you. A more diabolical hit against your children was never attempted and in justice to them I expect you will immediately comply with your husband's desire that you hand over all Renton's letters or cards in your possession.*

With shaking hands, she read the papers. Renton's lawyers argued that though Ker believed their client to be a man of great wealth, possessed of an income of over £2,000 a year, this was greatly exaggerated. Being forced to make a payment of £20,000 would severely injure his situation and deprive his descendants of their rightful due.

It was also asserted that Mrs Ker was 'a woman of gallantry' long before he had the most remote connection with her, and that she had committed adultery with a number of different men, receiving them at Broadmeadows when her husband was away on his muster master business. Renton also had reason to believe that she had connections with other persons at the time of having a connection with him. Moreover he was prepared to bring witnesses to swear that the marriage with Ker had been unhappy for a very long time before the divorce... *This would be a defence and a mitigation against Ker's claim of damages*, wrote Renton's lawyer, *because when the value of an article that someone has lost is proved to be low, how can they claim a large sum against it?*

She was being described in court as an 'article' like a damaged hat or a barren cow. It was difficult to believe that Renton was allowing this to happen to her. He could well afford £20,000, she knew that, but she also knew that it was a ridiculous claim on Ker's behalf and felt it right of Renton to fight – but did he have to fight it using what was left of her reputation as his weapon?

When you have read your lover's defence, you will realize the depths of his scorn for you, wrote her brother. *It is necessary to stop this becoming public and you must cooperate it us* by *sending me his letters and being prepared to attest that Renton alone seduced you from your husband's affection. If you do this, I will make arrangements to send you to live in Lisbon and provide you with an annuity.*

–

The magnificent cathedral standing high and proud on the top of the hill awed and fascinated Helen although she was sceptical about religion and had always viewed the crowds of solemn-faced people flocking into Edinburgh's churches on Sundays with a satirical eye. She knew that by Monday morning they would all be back to their old ways of living – pious faces were kept for church-going only. But the memory of her grandfather eagerly receiving the host from the shabby-coated priest had stayed in her mind – the exaltation on the old man's face as the priest made the sign of the Cross over him had left a deep impression.

Some of that feeling of reverence and mystery came over her when she stepped inside St Cuthbert's Cathedral. When despondency overcame her she wandered up the hill and across the expanse of grass to the heavy wooden north door with its grinning knocker. She pushed the door open and slipped inside, happy to wander up and down the dim aisles, tracing her finger along the incisions in the massive pillars or trying to read the words inscribed on the gilded tombs of bishops erected beneath the soaring roof. The cathedral filled her with an unspecified longing and a sense of wonder. It was astonishing to her that men could feel so strongly about their God that they had raised such a monument to him.

The vergers became used to the girl in her dark clothes flitting up and down the aisles, sitting peacefully in a pew listening to the practising choristers or toiling slowly up the steep stairs to the top of the steeple from where she had a view over the countryside. She loved the steeple stairs, because they reminded her of her tenement home.

An old beadle in snuff-stained black robes befriended her and when she came in he would quickly appear at her side, eager to tell, her stories about the church. He pointed out, the black slab of stone that marked the grave of St Cuthbert and she listened to him with flattering attention, drinking in his story of the blessed Cuthbert whose body had been brought there by wandering monks after years of travel. 'Cuthbert was from Scotland like yourself, you should be proud of him. He was a poor boy who started his life as a cattle herd and ended up the most holy and respected man in Europe,' said the beadle. Proudly then he went on to show her the cathedral clock with its different painted dials that could tell the day and the month as well as the hour; he took her into the treasury, full of silver and golden vessels that sparkled and shone in the dimness; he showed her ancient books and manuscripts written in strange letters and illuminated with fascinating little drawings. She was most interested however when he told her the story of the big verdigris-green knocker on the north door. It stared down at her, a frill of what looked like flames around its head, pointed ears like a cat's, huge empty eye sockets and a grin that held the metal bar of the knocker.

'I think it's frightening,' she told her new friend but he shook his head.

'Oh, no, it's a kindly face. It's the sanctuary knocker, you see.'

'The sanctuary? What's that?' she asked, standing on tip toe to lift the knocker bar, but the old man restrained her hand before she could let it fall.

'Don't sound it. Only people in need of sanctuary ever sounded it. The monks took them in and kept them safe from those who sought them. If they repented of their sins, they were allowed to go into exile.'

The girl turned her face to his and said slowly, 'My poor Miss Vee's in exile and she's sorry for what's happened but she's not been treated well. I wonder if sounding this knocker would help her?'

But he shook his head sadly. 'The right of sanctuary has gone now, I'm afraid. No one comes knocking here any longer. But perhaps if your lady would come to pray it might help her.'

'I'll ask her to come,' Helen told him, 'and I'll tell her about the sanctuary knocker.'

She went back with him into the church and sat for a while listening to the music, her eyes closed and her mind far away. When she was about to leave, she caught sight of a figure standing behind one of the massive pillars near the main door. Her native caution, bred of years in Edinburgh's streets, made her avoid the watcher, and she was veering off to use another door when a voice whispered, 'Won't you stop and speak to me, *a luaidh*?' Startled, she spun round and a man stepped into the brilliant light cast through the high windows. It was Peter Grant, his face beaming with smiles. She was not very surprised.

'I wondered if we would meet again. I recognized your voice that night on the moor when you said "God" in Gaelic. You gave yourself away, Peter,' she told him.

'It's a good thing that no one else in the party knew the Gaelic then, isn't it? But you didn't tell anyone, did you?'

'No, of course not. Why should I? You're my friend. Besides, the old man with the jewellery in his hat could afford to lose some of it. He'd hidden more in his shoes.'

'Had he, by God? Next time I'll have them off his feet as well. Did my little present reach you?'

'Yes. I guessed it was you who sent the money. "Mr Deacon" gave you away. That was taking a chance, wasn't it? But I didn't tell Miss Vee, she was so happy to think it came from Renton.'

'I sent it because I could see you both needed it. I made inquiries about you and I felt guilty at robbing you. I've brought some more with me today because I've done well this month. There's plenty of army money carts on the road these days…' He held out a small leather purse and she glanced over her shoulder to make sure that there was no one around.

'Oh thank you, Peter, I shouldn't take it but we really need it. Don't do it again, though. Why are you taking such chances? You know what happens to highwaymen, don't you? There's a gibbet at the other end of the Prebend's Bridge right now with a highwayman's body hanging on it. You don't want to take his place when the crows have eaten him, do you?'

The memory of his father swinging from a rope's end had never left her and she still sometimes woke shaking with terror when she dreamed of it.

But Peter only shrugged. 'I have an aim. When I've made enough money, I'll stop. I'm going to do it the other way round from my father – he had money when he started, and became a robber afterwards. I have nothing now so I'm a robber to help me become a gentleman.'

'You might not live that long,' said Helen, always a realist.

–

She was surprised that Peter was not afraid to walk openly in the street, but he calmed her fears by saying, 'It's all right. No one knows me here. I usually work alone and I use different inns up and down the district, but none in Durham.'

She stared at him curiously and with admiration for his boldness and capability. He had not changed a great deal and still looked so light-hearted and carefree that it was difficult to believe there was a price on his head. 'But the innkeepers must guess what you're doing?'

He laughed again. 'They have their share of the spoils so they're not going to talk to the wrong people. I don't feel a bit guilty about this, Helen, so don't start trying to preach to me.'

His youthful, open face beaming down at her made her heart lighten. He didn't look like a highwayman. Being with him was like being out on a childish prank, something exciting but not very serious. The worries and anxieties that she had been shouldering for the past months were suddenly lightened and Peter's devil-may-care spirits infected her so she laughed, too and took his arm. Slipping on the cobbles and giggling like a couple of children, they ran back down the hill to Helen's lodgings.

At the door of the corn merchant's house he bent and kissed her cheek. 'You've grown into a real lady, little Helen. I'm going off now but I'll come back for you, so don't go away.' Then he strode off, an upright figure with a determined set to his broad shoulders and she watched till he was out of sight. She found she was full of admiration and without any disapproval of his way of life. In fact she found herself longing to call after him, 'Take me with you, Peter.' But that was impossible, she was too much needed by Miss Vee. Besides it would never do for a woman to take to the roads and hold up coaches at the point of a gun.

—

Veronica was lying on her bed weeping when Helen entered their room. On the floor was a crumpled letter.

'Read that, read that,' sobbed Veronica. 'They want to send me to Lisbon – so far away!'

Helen read the letter with a sad heart. If Dr Thomas sent his sister across the sea, she too would have to go, and she hated the idea.

'Write to Renton,' she told her mistress. 'Write and tell him what they're planning. Ask for his help, he owes it to you.'

The next week was purgatory for both of them. Veronica refused to leave the house, spending her time sitting in the window which had a long view down Saddler Street, but no message came for her.

'Write again,' urged Helen.

After an insulting passage of six more days, the second letter eventually elicited a response but Veronica's delight at receiving it soon changed to despondency. There was no message of love, none of the tenderness for which she longed. The damages that Ker was claiming worried him most of all:

> The demand for £20,000 from the one whom you used to style your Tyrant, would so injure my fortune that it would put it out of my power to assist you which I should so much regret… You can however assist me and there would be less effect on your children than any prosecution I would have to adopt on my own behalf. Do not give your brother any of my letters.

'What does he think of me? Does he imagine I would betray him?' The lover she had known couldn't have changed towards her. If she could only touch him, put her hand in his, he would remember their happy times. Taking paper from her wooden travelling desk, she poured her heart on to the page:

> My Dear Love, As long as you love me everything is indifferent to me. Your silence till now made me very unhappy but the letter today was a relief to my mind. My brother assures me that your letters can do little good in Mr Ker's case, so why does he want them so badly? I wrote an answer back saying that I never intended to hurt you that I had been your friend and that I would remain so, so you see that I have declared against them. The moment you receive this set out to see me. I shall look for you every day… I hardly know what I am doing or writing but this I know that I prest your letter to my heart. I have much to say but must delay it till we meet my hardships have been great and more than bodily

strength can sustain. Let the world say as they please I
am your friend… V.K.

The cover was addressed by Helen and it went north that night.

-

Ker and Dr Thomas were trying to starve Veronica out and would have succeeded but for the money that Helen received from Peter. She had taken it gratefully, not caring how he came by it because she felt that using it to help Miss Veronica made everything right.

They met again twice in the cathedral where shadowy and secret corners made perfect places for assignation, and when they sat whispering together she was filled with relief at having someone to rely on. She talked about Veronica's problems and he nodded in sympathy when the maid described her mistress's absolute refusal to consider that Renton was no longer as ardent as he once had been. For in spite of her loving letter of support and plea for a meeting, Renton made no attempt to contact her.

When problems hit too strongly Veronica invariably found something to drink, and Helen returned to find her sprawled asleep in a chair with an empty bottle by her side. The lady was a pathetic figure for she had stopped caring about her appearance, her dresses were crumpled and her hair untended. She was only a shadow of the beautiful woman she once had been.

-

'I can't tell you what a comfort it is to meet you here,' Helen whispered on their third meeting when she slipped into the cathedral pew beside Peter. He turned his head and smiled at her but it was not his usual carefree grin, something was different. Her heart lurched in fear.

'What's wrong?' she asked in a low voice. 'You look as if you're in trouble.'

'I've just heard that they've caught my friend Irish Jack. He and I started on the road at the same time and we've done some night work together. They caught him yesterday and they hanged him this morning on the gibbet outside Lancaster. He's up there now...'

A terrible chill spread through Helen. Starting at her heart it seeped down her arms and legs and crept into the very marrow of her bones. It made her teeth chatter and her feet and fingers freeze as she looked hard at Peter, as if seeing him for the first time. She had been wrong – Peter Grant had changed. He was no longer the boy she had known in Edinburgh but a formidable-looking fellow with a determined chin and blue eyes that were now shining ice cold with anger.

She had never fully allowed herself to realize that Peter lived with danger as his constant companion. With her he was always so happy and carefree that he vanquished any black shadows, but now she saw that for him too their meetings had been a release and an escape.

'Poor old Jack,' he, whispered, and silently she slipped a hand over his in comfort. She kept her eyes fixed on Peter's face, afraid that if she looked away into one of the dark corners she would see the spectre of Deacon Brodie standing there. Was his awful fate to be visited on his son as well?

She immediately pushed away the thought. Peter was brave, resourceful, the best caddy in Edinburgh. Peter could look after himself. But still she was afraid. She bent towards him and pleaded, 'Oh, give it up, Peter, give it up now before it's too late. Don't end up on the gibbet like your poor friend. You're a clever man, there's plenty of other things you could do.'

He looked bleak, and she saw the pain in his eyes. 'What else? What do you suggest for a man who knows nothing but the life of the roads? Anyway, I don't want to stop – not yet. I'm used to the excitement. It's hard to explain, but Jack felt the same as me. I think that when they hung him he'd have accepted it as part of the game. It's easy for me to understand what made my father do it too… This must be my inheritance from him, Helen. Don't worry, I'll be all right – and if I'm not, I can't complain.'

Her heart was wrenched in agony. The tears were starting to gather in the backs of her eyes and a choking feeling blocked her throat. The idea of having to go on living without seeing Peter filled her with unspeakable dread.

As if he could read her mind, he told her, 'I'll have to go away for a bit. Jack knew I was coming to Durham and they might have made him say something, you never can tell. Will you and your Miss Vee be staying on?'

She shrugged, too full of emotion to speak. When she had quelled the strungling lump in her throat, she said, 'I don't know what'll happen. The damages case is going ahead and Miss Vee's brother wants to send her to Lisbon. She's not keen to go but if she agrees, he'll pay her an allowance.'

'Not much, I'll wager,' said Peter, who knew Dr Thomas of old. Then he asked in a softer voice, 'And what about you? Will you go to Lisbon too, *mo ghaoil*?'

The words of affection hung like iced diamonds in the chill air of the silent cathedral. She could almost see them sparkling between her and Peter as she looked into his eyes. Her unexpected reaction to him so surprised her that she mentally scolded herself: 'This is no time for falling in love – love's a delusion, look at the trouble it causes everyone, look at what happened to John Ker, Veronica and Renton all because they fell in love.'

She moved away slightly from him and said, 'Miss Vee needs me. I'd have to go with her. She hasn't anyone else.'

He was still looking intently at her. 'But I'll come back for you. I promise I will. Don't go away yet.'

'You're my friend, Peter. I couldn't have lasted these months without your help. Neither could Miss Vee. The money you've given us has kept us from starving.'

In a way Helen had convinced herself that Peter's kindness to them was partly because, like most men, he was infatuated with Veronica. They all fell in love with poor Mrs Ker; they were enthralled by her beauty and charm, and even though she had grown so thin and distracted she still retained her power to enchant. Sometimes it seemed that her anguish and pitiful state wakened love and admiration all the sooner.

Peter squeezed her hand, gently as he said, 'Promise me you'll not go to Lisbon until I come back. Promise me that, *mo ghaoil.*'

'Oh Peter,' she whispered in a stricken voice, 'don't call me that. My grandfather used to call me *mo ghaoil.* Don't say it to me unless you mean it.'

'But I do mean it. Why else do you think I've been coming here? Why else do you think I've risked my neck coming back to Durham? You are *mo ghaoil*, little Helen Cameron, don't you know that by now?'

'I thought it was Miss Vee… I thought you were like all the others, in love with her.'

'You and your Miss Vee! She's a fine woman, that's true, but she's not for me. She's a woman of gallantry who gathers men to her like bees round a honey pot, but you're gallant in a different way and I like that better.'

She promised that if they had to go anywhere before he returned, she would leave a message for him at the corn merchant's shop. Then they sat quietly for a long time, speaking little, only holding hands and breathing in the peace and tranquillity from the great cathedral. It seemed that hundreds of years of faith and worship had brought a quality of easement to the incense-scented air that calmed their fears and strengthened their resolution.

When it was time to go, parting was painful. They could never be seen leaving the cathedral together so, when the ancient clock chimed noon and the bells began ringing out in the steeple above their heads, he gathered up his possessions, kissed her lightly on the cheek, passed a gentle hand over her bent head and walked up the aisle without a backward glance.

He was so bemused by what had happened, so transported by the atmosphere of the cathedral that he seemed as sightless as someone going into a darkened room from brilliant sunlight. She watched him walk away and her heart was full of a mixture of feelings, love and longing, fear and a fierce protectiveness.

A short time later, when she felt it was safe, she followed him out and it was then that she noticed a dark-cloaked man who had slipped out of the shadows of one of the massive pillars, hurrying out behind Peter whom she could see walking briskly across the cathedral green. A sharp spasm of fear gripped her heart, for she could see that the cloaked man was intent on his prey. Although he was trying to appear nonchalant, there was an intensity about his back that alerted her suspicions. And there was something else: she knew the stranger, she had seen him before. All the way home she fretted about him. Why was he following Peter? Who was he?

When she reached the house in Saddler Street, however, all speculations were driven out of her mind. The place was in an uproar and frantic Mrs Winters met her at the door.

'Thank God you're back. There's been terrible trouble. Your lady's been taken away. A man came and arrested her for debt. He's taken her to the prison.'

Helen clutched her hands together in anguish. 'What debt? There must be some mistake. She doesn't owe any money. Where's the prison? I must go to her...'

The corn merchant's wife and Helen ran together to the city lock-up where a gruff bailiff told them that Veronica Ker was indeed inside and a summons for the debt of £50 had been issued against her by a man called Jackman in London. She had no money with which to pay so she was arrested.

Helen looked completely bemused at this news. 'In London.? When could she have had fifty pounds from anyone in London? I've never heard of Jackman. I don't understand this. Please let me speak to her.'

The bailiff was not as hard as he appeared and, like so many others, felt pity for the stricken gentlewoman in the cells. 'Go on in, then,' he said. Helen ran to the door of Veronica's cell and shouted through its peep hole, 'I'm here. Miss Vee, don't worry. I'll find out what this is all about.'

Veronica's voice was remarkably controlled when she replied. 'I've been expecting something like this. It's Ker and my brother who've done it. They've been trying to force me to give up Renton's letters. Write at once to Renton and ask him to send the money or I'll have to do what they ask.'

'But you don't owe anyone fifty pounds, do you?'

'I had a debt two years ago to a moneylender in London but Thomas said it would be paid off at the time of the divorce. Obviously they haven't cleared it and now they've told the man to arrest me. There's no use pleading with them – Ker's heart is made of adamant. He won't yield until I do what he wants.'

Back in their lodgings, Helen poured their money on to the table and counted it with anxious fingers. It only came to a little over twenty guineas. Mrs Winters offered another five, and in, desperation the maid went to the home of Veronica's aunt and pleaded with the old woman to make up the deficit. When she heard what had happened, the aunt conveniently fainted away and Helen was ushered out of the house empty handed.

Back in Saddler Street again, Mrs Winter wordlessly held out a sheet of paper which the court bailiff had brought down from the lock-up.

Helen read the note. *If Mrs Ker will deliver up all the letters she ever received from Renton, I shall take upon me to settle the debt due to Mr Jackman, signed John Bogue, Edinburgh, 5th July, 1801.*

'Miss Vee's right. It's all a plot. Bogue is Ker's agent in Edinburgh. I'll have to write to Renton,' Helen told Mrs Winters. 'But he won't take any notice of a letter from a maidservant. Do you know anyone who could write an official letter for me?'

Attorney John Ward was Mrs Winters' brother and when he heard the story he immediately took up his pen and asked Helen, 'What do you want to say to him?'

'Just tell him what's happened and ask for his help.'

It was a short and to-the-point note that went to Renton:

> *I beg to inform you that Mrs Veronica Ker was arrested here on the 6th inst for a debt of £50 which is a scheme to prevail on her to give up your letters. Thomas Hay, her brother, says that nothing can be done to help her until she gives them up. The poor woman has been greatly imposed upon by her pretended friends and betrayed by her relations. You can not be so devoid of sympathy that you do not know how she must feel. Clear yourself by sending her the money to pay this debt otherwise she must give up your letters and this she does not want to do. Signed John Ward, Attorney in Durham.*

-

The Durham prison for common debtors was housed in a grim building up an alleyway off the main square. When Helen walked towards it carrying a bowl of soup, she could hear the yells of people incarcerated there, and shook her head in sorrow that her dear mistress was reduced to such a desperate situation.

The jailer knew her by now and he held the heavy wooden door open with something like respect. Veronica was in a cell on her own, a privilege granted to her through the intercession of Margaret Winters who had many friends in high positions in Durham.

Veronica was huddling down in a corner among deep straw when Helen went in and the girl thought that she looked like a wounded animal – perhaps a hind that had been shot and abandoned by a cruel hunter. Her lovely hair was loose and undressed and her stained grey satin gown dotted with frivolous ribbons and loops looked incongruous in such a setting.

'I've brought you food,' said Helen gently, going across to the crouching figure. 'Sit up and eat it, please.' Veronica lifted her ravaged face. 'Has he written? Has he come?'

'No. Please eat.'

'I can't eat.'

'You must or you'll die.'

'That would be best. No one would grieve for me.' The maid put down a firm hand and lifted Veronica to her feet. 'I'd care. Eat this for me.'

The plate was almost empty when the jailer came to the door and announced, 'There's a man come to see the lady.'

Immediately Veronica changed, straightening her back, life returning to her face. Putting up a hand to arrange her hair, she said, 'I will see him. Send him in.'

But despondency returned when the man who entered was not Renton but a coarse, red-faced man who had often been at Broadmeadows: John Bogue.

He had no graces and no discretion, and without lowering his voice he told Veronica, 'If you give me the letters, I'll pay the fifty pounds and you'll be let out of here. My master thinks you'll have had enough of a prison cell by now.'

The two women stared at him and then at each other. Helen saw the conflicting emotions on Veronica's face: the defiance, then the fear; the hope and then the disillusion. Veronica looked around the cell: at the rough wooden stool and the straw-covered floor; she looked at the wooden shelf that served her as a bed and at the anxious face of her maidservant. It was to Helen that she spoke.

'In my travelling box there is a bundle of letters. Bring them to me, please.'

Helen ran all the way to the lodgings and all the way back. When she handed the sheaf over to Veronica, there was such a pain in her side that she could hardly breathe. Without reading them, Veronica handed the bundle over to John Bogue who smiled triumphantly and gave a money draft for £50 to the jailer, who had been watching the drama with unconcealed curiosity.

When Bogue strode away down the stairs without a word of farewell, the jailer said to Helen, 'You can take your lady home now.'

The journey back to Saddler Street was slow, with Veronica leaning heavily on her maid's arm. She said nothing till they were within a few yards of their door, when she asked, 'Did you bring them all?'

'I left out the poems,' said Helen, who knew how much they meant to Veronica.

–

Though it was high summer, a terrible sense of dread descended on the normally resilient Helen. Day after day shut up in their room with a despondent – and often unfortunately drunk – Veronica was too much to bear, so she wandered the river banks of Durham picking wild flowers.

She longed for Peter but he had disappeared completely. Going to the cathedral made her unhappy because he was not there. Its soaring roof now looked dark and threatening; its music seemed like an endless dirge without him.

As she walked she did sums in her head. How much money was left? How long would it last? Without Peter's help something had to be done if they were not to starve. Margaret Whiters was kind but it was impossible to rely on her benevolence for ever. Sitting under the trees and watching the river flow past her feet, Helen determined to take the burden on her own shoulders.

Margaret Whiters was bending over a big leather-bound ledger in the back shop when Helen reached home that night. When she heard the girl enter, Margaret raised a worried face and said, 'I can't be in the shop and do the books at the same time. I find them so difficult but my husband's not well, he has a bad cough and his chest's wheezing.'

Helen grasped the opportunity. 'I can write a clear hand and I'm very good at keeping accounts. Old Mrs Ker at Broadmeadows trained me up. I could do that work for you.'

Margaret had a deep respect for the girl and she hesitated only for a moment. 'All right. I'll let you try. If you keep them well, I'll not take any lodging money from you.'

—

She kept them so well, with such meticulous attention, that other shopkeepers in Saddler Street starting bringing their account books for her to add up the columns of figures and send out their bills. This work was both a means of earning money and a way of filling her mind, so that she had no time to brood on the possibility of Peter having been hung as a highwayman. She also did not notice that Veronica seemed preoccupied with some project which she would not discuss with her maid.

Secretly, when the maid was out, Veronica was writing to Renton, covering page after page with her careless scrawl. She had already arranged for one of the corn merchant's assistants to take her letter to the post office, and she no longer cared whether spies in Berwick would recognize her hand on the cover. It was important to explain to him – to make him understand her desperate position – to tell him her greatest secret:

> *My Dear Friend, I positively refused to give up the letters till I was obliged. On Tuesday when the man arrived from town my poor unhappy fluttered heart, the demand was for your letters or no mercy was to be found, what could I then do? No letter from you my dear friend. I waited till the last moment but still I wished to deal with honour with you. They paid the debt. Renton write, do write to tell me the reason for your conduct.*

I can win your case for you but what I am about to tell you must be kept secret and not made public for it would hurt my children My poor heart trembles yet I depend on your honour, I never was Mr Ker's lawful wife, I was married at seventeen to a young gentleman who my friends had in though for reasons they never knew it, I was forced to marry Mr Ker without mercy, think then my dear friend what were my feelings.

A few days after he was gone they told me the ship was lost he was in Poor Man I cry Day and Night for his loss. On my knees I confessed to my mother. She but begged me to be silent as it was all over and that now there was no saving my husband, her good advice had the effect but still my health suffered in the cause when Mr Ker made his address in my brother's orders I was obliged to give my hand, think then of my feelings yet I believed he was dead. Cruel now I believe he is still in life and for all he suffered he has suffered more on my account, it would hurt my children, be secret my love and don't let a word of this transpire. I am my dear friend yours VK.

Renton was in Edinburgh, at his new home in George Street, when the letter arrived at Mordington but it was directed on to him. He, left it lying for a long time on the table at his bedside for he was tired of her complaints: *Why have you not written to me? Do you still love me? Have you forgotten all the things we did together?* Eventually, his face betraying annoyance, he reached out for the letter, roughly slitting the seal. Why was it that women were less realistic about passion than men? The affair had run its course. Why did she not accept that with grace? It would be a bitter blow to pay out a fortune of money for having seduced a woman that one no longer lusted after... He had to find a way out of that.

As his eye ran down the pages of scrawled writing, however, he sat up in attention. This was not her usual letter. This was something very different. He read it again and then jumped to his feet.

In MacKenzie's office he flung the pages down on the desk, almost crowing in delight. 'Look at this, read it, what do you think? I think it means we've won.'

The lawyer carefully adjusted his gold-rimmed spectacles and lifted the paper. 'It has to be read aloud to make sense of it,' he commented.

Renton, striding up and down, turned abruptly. 'Then read it aloud – in court. But she hasn't told me all. I'll have to force her to reveal his name, where he can be found. If we can persuade him to give evidence, Ker is damned.'

'But she asks you to keep it secret...' Even MacKenzie felt it callous to ignore her plea.

'If she wanted it to be kept secret, she should never have told me. I'll have to make it public if I'm to see Ker off.'

'Perhaps we should warn him of the consequences if he continues with his case. Perhaps that's why she's told you. To give you a weapon to use in private,' offered the lawyer.

'Send a letter to Ker, then, but I'm going to see her. I have to find out more about this, none of those hints and whispers. I'll ferret out all of it, she'll tell me the truth.'

MacKenzie glanced over his glasses and warned, 'Be careful. Don't promise anything.'

'I'm not a madman,' said Renton.

MacKenzie's letter to Ker's lawyer was short and menacing. It said that new information about the situation had come to light and he would be under the disagreeable necessity of making it public to the world as a defence or mitigation against Ker's claim for enormous damages.

John Ker committed his most grievous error of judgement when he instructed his lawyer to ignore the threat. 'Tell them to go to hell. We'll fight on,' he ordered.

–

Alexander Renton had reached thirty-eight years of age and, though he was still enjoying bachelorhood, his mind had turned to the necessity of providing an heir for his estates.

'I'm going to have to find a bride,' he told his lawyer. 'This damned suit has cost me dear. She'll have to be a girl with money.'

His sister, a woman of fashion, kept a house in Edinburgh and moved in the highest society.

'I'm looking for a wife,' he told her over the tea cups. 'She has to be young – pretty if possible – and she has to have a good income…'

'Then you must go into society, attend the balls and soirées,' she said. 'I'll arrange it.'

Dressed in his finest clothes, he cut a dashing figure. The young ladies fluttered like cage birds at his approach, and the eagle-eyed dowagers responded to his charm as he sat beside them, flattering them with his golden tongue – and finding out how much every girl was worth.

At the Grand Ball in the New Assembly Rooms fronting on to George Street, he moved with the bucks, taller than any of them and far more confident.

In one of the anterooms he brushed past Dr Thomas Hay, who stared after him with open hatred. 'That seducer, that rake. He's without shame or discretion,' he said angrily to his wife. His anger was not for his sister but for her husband and the Hay family reputation. It galled him to see all Edinburgh fawning on Renton, though many of them knew the story of the Ker divorce.

'He can afford to be,' she said, fanning herself, 'he's rich. Your sister should not have been such a fool, but it's easy to see why when you compare him with Ker, isn't it?'

–

As he danced and flirted, picking out a bride for himself, Renton gave little thought to Veronica. He had loved her once

– he had certainly lusted after her – but that was finished. Yet, the business had to be concluded before he could finalize his plans to marry the only daughter and heiress of a large landowner in the West of Scotland who had taken his eye at the Michaelmas Ball.

He wrote a honeyed letter of assignation to Veronica, suggesting a meeting at an inn in Newcastle where neither of them would be known. As he made the arrangements he felt a voluptuous kind of anticipation and could not resist slipping in an erotic note: *Don't forget to wear the black habit, you know what an effect it has on me.* What was the harm in making the meeting enjoyable?

His letter arrived on a sunny morning before Veronica was out of bed. Helen almost hid it, but her conscience made her carry it up the stairs from the sweet-smelling shop with its bins of oats and corn. She laid it on Veronica's pillow and said shortly, 'He's written to you at last.'

The change that came about, when the short letter was torn open was almost miraculous. Veronica's skin glowed as in the past; her hair seemed to spring up with new life and vigour as she pushed it back from her excited face. She looked young and agile again as she jumped out of bed and ran across to her trunk. 'Where's my black riding habit? He wants me to meet him in Newcastle – and he specially asks that I wear the black habit.'

–

Next day Helen felt full of dread when, looking like a triumphant Diana with cheeks flushed and eyes sparkling, Veronica rode off to keep her tryst. She had the horse galloping within yards of leaving the stableyard gate.

She arrived back in Durham jubilant, transformed by the certainty that he loved her, he loved her yet. All her fears were stilled after the day and night they had spent together. When they parted she had promised that she would try to remember every detail about her husband Henry Stewart, and would write to Renton. He kissed her fondly and gave her some money, which she tried to refuse but allowed herself to be persuaded to keep.

'You'll remember where Stewart can be found now, won't you?' he had persisted, and she had smiled. 'Perhaps.' It was a pleasure to know that she had such power over him. He wanted her information so much that she could dangle it in front of him like a bait.

The elation that gripped Veronica worried Helen as much as the old depression had done. Her mistress was acting very strangely, as if hiding a secret, and the maid resented the change in their relationship.

Eventually she challenged Veronica. 'Why haven't you told me what happened at Newcastle?'

'We met. That was all. It was lovely to see my dear Renton again.'

'Did he say he'd help you? Did he have any suggestions about the future?'

'We must wait – to see how things turn out.'

'What things? What do you mean?'

Veronica was standing at the side of her bed and now she turned slowly and faced Helen. Her mood changed as she said slowly, 'I don't want to make my children bastards, Helen.'

The women stared silently at each other and Helen's mind was alive with memories of little Edward and Elizabeth whom she had looked after with such care. Her heart gave a wrench of pain.

'They're not bastards. What do you mean?'

Veronica wanted to unload her secret now. 'When I married their father, I was already a married woman. The marriage with Ker was invalid. That would win Renton's case if it came out in court.'

'For God's sake, you didn't tell him that?' asked the maid in horror.

'Yes, I did. I told him about Henry Stewart.'

'Henry Stewart?' Helen's mind went back to the summer when she had followed Veronica and watched her meeting the blond young man. His name had been Henry Stewart... 'But he disappeared. He was sent away to India, wasn't he?'

Veronica was weeping, wiping her tears from her eyes with trembling hands. 'Oh, they should have left us alone. If they had, none of this would have happened, would it? When he knew they were sending him away, he persuaded me to marry him in front of a clergyman in his sister's house.' She took her hands from her eyes and looked to see Helen's reaction. 'Would you believe it, Helen, the clergyman who married me to Stewart was the same one who married me to Ker? MacRoberts was his name.'

Helen was not sure if she was meant to take this story seriously, and she made a noise of scoffing disapproval. 'I'd believe anything of some of those Edinburgh ministers.' As she spoke she had a sudden vivid memory of the glum-looking cleric who'd conducted Veronica's marriage ceremony in Lady Huntingdon's flat. If what she was hearing was true, no wonder he looked so depressed!

'But I can't understand this. Why did you marry Ker when you were married already?'

'They made me do it. Thomas owed old Ker money – though I didn't know that then. And they told me Stewart was dead, his ship lost.'

'But this means that Ker can't sue for damages if you were never legally his wife. He couldn't even sue you for divorce, by rights. Why did you not speak out then?'

'How could I, and what point would there have been? I wanted rid of him. My brother said he could go to prison if it was found out – I didn't know if it was true, but he's my brother... And, worst of all, my children would be bastards. I couldn't do that to them.'

'And now you have,' said Helen flatly. 'Let's hope he keeps his counsel and doesn't drag it out in court.'

Veronica still refused to hear ill of him. 'Oh Helen, he loves me. He truly loves me. If you only knew the things he said in Newcastle. I know that he'll come for me when all this is over. It's just that he cannot do it at the moment or his case'll be lost. I had to help him, it doesn't matter what you say. He's promised that he won't make it public. He'll only use it to force Ker to give up the case. He promised me that he'd take care not to besmirch my children,' she protested.

'And do you seriously think that Ker'll give it up? You lived with him for nine years but you don't know him if you think that. Renton's promise will be worth nothing if he's faced with a bill for twenty thousand pounds. Do you really think that he'll keep such a story to himself if it means he'll lose his case unless he tells?' asked the angry maidservant.

But Veronica was not convinced. She believed in her lover and thought that if she made it possible for him to defeat Ker, they would be together at last. Her months of loneliness and poverty-stricken exile in Durham would come to an end.

The investigators sent out by Renton's lawyer in pursuit of Henry Stewart had only limited success. They discovered that in some details at least Veronica had been speaking the truth, for they traced his sister and her sea captain husband only to find that both were dead.

The Reverend MacRoberts who married her both to Stewart and to Ker was also dead.

It was impossible for anyone to question the very superior Dr Thomas Hay for he would talk to no one about his sister. After a long search Stewart was traced to Bombay where he had worked as a clerk for the East India Company, but he had stayed there, for only three years before returning, and after that he simply vanished.

Renton wrote to Veronica pleading with her to provide further details, asking her to tell him why she was so confident that he was still alive and for any documentary evidence of the original marriage or details of witnesses with whom Stewart might have shared confidences.

She wrote back: *His friend and witness was a West Indian and I do not know his name. After the marriage Mr Stewart give me a paper in which he took me for his wife but when I married Mr Ker I burned it.*

Renton and his lawyer puzzled long and hard over her replies. They could not be sure that she was telling the truth, and Renton was furious at the thought that she was either keeping something back or, what was more likely, she had no idea where Stewart was but would not admit her ignorance. In the end they decided to proceed with the revelation of her bigamous marriage, and papers were sent to Ker telling him so.

The dream ended for Veronica when her brother wrote from Edinburgh: *Your lover Renton is preparing to blacken your name as a bigamist in court. Not content with calling you a woman of loose morals, he is making you out to be a liar and a cheat. There is even talk of bringing proceedings for wrongful marriage against you. Have you any idea of what this means for your children and your husband Ker? The scandal will resound throughout Scotland.*

Renton's letters had stopped altogether. *You have used me cruelly. Write me,* she pleaded.

Finally, in an effort to shock him into replying, she sent a note saying: *It is nearly three months since we met and I dread the effects I dare say no more until I am certain but I have my fears.*

And her fears were justified. In the early morning Helen would waken to hear Miss Vee retching violently into the wash bowl by her bedside. Neither of them referred to this, though Helen watched Veronica closely and saw with despair how pale and shaken she looked. It soon became an effort for her to go out even for the short distance to the bridge over the river, where they had been in the habit of taking the air in the evenings. Her appetite dwindled and disappeared, and she was subject to fainting fits.

'You're not pregnant, tell me you're not pregnant,' pleaded Helen at last.

In a burst of sobs, Veronica nodded. 'I am. It's true. I think I'm having his child and he's abandoned me completely.'

Helen put her hands to her head in an attitude of despair. 'Oh my God, you should have taken care. Why did you not take care? Why did you go to bed with him at all?'

Veronica shook her head. 'I thought I was safe. I hadn't any monthly bleedings for a long time… I thought they were finished. And when we met, it was so wonderful. I couldn't deny him and I had no thought of taking care… Perhaps when he knows I'm having his child, he'll come to me.'

As she saw Helen's disbelief, Veronica wondered if she had any idea of what it was like to be swept along on a riptide of passion. It struck her that she still knew very little of her maid's life – had she a beau yet? Did she long for marriage and children? This stalwart little person who stood beside her with such an angry face was keeping her, working as a scribe and book keeper for local businesses and being paid in food, fuel and clothing. Thomas' stipend had ceased and would not be continued unless she agreed to go to Lisbon. They were poor, really poor, and what money they ever had came from Helen now.

Suddenly Veronica was afraid, very afraid, and she reached out her hand to grasp Helen's. 'You won't leave me, will you? I've no one to turn to. Don't leave me, Helen. What are we to do? How will we live?'

'We'll fight for your rights, that's what we'll do,' said Helen.

Back to attorney John Ward she went, her face tight with fury, and told her story. The kindly man returned with her to the lodging and sat beside Veronica's bed listening to her. She lay propped up by pillows, her swelling belly giving away the advance of her pregnancy, and turned the packet of Renton's remaining letters over and over in her fingers as she talked. Nothing else seemed to interest her any more – not the newspapers with their fashion columns, not the little bits of gossip that Helen brought in from downstairs. She had reached the nadir of her fortunes.

'I can't believe that he'd betray my trust,' she told Ward, 'I've been reading his letters. Listen to this: *You are safe in my hands*

– nothing on earth would tempt me to make the smallest use of any information you furnish me with – Fear nothing…'

'I'll write to him and tell him how sadly you are placed,' Ward offered.

'I don't want to threaten him. That would antagonize him completely. There must be a reason why he hasn't written to me. It must be because of the case.'

'Do you want to tell him that you're carrying his baby?'

She shook her head. 'No. I've already hinted that may be the case and now I'm waiting… He'll write me tomorrow, I'm sure.'

But Ward decided to write a letter anyway, a plea for help for a woman who, in his mind, deserved better treatment than she had been accorded by everyone except her maid. This time there was a note of genuine involvement in his words, it was not just a business missive:

> *I think I am duty bound to inform you that Mrs Ker is threatened with a decline. She is badly in need of funds and if remedy does not come Lisbon is the last resort. We strongly suspect that there is something affecting Mrs Ker's mind but she is as silent as the grave and is of a mild and gentle disposition which never seems willing to give pain to anybody. By her maid I am informed that she has suffered many hardships but never a word from herself. I have directed other letters to you sir and I would suppose that you was her friend therefore I think it is right that you should write and advise her how to act. She does not know that I am applying to you. I beg an answer by return of post…*

Renton sent a money draft for £10 but no letter. In the same week's *Edinburgh Advertiser* the betrothal was announced of Sir Alexander Renton to eighteen-year-old Miss Susannah Simpson, only daughter and sole heiress to the vast estates of a wealthy landowner in the West of Scotland. It was an advantageous marriage, the uniting of two very rich families, and it was the talk of Edinburgh. Dr Thomas wasted no time in sending newspaper clippings to his sister.

Your lover's fortune is doubling with this marriage. He is even more capable of paying your husband the damages he owes for seducing you from your marital duties. Perhaps now you can see that you put your faith in the wrong man, wrote her brother.

Veronica lay in bed, bloodless and without reaction to any of the blows that rained down on her.

As Helen bustled about trying to make her mistress eat, trying to breathe some life and hope into her, her anger was so strong that it almost choked her. So many people were washing their hands of poor Miss Vee – they had dropped her like a broken doll and now they wanted free of their responsibilities towards her.

–

'Will you watch my mistress while I go north to try to find some help for her?' Helen asked Margaret Winters. She did not know exactly who to ask for help but there had to be someone who cared enough for Veronica to save her from starving to death.

As she travelled to Berwick on the mail coach, remembering the night of the highwayman, her mind dwelt on Peter. Where was he now? Was he still alive? She was thinking about him, trying to imagine what his life on the road would be, when on the moor near Morpeth they passed a gibbet with an emaciated body in tattered clothes swinging from its rope. The other passengers leaned forward at the windows and speculated about the dead man but Helen did not join in. She had to turn her head away for fear that it would be Peter hanging there. But then she had to look, had to know – and it was not him.

Berwick was as busy and as full of soldiery as ever when she alighted from the coach. The loyalties of Veronica's old friends had swung over to Ker – some of them because they owed him a favour and others because he was one of themselves, a local man.

Dr Kellock, on whom she had relied, refused to listen to Helen's plea for help. 'I want nothing to do with her,' he said, 'I don't want to be hauled up in court again on any account.'

He had already been called as a witness on Renton's behalf, in an attempt to prove that Veronica had been morally lax when she was living in Berwick, and the experience rankled. The gossip it had caused was only just beginning to die down, and no one believed him when he swore that she and he had never been lovers.

How quickly love and desire were forgotten, reflected the girl as she turned away from his house, for she well remembered the doctor's look of starry adoration in the days when he came calling on the adorable Mrs Ker.

Her next stop was at Broadmeadows where the staff took her into the kitchen and crowded round with questions. Distance and time lend enchantment, and in the minds of the maids and Mrs Eliot, Veronica had taken on the status of heroine. After all she had been a considerate and undemanding employer – for more so than the penny-pinching Susan.

'How's the poor mistress?' asked the cook.

'She's sick,' Helen said, careful not to reveal anything about the baby.

'Oh poor soul, and who's looking after her?'

'We've a kind landlady. But I've come up to ask her husband to give her some money. She's badly in need.'

'What about Renton?'

Helen wordlessly shook her head and the servants nodded in understanding. 'Oh, they're an evil family, the Rentons… there's an old rhyme about them: "Renton Barns and Renton Bell, Harelaw side and Renton cell, the de'il tak them all that in them dwell"…' said Mrs Eliot.

'We heard he's marrying soon,' said Christine Branxton.

'Aye, so we heard,' agreed the cook, 'a rich lassie with even more land than he has. Does the mistress know?'

Helen nodded. 'Yes, she knows.'

'Oh, the poor mistress,' chorused the maids who once had not a good word to say for Veronica.

—

John Ker and Susan were finishing a meagre supper when Helen was shown into the parlour. They stared at her as if at a ghost, and Susan was the first to speak.

'What do *you* want?'

'I've come to ask a favour,' said the girl.

Ker lifted his red face from his plate and fixed wounded eyes on her. 'What sort of favour?'

'My mistress is sick and she has no money. In God's name can you spare a few pounds for her, sir?'

'Your mistress is no concern of my brother's,' said Susan sharply. 'Their marriage is finished, she has no call on him now. She's ruined my brother. The court case has cost him a fortune… she's ruined us all.' There was a note of hysteria in her voice, and a brilliant little spot of scarlet burned in the middle of each cheek.

Ker was staring at his plate again and Helen wished she could have found him on his own. From the way he slumped into his chair she could tell that he was torn in his feelings, and if they had been alone she might have persuaded him to help Veronica.

But Susan was in charge now and she rose in a fury, pointing a knife at Helen. 'Leave this house right now. Take yourself off down that road. You're as big a whore as your mistress.'

'Can't I see the children?' asked Helen, backing towards the door.

Susan let out a screech. 'Don't you let me see you near the children. They don't want to know anything about their mother.'

'But I love them very much and I'm sure they'd remember me.'

It was useless. 'Certainly not! Certainly not! Such shame she's brought on them. My brother's going to have to abandon his case just so they won't be publicly branded as bastards. He cares for his children, their mother cares nothing. They know what she's worth. They don't want anything to do with her or her maid.'

Mrs Eliot was waiting in the kitchen passage when Helen came out of the parlour wiping her eyes with the backs of her hands.

'Don't cry, lassie,' she whispered, 'I'll take you up to see the bairns. But for God's sake be quick, she'd kill me if she knew.'

Though Edward spent his time outdoors, six-year-old Elizabeth continued to live most of her life in her old nursery. She was kneeling on the window seat staring out when Helen pushed open the door.

'Oh, you've grown so tall,' cried the maid and rushed forward to grasp the girl in her arms.

Elizabeth was a Ker, heavy like her father with his rosy cheeks and turned-up nose but she had a trusting, tender look in her big blue eyes and she recognized Helen at once. They clung to each other and wept with emotion for a few minutes before. Elizabeth stood back and said, 'Has anyone sent for Edward? He'll be in the yard. I hope he knows you're here, Helen.'

'Smith went to get him, I think,' said Helen. 'Oh, my dear, let me look at you. Are you happy, sweet? I'll tell your mother I've seen you. She misses you very much and cries for you so often.'

Behind her a boy's voice said, 'She doesn't. That's a lie, she doesn't care for us. She left us so that she could go away with Renton from Mordington. Aunt Susan told us all about it.'

Helen turned and stared at the boy in the doorway, such a handsome boy, with his mother's brown hair and well-bred features, the long nose and the sweetly curving lips.

'Edward,' she entreated and stepped, towards him to hug him, but he drew away.

'What do you want, Helen?' he asked in a hostile tone. 'Why's she sent you here?'

His sister looked confused now, staring from one to the other. 'Why doesn't Mama come back?' she asked.

Helen shook her head. 'It's because she's not allowed to – your father won't let her into the house. But, oh how she longs to see you both. When you're bigger you can go to see her.'

'We'll never go to see her, we don't want to see her,' said Edward, putting an arm protectively around his sister's shoulders as if he feared that Helen would take her away.

'Edward, don't be so bitter. Your mother does love you. I swear it. She loves you and she loves Elizabeth and she longs for the day when she can see you again.'

But Susan's persistent poison had affected Edward too deeply. He remembered the terrible day when his mother left, and ever since then he had felt betrayed by her. His heart, as his mother had said of his father, was made of adamant as far as she was concerned.

'Go away, Helen, we don't want you here. We don't want to hear anything about our mother. She's gone. We don't care if she never comes back again.'

–

William Smith saw her tears as she re-entered the kitchen. 'You can't go back to Berwick now, it's too late,' he told her. 'They can't keep you in the house in case Miss Susan finds out, but you can sleep in the hay loft. It's warm and quiet and I'll make sure you're not bothered by any of the laddies.'

In spite of her tiredness and unhappiness, she slept soundly, burrowed like an animal in piles of sweet-smelling hay that tickled her nose and made her wake up sneezing.

She lay quietly for a while, listening to the noises of men working in the carthorse stables beneath her, but soon the trap door opened and William's head peeped through. 'The coast's clear, run across to the kitchen and Mrs Eliot'll give you something to eat, but then you'll have to be out of here. Where are you going now? Back to Durham?'

'I don't know. I came to find some help for Miss Vee but I've not been very successful. It seemed a good idea at the time – she had so many friends and she's so in need…'

William still had only his head, showing at floor level but she could see that he too was sorry for Veronica. 'It's a bad business. Poor woman. Have you tried Mordington? Sir Alexander's over there now, and surely all this is his responsibility. He's the one who ought to help her.'

After eating she set out to walk the four miles to Mordington Hall along the pretty lanes, bare of leaves now, that Veronica used to travel to keep her illicit trysts.

The gatehouse at Mordington was unmanned and the gate was swinging half open as if the keeper had been urgently called away on some business. Pushing through, the girl slipped in unseen and trudged up the drive that curved elegantly for nearly half a mile before the house came into view. There was a frenzy of activity going on at the front portico, men were rushing in and out with planks and paint brushes. Framed in the doorway stood Sir Alex who had come down to see that his project of redecoration and refurbishment for the reception of his young bride was well under way.

He had a good memory for faces and knew at once that the young woman staring up at him from the gravel drive was Veronica Ker's maid but he kept his composure, running a bold eye up and down her like a man appraising a horse. 'Quite a neat little thing with a pretty face, a good armful. And a full and luscious mouth – pity I've not the time to waste with her now,' said his confident stare.

She stood looking at him with equal boldness and said, 'Good morning, sir.'

'What's your business?'

'I came to tell you that my lady is ill and has no money.' Renton's lawyer had only two days before told him that there were rumours of Ker's intention to draw out of the case. His rival in the courts had not only taken fright at the prospect of dirty linen about his wife's previous marriage being washed in public, but had run out of money and was on the verge of bankruptcy. Knowing that if the case foundered, he could put the whole thing behind him made Renton indifferent to what had happened in the past. He was not prepared to waste any more time or worry on Veronica Ker.

'I'm sorry to hear that, but I'm not able to help her, I'm afraid,' he said.

The girl stared hard at his arrogant face, her blue eyes blazing like the eyes of a furious cat, but her tone was mild. 'You're to be married, sir?' she asked.

'Yes,' was the short reply and he was on the verge of turning away when she suddenly stopped him with a flashing look of such hatred that it rooted him to the spot.

'And in a few days you'll become a father,' she announced.

He reeled. Veronica had written rambling drunken letters hinting that she was pregnant, but he thought it another of her stratagems for gaining his attention. He had ignored the letters and they had ceased. He hadn't heard from her for many weeks.

'Clear off my land, be off or I'll set the dogs on you. She's no proof that I'm the father. It could be anybody.'

He put his hand in his pocket, pulled out some money, and raised the hand threateningly.

The girl took a step back and the money fell on the ground between them like golden rain. She looked down at it and knew how much it would ease their lives if she were only to bend down and pick it up, but she could not do it. She could not stoop in front of this scornful man and gather up his money no matter how much it was needed. Her practicality fought hard with her pride, but the pride won and with a flashing look that seemed to pass right through him like a bolt of ice, she turned on her heel and walked away, leaving the money at his feet.

With a bland face and a bright smile, Helen lied to Veronica.

'The children are looking well. Edward's grown so tall and handsome! Elizabeth's very pretty. And clever with her needle, Mrs Eliot told me. They sent you all their love and they each gave me a kiss for you. They remember you very well. You'd be so proud of them...'

Veronica lay in bed, a waxen ghost, drinking in the story. She was avid for every detail that Helen could remember about her children.

'What were they wearing? Tell me exactly. What colour is Elizabeth's hair now? Still butter yellow, I hope. Has that little red birthmark on the back of her neck gone away? Does Edward still dream about witches? I hope Susan lets him have a night light. She said I was stupid to indulge him so... Oh God, if I could only see them again. If I could only hold them...'

Helen ignored any signs of tears and kept on being bright and businesslike. 'Your Edward's grown into a real little man. He wouldn't need a night light any longer. And Elizabeth's hair's a golden colour, all in lovely tight curls, like yours.'

The description of them made Veronica's tears flow more copiously. 'Oh, I miss them so much. It's a terrible pain inside me. I've brought all this on myself. I wish I was dead.'

-

The labour, when it started ten days later, was surprisingly easy considering the anguish of the waiting months. Veronica had her first pains in the early morning and by noon, with the assistance of a friend of Margaret Winters and Helen, baby Charlotte Louisa was born. From the beginning she was a placid child – and again that was surprising for her mother had fretted her way through the pregnancy. But Veronica had no milk, for she had grown so thin that her once fine breasts seemed to have sunk into her chest, so a wet nurse was found whose own baby had died, aged only a few weeks and who was brimming over with nourishment for the sweet-faced baby with its tight-fitting cap of dark hair, its long elegant hands and feet. Helen and the nurse exclaimed in admiration at the perfection of the child but when they tried to display her to Veronica they were met with blank indifference.

'I don't want to see her now, take her away,' she said, turning her face into the pillow.

From the beginning it fell to Helen to dress and bathe the child, to carry her out into the sunshine and cuddle and play with her. She knew that she was giving all her pent-up love to this unwanted baby, and that she was once again putting herself into a position of terrible vulnerability. Like Edward and Elizabeth, Charlotte was not her own child and could be taken away from her.

--

At Broadmeadows, John Ker was shut up with his advisers. 'Renton's determined to try to prove your wife was already married when she went through the ceremony with you. His people say that even though they can't produce the man, there's enough evidence to support it, but I'm not so sure. I think we could fight. Unless they find Stewart – and they haven't traced him – their case is shaky,' said his lawyer.

Ker shook his head. 'I'm stopping the case. I'm withdrawing. I can't risk this news spreading about. There's my children to think of. My son and daughter would be bastards…'

The lawyer looked sceptical. 'There's enough talk around now,' he said.

But Ker was determined. 'No, it's all just rumour. If we let it come out in court the whole world would know for sure – and Edward and Elizabeth themselves would find out. No, I'm withdrawing.'

'But their case is not sure unless they can produce Stewart. And this has cost you a fortune. With Renton it's come off a broad back, but you've had to raise so much money – and you had to give up your muster master position too. It seems a pity to have gone in so deep and come out now.'

'If I don't come out it'll cost me more, won't it? But it's the bairns that matter most.' The heavy farmer thumped his fists on the table in frustration. 'From the day I set eyes on that woman, I've had nothing but trouble. She's ruined me.'

In confusion he thought about his troubled affairs – the debts, the heavy outgoings, the summonses for unpaid bills. It was true, he was deeply in debt. He began divorce proceedings with a borrowing of £300 from a neighbouring farmer; then, to pay that back, he borrowed another £600 from a colonel of the Dragoons who demanded a high rate of interest. So it had gone on, borrowing to repay debts, borrowing to meet new expenses until he was engulfed by liabilities of more than seven thousand pounds – and every day the sum was growing.

'Give notice that I'm dropping the damages suit against Renton,' he told his lawyer.

–

The financial position of the two women and the baby in Durham was beggarly, depending entirely on the pittance Helen earned. When there were only a few coins in her purse she regretted her gesture of defiance towards Renton and thought longingly of the money that she had spurned. Veronica was still ill, lying weakly in bed, and Helen was sadly wrapping Charlotte up in her old plaid for warmth one grey morning when Margaret Winters came up the stairs.

'Helen, oh, Helen! I didn't know you had a suitor. A fine-looking young fellow came to the door this morning before you were awake. He said he'd wait for you in the cathedral.'

Helen's heart beat so fast that for a moment she thought she might faint. Putting one hand on the table for support, she whispered, 'Did he say when?'

'No, he just said in the cathedral.' The goodwife had a romantic heart and thought it a fine trysting place. Besides she admired the staunch Helen and had thought for some time that the girl ought to have a man to look after her.

As soon as she could, Helen wrapped Charlotte tightly to her breast beneath the plaid and set out up the hill, keeping the tall spires of the cathedral in view as she walked. Her heart was singing a happy refrain: Peter's back, Peter's alive. It must be him who's waiting there for me.

Her joy was intense, not only because she knew he would help her, but by her delight to be seeing him again, safe and well. Yet the exaltation that filled her as she walked along confused her, for she mistrusted love. What was wrong with her? All her life she had watched people fall victim to love's wiles and she deplored the abandonment of common sense that it always brought to them. She dreaded being caught up in love's toils, yet all her troubles seemed miraculously left behind in Saddler Street and she glowed with anticipation.

The sweet smell of incense met her at the church door and made her already heightened senses swim. Inside it was dark because the day was overcast and only a few candles guttered in their sconces. There was no one in any of the pews as she walked slowly down the side aisle, so she turned and began looking for him in the side chapels, but the cathedral seemed empty and echoing. No one was there. Heart sinking she walked right round and was about to leave when she heard a soft whisper: '*Mo ghaoil, mo ghaoil…*'

In a dark cloak and with a hat pulled down over his face, he stood beside a shadowed tomb in the darkest corner. With a stifled sob she rushed towards him and he hugged her tight, holding her and the baby to him with gloved hands. She stood in his arms for a long time with her face against his chest, listening with a deep feeling of peace to the slow thudding of his heart. Then, at last, she slowly drew away to ask him, 'What's wrong, Peter? Why are you hiding?'

His face was tired and worried. 'There's a man after me. He's one of those thief-takers from London. They're paid a bounty of forty pounds if they turn in a highwayman. He's been following me for months, at my heels all the time, ever since the last time we met here. That's why I've not been able to come back, he knows that I have an interest in Durham.'

'But is it safe to be here now?' She glanced over her shoulder to see if anyone had come into the church behind her but it still seemed deserted.

'I can't stay long, but I wanted to see you. I've brought some money for you. I heard that your lady was ill and that the damages case is all over. Her husband's so burdened with debt that he could lose his lands as a result.

She nodded. 'It's brought sorrow to everyone – except Renton. He's the only winner.'

Peter gave a short bitter laugh. 'People like him usually are… By the way, whose is the baby?'

Charlotte, who had been sleeping in Helen's arms even during the embrace with Peter, woke up and gave a few happy gurgles, glad to be so closely cuddled and sensing the love that flowed around her.

'She's not mine, if that's what you're thinking. She's Miss Vee's – and Renton's – but he won't acknowledge her, of course.' With one hand she proudly drew back the shawl from the baby's face.

Peter laughed more happily this time. 'She's going to take after her mother and be a beauty. I hope she has more luck with it.'

'I love her,' said Helen, looking at the baby with adoring eyes. 'She's a wonderful baby. She has Miss Vee's nature – so sweet and loving.'

'So now you've got three mouths to feed have you, my little treasure?' said Peter, reaching into his pocket and pulling out a pouch. 'Here, take this. It's what I came to give you.'

She was reluctant to take the money, though she needed it badly, 'Perhaps you should keep it if you're on the run. You might need it yourself,' she said.

He thrust it at her. 'I can always find more. You take it and hide it. There's forty pounds there and I've hidden more outside the city. I'll bring that to you tomorrow. I had a good haul yesterday – a friend and I robbed an army wages wagon.'

As he held out the bag towards her she noticed a dirty bandage on his arm. 'Oh, you've been hurt,' she cried.

'It's nothing. We had a bit of a fight for the money.'

His dejection was more obvious now and she knew he was keeping something back. 'What happened?'

'They caught my friend. Just like Irish Jack. They'll have made him talk and they'll be looking for me now. That thief-catcher's close on my trail as well. I can't stay, Helen, I have to go but I'll be safe, I've a good hideout. I'll come back here tomorrow before I go for good. Meet me again at the same time.'

She nodded silently and pressed close to him. For the first time he kissed her on the lips and then, like a wraith, slipped out of her grasp into the shadows and disappeared.

Something told her to wait in the church for a while to give him time to depart and, shivering with nerves, she wandered around reading the names of the men buried beneath the imposing tombs. After half an hour in the chilling cold, surrounded by the dead, she thought it safe to leave but as she was pulling the heavy main door open, she was almost knocked over by a man in a hurry who came rushing through it. Like Peter he was wearing black. Like Peter, he had a hat pulled down over his eyes. He lowered his head as he passed her so she could not see his face but she felt as if she knew him and a little bell of memory rang in her mind.

Back in their lodgings Veronica had dressed for the first time since the birth of the baby and was watching from the window for their return. She was hysterically glad to see them.

'Every time you go away, I'm afraid that you're going to leave me, that you won't come back,' she said. 'The landlady said you have a beau. I'm so frightened, Helen. I don't know what to do.'

'Don't worry about it. I won't leave you,' the girl reassured her, disappointed that Veronica's anxiety did not include losing her child as well as her maid. From the very beginning she had acted as if the baby did not exist.

'But what am I going to do? Where am I to go? What's to become of us? I think I'll go to Lisbon after all. There's no other way.'

Helen did not want to go to Lisbon. If she had a choice she would go back to Edinburgh – with Peter if possible – and live there in the High Street for the rest of her life. She'd had enough of roving, and longed for the security of the close-packed ancient town that she knew so well. They had this conversation frequently, however, so she just nodded.

'Well, we don't have to do anything today. I have some money and we'll wait here till you grow a little stronger,' she said cheerfully, taking the bag of coins from her skirt pocket. 'Look at this. It's enough to keep us for a long time if we're careful.'

She pulled open the string that bound the neck of the pouch and poured the coins on to the table.

Veronica asked, 'Where did it come from?'

Helen decided to tell her about Peter.

'From the beau the landlady said I had. He's the one who sent money to us when we first arrived. Don't you remember, it came in a little box? He held up the coach we were in – you remember the highwayman? Well it was Peter Grant, Deacon Brodie's son. He's an old friend of mine from Edinburgh.'

Veronica was wide-eyed with amazement. 'So the box of money that I thought was from Renton came from the Deacon's son! Which of the Deacon's boys are you talking about? The Cant's Close ones or the Libberton's Wynd ones?'

234

'Cant's Close. Anne Grant's eldest boy.'

With a pale hand, Veronica stirred the heap of coins. 'How amazing. What a surprise. He must care about you a great deal, Helen.'

She shot a glance at her maid and saw the telltale look on the girl's face.

'And you care about him, don't you? It must be awful for you, having to stay here with me and knowing that you can't go with him.'

'It's not like that. I don't know how I feel about him, really. He's my friend and I worry in case he's caught but... that's all, really.' Helen's voice betrayed her confusion of feelings.

Falling in love was something Veronica Ker knew a lot about and she said wearily, 'Oh, you must be in love. It makes you feel as light as a skylark one minute and as heavy as a stone the next. Your heart almost chokes you when you think of him or catch sight of him; you dream about him at night and your body yearns for him all the time – that's love, that's what it feels like.'

'But there's other things to think about. I can't bear loving him so much that my world would collapse if lost him. I can't bear worrying every day in case they're going to string him up on a gibbet like his father. That would kill me. I can't open myself to that... So I've decided it's best to forget love and all its troubles. I've done well enough till now without being in love. Why should I want to cause myself all that trouble?'

Veronica pushed a strand of hair back from her face and said, 'Take it from me, try as you may, it happens, it just happens. It entangles you. It's like falling ill.'

'I'm not going to fall ill either. That's a luxury I can't afford,' said Helen, and hurried off to tend the baby.

–

When the birds were chirping their early morning chorus in the trees, Helen woke with a start and knew instinctively that Peter was waiting for her. Charlotte was still with the wet nurse for the night and Veronica was deeply asleep, so she dressed and silently let herself out of the house. A few people were starting to go about their business when she reached the cathedral, and high up in the steeple the morning bell was beginning to ring, a light-tongued bell calling the devout to early worship.

She pushed open the north door with its grinning gargoyle knocker and inside the dark, cold cavern a man in a black cassock was bustling about putting a taper to new candles. He did not notice her as she slipped into one of the pews near the high altar and buried her face in her hands. Praying was something she did very rarely. The child of a Catholic family which had ostensibly renounced its faith, she was without any true religion, but some deep yearning and belief made, her pray now.

'Hear me, hear me God if you're up there. Look after Peter. He's in danger, I can feel it and it doesn't matter if I never see him again, but look after him, keep him safe.'

She repeated the prayer inside her head over and over again and as she knelt in the pew the brightening light of the morning spilled through the stained-glass windows, gilding her hair with a halo of shining blue and gold and deepest ruby red.

After what seemed like a long time, she felt someone slip into the seat and kneel down at her side. Then a hand moved along and grasped her folded ones and Peter's voice said, 'I knew you'd come – at least I hoped you would. I've been thinking about you all night and I wondered if my thoughts would reach you.'

Without lifting her bent head she nodded and whispered, 'Yes, they did. I knew to come now. I knew you were anxious to leave Durham.'

He was whispering too though there was no one near to hear them. 'Yes, I must go. It's dangerous, will you come with me? We could easily travel together, we could go to London… they'd never find us there.'

She slid a look at him over their linked hands. 'I can't leave them,' she said softly.

'You'll have to leave some time. Your Miss Vee will find another man to look after her. She's still a fine-looking woman.'

'But the baby. Who's to care for the baby if I go?'

'The mother will care for it, surely.' He was pressing her hands urgently.

She shook her head. 'Oh no, Charlotte's mother has no love left for any more babies. Sometimes I watch her with it and I think she hates the child. She's given too much to her other children and had them taken from her. Louisa died and now she's lost Edward and Elizabeth too. She's afraid to love Charlotte, I think…'

'Come with me,' he interrupted quietly.

'I can't, I can't. I'd never have a minute's peace of mind if I did. I'd be worrying about Charlotte and Miss Vee, but worst of all, I'd always be waiting for you to be caught. I'd live in constant fear that they'd hang you.'

'I'll give up the road if that's what you're asking,' he said, 'I'll give it up when I've made enough to set myself up properly, but I have to keep on going till then – and I'll do it, I know I will.'

Helen sank her forehead on to the shelf at the front of the pew. 'I can't bear hearing you talk like this. All the men you see swinging on all the gibbets thought they'd be the ones to escape the law! I couldn't live with the fear of you being strung up too. If you hadn't been giving us money you might have had enough to stop by now, so let me give you it back. And stop, Peter, stop.'

'Not yet. I've a little longer to go and then I'll stop. Come with me, Helen. I promise I'll take care of you and in time you'll live like a lady.'

In spite of the precautions they had been taking not to be heard, her voice rose as she replied, 'I don't want to live like a lady. I don't like ladies. I'm a poor lassie from Edinburgh's High Street and I don't want to be anything else. I'm proud of where I come from and you should be proud too.'

In her passion she stood up and a watcher in the shadows moved towards her. Too late she saw him, too late she pulled Peter by the arm, crying, 'It's the man, it's the man I saw yesterday. Run for it.'

Swift as a deer, he leaped over the pew top, his cloak flowing out behind him as he headed for the sanctuary door. She ran after him, her heart pounding. They reached the door together but the pursuer was close on their heels and just as Peter hauled it open the pursuer grabbed him by the arm and cried exultantly, 'Caught you, caught you at last.' Then he pulled a long-barrelled pistol from the breast of his overcoat, and Helen felt her body stiffen with terror.

But Peter seemed suddenly very cool and self-possessed. With a smile he leaned against the red sandstone plinth at the side of the door and said, throwing up his hands, 'All right, so you've caught me. You've had a long run for your forty pounds, my friend.'

The pursuer cocked the tall trigger on the gun. 'Come on, we'll walk down the hill, just come along quietly. I don't want to have to shoot you here.'

Her brain was racing as she watched. Would it be possible for her to knock the thief-taker off his feet?

But his sharp eyes were watching her carefully too and he gestured towards her with his head. 'You can come or you can go away, please yourself. I'd go away if I were you,' he said.

'Don't take him, let him go,' she pleaded but she knew that it was useless. The thief-taker's face was jubilant and the two men stepped out of the porch and the heavy door swung closed behind them. The knocker seemed to be laughing widely at the scene enacted beneath its hollow. Its huge mouth turned up in a rictus of scornful laughter. Then, all of a sudden, she remembered the story she had been told about that knocker. Any miscreant who rattled it would be given sanctuary, they would be safe from the law. With a leap and a gasp she threw herself between the men and clanged down the ancient green clapper – once, twice, three times, using both her hands and bloodying her knuckles in the effort. The knocker's voice, silent for so long, shattered the stillness of the cathedral and everything seemed to go into suspension while the sound rang up and down the shadowed aisles. She clattered it again and then, one hand still hanging on to the clapper bar, she turned towards the startled thief-taker.

'You can't take him now – I'm asking for sanctuary for him, you can't take him. This is a holy place and they'll keep him safe.'

A trio of black-robed clerics came hurrying towards the door, shocked expressions on their faces. In scandalized surprise they looked at the two dark-clothed men in the porch, one with a gun held to the other's head; they looked with disapproval at the frantic, weeping girl clinging on to the knocker and they demanded in one voice, 'What do you think you're doing? Leave that knocker alone.'

Helen rushed towards them, gasping and pointing back at Peter. 'He wants sanctuary. Give him sanctuary. I want you to take him in like you used to do long ago!'

The senior cleric was dumbfounded. 'But – but – that doesn't happen now. It hasn't happened for at least a hundred years. Go away. Take your hands off the knocker. Go away from here, all of you. Leave the cathedral.'

Peter recovered his composure first and, ignoring his captor, doffed his hat to the angry officials and then to Helen, saying, 'Leave it be, my dear. I'll take my chance. He's caught me fair and square. Go back now to your Miss Vee and the baby. I'll be all right…'

His calmness in the face of evil fortune reminded her of the terrible day she witnessed his father's bravery on the gallows, and as the huge door was clanged shut behind her she turned in frantic desperation towards the thief-taker who was blocking their way out of the porch, half hidden by the shadows.

'Oh, let him go, let him run this time. I'll pay you everything I have if you'll only let him go.'

It seemed she had struck home, for the stranger dropped his hand holding the gun and stared fixedly at Peter, who was standing with his blond head bare and his cocked hat in his hand. For a few seconds they were all frozen in fixed attitudes like the carved figures of saints standing in niches around the walls above their heads.

The thief-taker's voice was hoarse, cracked with some unexpected emotion as he asked Peter, 'What's your real name?'

Helen looked from one man to the other as Peter turned to face his captor. 'Why? They call me the Morpeth Raider on the road, and that's all you need to know.'

'But your real name – your given name – what's that?'

'William Pitt!' snapped Peter. 'Any name you like. I'll answer to anything.'

The man with the pistol suddenly seemed less menacing. The hand holding the gun stayed lowered and the barrel was pointing at the ground. Helen saw Peter's eyes on it and guessed that he was thinking of trying to wrest it from the other man's grasp.

To give him cover she turned towards the thief-taker and said brightly, 'My name's Helen Cameron...'

He looked towards her and with a shudder she saw that his eyes, deep fringed with heavy lashes, were lustrous black and his brows were arched like a raven's wings. It was a face she had seen before, a face that haunted her dreams. It was the face of Deacon Brodie.

She had no time to signal her astonishment to Peter, for when the thief-taker saw her staring so fixedly at him, he also pulled off his deep-brimmed hat and said to Peter, 'Look at me, highwayman, don't you know me now?' Then he stood in front of them with his dark head bare and his proud eyes staring into the eyes of his brother.

In silence the two looked at each other, their faces working. Then, with a gasp, Peter took a step forward and put a hand on his brother's shoulder in exactly the same way as he had done on the day of their father's funeral.

'Andrew! My brother! My God, what a trick for fate to play on us.'

Then with a rueful laugh he stuck out both his hands, crossed them over at the wrists as if they were lashed together, and said, 'Go on, brother, take me. You've been following me for months. You've fought hard to take me.'

The dark-haired man was obviously deeply affected by their unexpected encounter and he pushed Peter's hands aside before hugging him in a tight embrace. Oblivious to watchers, they stood together in the church porch with their arms around each other for what seemed a very long time, and tears pricked Helen's eyes when she saw their shoulders shaking with the strength of their emotion.

Andrew was the first to break away, stepping slightly back from Peter and saying, 'I've hunted you for over a year. I've followed you like a terrier after a rat. I've dreamed about catching you but I'd no idea that you were my own brother. Now that I've caught up with you, I can't take you – not my own brother.'

'I'll give myself up to you,' offered Peter but Andrew shook his head.

'No, I can't take you. We have the same blood in our veins – and more than that, you're my friend. I can't take you, Peter Grant, but for God's sake go away from here before I change my mind or someone else scents you. There's a lot of them on your trail!'

He pushed Peter in the chest and pointed with his gun at a little path running towards the back of the cathedral. 'Go that way – now. There's not much time. I was with some others in the town and they'll be up here any minute.'

Helen was shocked and shaking but she gathered her wits sufficiently to join her pleadings with Andrew's and plucked at Peter's sleeve with frantic hands. 'Oh, go away, Peter, go now. Run, run for your life.'

He was still staring into his brother's face and once again he hugged him close. Then he turned to Helen and bent to kiss her on the cheek before leaping into life like a wild animal freed from a cage. She drew back against the sanctuary door and stared after him as he sprinted down the side of the cathedral, vaulted like a stag over a little wall and disappeared with a crashing of branches into the tree-filled river ravine. When the sounds of his escape died away, she turned to Andrew Watt.

'I saw you yesterday at this door and I thought I'd seen you before, but I never guessed who you really were. I'm glad it was you, Andrew. That was a fine thing you did.'

He shook his head and his lustrous eyes were bright with unshed tears. 'He's my brother. I couldn't send him to the gallows.'

They stood awkwardly staring at the gap among the bushes where Peter had disappeared.

'Do you think he'll be safe?' she whispered.

He shook his head. 'I don't know... but come on, Helen, I'll take you back to your lodging. I saw you too yesterday and I didn't recognize you either.'

'It's a good thing I told you my name then,' she said with a laugh.

'No, I'd recognized you before that. I knew who you were the minute you started shouting at those vergers. You've changed a lot, but you're still Helen Cameron from the High Street!'

-

The baby lay at her side in the bed, making soft little noises of content, and Veronica felt herself cringing away from it.

The wet nurse did not notice, fortunately, but stood with her plump arms crossed over her chest, smiling down at them. She nodded to the mother and said, 'There, I'll leave her with you till Helen gets back. I've fed her and she'll sleep. She's a lovely baby, madam.'

Veronica turned her head and tried to smile as she looked at the child. In the tiny face she could see traces of Renton and also of her dead Louisa. How sad she'd been when Louisa died – but that was all so long ago. If this scrap of humanity died, she would hardly notice.

She felt immobilized and powerless, in the grip of a terrible malaise, a smothering depression. When she first opened her eyes in the morning and stared around the bedroom, her mind felt empty. Then, one by one, the memories came creeping in, tiptoeing like thieves, each one enforcing her feeling of desolation until she was back again, deep in her blackness. Helen, Margaret Winters, the wet nurse all tried to raise her spirits but though she pretended for their sakes, though she summoned up a smile and rose to dress herself when she felt like lying in bed for ever, she was going through the motions like an actress. Inside her head the bleakness remained, the bleakness and the indifference to this baby who had become a symbol of all the bad things that had happened in her life.

To escape proximity with the child as much as anything else, she rose from bed and began to dress herself, carelessly pulling a sprigged gown out of the dome-lidded trunk in the corner of the room. The lavender smell from her dresses assailed her as she rummaged among their silk and taffeta folds; she lifted up a length of velvet and fingered its intricately stitched decorations. How lovely it was, she remembered wearing it. She found the black riding habit but pushed it back down to the bottom of the pile. Her mind darted away from the memories and she stood up wearily.

'Oh my God, I must find some brandy,' she said aloud, but though she searched in every nook and cranny, there was none. Helen had thrown out every flask that she'd hidden away.

The need for a drink and the frustration of being shut up alone with the child made her desperate and she began again pulling things out of her trunk in an effort to occupy her hands. Dresses, shoes, lace caps and fichus, flowers and feathers piled on to the floor. Finally, in the bottom of the box, she found her miniature portrait painted by Caldwell so long ago in Edinburgh. How he had admired her, how his eyes had lingered on her face as she sat proudly posing for him! She knelt on the floor staring fixedly at the picture of a lovely girl, looking enticingly and obliquely out of the deep black frame. The girl in the picture had a flashing eye and a roguish smile on her softly curving lips, and it was obvious that she was full of confidence at her ability to win hearts. The poignancy of the contrast' between what she had been and what she had become was so heart-breaking that she laid her crossed arms on the trunk wall and wept, great sobbing, wrenching agonies of tears that convulsed her body.

She was still weeping when Helen came running up the stairs, hair flying, and knelt beside her.

'Oh, stop, don't weep, I didn't leave you. I was only up at the cathedral...'

Veronica's distress was so terrible that this was not the time to start talking about her own troubles, so she soothed the crying woman, led her to a chair in the window and rushed out to prepare her a cup of chocolate, a luxury which could be enjoyed only rarely.

When a measure of calm was restored the girl was able to give some attention to the baby who slept on, a faint smile on her doll-like face. Helen bent over the bed and as she looked lovingly at the child, a feeling of consolation claimed her. A wonderful peace descended on her soul. Gently lifting the tiny, tightly wrapped bundle she pressed the child to her face. Charlotte's blue-veined eyelids fluttered softly and she sighed like a satiated puppy.

'Oh, she's an angel,' sighed Helen, lost in baby worship, 'she's just an angel, like the ones in the windows up there in the cathedral...'

Veronica was watching them with a ravaged face and it struck the girl that if she could only interest the mother in the child, it could prove a consolation for her, so she walked across and laid Charlotte in the silken lap.

'Hold her for a moment, give her a kiss. She's the dearest baby.'

Veronica stared down at the child and reluctantly lifted her up, seeming as awkward as if she had never held a baby before. She was looking intently into the child's face and her own expression betrayed a violent mixture of emotions – fear, grief, anger – and something else...

When Helen realized that her mistress was pressing the child tighter and tighter into her breast, that her hands were growing white with the effort, she quickly snatched Charlotte away. The baby was crying at being handled so roughly and had to be soothed, and all the time Helen was walking up and down consoling the sobbing child, Veronica sat like a statue, staring out of the window with a set face.

Later that day she said to Helen, 'I don't understand what's wrong with me. I feel so strange. I think it would be best if you kept the baby away from me till I feel better... I'm afraid that I might hurt her.'

–

The sun shone, it was a lovely day, but Veronica made no move to leave the stuffy room, sitting immobile, staring sightlessly. Her unbroken depression made Helen frantic and she asked Margaret Winters for advice.

'Poor thing, she's had a bad time. I've known women going like her after giving birth...' said the kindly woman, who was genuinely concerned for them all.

Helen saw the expression that crossed her face with the last words, and persisted, 'What happened to them?'

'Some don't recover. Some go quite mad.'

Helen stood up and straightened her back. 'Miss Vee's not going mad. She's going to survive. I'll make her do it.'

When Helen went back upstairs Veronica was in her usual place, hands tightly knotted in her lap, the fingernails pressing into the soft flesh, her eyes blank.

'It's time we started thinking about where we're going next,' said Helen without preamble.

Veronica slowly turned her head. 'Leave here, you mean?'

Helen nodded. 'Yes, we can't stay here for ever. What are you going to do now?'

'I don't know. My brother still wants me to go to Lisbon – that's all he'll do for me, send me to Lisbon to be forgotten and die.'

'Will you go?'

'I don't know. I can't make up my mind.'

'If you're waiting for Renton, you should put him out of your head. He's married now. You'll have no help from him.'

Veronica nodded brokenly. 'Oh, I know that now.'

'Ker can't help you either, even if he wanted to. He has money troubles. They say he's going to have to sell Broad-meadows.'

Veronica stared and a smile showed on her lips for the first time in weeks. 'Sell Broadmeadows? He'd never do that. The farm's the most important thing in his life. He'd sooner cut off his right arm. Oh, if it's true it serves the brute right.'

'But there's Edward to think of,' said Helen angrily. 'If Broadmeadows is sold, he loses his inheritance. And he feels as much for the place as his father does, I'd say.'

Veronica's short-lived jubilation left her. 'Oh, poor Edward. I've done that to him, have I? But I'm not the only one to blame, Helen. Ker was too greedy – he thought he'd make a fortune out of me. He didn't do anything to stop me seeing Renton, really. When he found out about Kellock he told me he wouldn't divorce me because the puppy had no money. But Renton had money… so he pandered to us, in a way.'

'And you made it easy for him,' accused the maid. The time had come for a bit of plain speaking, she decided.

As she hoped, Veronica was jolted into full awareness and defended herself with more spirit than she'd shown for a long time. 'You don't understand, I loved Renton. I loved him with

246

all my heart. I miss him still, I think about him continually, you can't know how that feels.'

Helen was really angry now too. 'What I know about love is that it always causes pain – and it soon passes. Hasn't what's happened to you taught you that? They tell you they love you one day and the next they're off telling the same story to someone else.' The memory of her dramatic parting with Peter and her own confused feelings about it made her voice hard.

Her exasperation was not lost on Veronica, who realized with sudden remorse how blind she had been to her maid's feelings, so involved was she with her own. She rose with concern and said, 'Something's happened to you, something bad. What is it, little Helen?'

The girl looked desolate. 'I lost someone. Someone I'll never see again.'

'Was it the Deacon's son?'

Helen only nodded, a lump in her throat.

'Why did you lose him? Was it because you couldn't leave us?'

'No, of course not. I just lost him. Please don't ask me any questions about it.'

Their talk cleared the air between them and for the rest of the afternoon Veronica seemed less melancholy. She even made an effort to play with Charlotte, although Helen was never far away and hovered over them as anxious as a mother hen: she had not forgotten the strange tension of Veronica's hands when she held the child that morning.

When four o'clock came near, Veronica rose from her chair and dressed herself with unusual care, smoothing the blue silk gown over her thin body with hands that did not shake or quiver. She put up her hair and covered it with a white lace cap, arranged her best lace fichu over her shoulders and covered all with a fringed kerseymere shawl. As Helen watched, Peter's words came back to her mind and she wondered if Miss Vee had a new lover in view so quickly.

'Do you want me to walk out with you?' she asked.

Veronica shook her head. 'No, stay with the baby. Look after her well, Helen. I'm just going to take a turn in the fresh air – I might even pay a call on my aunt and uncle…'

She had not seen the old couple since her first day in Durham. Her letters had always been collected by Helen who was handed them by a maidservant. It was unlikely that the old couple even realized a child had been born to their niece. Perhaps, thought Helen, that was why she was going to see them now – to break the news.

She looked very fine as she walked slowly down the street. Heads turned as she passed by, for even illness and melancholia had not completely robbed her of her old elegance and style. That she was a gentlewoman was unmistakable, and a few gentlemen lifted their hats and saluted her on the pavement. She gravely returned their greetings but paused to speak to no one as she walked calmly along the gently curving street known as the South Bailey that skirted the southern side of the cathedral. The door in the arched stone gateway of her aunt's garden was open when she reached it and she paused, looking with appreciation at the semicircle of flowering trees set in the emerald grass of the garden, but she did not step inside. With a smile she kept on walking till she passed under an old stone gateway and reached the Prebend's Bridge that arched high over the gorge cut by the river Wear.

There, in the setting sun, she stopped at last and leaned her elbows on the parapet, gazing down into the fast flowing water. It was a beautiful evening, made fragrant by sweet-smelling air blown over to her from may trees heavy with blossom on the river bank. A few birds gathering flies swooped low over the water. A man was patiently fishing in the shallows and a carter driving a small herd of cattle passed over the bridge behind her. She breathed in the sharp scent of the beasts, a warm, friendly, milky smell that reminded her of the milking parlour in Broadmeadows, but the thought of the farm made her face contract. No matter how much she hated Ker, she did not wish the loss of the farm on Edward.

On her walk under the trees at the head of the bridge, she had broken a branch of white flowers off an elder tree and now she sniffed at them, enjoying their fragrance. Old Mrs Ker used to make wine from them, she remembered, a sweet, strong wine that tasted exactly as the flowers smelt and went straight to your head. With careful fingers she picked the florets off one by one and dropped them into the water far below. She could see some of them bobbing along like fairy boats for a long way before they disappeared beneath the frothing water that broke over a weir farther down. For the first time in many weeks her head was clear and her thinking completely lucid as she stood on the bridge in the gathering twilight.

It was necessary to start at the beginning – the first memories were of her mother in their cosy flat in Edinburgh; then of carefree days at balls and routs; of the gallants who came calling, the delicious games of teasing and flirting. The memory of it all was so strong that she almost essayed a few dance steps there in the middle of the deserted bridge.

Then her gaiety disappeared as she remembered Henry Stewart, so handsome and, she knew it now, so stupid. The family fury that erupted over her head when they discovered she had married him was terrifying. It was the first time she was made fully aware of her dependency on her mother and brother. If they were to cast her out, she would be lost, and worth nothing. She remembered her mother's scolding and her brutal insistence that Veronica had only one asset – her beauty. Any thoughts she had, any hopes she entertained were irrelevant. She was marketable goods and such goods had to arrive unsullied in the market place. She had to be presented to any potential husband as a virgin – or at least she had to act like one. Till that evening on the bridge she had not even been able to bring herself to remember that she was not virginal when she married Ker.

249

Not that he even noticed – at least not at first before his suspicions were aroused. Then, like a maddened bull, unable to express himself either in words or actions, when driven into a corner the only way he knew to react was to put his head down and rush at his attacker. Their marriage had been as big a tragedy for him as it was for her. Why had Thomas forced her into it? She would have been happier married to one of the High Street caddies and living in loving poverty than married to Ker. But happiness was not one of the things that were weighed in the balance when her future was being decided.

When she thought of Renton the memory could still make her thrill. So tall and straight, as well-bred looking as herself, so handsome, so suave, so sophisticated. He was the man she had been born for, her perfect partner. Both were voluptuaries in love; both were amoral in their way of treating others; both shared an understanding of physicality that made them mad for each other. She felt her skin contract all over her body when she remembered how her heart thundered when one of his notes was brought to her. Those notes – always so ambiguous, so teasingly suggestive, written from one sophisticate to another who knew the language. When she remembered their lovemaking under the trees by the river the skin on her back tingled and there was the old familiar lurching in her stomach. If he were to come back, she would yield to him again. She would not be able to help herself for, once having tasted love like that, the longing for it never left you. Oh, Renton! Why did you swear to love me and then break your word? 'Why, why, why?' she asked aloud but there was no one there to hear.

The last flower heads were stripped from the elder twig and she looked at its bare outline – just like a skeleton. 'What happened to my life?' she asked herself. And when the answer came she saw that every turning she had taken was the wrong one, and now it was impossible to retrace her steps.

This was the time for taking stock, and her eyes filled with tears when she remembered her children. The memory of poor little Louisa, so waxen and pale in her winding sheet, still made her sob. Then there were the stillborn babies that she had never seen and her son Edward with his sturdy body and his solemn stare. Elizabeth too, of course, with her blonde curls and her endearing way of talking. What had she done to them? Would they remember her with love or would they hate her?

She thought of Charlotte, Renton's child, a living reminder of her final act of folly. She found it impossible to love that child. When Veronica caught sight of her a terrible fury rose in her heart and she was growing horribly fearful that she would do the child some harm. It was a strain not to give in to the impulse to snatch the tiny, powerless body from Helen and smash it to the floor. She could imagine herself throwing it down and stamping on it, stamping until it disappeared like a dead fly or a trodden wasp. The fury that erupted in her head when she thought of Charlotte scared her and made her fear for her sanity. She had never felt like that before about anything or anyone except Ker – why should her fury now be directed at a helpless infant? Leaning against the bridge parapet, she put her hands to her head as if trying to still the throbbing in her temples, and attempted to rationalize what she was going through. She had been drained of all love before the child came along and it would be better off with Helen. Dear, loyal Helen with her lamp-like eyes and her compact body loved Charlotte better than her mother did. Veronica wished she could talk to Helen once again, but if she went home now her resolution might disappear. If she returned to the lodging there was no knowing what crime she might commit when the blackness descended on her again. When she had done what she came to do, Helen and Charlotte would be free of her, free to follow the Deacon's son and make new lives for themselves.

Moving with stately grace like a dancer in a masque, she looked to left and right to see if anyone was approaching the bridge. She was safe, she was alone, darkness was gathering and there was no one in sight. The birds had ceased swooping and the sun had disappeared below the horizon. The last notes of the cathedral bell died slowly away and when the air was quite still again, she found it so easy to climb up on to the parapet. It was best not to pause there but to leap straight out into eternity.

–

They buried her in unconsecrated ground, without any marker on her grave, and the only mourners were Helen, the corn merchant and his wife, and the wet nurse with Charlotte clutched to her breast. News of Veronica's death was sent to Edinburgh and to Broadmeadows but no message had been received in reply, and when Helen sent a note to Veronica's uncle and aunt in their peaceful house beside the cathedral they pleaded infirmity as their reason for not attending her interment. They were anxious to dissociate themselves from a woman who had delivered the final shame on their family. Not content with being an adulteress who was hauled through the courts, she had sinned against the Church's injunction as to self murder.

When the last spadeful of earth was piled onto the grave, Helen put a little bunch of flowers, tied with ribbon on top as a remembrance of a beautiful and unfortunate woman.

Walking back to the lodgings with the other silent mourners, she heard hurried footsteps behind her and felt a hand on her arm. Turning, she saw Andrew Watt gazing at her out of his soulful dark eyes.

'I'm sorry, Helen. I heard what happened. I was riding out of town when they were bringing in her body. They told me she was your lady so I waited to see if I could do anything to help.'

Helen's eyes brimmed with grateful tears. 'Oh, thank God you're here. I don't know what I'm going to do now,' she said in an unguarded way, for the focus of her entire life had been removed with the death of dear Miss Vee.

The mistress's legacy was the baby Charlotte. Something had to be done about her. When Helen called at the home of Veronica's aunt and uncle, the old couple hardened their well-fed, complacent faces at the sight of her.

Her aunt said, 'I don't know why you're bothering us any more. We can't do anything for you. You'd better go back to where you belong. Do you want a character reference or something? Is that why you're here?'

Helen shook her head. 'No, I don't want anything for myself. It's about Mrs Ker…'

'She was a stupid girl,' said the uncle. 'She'd have been perfectly well looked after if she had done as she was told and gone to Lisbon. Poor Thomas tried his best for her and she never appreciated a thing.'

'But what about her baby, what about Charlotte?' Helen asked, looking from one old face to another. They looked kind and cherubic until you noticed their hard little eyes. A chill immediately descended on the cosy room. 'What baby?'

'Miss Vee's daughter Charlotte, she's nearly three months old.'

'We understood that the child you've been seen carrying around the streets was yours, my girl. There's no way you're going to foist your bastard on our family, so you take care what you say.'

They did not want to know about Charlotte. As far as they were concerned she did not exist.

Bemused, Helen walked back through the town. How amazing that life in the streets and the shops could go on as if nothing had happened when Miss Vee was dead and her own life was in turmoil. The overriding problem, however, was what to do about Charlotte?

The room above the shop contained many visible mementoes of the dead Veronica, her clothes were piled on a chair in the corner, her pen and paper lay on the table under the window, her miniature portrait lay face down on the floor beside her bed. There had not been time to tidy up but now it had to be faced.

Before she started, Helen took the child out of her wicker basket and held her close. Charlotte laughed and gurgled, looking up into Helen's familiar face. What a happy child she was, so completely unaware of the tragedy being acted out around her. Her confidence that she was in good hands, hands that she trusted implicitly, transferred itself to Helen and immediately she felt stronger.

She held up the tiny body and the little legs kicked vigorously into the air. Then she put her face against the milky-smelling baby and felt a rush of love so strong that it almost choked her. She could not give up this child. If the old couple said the baby was hers, why not go along with the pretence? She would not abandon Miss Vee's child to people who did not want her, for they would almost certainly send poor Charlotte to a foundling home or a foster family, the fate of so many unwanted bastards belonging to status-conscious families. There was no chance of Renton taking the baby either. That did not even have to be investigated as a possibility. He was married now to his fine lady and would pack Charlotte off as quickly as possible in the same way as Thomas Hay would do if he were given his wayward sister's bastard. Helen's young life on the streets of Edinburgh had introduced her to many people who had undergone such harsh, unloved upbringings and she knew of the hardships and cruelties that could be involved. That was not to be Charlotte's fate if she could possibly help it.

There was money left, enough to take them back to Edinburgh. In her mind's eye she saw the city that she had known as a child, not the one she visited on the last time she went north. Edinburgh was her home, she would be safe there. It was better to be poor somewhere you felt secure than in a city full of strangers.

Without tidying up, she lay down on the bed with the child held close in the crook of her arm and fell asleep, exhausted by the emotional draining of the past few days. When she awoke, it was evening and the maidservant was tapping at the door.

'There's a man to see you, miss. He's in the shop downstairs.'

Andrew Watt, almost sinister-looking in dark clothes that matched his black hair, stood running his fingers through a bin of golden grain, and when he looked up at her approach she saw pity and compassion in his eyes. Her clothes were rumpled from having slept in them but she did not care about her appearance as she walked slowly towards him carrying the child in her arms. They stood looking at each other for a few moments before he spoke, clearing his throat as if nervous.

'Have you decided what you're going to do, Helen?' he asked.

'I've been thinking I'll go back to Edinburgh.'

'Is your family still there?'

She shook her head. 'Not really. My father married again after my mother died. His wife wouldn't want me but there's sure to be someone who'll give me – us I mean, because I'm keeping Charlotte – a bed. I'd feel safer in Edinburgh. After all that's happened, I want to feel safe again.'

'I'll come with you, I've been meaning to go back to see my mother,' he said.

'But when you left you were meant to be going into the navy. What happened about that?' She had forgotten to ask him this before but it had come to her mind after their last meeting.

'As soon as I found out how things were for ordinary sailors in the navy I thought better of it. I worked in London for a bit and then I drifted into this – the thief-taking.' He dropped his voice to a whisper and looked over his shoulder when he said that, as if anxious not to be overheard. 'It's been profitable, but finding Peter was the end of it for me. I couldn't take him, and letting him go made me realize that I wanted out myself. I've made a bit of money, enough to start myself in a business.

It might as well be in Edinburgh as anywhere else. I'll go back with you.'

She looked levelly at him with a million questions in her enormous eyes but she only asked one: 'Why?'

He lowered his own eyes and she saw that his lashes were as thick and black as a girl's.

'Just let's say I miss it as much as you do. I was angry when I left but I'm old enough now to stand up and prove I'm a man. I'm not just the Deacon's son. I want to show them that I'm somebody in my own right.'

'In that case, I accept. We'll go back together,' she said.

He arrived early next morning driving a green-painted cart in which was yoked a strong, broad-backed little mare with hairy hooves and sharp, intelligent eyes, called Bonny.

Helen held her fingers under the mare's nose and the soft lips nibbled gently at her fingers. 'She's pretty, where did you find her?' she asked.

'From a man at the inn. He says she can go on for ever,' he said proudly, jumping down from the driving seat and grinning like a boy again. 'Where are all your things? I'll load them up and then we'll be off.'

'I don't have much, just a wee bundle and Charlotte. But there's Miss Vee's stuff, what do you think I should do with that?'

He went up into the room with her and surveyed Veronica's two trunks, her travelling writing desk and the big wicker hamper in which she kept her hats and fragile finery. 'We can't take all that – besides, it isn't yours. Her family could accuse you of stealing if you took it away.'

'I've sent all the letters she kept back to Renton – they were his by rights because he wrote them. The rest is Charlotte's, I suppose, but I've decided not to let on about her in case they send her away to be a foundling. The old aunt and uncle thought she was mine and I'm going to let them go on thinking so. When we reach Edinburgh, Andrew Watt, I'll say she's my bairn and I don't want you to tell anyone she isn't.'

'Whatever you say is good enough for me. I'll back you up,' was his reply. Then he asked, 'But what about all this stuff? Do you need silk and taffety dresses and fine hats with feathers in them?'

When she giggled the sound of her own laughter startled her, it was so unusual in that room. 'No, I don't. I'll send a note to her aunt and say she can collect them if she wants them. Otherwise Mrs Winters can keep them. But, Andrew, do you think it would be safe for me to take the wee picture of Miss Vee, this one she had painted in Edinburgh? It's awful like her and I want to keep it. When Charlotte's grown I'd like to be able to show her how bonny her real mother was.'

She lifted up the black-framed miniature and handed it to Andrew, who stared at it for a while before saying, 'Aye, you keep it. She was a bonny woman. I mind seeing her often on the High Street and thinking what a beauty she was. You keep the picture, it doesn't seem that there's anybody else in the world who cares enough about her to want it.'

The early summer sunshine warmed them and made their young hearts light as they drove out of Durham with Helen sitting up beside him on the cart's driving seat and Charlotte, wrapped in the old plaid, asleep in a wicker basket just behind them. To the other travellers on the road, who greeted them as they passed, they looked like a young carter and his wife. But they still felt slightly uneasy in each other's company. She was grateful that he did not question her about Peter and at no time did she mention him either, though when they were in the middle of the moor near Morpeth where he had held up the mail coach, his name was on the tip of her tongue. Oh, where had he gone? He must have escaped clear away or else Andrew would surely have told her. She hoped he was safe, and in the soft soothing air she turned her face to the sun and sent up a little prayer of intercession for him. The memory of Peter made her heart ache but she was stern with herself and closed him up in her memory along with the sadness about Miss Vee, like precious treasures that she could share with no one else. Life had to go on, there was no time for languishing and Helen Cameron was definitely not the languishing kind.

Although she had known Andrew Watt since childhood, for as long as she had known his brother, she had never been as friendly with him as with Peter. He was far more of an unknown and mysterious quantity to her and so they were polite and respectful to each other, talking with a certain reserve as if they were strangers. This made their growing acquaintance an exciting thing. As the hours passed they learned more about each other and they liked what they learned.

When night fell they slept in the back of the cart under thick covers that Andrew had had the foresight to bring along with him. Knowing what to feed to Charlotte was a bother at first. But the wet nurse had been gradually weaning her and though she sobbed for the comforting breast, she eventually agreed to take cow's milk and slept at Helen's side when her little stomach was satisfied.

Daybreak was wonderful. When the rising sun warmed her face, Helen peeped out from under her blankets and saw that they were silvered all over with drops of dew that sparkled like diamonds. What joy it was then to stretch and sigh, coax Charlotte to take her milk and watch Andrew harness Bonny who had been set to graze for the night under a grove of trees.

The journey took them three days – days of golden sunshine and growing happiness. For the first time in a very long while Helen felt young and optimistic again. Her future stretched before her – mysterious and unsure it was true – but the prospect no longer scared her. As the sun and companionship healed her soul, she began to feel that everything would turn out well for them all.

They came into Edinburgh from the coast road and Andrew drove up Leith Walk gazing around in obvious admiration – such bustle, such prosperity, so many crowds thronging the pavements, so much exciting life going on. But when they turned off the North Bridge into the High Street, Helen suddenly remembered how much their special part of the city had changed.

She was right, the bustle had gone, even more dereliction seemed to have taken over since she was last there. Poverty and decrepitude were rampant; buildings were uncared for; the pavements and alleys were littered with piles of rubbish between which scrawny dogs and even scrawnier children roamed like pariahs.

'What's happened?' Andrew asked in perplexity.

'I should have told you but I forgot how bad it was. It was like this the last, time I came back. You must see a dreadful change. How long is it since you've been here?'

'Not since that silversmith accused me of stealing, not since the day you wished me well at the top of Libberton's Wynd. Do you remember?'

She laughed. 'Oh, yes, I'd forgotten that too. You looked so stern setting off with your bundle on your shoulder. But that's a long time ago. The New Town's where all the quality live now. You should see it, it's very grand. Our High Street's been abandoned, I think.'

His face betrayed the disappointment and nostalgia for a vanished past that she felt herself.

'Cheer up,' she said, laying a hand on his arm. 'Things never stay the same for ever. We can't expect it. But you'd like what's going on over there...' and she gestured to the north where, behind the tall houses, another town was spreading like an opening flower.

'Let's go and see it then,' said Andrew, reining in Bonny and turning the cart round to head back on to the North Bridge.

They drove up and down the new streets and as they trundled slowly over the cobbles, even Helen was struck dumb in admiration. Everywhere she looked there were more buildings going up. Gardens bloomed in the middle of elegant squares, carriages rattled proudly along the broad thoroughfares, workmen tramped to and fro carrying hods of bricks or long planks on their shoulders. Andrew was wildly excited at everything he saw.

'Look, look, what a fine place,' he gestured to his right and to his left, growing more excited with each grand sight. He was almost rapt with astonishment at the large building that stood half built opposite the old theatre in Shakespeare Square. 'My word, Helen, we've come back at the right time, there's so much going on that there's going to be plenty of opportunities. We'll make fortunes, you mark my words.'

She smiled in encouragement and said nothing but she had noticed how he had started talking about them as if they were a team.

—

As she had expected, her stepmother held the door half closed against her and Charlotte. But it was not too much of a worry because Andrew found her a room in the building where his mother lived. Agnes Watt had grown old, skinny and shrill, but she liked Helen and was eager to bring her up to date with all the gossip...

'The Grants have all gone, all except thon Cecil and she's raving mad. She roams the Street at night shouting up at people's windows. She used to make a real nuisance of herself to poor old Miss Brodie till she died, and now she pesters Jamie Sherriff. God knows what she wants.'

'She wants to find out who told the Town Council where the Deacon was when he ran away to Ostend,' Helen said, remembering the time she had spent with the distracted Cecil.

'Och, don't be silly,' said Agnes. 'She kens fine who told on him. She did it herself, the wee brat. Though she was only a bairn she was smart as new paint and she took his letter to one of the councillors. I knew the man she gave it to, and he told me so himself.'

'She did what?' Helen could not believe what she was hearing.

'She took the letter herself, I'm telling you. She was so angry when the news was out about us – about me and my bairns I mean – that the wee besom was jealous.'

'Oh, how she must have suffered when her father was hanged, then,' said Helen, remembering Cecil's stricken behaviour on the day of her father's death.

'Well she had nobody to blame but herself. He'd have slipped clean away if she hadn't told on him. Mind, it was his own fault. He shouldn't have written to that Anne Grant. He was tired of her and he only wrote because of his bairns. He was fond of all his bairns was the Deacon.'

–

The Old Town had always had its share of dafties and oddities wandering the streets. They were treated with tolerance, a few coins were given to them by the kind-hearted and their vagaries ignored until they became too outrageous. This tradition was at least unchanged in the shabby place that the High Street had become. Dirty, muttering Cecil was one of the local eccentrics, nobody took her too seriously. Her aunt Jamie Sherriff, who gave her money for food because of her brother's affection for his eldest child, gently shooed her away when she came hammering at her door demanding help to clear her father's name. Jean Brodie had been less tolerant because she was more intent on forgetting the fact of the Deacon's existence, and the sight of Cecil's ragged figure in Brodie's Close was guaranteed to send her into a quivering fit of nerves that reduced her already frail health and accelerated her death.

If Jamie Sherriff knew the story of Cecil's betrayal of her brother, she was too kind to charge the distracted young woman with it. That was a stone that was best unturned, she thought.

But Cecil could not forget. Her guilt turned into madness and by the time Helen came back to live in Edinburgh, she was sunk into a permanent blackness and depression that nothing would ever lift. She could not let the Deacon lie in his grave in peace.

Helen saw her often on the sunny evenings when she was taking Charlotte up to the Castle Esplanade for a breath of air. Cecil always carried an enormous black Bible and kept trying to stop people on the pavement to show it to them but they hurried past, shaking her off as they would a louse.

When Helen paused beside her one evening Cecil began muttering, 'Will you look at this book? Will you look to see where his name's been cut out? They won't even have his name in the family Bible.'

She did not look directly at the young woman with the baby in her arms but held out the Bible in its worn leather binding. Helen took it in one hand and asked gently, 'Cecil, where did you get this? It's Miss Jean's Bible, isn't it?'

'I took it from Jamie's house. Don't worry. I'll take it back. I just brought it out to show folk...'

On the flyleaf, in faded crabbed writing, was a family tree of the Brodies, starting with the Deacon's great grandfather. Towards the bottom of the page a neat little square had been cut out.

'She did that. She cut him out. But I should be in there and so should wee David and my brother Peter...'

'And the Watts,' reminded Helen, whose heart gave a sad little spasm at the mention of Peter's name.

'No, not the Watts. Just me and David and Peter, even though they're dead. We were his real family.'

'David's dead but Peter isn't.' Helen's throat was closing with fear as Cecil stared at her with eyes that did not seem to see, like one of the Highland spaewomen that her grandfather used to talk about with such superstitious dread.

'Oh yes he is. He's dead all right. There's only me left to fight for our father. Look at this Bible, they've cut his name out. Isn't that against the law? Can't I go to law about it?'

A black cloud suddenly obscured the sun and Helen felt her whole body go icy cold, but she collected herself enough to put an arm around poor Cecil, in whose face she could still make out the handsomeness that had once distinguished the girl.

'Come on, Cecil. Let's take the Bible back to Jamie's or she'll be very angry. She wouldn't want you showing it to strangers in the street. And don't think about going to law, there's nothing to go to law about.'

Cecil stared into Helen's face and said, 'Oh, you're wee Helen Cameron, aren't you? Helen of the red ribbons. Won't you help me? I'm awful sick, Helen…'

'Come on, Cecil, come with me to Jamie's and we'll put the Bible back. Then I'll take you home and make you something to eat.'

Cecil went with her like a lamb, clinging to the edge of her shawl. 'You were aye good at looking after people,' she said contentedly as they walked along.

–

Being back in familiar territory, among so many well-remembered faces, soothed Helen, and for several weeks she walked around like a child again, carefree and unworried about the future.

Andrew Watt, however, was different. It was vitally important for him to set himself up in business as soon as possible; it was even more important to succeed and make people forget he was the Deacon's son who'd run away because the silversmith said he was a thief like his father. Although he looked like Brodie – a fact that he secretly regarded as a handicap in his search for personal acceptance – he had none of the Deacon's showmanship or the daring flamboyance which had been inherited by Peter. Andrew's nature was more withdrawn and private, but he was lonely on his own and needed someone to back him up through life. When he met Helen Cameron again he thought that he had found the right person. With her he could cut his way through the world. With Helen beside him, he could succeed.

'There's so much building work going on now, I think there's great openings for hauliers. I have Bonny and the cart so I'm going to start hiring myself out with them,' he told Helen a few days after their return to the city of their birth.

'That's a fine idea,' she agreed, for it only took a glance from the window to show her that the streets were full from dawn till dusk with toiling horses hauling carts of provisions and materials to the New Town.

'But I need a partner,' said. Andrew sombrely.

'To drive a cart?' she asked.

He shook his head. 'No, I need somebody to keep my accounts and – and to back me up, really.'

She stared across at him from the table where she was peeling apples to make a conserve – one of old Mrs Ker's recipes which she remembered well. 'I'm good at keeping accounts but you'll not be wanting a woman partner, and besides I haven't any money to put in with you,' she suggested in a tentative way which showed that she too had been thinking along the same lines as Andrew.

His solemn dark face beamed into life. 'A woman partner's just what I do need – providing it's you. And forget about the money, I've enough to start. You'd make the perfect partner for me.'

He did not say that he dreamed of making the partnership more than a business one… that would come later. He knew Helen was not a woman to be rushed and he remembered only too well how stricken she had looked when his half-brother made his escape. Time had to pass before she would forget.

–

After they'd been in business as carriers and hauliers for some years, they had expanded from having only one cart and Bonny to owning five horses and the same number of sturdy waggons with Cameron and Watt painted in gilt along the sides. Andrew found a fine big yard in Leith which could hold far more than their present capacity and he was building up a business hauling heavy loads from the docks for contractors working on the buildings around Calton Hill and in the far-spreading boundaries of the New Town.

Because of Helen's accurate and honest estimating the prices of Cameron and Watt were keen; their financial dealings prompt and accurate; the service they offered excellent. They soon established their business as one of the most promising enterprises of its kind. Even the slump caused by the resumption of war with France in 1807 gave them only a slight setback because their clients were engaged in a wide range of small activities and could always keep them busy while other contractors, who concentrated on larger projects, hit hard times. Because they were competitive, young and hungry, they survived. After work was finished they sat for hours in the yard office discussing their order book. In the bleakest period their accounts gave them sufficient cheer to decide that if they could stay in business until things picked up again – as things certainly would – they would be in a position to challenge any other haulier in the district.

Gradually and without realizing it, Helen began to rely completely on Andrew. To her he seemed like a safe hillside against which she could shelter from any blast. Common sense and integrity were two of his finest qualities and she respected him more than any other person she had known since old Colin died. For his part he marvelled every day he saw her, found himself lost in admiration when he listened to her. Sometimes he longed to pick her up and put her in his pocket for she was as tiny and neat as a doll, with her smoothly parted hair and her fresh complexion. But it was her eyes that fascinated him most because they were the mirrors of her soul, reflecting her thoughts and revealing her true feelings even when she did not want them known. He learned to read her eyes every day as a Roman augur would divine mystical portents. He was deeply in love with her.

As far as the business was concerned, however, he respected her expertise and knew that their success was as much due to that as to his hard work. Her skill with the account books meant that bills were never late and their money balance was always on the credit side. If any customer was slow to pay, Helen would put on her shawl and trot along to their premises to collect what they owed. In this she was more effective than any bruiser of a money collector because she was both tactful and persistent. The slow-to-pay customers could not believe that their money was being magicked out of their pockets by such a scrap of a woman.

Their only day of rest was Sunday when Andrew and his four carters would take turns in cleaning out and feeding the horses while Helen and the others rested up from their exertions. After he walked up from his stint at the yard one brilliant sunny morning, he turned into their close and, on an impulse, decided to call on Helen and Charlotte instead of going back to his mother's rooms.

He found them enjoying the sunlight that came shafting through the window. Early morning was the only time of the day when the sun managed to make its way into their building. In a pool of light in the middle of the wooden floor, little Charlotte, five years old and sweet-natured as an angel, was playing with a kitten rescued from the army of stray cats in the High Street. Helen was working, writing in one of her huge ledgers, when Andrew pushed open the door and she paused, screwing up her forehead and eyes when she looked at him.

Then she smiled, laid down her quill pen and said, 'I think I'll have to buy a pair of those glasses old men wear. I'd look fine with glasses on my face, wouldn't I?'

He smiled back at her. 'You'd look fine any way,' he said. Then he bent down and picked up Charlotte, who clung lovingly to him, and Helen's heart filled with pleasure and gratitude as she watched them. Sometimes she had to pinch herself to remember that Miss Vee had been Charlotte's mother. She loved the child so devotedly that it felt as if she had given birth to the little girl herself.

Andrew put the child back on the floor and pulled a sugar mouse from his pocket for her, then he said to Helen, 'I thought we'd harness up Bonny – she's not worked much this week – and go for a drive in the country. There's a lot of building going to start soon in a wee village called Stockbridge, I thought you'd like to see it.'

It was good to drive out with him, and as Helen looked ahead over Bonny's cocked ears, she remembered their trip up from Durham. That had been a good time too, but now they were much easier with each other, not so tentative. Now they were friends, probably each other's best friend in the world.

Andrew was pointing downhill, drawing her attention to the bridge over the river called the Water of Leith and the clustering houses that lined the river bank. Helen had not seen so many pretty gardens or such a profusion of brilliantly coloured flowers since old Mrs Ker died.

'Oh, wouldn't it be good to have a garden!' she exclaimed. It would be especially perfect for Charlotte, she thought, for the courtyard outside their tenement home was filthy and slimy with stinking puddles.

In her own childhood, she remembered, the town had been less noisome, its streets and courtyards were washed down every day and though it always smelt a bit in high summer, the stench was never so strong as now. All care had gone when the quality left. The Old Town had become a slum.

Her companion was watching her face – reading her mind again, she thought – as he said, 'Perhaps you'll have a garden one day. Soon the business'll be in profit and there'll be money enough to buy a house.'

She dropped her eyes to her hands and said, 'Perhaps, but in the meantime we need to buy another horse, don't we? The big Clydesdale's going lame.'

She'd skilfully deflected an awkward moment, for Andrew was off discussing the business again. 'Yes, I'm not pleased with that stableman we've got. He's coarse with the horses. We should find a better man.'

'I wish we could send for William Smith who worked at Broadmeadows. There was a man who knew his horses, but he was part of the landscape round there – none of his family had left the village of Hutton for hundreds of years, I think. He was like an old tree, rooted in the earth.'

He laughed at that, and soon it was time to turn for home.

During the walk up from Leith, they passed Charlotte between them for she was too tired to walk the long way to the Old Town, and when they reached the High Street she was asleep in Andrew's arms. As she watched him cuddling the child, Helen made a decision.

'Come in and I'll make you some tea,' she told him, 'I think there's some things we have to discuss.'

In her room she pushed the softly steaming kettle on to the dying embers of the fire and said, 'Sit down, you're tired.'

He did as he was told, knowing that something else was coming and feeling as if he were being carried along in a rushing river. 'We couldn't have done any of this without you, you know that, Helen.'

'But it's you who carries all the real burden. I just keep the books and send out the accounts.'

'You're the brains and you know it,' protested Andrew, longing to leap from his chair and take her in his arms but immobilized still by his shyness of her.

She smiled at him from the fireside and his courage expanded inside him. Then she handed him a cup full of copper-coloured tea. 'Drink that up. It's good for you when you're tired.'

He stared into the cup while summoning up the courage to say to Helen, 'I want to ask you something.'

'What is it?' She sounded unconcerned although she was far from that way inside and had to keep turned from him because she knew how he could divine her secret feelings.

He coughed, 'Er, I wanted to ask you to marry me.'

She stood stock still, staring into the fire. It was what she wanted him to say but now that the words were out, she had to think about them swiftly, to examine her own emotions.

He spoke again, more confidently this time, 'I want to marry you, Helen.'

What a turmoil raged inside her. She respected and admired him; she thought him handsome and trustworthy, everything a good husband should be, but he did not make her heart race, thoughts of him did not stop her sleeping at night. In the back of her mind she had the memory of Miss Vee describing true love. What she felt for Andrew was nothing like that – it was far less violent, more peaceful and companionable. The memory of her short attachment to his brother and how that had moved her also came into her mind. Then she recalled Miss Vee's delirious infatuation for Renton – Andrew could never make her feel so wild, but perhaps that was a good thing. Frenzy and passion only caused trouble.

'I'm very fond of you, Andrew,' she told him in a formal sort of voice.

When he replied he spoke with such feeling that she was almost afraid of her own power to waken such a demon of love in him. 'I'm in *love* with you and I admire you more than any woman I've ever met. I love you, Helen – so much. The pain of it is killing me.' But though his words were ardent, he kept on sitting in the chair with the cup of tea balanced carefully in his hands and she suddenly wanted to laugh. They were being so proper about it. But to laugh now would put him out of countenance so she suppressed the smile.

'Aren't you going to give me a kiss to seal the bargain, Andrew?' She ran towards him and they were both laughing and happy when he caught her in his arms.

–

Now they were married, they were partners in every sense of the word. One Sunday, because they could not spare the time during the week, they moved Helen's possessions from the room in Libberton's Wynd across the Lawnmarket to a first-floor flat in Baxter's Buddings – a flat of three big rooms with long windows looking across the Forth to Fife, and fine oak panelling on the walls. Beneath her windows Helen could see the earthen mound that was soon going to become a proud thoroughfare down to Princes Street, and she calculated how many horses and carts would be needed to undertake the construction work. She walked around in the emptiness of her new home, feeling like a duchess, and every now and again would rush over to her husband to throw her arms around him and squeeze him tight. 'It's a lovely flat, it's terribly grand, even grander than old Lady Huntingdon's place upstairs.'

But Old Edinburgh had lost its cachet long ago. Filthy beggars and sickly children prowled round the once clean courtyard, the stairs were always littered and smelt of urine and excrement, the nights were made horrible by drunken shouting from the rooms above their heads. The discreet to-ing and fro-ing; the peaceful atmosphere that once prevailed in the stair had long ago disappeared. If Helen went out she had to make sure she double locked her door or every precious thing she cherished would have been plundered by her neighbours.

They hired a little maidservant, a pinch-faced child who reminded Helen of how she herself had been long ago, to look after Charlotte, and when Andrew rode out early in the morning Helen went with him, a bundle of papers stuck into her skirt pocket. He consulted her about every move he made in business – she stood behind him, evaluating what was going on, when he questioned people applying for work or negotiated with customers. It was not her practice to intrude but everyone knew that before any decision was taken, the two heads of Helen Cameron and Andrew Watt would be involved.

Often, when times were slack, they almost despaired but, due to careful money management and hard – very hard – work, they survived. Their marriage was a greater success than Helen, even in her most optimistic moments, had expected. Though she was never carried away on a tide of mindless passion, her affection for her black-haired man was a solid rock, and her respect for him grew with the years. He was kind, trustworthy, ambitious and reliable and his major care was always for her and Charlotte. Then, four years after their marriage, she found to her delight that she was pregnant. When three months passed without a bleeding, she put her hands on her belly and marvelled. This miracle was about to happen to her, she was going to be initiated into the world of real women.

When she told Andrew he was even more solicitous of her health than she was herself, making her lie abed in the mornings, ensuring that a sedan chair or a gig drawn by Bonny was at hand every time she wanted to go out. He watched anxiously over her morning sickness and rejoiced when the bloom of pregnancy came upon her. Nearly five years after they married, she gave birth to their son, whom they called Colin after her grandfather.

There were to be no more children, and when Helen asked her husband, 'Would you have liked a larger family? I don't seem to be capable of giving them to you, my dear…' he replied, 'What we have is perfect as far as I'm concerned. You're not a brood mare. I don't want to keep you at home supervising a nursery.'

Colin was a chubby, dark-haired baby with the same golden skin and well-marked eyebrows as his father and grandfather. Charlotte, now aged ten, loved him and nursed him continually, taking over his care when Helen went back to work six months after his birth. Everybody regarded the girl as Helen's child who had taken the name of Watt after the marriage. When her 'mother' looked at the girl she was always struck by the likeness with Veronica, for Charlotte was growing into a spectacular beauty and so resembled her real mother – with the same distinctive long-featured face, the crisply curling hair and tall elegant figure – that Helen lived in dread that some of the Hay relations would spot the girl on the street and recognize her as one of their own.

She often anxiously asked Andrew, 'Look at me and then look at Charlotte. A one-eyed beggar could see that we're not mother and daughter, what if people recognize who she really is?'

'Don't worry, people only see what they want to see,' was his reply. 'She's your daughter in every other way, she thinks like you, she talks like you, she acts like you…' For Charlotte had escaped the trivial upbringing that had helped to bring ruin to her mother. Having had to educate herself, Helen was keenly conscious of the value of learning and sent the girl to good teachers who had no prejudices about women as scholars. The money to pay them had to be scrimped but she considered it a good investment.

From time to time scraps of gossip about the people she used to know came to her ears. Long ago she had read in the newspapers that Renton's wife had given birth to a daughter – and shortly afterwards died of childbed fever – but there was no news from Broadmeadows till one day Andrew came back from taking a load of flax from Leith down to Berwick and told her, 'In Berwick they're saying that Broadmeadows goes under the hammer next month.'

Her face clouded. 'Oh, poor Ker and *poor* Edward.' Though Veronica's husband was a stupid, blundering man she couldn't help feeling sorry for him. 'He loved that farm, it represented success to him and to his father. They worked hard for it.' She knew what it was like to work hard herself, so her appreciation of old Ker's struggle to move out of a ploughman's cottage and into a farmhouse was all the keener.

'They say Ker's in a bad way. He's sick and so overwhelmed with debts that even the sale of the place won't clear him,' Andrew told her.

'That's because of that useless court case… It went on so long it must have cost him a fortune, and it brought damnation to all of them – except Renton of course,' she said angrily. For only the death of Veronica had finally ended the long-drawn-out legal wrangle, and even after that, lawyers suing for their money had set upon the hapless John Ker who staved them off by more and more borrowing.

'He's in so deep, he can't find his way out, but folk are sorry for his boy. He's going to be left with nothing,' said Andrew, who had been assailed by gossip in Berwick market.

Helen closed her eyes and thought of Edward and Elizabeth as she last saw them – little, defensive children with puzzled, confused eyes, their feelings torn between their father and their mother. Her heart ached for them, such innocent victims of their parents' misalliance.

'Can we spare the time to go to the sale?' she asked. 'I'd like to see Broadmeadows again. Perhaps I'll see the children.' She'd forgotten that they would not be children any longer: Edward would be twenty now and Elizabeth three years younger.

–

The grass park that stretched like a vast green carpet in front of the house was empty of cattle and, only a few sheep grazed under the massive trees. Some straggle-feathered bantams clucked up and down the weed-grown drive and Mrs Ker's beloved flower garden was engulfed in nettles, thistles and bishop weed, with only a solitary brave hollyhock or a flowering rose peeping up towards the light. As they turned off the road from Berwick, Helen saw with a sudden shock that the house looked shabby and much smaller than she remembered. The paintwork was flaking and the windows seemed smeared and dirty. It had been raining heavily for three days and the once spick and span yard was a sea of churned-up mud, but that had not stopped an army of carts, chaises, broughams and pony traps coming to the sale. Their passage had churned the muck into a reddish brown morass that almost sucked the shoes off the feet of the horses.

She and Andrew tied Bonny up under a tree at the side of the drive and picked their way carefully through deep water-filled ruts to the main hayshed from where they could hear the voice of an auctioneer selling the horses.

A man at the hayshed door turned to her and commented, 'Ker has only four horses left now but I remember when twenty pairs pulled out of this yard in the morning.' She nodded without speaking for she could remember that too.

Andrew helped his wife up on to a bale of hay from where she cast her eye over the crowd. They were nearly all men, eyes eager for bargains, gossiping and laughing, indifferent to the plight of the man who was being sold up. There were several faces she recognized, some of them friends of Renton's, farmers or landowners from neighbouring spreads, who were clustered near the door, chattering together. She saw Smith from Nanshaw; Henderson from Fishwick; the laird of Gainshaw and Major Patterson from Lilliestead; but in the middle of their group rose the head of a tall man, Thomson of Moorpark, Renton's closest friend in the locality and a man to whom John Ker was heavily indebted. Gossip had it that Thomson was the one who had finally forced on the bankruptcy and sale.

The first horse came into the centre of the sale ring with a disheartened-looking William Smith holding on to its halter rope. He was much the same, the blond hair still stuck up in spikes all over his round head and his honest face was even more weatherbeaten and apple cheeked, but its habitual cheerfulness had gone today.

She jumped down from her perch and pulled at her husband's sleeve. 'William Smith's here, remember I told you what a grand man he is with a horse?'

Andrew, much taller than his wife, could see over the crowd to where she pointed. He sized up the man so expertly parading the horse and marked him out in his mind, for he was the sort of fellow they badly needed in Cameron and Watt's yard. With Broadmeadows being sold up completely, the new owner would be unlikely to keep on Ker's staff. Smith might well be looking for another job.

The horses were all sold at very low prices to one of the men in the Renton camp, who jubilantly clapped their hands when the hammer finally fell. Then the audience, with Helen and Andrew bringing up the rear, flowed out of the shed behind the auctioneer and headed for the house.

It seemed like sacrilege to enter the familiar hall knowing that everything she saw had a price tag on it. It did not feel right that she should be intruding on such a terrible day in the history of Broadmeadows, but her scruples were useless because she was carried along by the press of people into Miss Vee's drawing room, where the furniture was piled up higgledy-piggledy in one corner. There were chairs and tables, a rolled-up carpet and stacks of heavy-framed pictures, a looking glass and a box of books, lots of china vases on top of a mahogany desk. When the auctioneer climbed onto the oval table to conduct the auction, Helen suddenly became aware of a door at her right slowly opening to reveal three figures.

There was no mistaking them, though Edward and Elizabeth were adults now. The boy had grown tall and handsome, a finer-looking man than any of the Kers. His face, distinguished by his mother's imperious gaze, betrayed anger and resentment that his home was being so publicly broken up in front of him. Elizabeth, her hair the colour of butter, had been weeping and she kept a loving hand on the third person's shoulder who sat between them in a wicker chair. It was their father John Ker and he was obviously ill. His huge hands were folded limply over the top of a cane and his face was strangely impassive as if he had lost the power of expression. She saw at once that he had been stricken with a palsy and the muscles of his red face had slackened so that his mouth hung half open but his eyes were still alive, gazing bleakly around the press of people in his drawing room. When she watched how solicitously his children cared for him, it struck Helen that Ker could not be such a bad man after all if they loved him so much.

The auctioneer was happily listing many things that Helen remembered – the silver tea service, the china Miss Vee had treasured, a brace of pictures which she had brought to Broad-meadows from the Hay flat in Edinburgh, some good-quality furniture with curved brass handles that the housemaids used to polish with many complaints.

A pair of prettily painted Sèvres vases that had been favourites of Miss Vee were held up and Helen saw Elizabeth stiffen. Bidding began briskly and the girl raised her hand but it was a tentative wave and she was soon outpriced. Then there were only two contenders left fighting over the vases, one a prosperous-looking woman in a straw bonnet and the other the wife of a local farmer. It seemed as if straw bonnet was about to win when Helen stepped in. Raising her arm high in the air, she called out a bid that was several pounds over the last one and the vases were knocked down to her.

She went on to use the same tactics to secure the Hay pictures, the table silver and a pair of armchairs. She was quite carried away with the surging adrenalin excitement of bidding, and Andrew at her side never said a word of demur though she sensed he must be wondering how she intended to convey so many things back to their flat in Edinburgh. It was already crowded to the door, for since they moved in she had been on a domestic spending spree.

When the furniture was sold up the crowd drifted off to the dairy, leaving only a few stragglers behind. Helen saw that the door where the family had appeared was closed, but she went over and opened it for she knew where it led. Everything was more familiar now as she hurried down the dark passage to the kitchen, unchanged she was glad to see, and there she found the sad trio in front of a dead grate. There was no sign of Mrs Eliot or any of the other servants she remembered from the past – just the Kers, who stared at her in surprise. Her first words were addressed to the father.

'Do you remember me? I was your wife's maid. I went with her to Durham.'

His eyes showed that he understood her but he could only mumble in reply. Elizabeth however stepped in front of him. 'Don't upset him any more than he's upset already,' she challenged in a quavering voice. 'Have you come to gloat like all the others? You should be ashamed to taunt a sick man. He's very ill.'

Helen was contrite. 'Oh my dear, I've not come to taunt him. I'm sorry if you think that. I came to say I'm sorry, and to see you all. I'm your Helen, don't you remember me?'

Edward turned and faced her. 'I saw you in the crowd out there. You shouldn't have come here. We didn't want that woman dragged into it today as well. They're all talking enough about this as it is.'

Helen was nonplussed by his violence. 'That woman? You mean your mother? Oh Edward, she loved you, she really did and she would've been broken-hearted to know what's happened here today. Her life was such a mess... things went out of hand for her and she regretted it so much. But she did love you and your sister. I came to tell you that.'

But Veronica's boy was unforgiving. 'I don't want to hear anything about her. I don't want to hear her name. She's ruined us all. If it wasn't for her we wouldn't be selling up today. I'd be taking over Broadmeadows and not going off to join the army. My sister would not be marrying a tenant farmer from down the road – she'd be a woman of quality.'

Helen was stricken with pity but she had to say, 'Oh, be fair. I know you love your father but he's as much to blame as your mother. If he hadn't tried to squeeze so much money out of Renton, things would be different. I know he's a sick man, but be fair at least.'

But his children would not hear a word against John Ker. Edward, a newly enlisted ensign, was bitter at the loss of his inheritance – and even more bitter at the knowledge that there was a doubt over his legitimacy. The documents of transfer of ownership of Broadmeadows only referred to him as 'apparent heir' to John Ker. He looked at his sister, seventeen years old and marrying a poor man without land because no one else would offer for her. Their father had raised his last loan to give her a dowry of £500 and it was that loan which broke him. Helen looked from face to face and recognized their anger.

It was obvious there was nothing more she could say in Veronica's defence, but there was something she had to do before she left.

'I bought some things out there in the sitting room but they're not for myself. I bought them for you because I thought they should stay in the family. I'd like to give them to you. Please accept them.'

Edward looked at his father for some guidance but John Ker's head had slumped so deep that it was impossible to tell if he knew what was going on any longer. The young man glanced at Helen and could see that she was sincere. Sensing his indecision, she hastened to reassure him, 'Please take them, Edward. If your sister's marrying she can have them – your mother would want that.'

Slowly and stiffly he replied, 'I'm leaving here tomorrow because I have a place as an ensign in the 63rd Regiment of Foot – I'll never come back and I don't want to take any memories with me but, as you say, my sister's about to be married and it would be good if something from our old home went with her...'

Elizabeth had always been tender-hearted and she was weeping again as she listened to her brother.

'Oh, Edward, don't talk about never coming back, just say that I'll keep some of the things for you. It *is* kind of you, Helen. It was awful to think that everything was going, that we'd have nothing left...'

At this Ker lifted his head and began to mumble, his eyes ranging from one child to the other with desperate urgency.

Elizabeth leant towards him. 'What is it, Father? Don't you want us to take the things?' But Ker shook his head, there was something else he wanted to say.

Though his speech was incomprehensible to Helen, Elizabeth was able to understand him. 'The box? What box? The deed box? I'll bring it.'

She ran out of the room and though Helen prepared to leave with her, Ker made a gesture telling her to stay, so she waited till the girl came back with a large grey metal box. She laid it on her father's lap and opened its lid for his fumbling fingers to reach among the papers, which he threw to the floor. Finally, at the bottom of the box, he found what he wanted – a pair of gold-encrusted combs, the combs that Veronica had worn in her hair the night of the party at Spital House and thought she had lost. Ker mumbled to Elizabeth and she took the combs from his hands to pass them over to Helen.

'He wants you to have those. How strange, I've never seen them before. He must have kept them for years. Take them, Helen.'

–

She heard her husband's pleasant, deep voice rumbling away as she walked back to their trap and wondered who could have Andrew talking with such volubility, for he knew no one at the sale and was usually reticent with strangers. As he came into view she saw with pleasure that he was deep in conversation with William Smith, who had a rapt expression on his honest face.

They turned to look at her, but were so engrossed in their discussion that neither noticed she was upset.

'I've been talking to your friend here about the business,' explained Andrew, 'and telling him how badly we need a good head man. He thinks he'd like a change now that Ker's going from Broadmeadows – apparently that friend of Renton called Thomson has the farm now. I've been persuading William to come to Edinburgh. That'd be good, wouldn't it?'

She smiled at William for she had always liked and trusted him, and those genuine feelings shone transparently from her face. 'Yes, William – come. With your help we'll do even better than we're doing now – and that's not been too bad.'

Next day William, in a rough corduroy suit with his spiky hair wetted close to his head and his worldly possessions in one small bundle, met them at their inn to set out from Berwick for Edinburgh.

They were so deep in conversation that they scarcely noticed when they crossed the border at the toll house on the Lamberton road, a road that twisted uphill over bleak fields to Mordington. Only a short distance beyond it Alex Renton was lying asleep in bed, happily contented that he had finally routed and ruined his rival. The contest between him and Ker had developed into a full-scale war.

Not satisfied with having the damages suit thrown out, Renton had concentrated on delivering the death blow. Ker was in debt to so many of his friends, that it was easy to buy up his promissory notes one by one until the total reached a sum that could not be paid off at a stroke. When that stage was reached, he pounced. At his insistence, his friends demanded payment, writs were issued and Ker succumbed to a crippling stroke with the worry of it all. Even then Renton was not satisfied – the coup de grace had to be delivered, the prize of Broadmeadows had to be sacrificed. Though Edward, the heir – if doubts about his legitimacy (which Renton took care to advertise far and wide) were cast aside – pleaded for a stay of execution to allow him to sort out his father's affairs, the note holders were insistent and the auctioneers moved in.

Revenge was sweet to the sleeping man and when he woke, he would meet his cronies to exult over the final outcome. He was grey-haired now and becoming slightly more portly, but these made him even more commanding and sure of his position.

The fortune brought to him by his bride had enhanced his prestige with people who weighed such things by bank balances, so he strode through the streets of Berwick and Edinburgh like a lord. Tradesmen touched their hats deferentially to him, gentlefolk curtsied or bowed in his direction, the poor dropped their eyes as if the sight of his glory were too dazzling for the likes of them to contemplate. Everyone knew who he was for Sir Alex had the gift of clerical livings in his grasp, the gift of patronage, the gift of work for high and low alike. His racecourse was now one of his chief concerns and four main events were held there every year to which thronged the fashionable and unfashionable alike. With his estates straddling the border between England and Scotland, he was the lord of his own principality and if he was the lord, his daughter Annabel was the princess.

But she was a flawed princess for Annabel was slightly simple, though no one would ever have admitted that. Her tutors and governesses fudged the issue of her inability to learn by calling her 'dreamy, not bookish', carefully avoiding words like 'slow' or 'stupid'. Her father was well aware of the truth, however, but he did not care much – she was not an idiot, she looked quite normal, it was just that her thinking was simple.

His sister was convinced that one of the nurses must have dropped the girl on her head as a baby – but if anyone had done such a thing, they were never going to own up to it.

She was a happy, smiling girl, bouncy and eager to please her remote father who treated her like an overplayful puppy. She was very fond of her food, grew fat, and had to be restrained from polishing off every scrap that appeared on the table. Annabel's happiest hour was tea time and when the laden tray was carried in her eyes simply shone with delight at the sight of the crumpets and cakes.

'She's rich, she'll be married off quickly, they're usually quite sensual when they're like that,' her father said to his critical sister as if he were discussing a piece of breeding stock in his stable. She suggested that he marry again and try for a more suitable successor than Annabel, but he refused to consider the very idea. 'At least I'll be able to fix up a husband for her – I'll be able to select my own successor, not many people can do that. She's perfectly healthy, she'll breed well. I don't want to risk the marriage market again, I'm not suited to matrimony.'

It was true. When he thought of his wife he had difficulty in remembering what she had looked like, and sometimes even forgot her name. She'd been around for such a short time and even then spent a good part of it in bed awaiting the doomed delivery.

He hadn't missed her. She was boring and trivial in her mind, ingenuous in her approach to people and totally unadventurous in bed. Her death caused him no grief at all, only jubilation that he had his hands on her vast possessions without any inhibition, for though her trustees had left a good part of them to Annabel, her inability to grasp affairs meant he ran everything for her and fully intended to go on doing so. Alexander Renton was a happy man. If he ever thought of Veronica Ker it was only with the faintest twinge of regret or compassion, like a slight pain of indigestion that gives warning of a stomach ulcer – but somewhere deep inside him these feelings did exist and, being loth to admit to them, he thrust them out of his mind.

1813 – 1821

When news of Napoleon's ignominious retreat from Moscow reached Edinburgh, a tremendous boost of confidence swept the business community. Half-finished projects were started up again and as schemes dropped during the course of the long-drawn-out war began to recover from years of blight, the Cameron and Watt enterprise benefited. When the Treaty of Leipzig was signed, people were finally convinced that peace had come for ever. The bogey Boney was banished to the island of Elba, French soldiers went dejectedly home and the allies rejoiced. Nowhere was the rejoicing more enthusiastic than in Scotland's capital where fireworks brightened the night skies and cannons boomed from the top of the Calton Hill. There were plans for monuments and commemorative schemes – all of which would require contracting services – and the optimism and enthusiasm of all the people were unbounded.

From the window of their flat in the High Street the Watt family looked out over to Princes Street and watched the brilliantly coloured fireworks arching into the sky. They cheered loudly and toasted each other in wine, feeling rich and expansive for, with the recovery of the business, their success was secured.

For a long time their capacity had remained at five horses and carts but now, besieged with orders, Andrew and William went out to the horse markets in Fife and the Borders to increase their stock, and they bought carefully. The Leith yard soon resounded with the clattering of hooves of eight massive Clydesdales, magnificent animals with glowing brown coats and tightly braided black manes and tails. They were harnessed in pairs into long waggons with wheels like those on Roman siege engines; their horse brasses shone and tinkled as the great horses lowered their heads to haul against their shiny black collars. The waggons, glittering with unchipped paint and bearing the firm's name, filled Helen with pride and – admiration when she watched them rumbling out into the city streets.

Charlotte and Colin shared their parents' fascination with the business and accompanied them often on their trips to Leith. As Helen watched her son, trailing along behind his father, listening with an intent expression to Andrew's conversations with customers and stable men, she was reminded of Edward Ker as a boy. Poor Edward had been cheated of his inheritance, and she hoped fiercely that her Colin would not be cheated of his.

Charlotte was nearly thirteen years old, older than Helen when she first went to work as a maid for Miss Vee. She had been carefully brought up, loved, cherished and encouraged to stick to her books, but, Helen realized suddenly, was no longer a child. Her dear Charlotte was becoming a woman, her face and body were changing. The time had come to tell her the true story of her parents. There had never been any pretence made in their own home that Charlotte was Helen's child, but that information was not shared with strangers, and Charlotte's parentage was never challenged publicly. From time to time, when Charlotte was small, Helen would cuddle the little girl and tell her stories about her beautiful mother, so that Veronica became like a character in a fairy tale as far as Charlotte was concerned. She did not long for Veronica, she rarely asked about her – Helen was her mother in every sense apart from the birth giving.

One dull November day when Helen was not at work and the rain was drizzling down outside, she made a decision and suddenly said to Charlotte, 'Look, I've a present for you. You're growing up now and they'll suit you.' With the same care as she once used on Miss Vee's luxuriant hair, she combed out Charlotte's locks and pinned them up on her head with the golden combs.

The girl turned to look with delight into the mirror glass. 'They're lovely, did you buy them for me?'

'No, they were your mother's. I was given them by her husband just before he died.'

The news of Ker's death had reached William only two months after the dispersal sale. The bringer of it said that Elizabeth had gone to live with the even more embittered Susan in Hutton until she married her tenant farmer, and Edward was off in the army fighting in Spain.

Charlotte turned to stare at Helen. 'Was John Ker my father?'

'No, he wasn't. Your father was another man called Renton.'

'You mean my mother married twice?'

There was no point beating about the bush. 'She didn't marry Renton. You're his child but she didn't marry him.'

'So I'm a bastard?'

That cruel word.

'I suppose in law you are, but you're my daughter. I've taken you as mine. You have my husband's name.'

The girl rushed to Helen and threw her arms round her shoulders. She was taller than Helen now. 'Oh, my dearest mother – and you *are* my mother as far as I'm concerned. I don't care what you tell me, you're the one I love. You're the one I remember from the very beginning. You mustn't worry about this – and I know you have been worrying because I've seen you. But stop, it doesn't matter to me. I'm just glad that you and my father took me in. I'm very lucky.'

Helen sighed. 'Oh my dearest, you come from such well-born people. I wanted you to know that. Your mother was a lady of quality – and your father's a gentleman. Andrew and I are just town sparrows compared to them.'

'What nonsense. I'm terribly proud of both of you, and don't think I don't know that Andrew is Deacon Brodie's son. I've heard all that story, I think it's very romantic. I don't care about this lady of quality and the well-born gentleman… I'm your child and I don't want to be anything different.'

Helen went to her cabinet and opened a tiny drawer at the top where she kept all her treasures. 'I've never shown you this before,' she said, putting the miniature into Veronica's daughter's hands. As it was unwrapped, Helen was struck again by the startling likeness between mother and daughter. The girl gazed in wonder at the glowing portrait which still had an enamelled look – its colours had not faded with the years. There she was, dear Miss Vee, caught at the peak of her beauty, immortalized for ever by an artist who had fallen in love with her as every man who saw her did. She was looking coquettishly over her left shoulder, smiling a half smile with her fine hazel eyes dancing in mischief. Her curling hair tumbled carelessly from beneath the stiff lace of her married woman's cap and her white neck and shoulders rose in creamy luxuriance from the soft gauze over her shoulders. A rosebud was tucked into her corsage, emphasizing the cleavage of her breasts which were laced beneath with blue ribbons that made them point upwards under the white lawn dress.

Helen's heart felt sore as she looked at the picture and contrasted it in her memory with the gaunt ghost that Miss Vee had become in Durham. Her flowering time had been so short – and so bitter sweet. A fierce determination that nothing like that would happen to dear Charlotte gripped her heart.

'You're so like her, it's uncanny,' she told Miss Vee's daughter. 'You have her hair and eyes and her lovely long straight nose… look, you must see how like her you are. You're a swan in a duck's nest, my darling. Your blood entitles you to more.'

'Rubbish. What blood? Don't talk nonsense. I believe you when you say this pretty lady was my mother but she only gave birth to me. I owe everything else to you.'

It was a relief to Helen that Charlotte did not ask about Renton, for she would not have known how to tell their story without painting him as the blackest villain.

The victory at Waterloo and peace with France in 1815 gave an even greater impetus to the building boom in Edinburgh. Cameron and Watt were stretched to full capacity to meet the demands on their services. It meant that Andrew and Helen were out from early morning till late at night. Their coffers brimmed over with money which they did not have time to spend.

One night he came home jubilant and announced, 'I've a surprise for you. Tomorrow morning, you're to dress in your best and we're going on an expedition.'

Though they pleaded for details, he enjoyed teasing them and refused to divulge any more. 'Just wait. I want it to be a surprise. I'm sure you'll like it.'

He drove his excited family to Stockbridge – down the hill from George Street, over the Water of Leith and up a curving hill to their left. There were some fine old houses there, and Helen's heart longed a little as she looked at them. Then, on top of the hill, he turned his horse into Ann Street – a long narrow road lined by pretty houses fronted by flower-filled gardens and wrought-iron railings.

Helen and Charlotte looked around in delight – 'It's just like a village, it's like a street of dolls' houses,' they said together.

Andrew laughed. 'Would you like to live in a doll's house, my little one?' he asked Helen, who turned her face to him with the light of realization dawning in her eyes.

'You haven't! You haven't bought one?'

He was beside himself with pleasure at his success. 'I have that. I've bought this one here, We'll be living with the quality,' he said proudly. The Deacon's son had made it at last. He drew the horse up in front of a delightful house with a wilderness of a garden right in the middle of the row.

How surprising, after having dreamt for a long time about leaving the High Street, that Helen's feeling were mixed about packing up her possessions and moving out of Baxter's Buildings. The stair smelt foul when she climbed it for the last time but it held so many memories for her that, before she finally went away, she had to climb on up past the filthy doorways that had once housed genteel people, to the little alcove where she used to hide and spy on Miss Vee. It was still there, dusty and marked with candle drips. She rubbed at them with her fingernails – some of that candle wax must have been put there by her. It seemed so long ago. It seemed as if another person, someone she had read about, lived up there in the attic and worshipped the beautiful Miss Hay.

But Andrew was so delighted with his purchase and she too was looking forward to living in a neat street, to leaving the squalor of the slums behind her. The garden would be a delight, and Charlotte and Colin would have respectable neighbours, for it was a good address. No young man of quality or respectable family would consider marking a girl from the High Street, and the time was coming when Helen would have to start thinking about finding a suitable husband for her dear daughter.

Yet, in Ann Street, as she walked through the comfortable rooms of her new home, something worried her, a worry was niggling away at the back of her mind. She'd had thoughts like this before and they always presaged some important event – what was it this time? In the middle of the upturned furniture and boxes, she sat down with her head on her fist and concentrated. What was the trouble? She loved this house, she was happy to leave Baxter's Buildings, the business was thriving, she and Andrew were contented together... what was wrong? Yes, it was Andrew. He looked so tired; his face was often drawn and his breathing came in worrying short gasps sometimes. She was not a believer in doctors – Thomas Hay had put her off them for life – but she longed for her husband to take a rest. He would not listen to her, his ambition made resting impossible.

He was eager to ride the tide in business that they had awaited for so long; the challenge the new situations presented forced him on to ever greater efforts.

'I'll take a rest when we're the biggest contracting business in Edinburgh,' he told her confidently.

—

They were happy in their new house and Helen found herself making excuses to avoid going down to Leith so that she could potter about in her gardens – one in the front of the house and the other at the back beside the stable. She pruned and trained back tumbling roses, planted heady-scented lilies and clove carnations, grew lavender bushes and the same herbs as old Mrs Ker had cultivated at Broadmeadows. As she put her hands in the warm brown earth, the memories of what she had seen the old woman do came rushing back to her and she rediscovered a talent she had forgotten.

Andrew spent more time with her too for, in the attic at the back of the house, he installed a ship's telescope which he kept trained on the waters of the Forth outside Leith docks. When he saw a ship approaching that he knew was carrying a load which he was contracted to deliver, he would saddle up his horse and go down to supervise operations. William Smith, who had proved a tower of strength and their valuable third hand, ran the day-to-day business.

Sometimes Helen would hire a sedan chair and go back to the High Street to visit old friends or to see Andrew's mother, old Agnes Watt, growing frail but as sharp-tongued, full of gossip and cuttingly amusing as ever. She and Helen were always friendly for Agnes reminded the younger woman of her mother's bevy of indefatigable, quarrelsome sisters, most of whom were now dead. For Helen, Agnes was a symbol of the Edinburgh of the past, an Edinburgh that could never be re-created. Though Helen's neighbours in Ann Street were pleasant, they were remote and terribly respectable. Not for them the raucous shouting, noisy loving, tearful reconciling that had been the music of her growing up.

Since the news went round that Helen Cameron had married the Deacon's son by Agnes Watt, Cecil Grant had avoided her, crossing to the other side of the street if she saw her approaching and refusing to answer even when Helen spoke directly to her. Her strangeness had grown more marked with the years and when she went out she was followed by a line of chanting urchins, mimicking her strange spasmodic movements and grimaces. She seemed impervious to all this, however, for she was still totally preoccupied with hanging around Jamie Sherriff's house shouting insults up at the windows. Her aunt had tried to shake her off by moving out to Brown's Square on the south of the city, but the walk was nothing to Cecil. She seemed to enjoy it and trod to and fro every single day.

Sundays included. She had also begin waiting at the gates of the court house, waylaying various advocates and attempting to persuade them to take up a case against her long-suffering aunt.

'I'm the Deacon's legal heir. I should have what's left of the money. Neither Miss Jean nor Mistress Sherriff had any sons. I'm the Deacon's eldest child,' she told them, wringing her skeletal hands and fixing them so fiercely with her terrible eyes that they roughly shouldered her aside and refused to listen to her.

Agnes told Helen that nothing had been heard of Cecil's brother Peter for a long time, though it was suspected that he sent money to his sister. When she heard this, Helen's heart gave an involuntary leap in her chest that surprised her.

'But Cecil said he was dead,' she told her mother-in-law, trying to keep her voice indifferent.

'That one'd say anything. She'd tell the King she was his sister if it suited her. But she'll not let on if she's being sent money, she's not as daft as she's seemed to be all these years. The parish feeds her now,' said Agnes Watt with a wise nod.

One afternoon Jamie Sherriff's married daughter came down to Ann Street to see Helen and ask if Andrew, as Cecil's half-brother, could intercede to stop the pestering of Jamie, who was growing old and had recently been ill. Helen was reluctant to raise the subject with him for he never talked about his link with Cecil or the Sherriffs and, moreover, was working so very hard that he always looked tired. One evening, however, after a second visit from Jamie's daughter, she raised the subject and found that he was prepared to speak to Cecil.

It was a Sunday afternoon in spring and the daffodils were banked in Helen's garden when they set out to walk to Cant's Close where Cecil still lived in the same flat – and in the same state, they quickly found, of filth and decrepitude.

When she opened the door and saw them, Cecil tried to slam it shut again, but Helen pushed against it with her shoulder and ordered, 'Let us in Cecil, we have to talk to you. It's in your own interest.'

The smell in the room was indescribable but they forced themselves to enter. The place did not look as if it had been tidied up or cleaned since Helen had stayed there so many years before. She could almost swear she recognized the spiders that lurked as big as farthings in the middle of the lace-like webs. Cecil was rolling her eyes like a maddened horse, and had backed herself into a corner as if afraid they were about to attack her.

Helen did not beat about the bush. 'We've come to tell you that you must stop bothering Jamie Sherriff or she'll have you put away in Bedlam. You've troubled her enough over the years and it's to stop now,' she warned.

'Who are you to tell me what to do?' cried Cecil. She was not looking at Helen, however, but at Andrew.

'I'm your half-brother whether you like it or not. I'm trying to help you. For God's sake, woman, we'll give you money if you're in need. Just stop this carry-on. It's not doing the family any good,' he told her.

Cecil laughed in scorn. 'The family! Your mother was a whore, did you know that? She was walking Niddry Street at night when my father met her. She walked it after he was dead as well. There's no guarantee that you or your brother are his. You could be anybody's. I'm going to prove that in my case.'

Andrew rarely lost his temper, hardly ever raised his voice above a well-modulated tone, but now Helen saw a dark flush creep over his cheeks. In an instant it was replaced by a terrible ashen white that frightened her, so she hurriedly interrupted, 'Cecil, be quiet. Stop shouting. There's no good bringing up the past. None of us has ever held it against you that you were the one who showed your father's letter to the Council. Listen to what my husband is saying.'

Cecil's eyes dilated like the eyes of furious cat and she shrank back against the door. 'What do you mean? How can you say I showed them his letter? How was I to know what would happen? I just thought they'd bring him back to us...' She sank her head into her filthy hands and sobbed, 'I didn't mean it, I didn't mean them to hang him. I prayed to God to stop it but He didn't listen – I don't' think there's a God, do you? Do you really think there's a God? I don't!'

No matter how they tried to talk to her after that, they could obtain no sensible reply. She parried everything they said with an irrelevant comment and retreated into her secret world. All they could do was leave.

Without speaking they climbed the short distance from the mouth of Cant's Close up to the broad thoroughfare that led to the North Bridge. Sensing her husband's anger, Helen silently took his hand and she was still holding it when she felt him flinch as if someone had hit him. She looked anxiously at his face as he gave a gasp and paused in mid stride with one hand against his chest.

'Oh, Helen, my dear wee Helen, I've an awful pain in here, it's like someone's stabbed me,' he said in a strangled voice.

She was terrified but knew how important it was to hide her terror from him. 'Don't worry, just take a rest. It's only because you grew so excited about what Cecil said,' she consoled him and slipped her arm into his to help him to their fine new house.

There was a strange menace in the bedroom when she woke with a start. Terror seized her heart as she sat bolt upright and stared around for a second – but it took only a second before she realized what had wakened her. Andrew was thrashing around beneath the covers like a man possessed of a demon. When she put her hand on him, his body was wet with sweat. She asked what was wrong, but the only reply was an agonized, 'Helen, oh, Helen...'

With trembling fingers she struck a light for their bedside candle and, holding it up, saw his face, grey-white and contorted, looking towards her. One clenched fist was held tight against his chest and he managed to whisper, 'It's that pain – worse...'

'Lie still, my dear, try to lie still,' she said and flew downstairs to find the brandy bottle which she uncorked as she ran back to the bedroom. He was trying to be still but his eyes, staring at the ceiling, gave eloquent silent testimony of his suffering. Kneeling on the bed, she lifted his head in her arm and tried to pour some of the brandy through his slightly parted lips. It spilled over his nightshirt and the pillows because he seemed to find it difficult to swallow, and she saw with horror that his lips were bright blue.

'Swallow it, try to swallow it, Andrew,' she whispered and when he painfully did so, she tried to give him more. He turned his head wearily away and whispered, 'No, no, the pain's worse...'

His consciousness was going and his breathing became rasping and laboured as she clutched him to her, trying to take some of his pain into her own body. Her whole life force was concentrated on keeping death away from him and, as she smoothed the hair from his soaking wet face, she whispered urgently to him, trying to fend off the approaching spectre. But it was stronger and more inexorable than she – death was in his face. His hands were clasped tight round hers and she laid her face against his, whispering endearments which she had always found difficulty in saying to her husband.

'Oh my darling, don't leave me, don't go. I can't carry on without you. Oh, don't go, Andrew, I love you. I love you. I love you so much...'

He lapsed into unconsciousness and she was still whispering endearments to him while he died in her arms five minutes later.

–

The grief she felt was devastating. She lay beside him, stiff and silent, with such a pain in her heart that she prayed death would claim her too. He had been her supporter and her friend ever since the day they met at Durham, and though she had married him not because of passion but because of respect and mutual understanding, their marriage had been a resounding success. The realization that he had gone, that she was alone, made Helen Cameron feel like a tree split down the middle by lightning.

When morning came she released him from her arms and went downstairs to break the news. She was calm but white-faced, and totally numb inside. Her only comfort was that she had been able to tell him how much she loved him while he was dying.

–

'You'd think she'd stay at home longer than *this*...' Mrs Buchanan, a prim-mouthed lady whose husband was a Writer to the Signet and came from what she was keen to describe as 'a very good family', watched the little party set out from the house next door two days after Andrew's funeral.

Helen, in her working clothes, paused on her doorstep oblivious to her neighbour's disapproving stare and bowed her head before the wind that came rushing up the hill. She put out a hand to push Charlotte back indoors before the onslaught hit her.

'You stay at home, my dear. I'll go down myself. There's nothing you can do. I want to speak to the men.'

Charlotte firmly shook her head. Like her mother she was dressed in black, and her eyes were sad and concerned for Helen. 'Of course I'm not going to leave you. Come on, climb into the gig and we'll do it as quickly as possible.'

Over Helen's shoulder she could see Mrs Buchanan's silhouette behind the lace curtains of her drawing room window. Her heart sank for she knew what would be said to the Buchanans' son George when he came home from the college that night: 'I saw the pair of them, mother and daughter, dressed like paupers, going out driving only two days after the funeral. A decent woman isn't seen on the street for at least three months after her husband dies! Scandalous.'

From Mrs Buchanan's cold smile Charlotte could tell that the Watts were not the sort of people she preferred to have living next door to her. The families exchanged nods but not social calls, and Mrs Buchanan always cast horrified eyes at Helen in her working clothes. Her expression said, Why can't the woman dress like a lady?

But their son George was different to his prim parents. He was light-hearted and smiling, so handsome that just a glimpse of him was enough to make the strength go out of Charlotte's legs. George Buchanan was studying medicine and went off every morning carrying an armful of important-looking books. The girl next door had started waiting at her drawing room window in the evening to catch sight of his slim, athletic figure coming back up the hill from his classes. But though he never glanced her way in anything but neighbourly politeness, she thought she had never seen anyone she admired as much as George. Her heart was totally given to him.

Before Andrew's sudden and devastating death, Helen had watched Charlotte's growing infatuation with amusement.

Now all such concerns were pushed out of her mind by worry about what was to happen to the firm of Cameron and Watt. Without her man would she be able to carry on – as she had boasted to his rivals who had come to pick over what was left of his business? Suddenly she felt very, very alone and unsure of her own abilities and, in an effort to reassure herself, she sat up very straight in the gig, tightening the muscles along her shoulders under the dark shawl. She had deliberately dressed herself in drab workaday clothes for she always liked to appear as an ordinary working woman when she went to the yard. A resolve took form as she stared grimly ahead, holding firmly on to her dear daughter's hand. She was not going to give in. She was going to have a damned good try at keeping the business going, for she and Andrew had worked too hard to throw it away to his eager rivals now.

The driver took them down to Leith at a spanking pace and turned their gig into the stableyard with a flourish that made Helen feel like Queen Boadicea arriving to rally her troops. Work appeared to be going on, but there were more people than normal about in the yard at that time of the morning. Men were leaning on the doors of the horse boxes, men were standing on the pavement, men were pretending to fork straw from the haylofts, but she well knew that they were all straining their ears to hear everything she had to say.

'Where's William Smith?' she asked in a clear, high voice when she and Charlotte had climbed down from the gig.

'I'm here, Mistress Watt,' came William's voice as he stepped slowly out of the harness room, a white apron round his waist and a solemn expression on his face. They looked at each other and a feeling of understanding flashed between them. As always she was favourably impressed by the rugged sincerity of his expression. He had been as broken as a straw man when Andrew died but, like her, he knew that grief had to be borne and work had to go on. Now she was going to put him to the test.

'The men all want me to say how very sorry they are about Mr Watt, Missus,' William told her, and she could see tears

297

glittering in his blue eyes. 'Like me, none of them could believe it when they were told. As for me, I still couldn't believe it at the funeral. He was too young and too much needed.'

A hiccup of pain gathered in her throat and she swayed so on her feet that Charlotte put out a hand to steady her. But she straightened quickly. This was no time for weakness.

Stepping forward she laid a hand on her foreman's arm and said, 'Oh, thank you, Smith. He had such a respect for you, I know that. Let's go somewhere to talk without being overheard.'

William ushered her and Charlotte into the tackroom, which was warmed by a charcoal stove in the corner. As if seeing the familiar place for the first time, she stared around, taking in the piles of harness waiting to be cleaned, breathing in the smell of leather and saddle soap, a smell that brought back so many memories of Andrew. She thought of their drive from Durham behind Bonny, Charlotte lying in a wicker basket at their backs, and she sobbed out loud in sheer agony.

'Oh, no, oh, no. It can't have happened!'

William hurriedly pulled an old wooden stool out of a corner and gestured for her to sit down, but she gathered her composure again and shook her head.

'No, I'd rather stand. I've been sitting down for two days.'

He looked at her with compassion showing so clearly on his face. 'I know what you've come about. There's been a lot of talk, missus. The men are saying you're going to sell up to one of the other contractors. I've had a job keeping them all at their work today.'

'Yes, that's what I've come about. I knew you'd be wondering. I have been approached to sell the yard but I've decided not to – I'm going to run the business myself, so I'll need your help more than ever. I can only do it with you. Will you stay with me?'

Only that morning William had been offered a considerable sum of money to quit the Widow Watt. He knew that without him the business would founder, for though Colin was keen he was too young, and Helen could not manage the horses on her own. Most of all she needed a strong overseer to control the men, some of whom could be unruly, especially when they had too much to drink.

But William respected Helen Cameron whom he had watched grow from a skinny little waif to the dignified, handsome woman of today. He respected the power of her determination and her considerable intelligence. If she said she was going to run her husband's business, he was prepared to give it a try and help her. It was not a dilemma for him. His mind was instantly made up.

'I'll stay with you,' he said, awkwardly rubbing his gnarled hands together as if to clean them before thrusting one out to shake hers.

Her solemn face came alive with relief and gratitude as she stepped towards him and stood on tiptoe to put one hand up on his shoulder. 'Thank you, William. With you, I'm sure we'll do well. We owe it to Andrew. He'd be so disappointed if it all ended now. Come on, let's tell the men.'

The plump man sitting opposite her wore an unctuous expression, but satisfaction still shone through his assumption of fake mourning.

'He was a grand man was Andrew Watt. I've known him since he was a laddie. Aye, he'll be much missed. As an old friend I thought I'd just come along and give you, my condolences Mrs Watt.'

'Thank you,' she said coldly, sitting passively with her hands folded in her lap waiting for him to reach the point – as she knew he would, as they all had in fact.

'You'll be giving up the business now, I suppose. A woman on her own couldn't run it and your laddie's still only wee, isn't he?' he pursued, with false concern on his broken-veined face.

'My son's at the High School,' she agreed.

'It's a terrible thing for a laddie to lose a father so young,' said the fat man.

'My husband was only thirty-nine,' she said in a level voice though she was screaming inside at the terrible injustice of it all. Why should this fat man, who so obviously drank and ate to excess, be spared when her dear Andrew was dead?

'I know, I know, a terrible young age. You'll not be wanting all those work horses that's stabled down in Leith, will you?' He was implacable.

'Have you any suggestion what I should do with them?' She sounded mild and innocent.

'Well, they'll be eating their heads off down there, standing idle. I'd be prepared to take the business off your hands at a good price, Mrs Watt, because I was an old friend of Andrew's?'

That was it. He'd come to the point at last.

She lifted her eyes to his and shot him her most gimlet stare. It made him flinch, she noticed with satisfaction. How good it was to know her eyes had not lost their old power in spite of all the tears she'd shed.

'I don't think I'll be wanting the business taken off my hands. I'm carrying it on myself,' she told him as she had told those who had come before.

He was intimidated by her and lifted his hat from the floor, preparing to leave. 'Oh well, we'll just have to see about that. It's a pity you've turned down a good offer. You might be sorry later.'

She gave a cold smile. 'Yes, I might, but I'll take that chance. Good day, Mr Scrimgeour.'

–

Immediately after her husband died she had been numb with shock. His heart, seizure was so unexpected, the swiftness of his end so cruel and inexorable that it seemed as if one minute she was talking to him, and the next she was following his coffin into the burying ground. Colin and Charlotte watched her for a lead, a guide as to how they should react to this cataclysm in their lives, so she fought back her tears and took up the reins of the business. Colin was a responsible lad, and on every weekend and every school holiday he was at her side in the yard, trying to step into his dead father's boots.

It was only in the middle of the night, when she awoke alone in their vast bed, that she allowed herself to examine her feelings. She was angry about Andrew's death, very angry, and the centre of her fury was directed at Cecil Grant. If it had not been for that foolish woman and her wicked tongue, he wouldn't have been so upset that day. Cecil could go to hell as far as Helen was concerned, and the quicker the better. It was a relief to let her fury loose by pummelling a pillow as if it were Cecil's inert body. When she had thumped at it until the seams split, she felt a lot better.

But it was undeniable she missed him badly. She missed their ability to talk to each other without awkwardness. She missed their long discussions about the business, their mutual regard for each other's opinions and feelings. She missed his support and the sure knowledge that he was a rock behind her. She missed his friendship because throughout their marriage he had been her best friend, the best friend she had ever had in fact. Till she married there had been no one since her grandfather in whom she could confide. True, she had loved Veronica, but that love was mixed with pity and often with exasperation. Helen had looked after Veronica almost as if she had been a child, and it would have been useless to look to her for practical support. The relationship with Andrew was different. He was the one who did the looking after and she had been the one who was loved.

Throughout long sleepless nights she lay with her arms behind her head, staring out of the two big bedroom windows or watching the light of the moon silvering everything in the room with an eerie glow. If she stared long enough at the shadows, she could imagine people there, always people from her past.

Once, she was sure she saw old Colin Cameron hunched in the armchair beside her fireplace, and it struck her that her grief for her grandfather was very much the same sort of pain as her grief at the death of her husband – a slow, aching sense of loss, but not a fury of anguish. No, not that, what she felt now was more a sad acceptance of inevitability.

As the months passed Helen grew to realize that she was mourning him like a friend and not a lover. Her vital force, her passion, was taken up by the business. She worked at it as if besieging a lover. From time to time she thought that deep inside of her there was a part that had not been fully expressed, and now probably never would. When she thought of the brief time she had known Peter Grant, she recognized that this strange part of her, had almost seen the light of day, but after he disappeared it had been firmly repressed.

As dawn began to break sleep would start to claim her and she would turn over on the pillow, pressing her face against the cool linen, hoping for a few hours' sleep before work started again. I have so much to do she thought. I have to prove myself. There's no time for weeping and wailing and thinking about what might have been. I don't have time for love – look what it did for poor Miss Vee! As a way of comforting herself she almost came to believe that her grief would have been much worse if she had been passionately in love with her husband.

After he died business dropped off, as she had expected, because many customers could not believe that a woman, especially so young a woman as Helen, could continue giving them the service they expected from Cameron and Watt. They shook their heads when she presented tenders for work and said in kindly tones, 'We have great respect for what you're trying to do, but how do we know you'll be able to carry this out? It's a job that's going to last a good eighteen months. You might well be out of business by then...

They meant: 'You'll be gobbled up by one of your rivals or you'll be driven into bankruptcy. On the other hand, because you're a woman, you might become tired of it all, give it up and marry again, for you're not such a bad-looking wee thing.'

She was acutely conscious of the way men were sizing her up, not as a contractor but as a woman, and she longed to be old and ugly. Perhaps they'd trust her then. Deliberately she dressed in fustian clothes, deliberately she dampened down her femininity, deliberately she turned aside any look that implied she was something other than a business person, and presented herself as a sexless, cold being.

Her mind was taken up day and night with her problems. Without Andrew to leaven her anxieties by his own special brand of common sense, she worried every week in case she would not make enough money to pay her men. She was always checking and re-checking that there was enough hay in the sheds and corn in the kists to feed the horses. If an unexpected bill came for saddlery repairs, for refurbishment of her carts and carriages, it threw her into a panic. She sold her best pair of horses to raise funds as one by one the big building contracts went to other people.

One day Scrimgeour, the fat man who had offered to buy her out, called in at the stables to gloat over her dwindling stock of horses, some of whom were stamping idly in their boxes.

'Aren't you sorry you didn't take up my offer?' he asked her. 'I wouldn't be making such a good one now. In fact I won't have to pay for the business. I'll just have to wait…'

Fury turned her face red and she almost spat at him. Memories of her mother and aunts fighting at the well head sharpened her tongue. 'Take yourself out of here, before I kick you out. I'll see you in hell before you put your hands on this business. I'm not going out of business. Clear out of my yard and don't come back or I'll run you out on the end of a pitchfork.'

He went away pretending to laugh but it was easy to see that he was shaken at her unfeminine vehemence.

William Smith came in one morning with the news that one of their old customers was preparing a plan for building streets of houses on the slope of the Calton Hill overlooking Holyrood.

'They're needing stone brought in from quarries all over the place and timber carried up from Leith. It'll provide good work for a long, long time,' he told her.

She looked up from the pile of bills on the yard office table and frowned. 'Have we enough men and carts to do it? Will we be able to offer for the work?' Their staff had gradually been whittled down.

'Yes, we could do it if the men worked long hours and we bought another two pairs of horses. I'll ask them what they think.' He ran out and a short time later he came back nodding. 'They're with us. Work out your offer, missus, and let's try for it.'

She was bent over her books for hours. With Colin and Charlotte she walked round and round the Calton Hill, inspecting the site of the new streets. She had a dog cart hitched up and drove to the best quarries, carefully noting each gradient, each corner on the way, for such things meant time in the transporting of stone.

Even when she went back to her house at night the lamp burned for many hours in her parlour, showing passers-by the figure of a woman bent over a desk at the window. Then, at last, she was ready. Her papers were in order, her estimate prepared with every cost pared down to the barest minimum.

William drove up early in the morning to take her to the contractor's place of business. 'There's plenty of competition. Work's been slack and they're all after this one,' he said.

She knew he was trying to prepare her for losing the contract, but she sat up straight and said firmly, 'I just have a feeling that we're the ones who're going to win it. Don't worry.'

He saw she didn't want to discuss it any longer so he changed the subject. 'Your man was one of Deacon Brodie's laddies, wasn't he?' he asked.

As always when that subject was brought up, she stiffened suspiciously while she replied, 'Yes, he was, what of it?'

He was anxious to reassure her. 'Oh, nothing, it's just that the Deacon's girl's pretty sick, they say. A woman came down to the yard last night after you'd left and said that Cecil Grant was fading away. She said to tell you that she's a poor mad soul and she's growing worse.'

Helen turned her face away and looked at the traffic filling the road beside them. 'So what's that to me? She's beyond help anyway. She never listens to what anyone says to her.'

'I just thought because she was sort of related to your man that you'd want to know.'

Her voice sounded as cold as ice. 'Well I don't, really. He was only her half-brother and she never gave him a good word. I can't help blaming her for making him die.'

There was a crowd of other people – all men – besieging the contractor's office in hopes of being awarded the work. Among them was Scrimgeour, who smirked to his friends when he saw Helen drive up with William, but she ignored him and silently waited until her name was called.

When she was ushered into the great man's presence she noted that he was a thin, intense-looking person with a long white face and straggling grey hair, very much an Edinburgh type. She could walk past a dozen men like him if she took a stroll along Princes Street or up the High Street. He did not even glance at her as she entered but gestured briefly at the chair in front of his desk and returned to his perusal of a pile of papers. His cavalier attitude made her quail in spite of her determination to succeed and she sat down nervously on the edge of the seat. He kept on reading so she gave a little cough to make him look at her.

'I'll be with you in a minute, Mistress Watt,' he said shortly and she relaxed because she recognized that he was subjecting her to the breaking-down treatment. The knowledge that they were playing a game helped her to compose her mind and she stared out of the window, mentally battling with him to give in first.

Eventually he straightened up and said, 'Have you brought your offer?'

Without speaking she laid her packet on the desk and he opened the carefully written sheets which had occupied her for so many long nights. She knew by heart every figure inscribed on them, every ink blot, every place where her pen had faltered with tiredness. The man sat running his eye down the columns and shaking his head as he did so.

'Mmm, it seems a lot of money,' he said at length but she knew that this too was a ploy. Her estimate was as low as possible. No one could do better.

'It's not a lot when the work's well done,' she told him in a confident voice, and he gave a reluctant smile.

'Yes, that's true.' Then he lifted his hollow eyes and stared at her for a second. 'People tell me you give a good job for your money. I've heard that.' He sounded slightly surprised at the idea.

'I do – when I'm given the chance,' said Helen, and the note in her voice made him look at her more closely.

'I know you, don't I? You're Helen Cameron. You're the granddaughter of old Colin Cameron who used to be head of the High Street caddies?'

She raised her head proudly. 'That's who I am.'

The contractor leaned forward on his elbows, relaxed enough to speak more freely. 'Of course, I thought I knew your face. I was a caddy when your grandfather was alive. We used to come up all those stairs to your room on Friday nights and carry him down to the ale house. Don't you remember?'

She smiled and looked more closely at him. Yes, she did remember a long, lanky youth who came with the others for her grandfather. This must be him. The man was still reminiscing about the old days and she could see that, like her, he recalled their High Street days with nostalgia and affection.

'My, he was a big man and he was some weight. We didn't mind, really. He was a good man. I remember you too – a skinny wee thing…'

'I'm still pretty skinny,' laughed Helen, 'but that's not what I've come here to talk about. Give me the chance to do your transporting – or at least some of it. I've a good staff of men and we'll do it well, I promise you, you'll not regret it.'

'Well, I'll be honest with you. Cameron and Watt weren't going to win the work when this all started, but now that I've read your estimate – and now that I've seen you and know who you are – I'm prepared to take a chance on you. You can have half of the work for a sixmonth and if everything's all right at the end of it, I'll give you more. My partners and I have big plans – we'll not be stopping with one project.'

William was anxiously holding the pony's head when she walked back across the contractor's yard and she felt his querying eyes, as well as the eager eyes of her rivals, fixed on her from the moment she stepped out of the office door. This was all part of the play-acting and she enjoyed deceiving them. With her head lowered and her face solemn, she walked slowly and sadly till she was alongside William and then she suddenly broke into a grin, giggling like a child. 'Don't look so glum, William. We have it, we have it!'

They drove back to Leith in such jubilation that people on the street as they passed stared after them wondering what had caused the pair to radiate happiness so openly. William drove the horse like a charioteer and Helen clung to the seat beside him, her face alight and her bonnet flying from its strings at the back of her head. Her hair, usually so orderly and neat, was flying about her face and she was conscious of feeling the liberation of true delight for the first time since Andrew died. Her workmen were waiting anxiously in the yard, knowing that if this order was lost the firm would be cutting its staff to the bone. As their pony turned in at the huge gate Helen could not resist standing up in the cart and waving her papers at them like a victor returning with the trophies of war.

'Send out to the ale house for jugs of porter, we've won the contract,' she called, ignoring her own ban on anyone drinking in the stables. Her workers cheered her till the horses began kicking at their boxes in fright.

When she and William were closing up the yard later that night she walked with him from box to box, inspecting the horses and making sure they were comfortable. These huge, kind animals, stamping quietly in their bedding straw, were her bread and butter. They were fed like kings and any scratch or sore was immediately treated with loving attention. She thought Cameron and Watt looked after the horses better than she looked after her children, for her absorption with the yard was so intense that she spent less and less time at home with Colin and Charlotte. They locked the gate and she looked at Smith with gratitude in her face. None of this, none of her success that day would have been possible without his help.

'Thank you, William. Thank you so much. I rely on you completely now that Andrew's gone, you know.'

As he looked down at her, a mixture of feelings showed in his face. It was difficult for him to find the words to express them, however. 'Oh, that's all right. You know I'd do anything for you, anything I could. You've only to ask. I hope you know that.'

All of a sudden she felt that she had failed him in some way. She had been so taken up with her own affairs that she knew very little of how he lived when he was not in the stableyard. 'Where's your home, do you have a house?' she asked.

'Oh aye, I've a cottage down near the docks. It's wee but it suits the wife. She comes from down there.'

The wife! She hadn't even realized William was married. He'd never mentioned it. In her mind she had categorized him as a perpetual bachelor, had decided he would never marry because of his intense feeling for Veronica. It had been obvious how smitten he was with Miss Vee. She'd never seen a man so lovesick.

'You're married, then? What's your wife's name?' she asked in surprise.

He laughed. 'Oh aye, I'm married. We were married two years ago – just before, er, just before your husband died. My wife's expecting a bairn any day now. Her name's Rachel.'

She was astonished. But she did not mean him to see that, so she kept her voice level as she answered, 'Rachel. That's a nice name.'

He nodded. 'She's a nice lass. I'm lucky. She's a good friend to me.'

The tone of his voice made her think of the way it had been between her and Andrew and she recognized that William had married for company and comfort. Of course, it would have been impossible to find a wife who would awaken in him the same feelings as he had for Veronica. He was a wise man and had looked for something different – just as she had done in a way, for there was a part of her that would never feel again what she had felt for Peter Grant.

As she rode home in her sedan chair she found herself thinking about Peter. She wondered if he was dead and how his fate had overtaken him. Or had he escaped? Had his devilish luck sustained him? She looked up at the stars and wondered if they were shining down on him, somewhere. She hoped so, oh, how she hoped so, even though she would never see him again.

–

That night she slept soundly, the first unbroken sleep she had enjoyed since Andrew died. When she woke she felt strangely light, as if a weight had been lifted from her shoulders. What's happened to me? she wondered, and for a while she lay happily going over the previous day's events. Then she realized that her contentment was not only due to the triumph of securing the contracting work. Her anger had miraculously seeped away, taking with it the rage against Cecil Grant. It wasn't Cecil's fault really that Andrew had died. The doctor had said his heart was very bad and must have been bad for a long time. She jumped from bed, anxious to make amends to Cecil, and as soon as she walked into the yard that morning she shouted to one of the men, 'Put a pony in a trap and take me up to the High Street. I'm going to Cant's Close.'

It was even more depressing in the close than on her last call. Ragged children held out their palms to her as she passed and their eyes told her that they were begging through necessity. She emptied her purse for them and then climbed the filthy stairs to Cecil's door. It was unlocked and she could see the mound of a body beneath the covers of the filthy bed beside the fireplace.

'Cecil, Cecil,' she called softly. 'It's Helen Watt – Helen Cameron. Are you awake?'

There was a movement beneath the tattered cover and a head peeped out. It was a terrible head like something from a nightmare, for the black hair was so tightly matted that no comb would get through it now; the skin was drawn like dry parchment over the cheekbones and the eyes were red-rimmed and staring. Helen felt weak at the sight of those eyes because she saw death in them.

Cecil stretched out a naked arm that was nothing more than bones and long pointing fingers. 'Go away, go away. I don't want to see you, go away.'

Helen stepped closer, shocked into silence. There were dark purple stains discolouring the skin beneath Cecil's eyes, as if she had rubbed elderberry juice on to her face. From her came a feeling of desperate weariness which told only too clearly that she had given up on life.

'Oh, you need a doctor. You're ill. Do you want me to bring you something to eat, something to drink? Let me help you, Cecil,' pleaded the visitor, advancing, across the littered floor. As she approached the bed a trio of hissing cats leaped from the covers and fled for the daylight. The stench was overpowering.

'I'm not ill and there's plenty of food here, too much of it.' Cecil gestured across to the table where a few wizened apples and a dried loaf lay beside a piece of rotting meat with huge bluebottle flies buzzing lazily around it. Helen flinched from the sight.

'You can't eat that. I'll find you some fresh food. I won't be long,' and she ran from the room, gratefully gulping the fresh air as soon as she was back in the courtyard. But even when she returned with new bread, a bundle of green vegetables and a steaming pie from the hot pie shop, she could not tempt Cecil to eat. The very sight of the food seemed to make her nauseous and she gestured it away.

'Ugh. It makes me feel sick, I don't want it, take it away, give it to the cats,' she ordered and Helen was forced to lay her offerings down beside the rotting remains of previous meals.

'What's wrong with you, will you let me bring a doctor?' she pleaded.

Cecil wearily turned her face to the wall. 'No, I won't. I don't need a doctor. Leave me be. I know what I'm doing.'

And in truth, her voice was more sane and logical than at any time in the past few years. She sounded like someone who had taken a decision and was sticking to it.

Feeling disconsolate and inadequate, Helen stepped out on to the landing and knocked on the door of Cecil's neighbour, a woman who had lived there since Anne Grant's day. She was old now and bent but her eyes were as sharp as ever and she knew Helen at once.

'If you've come to see her next door, don't waste your time. She's starving herself to death. You'll not stop her now, she's past the saving point. I've seen it happen to others like her...'

'But why? She seems more sensible than she used to be. She's not raving any more.' Helen was bewildered.

'Being sensible makes it worse for her. She sees it all too clearly. She's not eating anything, she's growing thinner every day. Just let her be. You can't stop her. Go away and leave her in peace. I'll let you know when it's all over.'

It took a week and when the news came Helen was deeply involved in the organizing of her new contract. In spite of her preoccupations, however, it was a shock to realize that Cecil Grant had gone, unmourned by anyone. Jamie Sherriff was too ill to have anything to do with the funeral arrangements even if she had wanted to, and her daughter reacted in horror at the suggestion that she should associate herself with the madwoman Cecil Grant.

It was Helen who gave the orders for the burial. After it was over she went back alone to the filthy flat. If he was alive it was Peter's property, she supposed, but no one in the stair had heard anything of him for years. Cecil had never talked to them about her brother or anything else. Privacy had been a mania with her.

The task of cleaning the flat was too much for one person and Helen asked Charlotte for assistance. Wearing huge white aprons, with their hair tied up in nets and their hands in gloves, they set about the horrible task. Everything had to be burned, but under the bed Helen found a locked box which, when forced, revealed golden coins wrapped up in softest velvet – some of them from France and Austria, others from Spain, even a few Indian pagodas.

'Where do you suppose all this, came from?' she asked her daughter in amazement as they looked at the glittering hoard. It was a problem to know what to do with it, but in the end, she converted some of the coins into Scots pounds which she distributed among the poor of the High Street and the rest she deposited with a lawyer in the name of Peter Grant or any of his heirs.

–

William came out of the largest stable hauling a man by the ear. His face was dark red with anger and it was obvious that it was all he could do not to murder his captive.

'I caught him trying to lame Bess,' he told Helen in a trembling voice. Bess was one of their best Clydesdales, an enormous, gentle horse, and the thought of anyone deliberately injuring her was almost unthinkable as far as he was concerned. Helen was equally shocked.

'Why did you do it?' she asked the man, a dissipated-looking character who had recently been taken on to clean out the stables.

'I wasnae, I wasnae...' he protested.

'He was,' said Smith stoutly. 'He had a knife and he was going to stab it into her frog. It's a good job I was watching him. I've been thinking for a couple of days he was shirking the work.'

Helen caught hold of the miscreant's shirt front with her two fists and shook him like a rat as she hissed, 'Get out of my yard. If we ever see you here again, my men will beat you within an inch of your life.' Her fury was so impressive that his legs were making running motions before she even let go of him. As he disappeared through the gate, she called after him, 'And you can tell whoever hired you that we can play as dirty as them – but one thing we'd never stoop to is harming an animal.'

It was not the first attempt at undermining her business. Horses went mysteriously lame; waggons were overturned by careless drivers; deliveries were unpunctual and men hired to meet the increased demands of the business did not turn up when they were most needed. It was a constant battle to keep up to schedule and placate the contractors every time anything went wrong – which seemed to happen far too often for Helen's peace of mind – but she and William battled on, gradually gaining ground as far as the respect of their client was concerned.

When she lay awake in her bed at night she was not kept from sleep by sorrow and a sense of loss but by the columns of figures that ran continually through her head. She was doing her mental arithmetic one night before Christmas when she was roused by a terrible hammering at the front door. It was two o'clock in the morning and a messenger had come to tell her that the hayshed at Leith had caught fire. When she reached the yard she was horrified to see black-faced men leading the horses into the street and others trying to douse the last flames that licked around the burnt spars of what had once been her hay store. What was worse was that it had been packed to the doors with enough bales to last them through till spring. It was a miracle that the horses were saved and only two big waggons were damaged by the conflagration, which had been spotted by a passer-by weaving his way home from a tavern in the early hours.

They were just recovering from that blow when the corn kist was found to be contaminated and hundreds of pounds of corn had to be thrown away.

'Who's doing this? How can we protect ourselves?' she asked William, who shook his head grimly.

'We have enemies. They're trying to put us out of business. But I'll sleep in the yard from now on, and we'll tighten up everything. We'll keep on only men that we can trust and pay the others off. We'll ask the ones we keep to work extra time. It's a pity Colin's not old enough yet to come in – another good head is what we need.'

Expenses were heavy and payment was slow but the various accidents which had befallen her meant that if Helen were to continue with the contracting business she had to find some ready money. There had to be some way of bringing it in, quickly and without too much outlay, she thought. Then she hit on the idea of developing the sideline in carriage hire.

Advertisements were inserted in all the Edinburgh newspapers and wall posters printed announcing a new carriage hire firm to be ran by the Widow Watt. It was to be of the highest quality and reputability – a service run by a lady for ladies and gentlemen. The horses were the most tractable, well mannered and immaculately groomed; the carriages were spick and span and up to date – no lord or lady could drive out in greater style than a customer hiring a barouche from Mrs Watt.

Even the most anxious husband or father could send his wife or daughter out with them, for Mrs Watt guaranteed it all. The ladies and gentlemen who flocked to her yard and drove out in her carriages did not realize that the respectable widow who courteously took their orders and collected their payments was also the person who rolled-up her sleeves and set about cleaning the carriages when they were returned.

She had no time for herself, no time to think about the future, no time to consider remarriage. The determination and drive that emanated from her, and her unsettling, critical eyes deterred many a would-be suitor who fancied setting himself up at the head of a thriving business.

She did not want either of her children to have to work as she did. Charlotte was sent to an expensive school ran for girls of quality by two well-connected maiden ladies in the New Town. They educated her in manners, deportment, music, sewing, reading, writing and arithmetic.

Colin still attended the High School of Edinburgh and was showing promise as a Greek and Latin scholar. Helen was painfully proud of both of them and, though she could spare little time to be with them, she gloried in their accomplishments.

One night when she arrived home late and exhausted, Charlotte hurried her up to bed and made her lie down, and a tray of food was carried up and placed in front of her.

The girl sat beside Helen and took her hand gently. 'I have something to ask you and I don't want you to say no at once. I want you to think about it. Will you?'

Helen nodded. 'Of course, my dear.' Was Charlotte about to announce she had found a nice young man? But that was not it at all.

Charlotte sat serious faced as she said, 'I'm worried about how hard you work. You seem to do everything from cleaning out the stables to dealing with the customers. The next thing we know, you'll be out here hauling stones if we don't stop you. Colin and I've been talking about it and we think you need help. I want to go down to the yard with you every day and take my share of the responsibility. After all I'm eighteen, well old enough to work. You went out to work at ten years old, didn't you?'

Helen sat bolt upright, almost upsetting her tray. 'It was different for me. You're a lady, Charlotte. I can't let you dirty your hands.'

'Don't be so silly. I want to dirty my hands. I want to learn how to run the business. I think you're wonderful to do it. Everybody respects you. I want to be able to do the same thing.'

Hearing this, a change came over Helen and she sank back against her pillows. This was not an empty offer. The girl was beautiful and stately but she had something in her that would not be satisfied with sitting in a parlour stitching at needlework.

When she looked back over her own career Helen was proud of what she had achieved, proud of the amazement in men's eyes when they realized that one of the biggest contracting firms in the city was run by a woman no more than five feet tall. Charlotte should also be able to earn the same, respect.

'All right, I'll give you a try. But remember, I'll be trying you out just the same as I'd try out any other person I take on. You can come with me tomorrow and we'll see how it suits you.'

—

While Helen and Charlotte were in the office next day William came hurrying across the yard and paused in the doorway, blinking to adjust his eyes to the dimness after the brilliant sunshine. Charlotte was standing behind her mother's chair, looking over her shoulder at one of the account ledgers, and at the sight of her he visibly reeled. Then he put his hands up to his eyes and rubbed them as if he could not believe what he was seeing.

The girl noted his surprise and asked in concern, 'Are you all right, William?'

He collected himself quickly, saying, 'Oh, it's you, Miss Charlotte. I'm fine, miss, it was just I couldn't see for a bit coming in from the sunshine.'

Later however he waylaid Helen and said to her, 'My word, seeing Miss Charlotte in there gave me an awful turn. It's a while since she's been down and the lassie's become the spitting image of Mrs Ker. I've never seen the like of it. When I saw her in the office, I thought it was Mrs Ker come back from the dead.'

Helen nodded. She had never confided the story of Charlotte to William, but now she said quite simply, 'She's Mrs Ker's daughter, that's why.' And she went on to tell him the whole story, for she had enough confidence in him to know that her trust would not be abused. Her irrational fear that Miss Vee's brother and his family, high placed in Edinburgh society now, might claim the girl if they knew the truth had never left her.

The realization that Charlotte had grown into a woman of startling beauty unsettled Helen. Soon her girl would want to be married, soon suitors would come calling, for she was almost the same age as Veronica had been when she married John Ker. Though Charlotte was a more reserved and less insecure character than her mother, Helen was terrified of her making similar mistakes. But Charlotte did not seem to have any problems of a romantic kind. She had many friends and went out socially to various parties and balls, but her main concentration was on work. Every day she accompanied Helen to the yard where, bit by bit, she had taken over dealing with people wanting to hire carriages. The customers appreciated being attended to by such a graceful, well-bred young woman, and her confidence rose as Helen left more of that side of the business in her control.

But one day she noticed a sad look in the girl's eyes and decided to find out why it was there.

'I'm driving out to Queensferry to speak to a ship's master who brings bricks across from the works in Fife. Would you like to come out with me?' she asked Charlotte, who brightened and nodded eagerly.

'Oh, yes, it's a lovely day. A drive would be pleasant. Besides I want to talk to you…'

Apparently her mind had been running along the same lines as her mother's so it did not take long to find out what the trouble was. It was that deceiver love, of course, Helen discovered with a sinking heart. She might have guessed that a creature of such perfection as her daughter would not be able to steer away from its stormy whirlpools for long.

'Do you remember George Buchanan?' Charlotte began by asking idly – too idly – as they drove along a long straight road lined with beech trees that were just beginning to show the first burnishing of autumn in their leaves. For a few moments Helen looked nonplussed so Charlotte persisted, 'He's the boy who lives next door…'

'The medical student one?' Helen had seen the young man coming and going but she was still only on nodding acquaintance with his snobbish mother and had never exchanged more than a few words of greeting with him.

'Yes, that's right. That's him…' Charlotte's voice went soft at the memory of George. 'I met him properly about six months ago at a ball. He's a very nice young man. Mother…'

She called Helen 'Mother' in spite of knowing about her parentage, and each time Helen's heart felt warm with pleasure and gratitude.

'I'm sure he is, my dear.' This was the time to be cautious and not jump to conclusions.

'We've become friendly,' continued Charlotte, watching for a reaction because she knew how little Helen thought of the Buchanan parents. But Helen remained impassive.

'That's good.'

'In fact, I'm in love with him.' There was silence between them for a long time and an unasked question hung in the air. Then Helen's hand crept along the horsehair seat to clasp Charlotte's.

'Does he love you, my dear?'

'Yes, he does. He's very much in love with me. He wants to marry me, Mother.'

Helen looked at her daughter, a woman now and ready to be married. She tried to remember more about Gorge Buchanan but all she could summon up was a dim memory of his tall figure striding along Ann Street in the evening, books beneath his arm. He's a respectable young man in a good profession. He'll be able to look after her, she told herself. Oh, but is he good enough for my dearest Charlotte? Is he kind?

The girl was watching her, waiting for a reaction. 'It's good that he loves you,' Helen said at last. 'I'm glad of that – just so long as you're happy, my dearest.'

This was the time when the old, long unspoken Gaelic words of affection and endearment sprang without thinking to her lips, but she bit them back. Charlotte would not understand what she was saying if she called her *a luaidh*. But what was wrong? Instead of being radiant, the girl was weeping, slow tears trickling down each side of her delightful nose. At the sight of them Helen became defensive and angry.

'So what's wrong? Has he hurt you in some way? My God, if he has I'll go round there and tell him and his parents a few things…'

'Oh no, George wouldn't hurt me. He's as unhappy as I am. It's his parents. They say I'm not good enough for him. They're absolutely against him seeing me. His mother's furious that he wants to marry me.'

Helen jumped up and down in her seat with rage, making the coachman turn round and stare at her in surprise.

'Drive on, drive on.' She gestured with her arm through the window in the cab hood, while to Charlotte she said, 'I've never liked that woman. You're for better than she is, I can tell you that. I know which family she comes from – a low-born lot. She can't fool me. I've a long memory. All her boasts don't impress me. Her father's grandfather pushed a barrow in the Lawnmarket selling ribbons and laces when my mother was a girl. Now she's married a lawyer and thinks she's very grand, but I know where she came from.'

She was almost incoherent with anger, her face flushed red and her fists balled as if to take a punch at her snobbish neighbour. In spite of her own sadness Charlotte almost laughed.

'Oh Mother, don't be so upset. I knew you'd be angry when you heard. But listen, this is serious. George says that his father and mother are refusing to buy him into a practice if he marries me.'

Helen sobered at once. She knew how expensive it could be to set a young man up in medicine in Edinburgh. 'How much does he need?' she asked.

'Oh, he wouldn't take it from us. He's terribly proud. But he's worked out a solution – he's going to sign on with the East India Company as a surgeon and go to Bengal for seven years.'

The memory of their long talks about this brought the sadness back to her face and Helen stared at her in horror.

'Is he planning to take you with him? India's a terrible place for women. They die like flies. You can't go to Bengal, my dearest child, you just can't.'

Charlotte shook her head. 'Oh, I wish I could. I'd go with him tomorrow. I wouldn't be afraid. I love him so much. And he'd take me if he could but the Company won't send out young men if they're married. He'll have to sign on for seven years and hope to make enough money during that time to set up on his own when he comes back here.'

'Seven years!' exclaimed Helen, thinking it was a very long time for someone in love at eighteen. Her heart ached for them. Poor Charlotte. Poor George. There was also the fear that George wouldn't survive Bengal, for though he was a tall and well-built young man, she seemed to remember there was a delicacy about him that the diseases of the East would search out.

Charlotte was speaking again, the words tumbling out of her. 'We went together to see his mother and she said awful things.'

Helen bristled. 'Like what?'

But Charlotte was not prepared to tell her. All she would say was that Mrs Buchanan had turned her down as a bride for George because she was of low birth and had no dowry.

'I know how hard things have been for you, Mother, though you've never spoken of it, and I don't expect you to give me a dowry so that George could buy himself a practice. So he's going to Bengal. We've both made up our minds to wait.'

Helen's heart was almost breaking with pity as she held her weeping daughter's hands. If life had been fair this child would have been eagerly sought after as a bride by people for superior to George's horrible mother. She could imagine the delighted reaction next door if he went home and announced he was engaged to be married to the daughter of the landowner and social lion Sir Alexander Renton!

'Tell George to come and see me,' Helen said. 'I'll have to think about all this, but you've not to worry. I'm sure we can work things out so that he doesn't have to sail off to Bengal.'

For the rest of their drive Helen was abstracted, sunk in her own thoughts – doing her usual calculations. Charlotte's bombshell had come at a time when there was no money to spare from the business. Every penny was needed to carry through the contracts they had undertaken and only that morning she had heard rumours that King George was planning a visit to Edinburgh soon. If he did come, Cameron and Watt's services would be in great demand from the fashionable throng – and the carriages would have to be in excellent condition, pulled by the best horses. To sell a horse or a carriage now would ruin all their prospects.

I could sell the house, she thought, but quailed at the idea of leaving pretty Ann Street and the house which Andrew had bought for her with such pride. She'd do that if necessary, but there had to be another way, there had to be…

Thinking of all this, Helen looked at the child of Renton and Veronica and felt a burning sense of injustice. Charlotte should have some claim on her father's vast possessions. If he were to see her, surely he would be proud, prouder indeed than he could possibly be of his lumpish legitimate daughter. For if he was anything, Renton had always been a connoisseur of beauty.

'It's not fair, it's not fair,' she said aloud.

Charlotte, misunderstanding her mother's cry, shook her head. 'Oh, don't worry. Mother. I shouldn't have told you about our troubles now when you're so busy. It'll work out in the end. I'm sure of that. Seven years is not a lifetime. And when George comes back, We'll be so happy!'

—

News of the people in Berwickshire came to William through his family in Hutton. He told Helen about Edward being sent with his regiment to the West Indies, and that Elizabeth had finally married. The girl had settled down very well. Susan Ker was still alive, more acid-tongued than ever.

On her return from Queensferry with Charlotte, who was only half reassured by her mother's confidence that some-thing could be done to prevent her darling George sailing for Calcutta, Helen sought out her chief assistant and asked him, 'Do you ever hear anything about Renton? Where is he now?'

'It's funny you should ask that,' was the answer. 'Only yesterday I heard he's pretty hard up in himself. Very ill, they say. He's been brought to his house in George Street so's the doctors can look at him, and to be near that daft lassie of his who's married to some fellow in the West. Folk think he hasn't long to go.'

He was surprised at Helen's reaction to this bit of news. She looked shocked.

'Oh, that's awful. He can't die yet. What number George Street is his house?'

'I think it's ninety, but why're you so worried about him? I'd have thought you'd have been pleased to hear he's on his last legs.'

She shook her head. That sort of revenge had truly never occurred to her. 'It's because of Charlotte. He's her father, I told you that once, didn't I? I want to talk to him about her. He's the only one who can help.'

Over the years Helen had listened eagerly to William's snatches of news about Miss Vee's lover. When she heard of his wife's death, only a year after their marriage, she was not surprised to learn too that he eagerly resumed his old rakish ways. He went coursing, whoring, cock fighting and especially racing more than ever; his enhanced estates supported him in splendour and his daughter was brought up by his married sister.

In spite of her simplicity the girl, sole heiress to vast lands in Ayrshire and Berwickshire, had been greatly sought after in marriage, and when she was sixteen a battery of lawyers had drawn up her marriage settlement. The lucky man who passed her father's scrutiny was an army officer called Edward Johnstone, possessed of a good blood line connected on both male and female lines to ducal houses. The fact that he had no money did not matter a great deal for he was docile and ready to do whatever Sir Alexander told him. Within a few months of the wedding the girl was pregnant and Renton was fully confident that she would bear a male heir for his possessions. She did as he expected, of course.

Ignoring any protests on the part of the parents, he stipulated exactly how this son should be brought up. He detailed how he should be educated – at Eton and in Europe – and, because the money was carefully tied up with trustees who were in his confidence, he was sure his wishes would be carried out to the letter. He ordered the child's parents to change his surname to Johnstone-Renton. The lands of Mordington and Lamberton were going to stay in Renton hands, even if he had to bend the facts.

–

The manservant who answered the door to Helen had obviously been drinking. His livery was stained and crumpled as if he'd slept in it, and just by the look of him Helen knew that Renton was beyond help. In health, he would not have suffered for a moment to be waited on by such a disreputable-looking character.

'The master's unwell, he's seeing nobody,' the man told her, casting his eye over her drab working clothes and dismissing her as not of the quality.

'He'll see me,' she said firmly and stood her ground on the wide doorstep. 'Just you go and tell him that Helen Cameron has come to speak to him about Veronica Ker.'

In the vast bedroom above the front door Alexander Renton's long body lay stretched on the bed, his head propped up on pillows so that he could see the changing sky over the roofs opposite. Piercing his view like a raised dagger was the steeple of a church, an unpleasant reminder of what was ahead for him.

He heard raised voices coming from his doorstep and listened intently, for although weakness was fast overtaking his body, his brain was as sharp as ever. The days were long for him, enlivened only by visits from his doctors or lawyers and with the occasional call by his boisterous daughter or her milk-and-water husband. The baby, his heir, was being looked after by an army of nursemaids and Renton gave regular orders about every detail of his upbringing – he had to be weaned early, to have a dog, to be put on a horse as soon as his backbone was strong enough to hold him upright. The grandfather liked to think that he was creating another version of himself to carry on when he had gone.

But, though he appeared indifferent, the thought of his approaching death terrified him and he was not deceived by the false reassurances of his medical men. They couldn't stop what was happening to him; they couldn't repair his faltering heart or bring strength back to his wasted body. At this thought, he raised one feeble arm and examined his hand. Liver spots dotted the loose, parchment-like skin, the bones showed clearly – and the realization of age and decay made a sweat of fear run down his back.

Like many men of fashion, Renton had only paid lip service to religion. He went to church when it pleased him and walked out if the sermon was too long. Because he had the power of appointing clergymen to the livings on his lands, he felt that injunctions from the pulpit were directed at other, more lowly people, not at him, for he was the squire, a man of property, who could do what he liked. Squires and gentlemen were above the prohibitions that lesser people observed. If they were not able to dodge death, surely they would be able to ignore retribution and hellfire. When he was younger, hellfire to him was the name of a club; heaven was a sexual transport with some complaisant woman. Even death had been unthinkable but now it stood in the corner of his room, mocking him, waiting for him. For the first time in his life he was worried about his immortal soul. When he dropped off to sleep he often dreamt that the flames of hell were licking round his body, and he woke in agony.

For the first time in his life, too, he sent for a clergyman and listened avidly for reassurances of life hereafter. If only the man wouldn't harp on sins and the need for repentance.

'Bring me another minister. I don't like the one you sent yesterday,' he told his vacant-faced daughter when she came in her rustling silks to sit by his bed.

But the second minister was even worse than the first; more insistent that nothing a man had ever done in his life would escape the notice of the Almighty. Renton didn't want to hear that sort of thing and it worried him greatly that he would not be able to buy or bully himself a way into heaven.

So it was a relief to be distracted from such thoughts by the voices of his man and a woman arguing beneath his window. He was waiting in anticipation of hearing what it was all about when his servant came reeling into the room and said, 'There's a common-looking woman at the door who says you'll speak to her.'

'*Sir*,' reminded Renton. He disliked this servant and knew of his drinking, but was powerless to take a horsewhip to him as he would once have done. When he complained to his sister she hushed him, telling him not to worry. It was difficult to find people to nurse her fractious brother and she had no intention of dispensing with the staff in the house. Better the thieves she knew, she felt, than the unknown ones who would move in on their tails.

'There's a woman called Helen Cameron asking to speak to you, *sir*,' said the servant in an insolent tone.

The response was surprising. 'Send her up,' said Renton.

The house was luxuriously furnished with swagged silk curtains and marble figures in the hall, large oil printings on the walls and a dark red turkey carpet on the floor of the bedroom where Veronica's lover lay, but Helen was obviously unimpressed by the grandeur as she marched like a soldier across the carpet towards the bed and sat down in the chair which Renton indicated.

'You haven't changed much,' he said to her without preamble.

'You have,' she told him bluntly. His undiminished size was evident from the outline of the long legs beneath the coverlet, but his substance had gone, the bones were fleshless and the face was worn and wrinkled. His once dark hair was steel grey. She could tell from his face that he was dying and his eyes gave away his terror of the prospect. Death was the only thing that could finally bring fear to Sir Alexander.

'I've come about your daughter,' she announced.

'Mrs Johnstone?' He was bewildered by why Veronica's maid was concerned about her.

'Not her, your *first* daughter – Charlotte, Miss Vee's child.' She sat firmly in her chair with her hands folded in her lap and stared accusingly at him.

He shifted uneasily in the bed and replied, 'We talked of that before, as I recall. I told you there was no certainty that child was mine.'

'I thought perhaps you'd think differently about it now. I was with Miss Vee all the time after she left Broadmeadows and I know the child was yours. I know where and when she was conceived – and so do you. But I've not come to argue about it. She's your daughter and she's grown into a fine girl. You ought to be proud of her.'

He turned his head on the pillow and stared out of the window. 'I've seen her. She's very like her mother.'

Helen was surprised and slightly angry at this. 'Where did you see my Charlotte?'

He turned his head back to look directly at her. 'At Leith Races two years ago. She was there with you. I recognized her at once. It was like seeing her mother again.'

'She's your child, you know that, don't you?'

'I don't deny it.' He sounded weary and she could see that he was already growing tired.

'I've come to see you because she wants to marry but the boy's parents won't agree. They think she's my daughter. They think she's beneath him – and besides she hasn't a dowry.'

A spark of interest shone in his eyes as he asked, 'Who's the man?'

She told him, adding the details of Mrs Buchanan's unjustified snobbery.

'Damned plebs,' growled Renton in as near an approach to his old way of speaking as she had heard that day. Then he asked, 'And what do you expect me to do about it?'

'I want you to give her a dowry. She's your child and she has nothing. You've never given her as much as a crust of bread and you've more than enough. You're dying…'

He flinched from the word. 'You mean I could assuage my soul by admitting to her parentage and putting her in my will? There's no way I'll do that, not even if it means I'll go to heaven for it. I've a grandson and he's having the lot.'

'No, I don't mean that. I just mean that you could give her a little money so that her George can buy a practice and not go to Bengal. That's a terrible place, I hear, and he might never come back. She loves him. If he died out there it would be a terrible blow for her.'

Love. The woman threw emotive words about – love and death. He sank farther down into his bed and closed his eyes. For a moment she thought he was going to sleep but he was only thinking about Veronica and her anguished lovemaking, all in the past now, all so long ago. He remembered the promises he had made to her; he remembered her tenderness and her trust. Why did this servant have to turn up bringing all those memories with her?

When he opened his eyes, he said, 'Ring the bell for my man. When this is done, don't come back. I don't want to see or hear of you or that girl again. I'm not going to acknowledge her openly, but I'll give her some money. I suppose I owe it to her.'

When the servant came sauntering in, Renton ordered, 'Go and fetch my lawyer. Tell him to come at once. I need him immediately.'

Then he said to Helen, 'Leave me now. I'll do what's necessary. The papers will be sent to you. Please go away, I'm very tired.'

Should she thank him, should she shake his withered hand? Awkwardly she stood up and stared down at the figure on the bed but he solved the problem for her by closing his eyes as if she were not there. Without a backward glance she left him and let herself out of the front door. On the pavement she was surprised to realize that her legs were shaking and she swayed, fighting back a feeling of faintness, but Helen Cameron had never fainted in her life and she wasn't going to start now.

–

The impressively sealed packet arrived at Ann Street two days later by special messenger. Helen had gone down to Leith as usual and came home in the afternoon to find her daughter sitting in the parlour with papers strewn over the table and a look of shock on her face. Her hands were trembling when she pushed them towards Helen.

'These came addressed to me. They're from some lawyer called MacKenzie. I can't understand it. It must be some sort of a hoax.'

Helen pulled off her bonnet and sat down beside the girl to read, the papers. Halfway through she gave a gasp of genuine surprise and looked up at Charlotte. 'I'd never have believed it! I never expected this!' she said.

The girl put out a hand to grasp Helen's. 'You had something to do with it, didn't you? Oh, my dearest Mother, how did you manage to work this miracle?'

Shaking her head for silence Helen read the papers again and then stood up with a look of sheer delight, crying out exultantly, 'I didn't think he had a heart but I was wrong. Your father's more than done his duty by you, my dearest girl.'

Renton had given Charlotte Watt the sum of £20,000, partly in cash and partly in securities. There were no conditions on the gift, it was to be hers without encumbrance.

He had given his daughter the sum of money that Ker had demanded for the loss of Veronica. He had made amends for the ruin of other people's lives by paying up in the end.

Charlotte was crying over the stiffly written sheets. 'But it's all so official. There's not a word from my father. It can't be true. It must be a dream. Why should he give me so much money – and so distantly? It's a fortune.'

And indeed it was. He had given her enough money to set her up comfortably for life. She could buy an estate and live like a lady if she chose.

Helen was not so impressed by the size of the gift as by the fact that it had been made. 'There's plenty where that came from. Your father's a very rich man. It's what he owed your mother, really. That's the value Ker put on her...' she told Charlotte, thinking it a pity that he could not have spared a fraction of the sum to help poor Miss Vee when she was so sorely troubled. However, that was all past and Charlotte's need was in the present.

Seeing that it was no joke, no dream, the girl became almost delirious with delight. 'But it's so much. I'll have to tell George. We'll go to see my father and thank him.'

Helen put out a hand to restrain her from jumping up there and then to go to George Street. 'You mustn't do that. He's handed some of his fortune over to you but he won't want to see you. He told me that.'

Then she remembered Renton's voice as he compared Charlotte to her mother. He was paying his debt to Veronica.

Charlotte was dancing around happily. 'Then I'll go into the garden and tell George. He won't have to go to Bengal now. Oh, I'm so happy. Thank you, thank you so much. Mother,' and she hugged Helen so tight that the breath was almost driven out of the woman's body.

'Let me come next door when you break the news to his mother. Let me hear you telling her. I'd enjoy that,' Helen pleaded, not wanting to miss the pleasure of seeing her neighbour's attitude change.

When they arrived on Mrs Buchanan's doorstep that evening she was at home but reluctant to see them. 'I can't spare time for that girl and her mother now. I've a headache with all this bother about you going off to India,' she told her son when the maidservant announced the callers.

'I'd like you to see them,' he said firmly, for he knew already of Charlotte's good news and had had difficulty all afternoon keeping his delight from his mother.

So they were shown in to be greeted by a stiff-backed Mrs Buchanan who did not offer them any refreshment but sat stonily in her chair regarding Charlotte and Helen as if they were scarlet women.

'What's the purpose of your call? If it's to plead with me to change my mind, I'm afraid that is impossible,' she announced in a haughty tone.

Helen saw the girl was nervous and took the initiative. 'Your son and my daughter would like to marry, but you know that already. I've come to talk to you about it.'

'There's nothing to say. George has told me about this infatuation but his father and I are convinced it would be a most inadvantageous match,' said his mother, glancing at her tall, mild-faced son who stood with one arm along the chimneypiece impassively watching her.

'It's a pity you feel like that because I'm much in favour of it,' Helen replied coolly, keeping her temper with difficulty.

'I expect you are. There's nothing but advantages in it for you – financially and socially, if I may say so.'

'Can you tell me exactly what objections you have against my daughter as a wife for your son?'

'Well Mrs Watt, that's rather embarrassing, but if you insist – first of all, her family is very obscure. We understand that your husband was one of Deacon Brodie's – er – sons.'

'He was one of the Deacon's bastards, if that's what you mean, but my Andrew wasn't Charlotte's real father. She only took his name.'

This was news to Mrs Buchanan who looked askance. Helen had given her more powder for her gun. 'Am I to take it she's illegitimate as well?'

Helen looked down at her feet in mock shame. 'I suppose you could say she is, yes, but there's a lot of it about. I remember your own grandmother who kept the lodging house in Blackfriars Street. I don't think she was married to anyone, though she had several children. Am I right.?'

The other woman's face reddened slowly and she swallowed. 'That's as may be, but at least my family gave their daughters dowries when they married.'

'If they *did* marry,' amended Helen. 'But don't worry. My Charlotte has a dowry all right.'

'Indeed? My husband and I understood that she has no dowry.'

'Why should we mention it? I don't believe in attracting the wrong sort of suitor for my daughter by boasting about her fortune. She's not up for sale. But Charlotte has a dowry. Quite a considerable dowry in fact.'

This changed the tone of the conversation slightly but George's mother was still very condescending.

'Mrs Watt, a few hundred pounds is neither here nor there to people like us, you know. My son can do much better than that. He's qualified as a doctor, he's a very good marriage prospect.'

Helen ignored that and said, 'I expect he's told you that he's going to marry Charlotte whether she has a dowry or not. I'm glad to say that they won't be poor. They won't have to scrape by on a doctor's fees or on a hundred pounds a year.'

'Oh, so you think he will marry her, do you? They'll have to wait for that if his father and I have anything to do with it, and time changes lots of things. If she's so well dowried, how much will she bring with her exactly?'

Helen sat back in her chair and paused for a moment, enjoying the satisfaction of delivering her knife thrust with skill and to the heart. 'Well, let me see. Um… how much was it at the last reckoning, darling?' This was directed at Charlotte, who shook her head dumbly, not knowing exactly what was expected of her. With a smile Helen continued, 'I think you'd find that today she's worth some twenty thousand pounds – and you and I both know that twenty thousand yields six hundred a year at a safe three per cent… They could live very comfortably on that, couldn't they? Your son's earnings as a doctor would give them just that little bit extra for fripperies.'

1822

The wedding was in the spring, a quiet affair that gave little hint of the riches possessed by the bride, though keen-eyed spectators recognized the splendour of her dress, made of heavy cream silk imported from France and decorated with flounces of Brussels lace which were available only from the exclusive, and very expensive, Miss Draffin of Princes Street.

Helen wept during the ceremony because it was a bitter sweet occasion for her. Although she had a firmer line to her mouth than Veronica, Charlotte looked so like her lovely mother as she stood before the clergyman that Helen's mind flew back across the years to the times she spent with Miss Vee – at Berwick and Broadmeadows, but most of all at Durham when she alone had the care of the poor woman. She remembered the day they brought her dripping body up from the tree-filled gorge of the Wear, the blue gown clinging to her like the skin of a limp fish. There had not been much chance to weep then, and the tears had been saved up inside her till now. She felt a vast release as she let them free.

At her side Colin glanced anxiously into her face. 'Don't cry,' he whispered. 'George is a good fellow. He'll be kind to her. They're happy, Mama.'

'It's not that,' she gulped. How could she tell him that some of her tears were tears of pride? Her soul soared with pure delight as she looked at her lovely daughter – for Charlotte was her daughter in everything but blood – and her pleasure was so intense that it brought tears with it.

The newly married couple rode to Leith Docks in a Cameron and Watt carriage, all decorated by Colin with white narcissi and hyacinths, to board a ship that would take them to France for their honeymoon. Waving them off from the quay, the wedding party commented about their destination – some with envy and others with patriotic disapproval, for memories of war were still raw. Helen's eyes were shining at the thought of Paris. To her it seemed like fairy land. The farthest she had ever travelled was to Durham – but foreign travel and fine clothes were what her Charlotte deserved, it was her birthright.

She turned to William Smith, awkward-looking in his best black broadcloth suit, and asked him, 'Don't you long to see Paris, William?'

He gave a snort. 'Paris, not me! I've enough trouble understanding the folk in Edinbury.' He always called the city that, as did everyone in rural Berwickshire.

Riding home in the dusk, Colin sat beside his mother and strove to divert her with interesting conversation because he feared that she would slip into the depression of anticlimax.

He was right, too, because as she gazed around the town through which they were driving she was noting the places for which her Andrew had carted the stones – this building and that bridge, this road and that gateway. Oh Andrew, I miss you! she thought. It would have been good tonight to sit with him beside the parlour fire and go over every tiny incident of Charlotte's wedding. But she had no one with whom to share her innermost feelings – only Colin, but he was still a child.

Helen saw his anxious face watching her and took his hand gently without speaking. She thought, There's still work for me to do. I must safeguard the business till Colin's old enough to take it over from me. And that would not be long, for her son was growing fast.

As if he could read her mind, the boy said, 'I've been thinking about how we're going to decorate our yard when he comes in the summer. He'll have to pass our gate on his way up to Edinburgh.'

She stared at him. 'When who comes?'

'The King of course, Mama. Don't say you've forgotten the King's coming in August? We'll have such a busy time when he comes. The yard'll have to be all decorated for him.'

'Goodness me, my grandfather would be awful angry if he knew I was putting flags out for a Hanoverian,' she said to her son with a laugh, imagining old Colin's reaction to the news of a visit from George IV.

Young Colin only grinned. 'But we'll have to do it. If it worries you too much, I'll think of some way of showing your Jacobite sympathies,' he assured her.

–

The warm summer days had turned Colin's skin to the same biscuit colour as his father used to be in the fine weather. One day she caught a golden glimpse of him, gleaming like a young god in one of her grandfather's stories, as he swam naked with a group of his friends in the Water of Leith that ran through its little valley near their house. At the sight of his long, lean body her heart gave a strange yearning twist and she looked hurriedly away. Her son was growing up fast, drawn towards the sun like one of the plants in her carefully tended garden. It made her feel proud but it also made her feel old and soon to be useless.

She looked at him with a new awareness as they sat together taking early breakfast in their parlour on the day before the King was due to arrive at Leith for the ceremonial visit that the whole of Edinburgh had been eagerly awaiting for months. Colin was greatly excited but the thought of seeing a king did not interest Helen much – her chief concern was that the business arrangements should all run smoothly. To calm her fears and reassure herself, she took a deep breath, gratefully inhaling the spicy scent of her pink and white moss roses. Her garden always calmed Helen, and when she had worries would go and sit beneath her rose arbour until they were smoothed away.

But there was no time to sit in contemplation of her flowers now. Colin was quickly spooning up his porridge, eager to go down to the yard and see what was on the schedule for that day. During his holidays from school he acted as her companion, trying to fill the gap left in her life after Charlotte married. But things had been less solitary recently since Charlotte and George came back from France, visibly enchanted with each other and full of stories about their travels. They had gone to live only a couple of miles across the town in one of the fine new houses that Cameron and Watt had helped to build on the side of the Calton Hill looking down at Leith.

Helen smiled at her son. 'Take your time eating, it'll be a long day,' she warned. He loved going with her to the yard and, recognizing his longing to take part in the business, she had begun consulting him and asking his advice about the day-to-day problems she and William encountered. Colin filled a huge gap in her widowhood because although William was a good reliable man, he was not 'family' and she found it impossible to reveal herself fully to him. Charlotte still came down to the yard from time to time but Helen would not allow her to continue with the hiring of carriages.

'It wouldn't be right. Your husband has a good practice, with people of quality as his patients. They'd be shocked if they knew that his wife worked in a carriage hiring yard!'

So, during the school holidays, Colin had taken over his sister's job and Helen saw that he was doing it well. She had a dilemma about him because he was a good scholar and his teachers were urging her to send him to the university.

But when she asked him what he wanted to do in life, he looked astonished and replied, 'I want to work with you, of course. I want to help you, run our business.'

'*Our* business' – the words warmed her heart.

In the gig Helen handed the reins to Colin and let him drive her down to Leith in the soft summer sunshine. She admired the deft way he handled the sprightly bay horse between the shafts. William had taught her son well, she reflected as she settled back in the seat. She had not felt so happy or optimistic for years. The anxieties that had haunted her for so long, ever since Andrew died in fact, were gradually receding.

Only last week Charlotte had whispered to Helen that she was going to be a mother when next spring came. A grandchild would be such a delight for Helen. She'd tell it all the stories her grandfather had told her, she'd buy it toys and penny candy and take it out with her in the gig. Her eyes shone with the anticipation of her pleasure.

The business, perhaps Helen's most major concern over the years of her widowhood, was thriving at last. Her enemies had finally given up trying to oust her. Scrimgeour, her chief rival, had died and his capacity for making trouble died with him. Success had come to her at last and she was able to look to the future with confidence. The contracting side of her enterprise was steadily profitable but the real surprise had been how the hiring of horses and carriages had overtaken it. The Widow Watt's equipages were now the most sought after in town. Anyone attending a prestigious event and wanting to put on a good show left their own dog cart and aged pony at home and sallied out in a four-in-hand driven by one of Helen's liveried coachmen.

The excitement when details of the King's visit were made official meant that her yard was besieged with prospective customers. Everyone in Edinburgh, it seemed, wanted one of her carriages to ride in behind their ruler. They tried to bully her and they tried to bribe her until she announced that priority would be given to long-established and respected clients. It was difficult sometimes to persuade the others that she would play fair by them and keep their names on her waiting list. That list had been growing in size over the past weeks until it would take treble the capacity of her yard to cope with them.

Throughout the early summer Helen and William, accompanied sometimes by Colin, made excursions into the countryside to buy more horses, and they were particular about the animals they took. To suit them a horse had to look splendid and be well mannered. Such paragons were few and far between, and Helen reconciled herself to turning away many customers. She would not risk putting inferior turn-outs on the road.

When Colin turned the pony's head into their cobbled yard she was presented with a scene of frenzied activity.

The men had been working since dawn, hauling freshly enamelled and shining carriages out of the sheds. Each carriage had the recently devised Cameron and Watt crest painted on its doors and they were lined up with their shafts pointing towards the sky while the workers crawled over them polishing and buffing, dragging out the seat cushions, shampooing out any stains and beating them so that the stuffing smelt fresh and sweet.

Inside the stables the hay nets and corn bins were brimming over, for horses that were going to work hard needed good feeding. The immensely muscled farrier strode past her with a respectful salute. He had donned his leather apron and was off to hammer out spare horseshoes that he would range in readiness along the beams of his blacksmith's shop at the back of the premises. A gaggle of young lads could be seen through the open door of the tackroom, polishing the saddlery till it sparkled and shone. Diminutive grooms hissed and crooned as they buffed the horses' coats to satiny perfection. Surveying all this, Helen felt like the Duke of Wellington marshalling troops for battle. Bursting with pride, she stepped down from the gig and bustled into the office where her trusty Smith was waiting.

He looked up at her with admiration. He'd known she'd arrive early, dressed for action. Her only concession to femininity and the gaiety that seemed to fill the city was a posy of fresh roses tucked into the band of her bonnet. William found it difficult to realize that nearly thirty years had passed since they first met in the kitchen quarters at Ker's house in Berwick. We've all come a long way since then, he reflected as his mind went back over the things that had happened to them. Now she was briskly taking off the pretty bonnet and shaking her head to loosen the curls tucked tight against her face. Though she must be forty, there was no grey in her hair; her skin was unlined and her eyes sparkled like a child's with the enthusiasm of feeing a huge new challenge.

'Let's put things in order, William,' she said, wrapping her tiny waist with a long white apron. 'We must work it all out in advance. I don't want to disappoint our customers. Nothing must go wrong, not one single thing. If anything does they'll be baying for our blood.'

—

The whole of Edinburgh was gripped in a kind of Royalty-worshipping madness by the beginning of the second week of August, 1822. There had never been such a demand for smart clothes, even from people who had no hope of being invited to any functions that the King would grace. Tailors and seamstresses worked all night through to fulfil their orders. In far away lands ostriches were robbed of their tails to provide fine feathers for Edinburgh ladies. Lace makers in France made their fingers bleed for the flounces. Florists rushed to and fro, stripping gardens for miles around, gathering up bouquets and floral tributes to decorate house fronts. Flag makers had a bumper time; boxes and crates of fireworks were dragged into the city and stored – often in highly volatile conditions – in every district. It was impossible to find a room to rent throughout the length or breadth of Edinburgh as visitors congregated in the capital, eagerly looking forward to the social whirl that inevitably attended on the presence of a court. Property owners fortunate enough to possess rooms overlooking the route of the Royal procession up Leith Walk to Holyrood Palace rented out seats in their windows for as much as they would previously have expected for renting the room for a year. Musicians practised, singers ran through their scales, the ballrooms and assembly suites of the city had their floors waxed till they looked like indoor lakes, mirrors were polished, furniture reupholstered, everything in sight was covered with fresh, new paint. There had not been such a rush and bustle in living memory.

It was not as if the good folk of Edinburgh were all enthusiastic supporters of the Hanoverians. Far from it. Fat King George, better known by his nickname Prinny, had been for a long time an object of some scorn because of his philandering with women, his grossness of body and his effeteness of manner – none of these qualities being things which normally appealed to the sobersided Scots. But at least he had agreed to pay them a visit, his first to Scotland. And he was a *king*. The snobbery of the upper classes was excited. They wanted to shake his hand and exchange a remark with him, even if they were to go away later and make jokes about what he said.

Helen Watt and William Smith did not leave the yard during the Tuesday night before the King was due to arrive at Leith. They sat up in their office, worrying about the line of carriages which were to troop out of their premises the next day. They consoled each other's fears and encouraged each other when doubts were voiced. William kept rushing into the stables to make sure that the horses were resting; Helen kept going over and over her lists of customers until in the end she fell asleep in her chair from sheer exhaustion.

When the Wednesday morning dawned it was raining, a fine wet, typical Edinburgh drizzle, sweeping in off the sea.

The time of the Royal arrival was set for two o'clock in the afternoon, and at eleven in the morning the crowd of watchers on Calton Hill, straining their eyes through the mist, spotted the first of the flotilla of ships escorting the *Royal George* yacht come tacking into view near Inch Keith in the mouth of the Forth. A huge cheer swept the city, rolling down from the hill to be taken up along the shore and the streets.

As time passed, the ships grew clearer… the King's yacht was being towed by *James Watt* and *Comet* steam packets, belching billows of white smoke from their short stacks. It was also solicitously surrounded by attendant ships, the *Phaeton* frigate, the *Egeria* sloop of war, the *Prince Regent* yacht, the *Calliope* and the *Chameleon* tenders, all enthusiastically firing salutes to announce their arrival at Scotland's capital city. At two o'clock the Royal yacht cast anchor in the Leith roads.

As soon as it came to rest an armada of little boats set out to bob up and down in the choppy waters around the sleek sides of the *Royal George*. People stood up on the tilting decks and waved their handkerchiefs in the King's direction.

They were eventually rewarded by a glimpse of his florid face at one of the portholes along the ship's side, but that was all they saw. King George IV was unwell. The choppy seas upset his delicate stomach. He was not going to risk his composure by setting out for the shore in such poor conditions. A message was sent out that they should all go home, for he would arrive in Leith tomorrow.

Such disappointment! The small ships turned for the shore, the crowds drifted off in the grey drizzle. Only a few hardy people stuck it out for a little longer, hoping against hope that the King might change his mind. A spluttering bonfire was lit on the top of Arthur's Seat; the illuminations in the city, especially the Royal Crown perched on the top of the gas works chimney, were set glowing and Sir Walter Scott, never one to miss an opportunity of hobnobbing with Royalty, hired a boat and had himself rowed out to the *Royal George* where he clambered up a rope ladder and ceremoniously presented the King with a silver cross which had been bought by a subscription raised by the ladies of Edinburgh. George IV, though slightly drunk by this time, appeared most gracious and promised Sir Walter that he would wear the cross when he arrived on land the following day.

Helen's yard had been organized like clockwork to dispatch coaches and carriages at three-minute intervals to eager customers waiting on the street outside. But as the news spread that His Majesty would not be setting foot on Scottish soil till the following day, the grooms, as disappointed as anyone, began unharnessing the fretful horses, and Helen had the task of consoling the downcast customers.

'We'll have to exercise the horses or else they'll kick the bottoms out of the carriages tomorrow,' said William in despair, and ordered cavalcades of riders to lead strings of bucking, kicking animals out of the yard. They set out for Leith Links to work off some of the high spirits and energy that magnificent feeding had brought.

When they had been exercised, groomed and fed, the evening was well advanced and Helen, who had not left the yard all day, suddenly felt deathly weary.

'Damn fat Geordie,' she said, wiping her brow, for the atmosphere, though overcast, was close and humid. 'I hope we don't have to go through this again tomorrow for no purpose. Pray God the weather'll be fine enough for him to risk his neck in the launch.'

William stood in the open doorway and sniffed the air. 'It's going to dry up. The rain's nearly stopped now, it'll be fair tomorrow. Don't, worry, everything'll be fine. Go on home and have some sleep. You'll make yourself ill fretting like this.'

She did as she was told, grabbing her shawl from the back of the door and telling one of her men to call a sedan chair, for no horses could be spared to carry her around. The chair men who eventually came for her were old friends whom she'd known as boys in the High Street, and the oldest of the two handed her into the chair with broad smiles.

'My word, Helen, your place's looking gey festive. But you're a Jacobite at heart like your grandfeyther, aren't you? So why all the roses and bunting on your gate?' he asked.

She looked apologetic. 'It's Colin, my laddie. He's awful keen to dress the yard up so's the King'll notice it. But he's not forgotten his grandfather. Can you read what he's put up on the gate?' she asked, leaning forward in the chair so that she could point towards Colin's handiwork. Because it was growing dark the lights in his decorations were glowing brightly, spelling out an illuminated message that would shine out even brighter as the darkness deepened: *Righ Albain Gu Brath*.

'He told me he'd asked someone to translate it into Gaelic to show that we're true Highlanders at heart,' she laughed, remembering Colin's delight as he recounted to her how he'd asked his grandmother old Agnes, for the name of someone who could devise a motto in Gaelic for him. Trust Agnes Watt, as resourceful as ever, she had not failed him.

The older sedan chair man read it and laughed, for he too could understand the Gaelic. 'German Geordie won't know what that means. He'll think you're being complimentary – but it can be taken two ways, can't it?' he said.

For *Righ Albain Gu Brath* meant *Scotland's King for ever* – Cameron and Watt were not hailing the King from London but the absent King Over The Water, the exiled Stuart.

When the joke was explained to him the younger chair man also laughed and told Helen, 'There's some other grand mottos in the town. They're stuck up on all the fine buildings. We'll take you the long way home and you can see some of them.'

George's subjects in Scotland had excelled themselves. They had built triumphal arches; put up flags and bunting; devised garlands of flowers and leaves; hung their premises with streamers and spangles. In the darkness, lighted silhouettes shone out showing profiles of George IV, his crest, the flag of St Andrews or welcoming messages. 'How's A' Wi' Ye?' adorned a perfumer's shop but more conventional ones like 'Hail to our King' or 'Scotland Welcomes Her Monarch' appeared in large numbers on all sorts of business premises and private houses. Few people had not taken the opportunity to express their pleasure at the Royal visit. As the chair was being carried down Leith's Constitution Street, the front runner turned his head to shout over his shoulder to Helen, 'Look to your left. Look at Reid the bookseller's.'

She leaned forward to spell out a transparency message that read 'Fair Fa' His Honest Sonsy Face'. She read it twice and then fell back laughing.

'Oh, that's a clever one. It's a good job they didn't put the line "…Great Chieftain O' the Puddin' Race",' she called when her giggles subsided a little.

She was carried swiftly along, laughing as she went, her tiredness almost forgotten, and did not notice the tall, well-dressed man who had been standing on the pavement outside Reid's, also reading the message. At the sound of her infectious laughter he turned round to share the joke, but started visibly when he saw her face peering out of the sedan-chair window. He seemed to lose his composure, then, collecting himself, raised an arm to hail her. But he was too late – she was gone, engulfed by the throng of people in the roadway.

–

At twelve o'clock precisely on the following day an expectant crowd was thrilled by the sound of a cannon firing from the *Royal George* to announce the moment when the King entered the barge that was to carry him ashore. King George IV was pale and felt very unwell when he finally put his foot on the heaving platform at the side of the quay. To the eager crowd he did not look very regal and imposing because his face was yellow, his eyes bloodshot and his expression so hangdog that his equerries felt it necessary to explain to the reception committee that His Majesty's stomach had been upset by the swell of the waves while crossing from his yacht. The fact of the matter however was that he had a hangover. Till late the previous night he had been sampling the best Glenlivet whisky with a crowd of cheerful, roistering cronies. While he was shaking hands with the worthies of Edinburgh his servants were engaged in throwing empty bottles overboard from the far side of his yacht.

The crowd who were watching his every move with bated breath trustingly took his pallor as a symptom of seasickness and gave him a sympathetic cheer. This grew in volume till it seemed to rival the cannon's roar and it was taken up by the people packed into the streets behind the quay, rolling away up through Leith into Edinburgh in an unending ovation.

'The King's ashore! The King has arrived! God save the King!' ran the call. Pleased, he bowed and smiled gravely, doffing his Admiral's hat with its sprigs of thistle and heather and putting a plump, appreciative hand on to the silver cross that was prominently displayed on his chest.

There had never been such a press of people packed into Bernard Street and crammed into the road alongside Customs House Quay. The next day the newspapers were to boast that three hundred thousand had turned out to greet their King, and when he received the keys of the city at the boundary of Edinburgh in Picardy Place it was generally acknowledged that there had not been known such an immense gathering since the hanging of Deacon Brodie in the High Street.

When dawn broke that morning everyone connected with the festivities had been relieved to see that the day was dry and sunny. The masses started collecting very early, filling the windows overlooking the floating platform that was to be the King's landing stage, climbing to the risk of their lives on to the tall red-tiled roofs above Young's Crown Tavern, Dickman the watchmaker's and the Leith Circulating Library. Their flag-waving became hysterical each time any little boat, no matter how shabby, bobbed about on the waters of the dock. Along the rigging of two huge men o' war tied up in the harbour, sailors in their best uniforms were sitting like swallows lining up for their autumn flights.

Helen, William and Colin saw none of this because they were rushing around in their yard. Some of the most important people in the royal procession would be riding in Cameron and Watt's equipages though the King himself, to Helen's regret, was to appear in a low-slung landau supplied from the mews of Holyrood Palace and driven by his own men from London.

She saw the royal carriage going down past her gate to Leith docks early in the morning and said with scorn, 'I could have given him a better one than that.'

Colin nodded in agreement. 'We could that. Our horses are just as good as his, too.'

Satisfied in their judgement of the opposition, they went back to work and neither lifted their heads again till they heard the cannon blast coming from Leith. 'That's him. He's arrived at last,' gasped Helen. 'Oh, my God, I hope everything goes well. I hope those horses behave themselves. I hope none of our coachmen get drunk.'

'Of course they won't,' William consoled her. 'Just keep calm. It's started now, all we can do is wait for it to finish.' When they heard military music and the clattering of thousands of hooves on the cobbles, they rushed to the gate and stood together waiting for the huge entourage to pass by.

Helen was so absorbed in noting which of the passing carriages was hers that she was oblivious to the fact that her hair was untidy and an apron was still looped up round her waist.

George IV was gratified at the crowds who had turned out to cheer him. Their raised voices and the benison of the sunshine soothed away his headache, and the waves he gave to his subjects increased in enthusiasm as he was driven along. Everywhere his eye fell there was colour and people – on specially erected scaffolding at the side of the roads, crammed into windows, pressed into alleys and side streets, on horseback, on rooftops, along the bridge across the dock, on each other's shoulders, on ships' rigging… In his long experience of official receptions this was the most enthusiastic welcome he had ever received. Scotland might not be so bad as he had feared after all. There were some damned fine-looking women among the crowd and his spirits lifted as he ran his eye over them.

He was smiling benevolently when his carriage passed Helen's yard. To her own surprise she found herself smiling back at him.

'Not so bad-looking after all, though he seems too fat for his own good,' she said to Colin in a placatory tone, as if apologizing for her weakness.

He laughed. 'Oh, come on. Mother, he's brought us a lot of business.'

They were staring in admiration at all the fine people when Charlotte's carriage, supplied by Helen of course, passed by. Dr and Mrs Buchanan were far back in the procession – which they had been invited to join because George, as an up and coming doctor, had been appointed one of the Honorary Medical Attendants to His Majesty during the Royal Visit. Charlotte gaped at the sight of her mother and brother capering in the yard, it was so unlike Helen to behave in such an undignified way.

She smiled and sat forward, waving her white-gloved hands and calling out, 'Mother, Mother, look here, don't miss us.'

Helen stopped stock still, suddenly sobered, and stared at Miss Vee's beautiful daughter. How lovely Charlotte looked with her perfectly featured face glowing beneath the leghorn-straw bonnet. Ringlets clustered on her cheeks and her eyes sparkled enough to rival the diamonds in her ears and at her neck. The pride that engulfed Helen made her almost faint with delight. It was one of the most delightful moments of her entire life.

'Charlotte, Charlotte, it's Charlotte and George,' called Colin, jumping up and down in excitement at his mother's side, but she could hardly wave her hand, so overcome was she with emotion.

If only her mother could see her, she thought – even Renton would have been proud of his daughter, but he had died, alone and bitter, only a few weeks before. Helen thought of her poor Miss Vee. If life had played her right she would have been riding in this entourage behind the King, dressed in satins and gauzes, waving to the cheering crowds. It never occurred to Helen to wish that instead of providing carriages for people of quality and standing in her gate to watch them drive by, she too might have been riding in style. But it occurred to her son and to her devoted Smith.

'You should have taken up Charlotte's invitation and ridden with her today. We could have spared you for once,' said William, thinking how fine it would have been if Helen could have dressed herself in finery from Miss Draffin's and joined the fashionable throng. She'd look as grand as any of them, he thought fiercely.

She shook her head. 'Och, don't talk nonsense. That's not the place for the likes of me.' In her heart it was sufficient for her that Charlotte was there among the elite, that Charlotte would be dancing at the balls graced by the King, that Charlotte would curtsey before him. She was satisfied that though fortunes had been spent on the clothes and jewellery which were displayed that day, not one woman in the procession looked finer or more aristocratic than her Charlotte. Pride flowed out of her like a broad river to embrace not only her daughter and son-in-law but the whole of her beloved Edinburgh which was showing itself at its very best, not as a dull provincial place but as a capital city bursting with pride and prosperity.

–

One by one the carriages began returning to the yard in the late afternoon and Helen greeted each with an eager face. 'How did it go? Was everyone quite satisfied?' she asked, anxious to make sure her customers were fully served and happy. As the reassurances flowed in she gradually relaxed and became convinced that her coachmen were truly to be considered the most skilful in the procession that had snaked its way up Leith Walk to Picardy Place, from there on along Regent Road and down to the Palace of Holyrood where His Majesty had been ceremonially presented with the Crown of Scotland. It was a relief to her when she heard that while waiting in the long line along Regent Bridge to descend into Holyrood, her carriages and their occupants were among the few to emerge unscathed from the ruck. Many others were involved in accidents caused by careless coachmen or frightened horses running into the back of the carriage in front. The weeks and weeks of careful training William had given his horses and his men had paid worthwhile dividends.

Her intense interest kept tiredness at bay until evening when all the horses were finally bedded down and the men paid a cash bonus with her thanks and congratulations. Then, in a state of exhaustion, she and Colin were packed off home to Ann Street.

William too was preparing to return to his Rachel when he heard a sharp rapping at the yard gate. Slowly he walked towards it, weariness bearing down on his shoulders like a heavy coat. Who could be knocking so late in the evening? It was nearly nine o'clock and all decent people were going to bed. When he drew back the bolt and opened the little doorway set inside the huge gate, a dark-cloaked man loomed up in the shadows.

'Is this the yard of Cameron and Watt? Is this where all the good carriages came from today?' he asked.

'Aye, it is that, but we're closed up for the night, we've nothing to hire. All our horses were out today.'

The man drew nearer. 'Let me in for a moment. I've a very special request to make… I'm from the King,' he said conspiratorially, 'just let me in, for a minute and I'll tell you about it.'

Though intrigued, William was reluctant to open the door wider but the man pushed his shoulder into the gap and stepped through, bending his head in its cocked hat as he did so. He looked around the tidy yard with approval, then at William – a long look, it seemed.

'I've come up from Holyrood. I'm in the service of the King. He sent me to ask if you would hire him a closed, plain carriage – nothing fancy, nothing that could be recognized – so that he can drive out, to see the illuminations without anyone recognizing him. We can't use any of the Palace carriages for people would know them, and you were recommended. Everyone says you're the best hirers in Edinburgh.'

349

Tired as he was, William felt a surge of pride at his words. 'Well, I don't know. The lady who owns the yard has gone home for the night.'

'Are you her husband?' The question was sharp and abrupt. William was just as sharp when he replied, 'No, I'm not... I'm her chief assistant, though. But, all right, I'll take the responsibility. I'll give you a nice gig and one of the horses that haven't been worked too hard. Come into the stables and take your pick.'

In the light of a swinging lamp the stranger looked at the horses standing in their well-filled loose boxes, pulling sweet-smelling hay from the nets tied to the walls. William, walking along at his side, could see that he knew a good horse from the way he sized them all up.

'There's Truebell or Templar, the greys. They were first back,' he offered.

The stranger shook his head. 'Not greys, people notice greys, dark horses are better.' And he gave a little laugh as he said the words as if he'd made a joke.

'Then, in that case, we've Daisy or Bella. They've not been over-worked either. They were pulling Miss Charlotte's carriage today. Miss Charlotte is Mistress Watt's lassie and she'd not be hard on them. I could let you have either one of that pair,' was William's next-suggestion.

The stranger nodded in agreement. 'All, right, let me have a look at them. I don't want anything too light. He's a bit of a weight to pull up the Edinburgh hills is our King George.'

In the end, he picked Daisy, a solidly built bay mare with powerful shoulders and a well-muscled neck. 'She'll do,' he said and then went to look at the gig. It pleased him. 'That's fine, plain and ordinary – and it's hooded.'

'Do you want me to drive?' asked William, hoping the answer would be 'no', and was pleased when the stranger shook his head.

'That won't be necessary. I'll drive myself. If you could help me harness the mare now, I'd be grateful. We might be late back

350

and you look tired. I'll keep the mare up at Holyrood for the night and bring her back tomorrow if it suits you.'

The offer was gratefully accepted and when the gig drove smartly off up Leith Walk, William was at last able to walk wearily home.

–

Full of dinner and with his mind made tranquil by brandy, Prinny leaned his vast bulk back in the corner of the gig and breathed a vinous sigh as he was driven slowly through the streets of Edinburgh. The buildings glittered with messages of light, all wishing him well, all enforcing his sense of wellbeing. From the point where the gig drew up on the Castle Esplanade he could look down across Princes Street to the glittering lights of the messages of goodwill on the front of every building. Fireworks arched across the blackness of the sky and bonfires blazed on the hills. When he closed his eyes, sparkles still danced tantalizingly beneath his eyelids.

It had been a most successful day and though he felt tired he was happy, but glad to be alone at last with his driver, whose dark shoulders rose in front of him. When they spoke to each other it was in a relaxed and informal fashion, for they knew each other well and George was not a man to disdain his servants.

'Hey, my goodfellow,' he called, 'you seem to know your way about this place pretty well. Why are you so familiar with it?'

Without turning his head, the driver said, 'Oh, I should know it well all right. I used to run those streets for a living. I was born here, Your Highness.'

'By God, you crafty devil. I never guessed you for a Scotchman. What's happened to your accent, then? You fellows are everywhere, aren't you? You have us all under your thumbs, I think,' laughed the King.

The driver laughed too. 'Maybe yes, maybe no, but we do like to travel. You know what Dr Johnson said about our best prospect being the road to England, don't you, sire?'

'Was that true for you?' asked the King.

There was a pause before the man answered, 'In a way it was – but only in a way. I think, a man makes his own prospects in life…'

They drove back down the High Street of the Old Town, and as they passed through the dark canyon between the tall houses, the driver pointed his whip and said, 'My father lived in that house over there.'

'Didn't you live with him then?'

'No, my mother and the rest of my family lived down the road a piece. They weren't married, you see…'

'So you're a bastard, like all the happiest people. My God, I've sometimes wished I hadn't a father either. It would've made for an easier life,' said the King with feeling.

He was asleep and snoring peacefully by the time the gig was driven into the inner courtyard of the Palace and a squad of hefty men in livery were waiting to carry him to bed.

–

It was still early when the King's man came driving skilfully into the yard with Daisy and the neat gig.

He was smiling as he slipped to the ground and shouted cheerfully to William as if he had known him for years, 'What a capital turn-out. His Majesty was very pleased. Is the lady here? I'd like to thank her.'

But Helen was still in bed exhausted, and Colin had taken care not to waken her when he slipped out of the house before breakfast. Now he was standing behind William, curiously eyeing the man who worked for the King.

William indicated the starry-eyed boy and said, 'She's not come down here yet but this lad's her son.'

The King's man looked at Colin in a strange way, almost as if he were affected by the sight of him. His composure was obviously shaken for some reason but he collected himself and walked across to put a hand on the boy's shoulder as if in friendship. He kept it lying there while he said, 'You're a fine-looking fellow. Tell your mother the King enjoyed his ride out in her gig. That's a good mare you have there. I'd come back to tell her myself but I have to go to Dalkeith with the court... Mind and say how much the King enjoyed himself.'

–

When Helen arrived the whole place was buzzing about the late-night customer and his glowing praise. 'Oh, I wish you could have seen him. Mama, what a grand-looking man he was! And he could handle a horse. You should have seen old Daisy stepping out for him! I've not seen her going like that since Father died,' an excited Colin told her.

The yard was almost as busy as the day before with the demands of people going to the King's grand morning levee at Holyrood. Ladies in court dresses crammed side by side in the seats of the carriages, their ostrich feathers and fans bobbing in the sunlight and their beautiful skirts spread out over their knees in falls of brilliant colour.

But the day was shorter because the King retired early to Dalkeith Palace and all the fashionable people who had been thronging along in his wake were happy to take a breather too, putting their elegantly shod feet up on their sofas and loosening their stays.

Nonetheless it was dark again before the work at Cameron and Watt's was finished. Eventually Helen and William stood together in the office, jubilant and smiling, for everything had gone like clockwork... their customers were satisfied, there had been no accidents, their profit was assured.

'We've made it, William, we've made it!' she cried in delight, and threw her arms round him, executing a jig on the paper-littered floor even though her feet hurt and her calves ached with weariness.

Their glee however was interrupted, for again there came a knocking at the stableyard gate. When William opened the inner door he saw the King's man waiting to be admitted. He was not very welcoming, saying gruffly, 'Oh, it's you. I'm hoping you're not wanting another gig the night.'

The stranger stepped into the yard, quite at home. 'No, it's not that. I came up from Dalkeith to speak to Mistress Watt, if she's here. I went to her house but her son said she wasn't back yet.'

William looked puzzled and suspicious. For a moment he wondered if he should turn the man out. Why was he bothering Helen, chasing her up at home and tracking her down so late at night? There was a note of caution in his voice as he replied, 'Aye, she's here, she's in the office. It's that door over there – but I'll take you across.'

He was not going to let this stranger go by himself into Helen's sanctum.

She was sitting on the stool in front of her high desk, her head supported on one hand and her skirts kirtled up almost to her knees. Her face was white with tiredness and she yawned as she gathered up the last of her papers.

No matter how much she would like to finish everything off, she had made a resolve to go home and sit at the fireside with Colin. She'd catch up with the paper work in the morning – and then she'd be able to confirm her expectations that the business balance sheet would show a huge profit.

'All thanks to German Geordie,' she told herself with a little chuckle. She was still smiling when she glanced up and saw William standing huge in the doorway, looking very solemn. 'It's the King's man again, mistress. He wants to speak to you.'

'Oh, must he? He's said his thanks. I'm too tired to talk to anyone now. Tell him to send us a medal or something…' she said, hopping down from the stool and taking her shawl from a peg behind her seat.

She was reaching out to turn down the lamp when there was a sound behind her of someone stepping into the office, so she called more sharply over her shoulder, 'Tell him to go away, tell him I'm not here, tell him anything you like, William… It's time to go home,' she said.

'I'll take you there with pleasure, *mo ghaoil*,' said a voice behind her. She stood stock still, frozen in mid movement with one hand reaching out to the lamp. It was impossible to move. A strange paralysis stilled her limbs and buzzing filled her ears. To clear her head she shook it slightly, for she could not believe what she was hearing.

'Let me take you home, *a luaidh*,' he said and, controlling herself with an effort she turned slowly to look at him, lifting the lamp up to illuminate his face.

He had not changed – still tall, still straight, still dashing and cheeky-looking. The grin he directed at her was challenging and his whole bearing showed the careless gaiety that he had displayed when he roamed the roads as a highwayman. It was her Peter, the man she'd thought about so often, the man she had feared was dead. Her voice when it came was little more than a whisper.

'It's not you, Peter Grant? It can't be you. Was it you who came here last night? Why didn't you say who you were then? Oh, I'm so glad they didn't hang you. I hoped you might have survived when I saw all the strange foreign money Cecil had – but she always said you were dead.'

He shrugged his, shoulders. 'Cecil was a problem. I sent her money through sailors who came into Leith, but she never wrote back with any news. Long ago I went to see the corn merchant's wife in Durham and she told me that you'd come back to Edinburgh with Andrew. But that was all I knew till I saw you in a sedan chair on the night before the King arrived.'

She could see he too was shaken, for his voice lost its lightness as he continued, 'I didn't know this place was yours – not at first, though the name should have told me. The sedan-chair men at the Mercat Cross told me to come to Cameron and Watt when I was looking for a carriage for the King. I saw your father there, but he never said the business was yours…'

The mention of her father brought her back to sobriety. 'He's forgotten I exist,' she said, and her expression clouded as she went on to tell him, 'Andrew's dead, and so's Miss Vee. Did you hear that?'

Peter nodded, his eyes fixed on her face. 'I know. I'm sorry about them both. I went to see Agnes Watt after I saw you. I didn't know till then if Andrew was alive and if you'd want to see me. I still don't know, but I had to try. I'm sorry, very sorry, about Andrew, my poor brother. When I saw his son this morning I felt as if time had turned back. It reminded me of the day Andrew and I went to the Deacon's funeral.'

His obvious feeling moved her heart and she stepped closer to him, still holding up her lamp, and stared at his face. Suddenly she became conscious that William who had been carefully watching them, was now tactfully stepping back and closing the door. He was leaving them together.

In soft voice she told Peter, 'I loved Andrew very much, you know. He was a good man and he was my friend as well as my husband.'

Peter nodded. 'I loved him too and I've never forgotten that I owe my life to him. That's why I wasn't sure that I should come looking for you. For years I've felt guilty about loving you.'

The words hung between them like golden orbs in the semi-darkness but she chose to ignore them, saying, 'I thought you were dead, Peter. I used to be afraid to look at a gibbet in case you were swinging on it. I was so sure they'd hang you. You took too many chances.'

When he grinned it was the same grin that used to lighten her spirits in the darkened pews of Durham Cathedral.

'Oh, they never got close to hanging me. I went to Newcastle and signed on a ship that took me to India. After a time I came back with a man who was a friend of the King and I've been in the Royal service for the past five years.'

She was hardly listening, just looking at him, feasting her eyes on him. His voice seemed for away and they were talking at cross purposes, each one conducting their own interior conversation... She felt strange, as if she were dreaming the whole thing.

It was difficult to follow what he was telling her now for his words about loving her sounded and resounded inside her head while her body seemed to have slowed down, as if she were taking part in a stately minuet.

Peter came nearer. His face was vibrant and alive, his eyes shining, and he seemed as entranced as she. Tentatively he put out one hand and took hers which lay in his confidingly, as natural as if it had never left its place there.

She sighed at his touch and said again, 'I used to wonder if you'd ever come back – oh, Peter, you've not changed.' The sight of him standing there was like a miracle.

Slowly, gently, he drew her closer to him and she could not have stopped herself going if she had wanted to, which she found she did not.

'Neither have you changed, Helen *mo ghaoil*...' His voice was low as he voiced the Gaelic endearment. 'I want to ask you something – did you hear what I said about loving you?'

'Say it again,' Helen whispered.

'I said that for many years I felt guilty about loving you. Ask me if I do still. Please ask me.'

She put her hands up to his shoulders and stepped up against him, laying her face on his chest. There was happiness in her voice as his arms folded round her and she said, 'Oh, I don't think I'll ask you right now. Just bend down that head of yours, Peter Grant, and stop talking – I want to kiss you.'